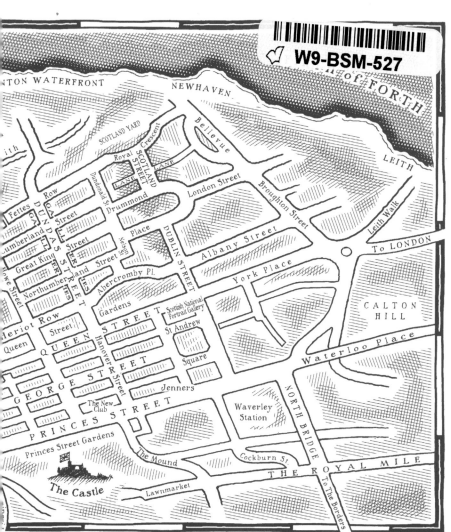

Central Edinburgh

Glasgow

44 Scotland Street

ALEXANDER McCALL SMITH

ESPRESSO TALES

The latest from
44 SCOTLAND STREET

Illustrated by IAIN McINTOSH

Polygon

First published in Great Britain in 2005 by
Polygon, an imprint of Birlinn Ltd
West Newington House
10 Newington Road
Edinburgh
EH9 1QS

www.birlinn.co.uk

ISBN 10: 1 904598 55 2
ISBN 13: 978 1 904598 55 8

British Library Cataloguing-in-Publication Data
A catalogue record for this book is
available on request from the British Library

Typeset in Janson Text by Palimpsest Book Production Limited,
Polmont, Stirlingshire
Printed and bound by Creative Print and Design,
Ebbw Vale, Wales

Preface

This is volume two of a serial novel which I started to write in *The Scotsman* newspaper and which, at the time of publication of this book, I am still writing. The enjoyment which I have obtained from spinning this long-running tale of a house and its occupants in Edinburgh is, I hope, apparent on every page. It has never been a chore. Not for a moment.

At the end of the first volume, *44 Scotland Street*, I left matters unresolved for many of the characters. Now in *Espresso Tales* we see the continuation of many of the themes begun in volume one. Bertie, that immensely talented six-year-old, is still in therapy, and his plight seems to get worse and worse. Bruce, the unbearable narcissistic surveyor, is still as irritating as before, perhaps even more so. If there is any justice, he will get his come-uppance in this volume (but don't count on that). And Domenica, that sage occupant of the top floor of 44 Scotland Street, continues to comment on the world with her mordant wit.

During the writing of this book, which appeared in daily parts in *The Scotsman*, I received comments from many readers. Some wrote in with suggestions; others occasionally upbraided me for the views which some of the characters expressed. I inadvertently ruffled the feathers of an entire Scottish town at one point, and at another I received a very reproachful letter from a convinced vegan. These, I suppose, are the consequences of writing a novel under the scrutiny of the public eye.

This is, of course, not a work of scrupulous social realism. However, unlike in many other novels, all the places in this book exist, and a number of the characters are real people, who currently live in Edinburgh and who agreed to appear, as themselves, in this story. Other people have, for some reason, imagined that they appear in this story, thinly (or otherwise) disguised. Alas, this is not true. There is no real Bertie; and even if there are many like Domenica, or Angus, or any of the other characters, I had no particular person in mind when writing about them.

When the last episode of this book was published in the newspaper, we had a party in the offices of *The Scotsman*. Many readers attended, and some gave me their frank assessment of what had happened in the series. Others came up to me and said, "You can't stop now. There will have to be a third volume." At the beginning of the evening I had decided that I would not write a third; by the end I had changed my mind. I am easily persuaded to continue to have fun. And why not?

This second volume is committed to press in gratitude to the readers of *The Scotsman* and in affection for this remarkable city and the people who make it one of the most vibrant and interesting places in the world. Again I express my thanks to those who accompanied me on this particular literary journey: to David Robinson, books editor of *The Scotsman*, to Iain Martin, editor of *Scotland on Sunday*, John McGurk, editor of *The Scotsman*, and Neville Moir of Polygon, that most perceptive and sympathetic of editors. And my thanks are given, too, to Florence Christie, leader of the fans of Bertie, and my friend, Michael Lamont, who has been one of the few readers who showed any sympathy for Bruce. And finally, I would like to thank William Lyons, arts editor of *Scotland on Sunday*, who gave me advice on wine matters and who features in the story as himself. Not having tasted *Chateau Petrus* myself, I assume that what he says about it is correct.

Alexander McCall Smith,
Edinburgh.

1. Semiotics, Pubs, Decisions

It was summer. The forward movement of the year, so tentative in the early months of spring, now seemed quite relentless. The longest day, which always seemed to arrive indecently early, had passed in a bluster of wind and light rain, but had been followed by a glorious burst of warmth that penetrated the very stones of Edinburgh.

Out on the pavements, small clusters of tables and chairs appeared here and there, populated by knots of people who could hardly believe that they were sitting outside, in Scotland, in late summer. All of them knew that this simply could not last. September was not far off, and after that, as was well known to all but the most confused, was October – and darkness. And Scottish weather, true to its cultural traditions, made one thing abundantly clear: you *paid* for what you enjoyed, and you usually paid quite promptly. This was a principle which was inevitably observed by nature in Scotland. That vista of mountains and sea lochs was all very well, but what was that coming up behind you? A cloud of midges.

Pat Macgregor walked past just such café-hedonists on her way back to Scotland Street. She had crossed the town on foot earlier that day to have lunch with her father – her mother was still away, this time visiting another troublesome sister in Forfar – and her father had invited her for Saturday lunch in the Canny Man's on Morningside Road. This was a curious place, an Edinburgh institution, with its cluttered shelves of non-sequitur objects and its numerous pictures. And, like the trophies on the walls, the denizens of the place had more than passing historical or aesthetic interest about them. Here one might on a Saturday afternoon meet a well-known raconteur enjoying a glass of beer with an old friend, or, very occasionally, one

might spot Ramsey Dunbarton, from the Braids, who many years ago had played the Duke of Plaza-Toro in *The Gondoliers* at the Church Hill Theatre (with such conspicuous success).

There was no such interest that day. A mousy-looking man in a blue suit sat silently in a corner with a woman companion; the silence that reigned between them being broken only by the occasional sigh by one or other of them. He looked steadfastly down at the menu of open sandwiches, as if defeated by the choice and by life; her gaze moved about – out of the window, at the small slice of sky between the Morningside Road tenements, at the barman polishing glasses, at the tiles on the floor.

As she waited for her father to arrive, Pat found herself wondering at the road which had brought them to this arid point – a lifetime of small talk, perhaps, that had simply run out of steam; or perhaps this is what came of being married. Surely not, she thought; her own parents were still able to look at one another and find at least something to say, although often there was a formality in their conversation that made her uncomfortable – as if they were talking a language, like court Japanese, that imposed heavily on them to be correct.

In Pat's company, her father seemed more comfortable. Leaning back in the bench seat at the Canny Man's while he perused the menu, his conversation took its usual course, moving, by easy association, from topic to topic.

"This is, of course, the Canny Man's," he observed. "You'll notice that the sign outside says something quite different. The Volunteer Arms. But everybody – or everybody in the know, that is – calls it the Canny Man's. And that pub down on the way to Slateford is called the Gravediggers, although the sign outside says Athletic Arms. These are verbal tests, you see. Designed to distinguish."

Pat looked at him blankly. Her father was intelligible, but not all the time.

"These tests are designed to exclude others from the discourse – just as the word discourse itself is designed to do. These words are intended to say to people: this is a group thing. If you don't understand what we're talking about, you're not a member of the group.

"So, if you call this place the Canny Man's it shows that you belong, that you know what's what in Edinburgh. And that, you know, is what everybody wants, underneath. We want to belong."

He laid the menu down on the table and looked at his daughter. "Do you know what the NB is?"

Pat shook her head and was about to reply that she did not; but he cut her short with a smile and a half-raised hand. "An unfair question," he said. "At least to somebody of your age. But anybody over forty would know that the NB is the North British Hotel, which is today called the Balmoral – that great pile down at the end of Princes Street. That was always the NB until they irritatingly started to call it the Balmoral. And if you really want to make a point – to tell somebody that you were here before they were – that it's your city – you can refer to it as the NB. Then at least some people won't know what you're talking about."

"But why would anybody want that?" she asked.

"Because we like our private references," he said. "And, as I've said, we want to feel that we belong. It's a simple matter of feelings of security . . ."

He smiled at his daughter. "Talking of the NB Hotel, there was a wonderful poet called Robert Garioch. He wrote poems about Edinburgh and about the city and its foibles. He wrote a poem about seeing people coming out of the NB Grill and getting into what he called a muckle great municipal Rolls-Royce. That said it all, you see. He said more about the city of his day in those few lines than many others would in fifty pages."

He paused. "But, my dear, you must be hungry. And you said that you have something to tell me. You said that you've made a momentous decision, and I'm going on about semiotics and the poetry of Robert Garioch. Is it a really important decision – really important?"

"It is," said Pat. "It really is. It's about my whole life, I think."

"You think?"

"Yes, I think so."

2. *Letting Go*

When his daughter had announced that she had made an important decision – an announcement casually dropped into the telephone conversation they had had before their lunch at the Canny Man's in Morningside Road – Dr Macgregor had experienced a distressingly familiar pang of dread. Ever since Pat had chosen to spend her gap year in Australia, he had been haunted by the possibility that she would leave Scotland and simply not return. Australia was a world away, and it was full of possibilities. Anybody might be forgiven for going to Melbourne or Sydney – or even to Perth – and discovering that life in those places was fuller than the one they had led before. There was more space in Australia, and more light – but it was also true that there was there an exhilarating freedom, precisely the sort of freedom that might appeal to a nineteen-year-old. And there were young men, too, who must have been an additional lure. She might meet one of these and stay forever, forgetful of the fact that vigorous Australian males within a few years mutated into *homo Australiensis suburbis*, into drinkers of beer and into addicts of televised footie, butterflies, thus, into caterpillars.

So he had spent an anxious ten months wondering whether she would come back to Scotland and upbraiding himself constantly about the harbouring of such fears. He knew that it was wrong for parents to think this way, and had told many of his own patients that they should stop worrying about their offspring and let go. "You must be able to let go," he had said, on countless occasions. "Your children must be allowed to lead their own lives." And even as he uttered the words he realised the awful banality of what he said; but it was difficult, was it not, to talk about letting go without sounding like a passage from Kahil Gibrain's *The Prophet*, which had views on such matters. The trouble with *The Prophet* was that it all sounded so profound when you first encountered it, and yet it was the sort of thing that one grew out of – just as one grew out of Jack Kerouac. It was entirely appropriate to have *The Prophet* on one's shelves in one's early twenties, but not, he thought, in one's forties, or beyond. One must be prepared to let go of *The Prophet*.

And although he gave this advice to people, he found it difficult – almost impossible, in fact – to practise it himself. He and his wife, Maureen, had only one child; she was their future, not only in the genetic sense, but in an emotional one too. In the case of Dr Macgregor himself, this was particularly true. He enjoyed cordial relations with Maureen, but there was a distance between them which he realised could never be bridged. It had been apparent from the earliest years of the marriage that they really shared very few interests, and had little to talk about. Her energies were focused on public causes and on her own, largely dysfunctional family. She had two difficult sisters and one difficult brother, and these siblings had duly spawned difficult and demanding children. So while she nominally lived in Edinburgh, in reality she spent a great deal of her time moving from relative to relative, coping with whatever crisis had freshly emerged. The sister in Angus – the one who drank – was particularly demanding. This manipulative sister really wanted Maureen to live with her, and to this end she longed for Maureen's widowhood, and said as much, which was tactless. There are many women whose lives would be immeasurably improved by widowhood, but one should not always point that out.

The absenteeism of his wife had its natural consequence. Pat became for him the focus of his family feeling; she was his best friend, and, to the extent that the father and daughter relationship permitted, his confidante. Of course he knew of the dangers of this; that the investing of one's entire world in a child was to give a powerful hostage to fortune, and that he should develop other friendships and ties. But he had somehow failed to do that. He was popular with his professional colleagues and he would have called many of these his friend, but there were limits to such friendships. People moved jobs; they went away; they developed new, outside friendships which were more absorbing than those of work. He should join a club, perhaps; but what clubs could he possibly take seriously? He had never had much interest in golf, and he was not sure whether he would approve of the ethos of a golf club, and what other clubs did people have in mind when they recommended membership as an antidote to loneliness? Perhaps they meant the Scottish Arts Club; he had walked past it one day and seen people having lunch in the dining room on the ground floor. He had stopped in his tracks and gazed in at the sight. A well-known journalist was holding court, it seemed, to an audience of antique dealers – he knew one of them, a man with an exemplary moustache – and portrait painters. They had full glasses of red wine before them and he saw, but could not hear, their laughter. For a moment he had been transfixed by this vision of fellowship and had thought: this is what I do not have. But although this sight had made him think that he might perhaps apply to join, he had done nothing about it, and he had gone back to his empty house that day (Pat had been in Australia and Maureen in Kelso, at her difficult brother's house), and he had sat and reflected on loneliness and on how few, how very few, are the human bonds that lie between us and the state of being completely alone. How many such bonds did the average person have? Five? Ten? In his case, he thought, it seemed as if the answer was two.

So it was natural that he should feel trepidation about any decision that Pat should make, because that decision could always be to go back to Australia. That was what he dreaded above all else, because he knew that if she did that, he would lose her. He wanted her to stay in Edinburgh, or go to Glasgow at the most. Her choice of St Andrews University was perfect in his mind; that was just up the road and completely unthreatening.

Now, in the cluttered surroundings of the Canny Man's, he steeled himself for impending loss. "You said that you'd made a major decision?"

Pat looked at her father. "Yes. I've decided not to go to St Andrews after all."

He caught his breath. She was returning to Australia. How few were the words needed to end a world.

3. *Narcissism and Social Progress*

Pat saw nothing in her father's face of the hollow dread he felt. He was accomplished at concealing his feelings, of course, as all psychiatrists must be. He had heard such a range of human confessions that very little would cause him so much as to raise an eyebrow or to betray, with so much as a transitory frown, disapproval over what people did, or thought, or perhaps thought about doing. And even now, as he sat like a convicted man awaiting his sentence, he showed nothing of his emotion.

"Yes," said Pat. "I've written to St Andrews and told them that I don't want the place next month. They've said that's fine."

"Fine," echoed Dr Macgregor faintly. But how could it be *fine?* How could she turn down the offer from that marvellous place, with all that fun and all that student nonsense, and Raisin Week and Kate Kennedy and all those things? To turn that down before one had even sampled it was surely to turn your back on happiness.

"I've decided to go to Edinburgh University instead," went on Pat. "I've been in touch with the people in George Square and they say I can transfer my St Andrews place to them. So that's what I'm going to do. Philosophy and English."

For a moment Dr Macgregor said nothing. He looked down at his shoes and saw, as if for the first time, the pattern of the brogue. And then he looked up and glanced at his daughter, who was watching him, as if waiting for his reaction.

"You're not cross with me, are you?" said Pat. "I know I've messed you around with the two gap years and now this change of plans. You aren't cross with me?"

He reached out and placed his hand briefly on hers, and then moved his hand back.

"Cross is the last thing I am," he said, and then burst out laughing. "Does that sound odd to you? Rather like the word order of a German or Yiddish speaker speaking English? They say things like, 'Happy I'm not,' don't they? Remember the Katzenjammer Kids?"

Of course she didn't. Nor did she know about *Max und Morris* nor Dagwood and Blondie, he suspected – those strange denizens of that curious nowhere world of the cartoon strips – although she did know about Oor Wullie and the Broons. Where exactly was that world, he wondered? Dundee and Glasgow respectively, perhaps, but not exactly.

Pat smiled. "I'm glad," she said. "I just decided that I'm enjoying myself so much in Edinburgh that I should stay. Moving to St Andrews seemed to me to be an interruption in my life. I've got friends here now . . ."

"And friends are so important," interrupted her father, trying to think of which friends she had in mind, and trying all the time to control his wild, exuberant joy. There were school friends, of course; the people she had been with at the Academy during the last two years of her high school education. He knew that she kept in touch with them, but were those particular friendships strong enough to keep her in Edinburgh? Many of them had themselves gone off to university elsewhere, to Cambridge in one or two cases, or to Aberdeen or Glasgow. Was there a boy, perhaps? There was that young man in the flat in Scotland Street, Bruce Anderson; she had obviously been keen on him but had thought better of it. What about Matthew, for whom she worked at the gallery? Was he the attraction? He might speculate, but any results of his speculation would not matter in the slightest. The important thing was that she was not going to Australia.

"Matthew says that I can continue to work part-time at his gallery," Pat went on. "I can do some mornings for him and Saturdays too. He says . . ." She paused. Modesty might have prevented her from continuing, but she wanted to share with her father the compliment that Matthew had passed. "I hope you don't think I'm boasting, but Matthew says that I have an eye for art and that the only way in which he thinks he can keep the gallery going is by having me there."

"That's good of him," said her father, thinking, but not saying, dependence: weak male, looking for somebody to look after him. "Mind you, I'm not surprised. You've always been good at art. You're good at everything, you know."

She glanced at him sideways, reproving him for the compliment, which had been overheard at a neighbouring table and had led to suppressed smiles. "And I think that I'll stay in Scotland Street," she went on. "It's an exciting place, you know. There are all sorts of interesting people who live down there. I like it."

"And you can put up with Bruce?"

"I can put up with him. He keeps to himself these days. He lost his job, you know, and he wants to do something else. He spends a lot of his time reading up about wine. I think he fancies himself as a wine merchant – or something of the sort."

Dr Macgregor nodded. He had not met Bruce, and had no real interest in meeting him. He was accustomed to psychopaths, to those whose selfishness was so profound that they tipped over into a clinical category; he was patient with neurotics and depressives and those with schizoid disorders; but he could not abide narcissists. From what his daughter had told him of Bruce, he was a classic narcissist: the looking in mirrors, the preening, the delight in hair gel – all of this was pure narcissism. And the problem was that there was a positive epidemic of narcissism, encouraged by commercial manipulation and by the shallow values of Hollywood films. And interestingly enough, the real growth area was male narcissism. Young men were encouraged to dwell on themselves; to gaze at photographs of other young men, looking back at them as from the mirror. They loved this. Edinburgh was full of them.

Hundreds of them, thousands, attended to by an army of hair-stylists, and outfitters. Yes, it was a profound social pathology. Reality television, which turned its eye on people who were doing nothing but being themselves, was the perfect expression of this trend. Let's look at ourselves, it said. Aren't we fascinating?

Dr Macgregor found himself thinking these thoughts, but stopped himself. It was true, of course, there was an abnormal level of narcissism in our society, but it did not do, he told himself, to spend too much time going on about it. Society changed. Narcissism was about love, ultimately, even if only love of self. And that was better than hate. By and large, Hate, of all the tempting gods, was the unhappiest today. He had his recruits, naturally, but they were relatively few, and vilified. Did it matter if young men thought of fashion and hair gel when, not all that many years ago, their thoughts had tended to turn to war and flags and the grim partisanship of the football terrace?

4. On the Way Back to Scotland Street

Pat left the Canny Man's and walked back up Morningside Road. She was accompanied, as far as Church Hill Place, by her father, who said goodbye to her and turned off for home, elated by the news she had given him. She toyed with the idea of a bus, but it was a fine, late August afternoon and she decided to walk all the way back to Scotland Street. She was in no hurry to be anywhere. In fact it occurred to her that between then – Saturday afternoon – and the coming Monday morning, when she was due at the gallery, it made no difference at all where she was. She had nothing planned. She was free.

It was the final week of the Festival, and of its burgeoning, undisciplined child, the Festival Fringe. In a corner of the Meadows, under the shadow of the University Library, a large tent had been pitched, hosting an itinerant Polish circus, the Great Circus of Krakow. A matinée performance was in progress and she heard a burst of applause from within the tent, and then laughter. As the laughter died down, a small brass band inside the tent struck up, playing at the frenzied pace that circus music seemed to like, a breathless, hurried march that accompanied what feats within? A troop of performing dogs? No longer allowed, she thought; frowned upon by protesters who had successfully lobbied the Council, although everybody knew that the one thing which dogs liked to do was to perform. Was it demeaning to dogs to be made to jump through hoops and stand on their hind legs and push prams? Making a lion jump through a hoop was one thing – that was undoubtedly cruel – but could the objectors not see the distinction between a dog and a lion? Dogs are in on our human silliness; lions are not.

She paused, standing underneath a tree, watching the sides of the circus tent move slightly in the breeze. To its side stood a row of large motor caravans and a small catering van. A door suddenly opened in the side of one of the vans and a man tumbled out, as if pushed from within. Or so it seemed to Pat, who saw him fall, as if to regain his balance, and then convert the fall into the most extraordinary gymnastic display. He rolled forward, somersaulted, stood on his hands, his legs pointed skywards, and then flipped over onto his feet. The entire manoeuvre took less than a couple of seconds, and there he was, standing only a few yards away from her, facing her. He seemed as surprised to see her as she was him, and for a moment they stared at one another, speechless. She saw that he was wearing what must have been his performing outfit – a body-hugging stocking that covered him, shoulder to toe, in a glittery, red material.

He smiled at her and she saw that he had perfectly regular teeth, polished high white. She was struck by this smile, and would have been less so had he opened his mouth to a vista of dental disaster. Somehow that was what one expected of the circus; external glitter, but decay and pain within.

The performer took a few steps back, still looking at Pat and holding her gaze. Then, reaching behind him, but still facing her, he opened the door in the van which had slammed shut behind his undignified exit.

"Please?" he said to her. "Coffee? Or maybe a glass of wine?"

He gestured to the interior, which was lit, but only faintly. Pat made out a table and a rail of bright outfits similar to the one he was wearing. At the side of the table were a pair of high-heel boots and a small side-drum.

He repeated his offer, bowing as he did so, the Spandex outfit spreading obligingly to accommodate the rippling of muscles which the manoeuvre involved.

Pat hesitated. He had recovered from his bow and was standing straight, but was slightly shorter than she was, and she noticed that he now raised himself on his toes for the extra height, effortlessly, as might a ballet dancer, but spotted by her, and it was this that broke the sudden hypnotic spell which had fallen upon her.

She laughed. "No thank you," she said, realising that the addition of the thank you marked her out for what she was – and her Edinburgh origins.

He took her refusal in good spirit. "God be with you," he said, and jumped back into the van. The door closed, and the moment was lost. Pat thought, as she walked away: I shall never be invited again into the living quarters of a Polish circus performer, and she laughed at the idea. Had she gone, then her life might have been different. She might have gone off with the circus, and married him in a dark church in Krakow, and borne the children of the gymnast, tiny, lithe children who would have been taught to leap from her lap and turn somersaults in the bath. And what was more, she thought: I might have become a Catholic.

It took her forty minutes to reach Scotland Street, as there were other Fringe performers to watch as she made her way down the hill. On the steps behind the National Gallery, she stopped for a moment while a group of students enacted a scene from *Macbeth*, a taster of their show that evening. There was an element of desperation in their performance, which suggested that they were at the end of an unrewarding stint on the Fringe. Lady Macbeth upbraided her husband, a tall young man with the residue of teenage acne about his chin. Pat watched for a few minutes, trapped in a small audience. But then her chance to leave came: she had spotted Domenica Macdonald, her neighbour from across the landing at Scotland Street, and she could slip away to join her. Domenica was on the edge of a growing crowd that was surrounding a man dressed as Punchinello and who was about to swallow a sword. The performer held the sword above his upturned mouth and it glinted in the afternoon sunlight.

"Domenica," she whispered. "Is he really going to do that?"

Domenica turned and smiled warmly. "How nice to see you," she said.

"I have always loved a spectacle, and there are spectacles galore at the moment. Of course he's going to swallow it. And then we shall all applaud. We are very vulgar at heart, you know. We love this sort of thing. All of us. We can't resist it. Behind us in the Gallery are all the treasures of Western art, as assembled for us by Sir Timothy Clifford, and we choose instead to watch a man swallowing a sword. Isn't that peculiar?"

Pat nodded. It was very peculiar; of course it was; she began to say this, and then she stopped. Wasn't that Sir Timothy Clifford himself, on the other side of the crowd, watching the sword swallower? She nudged Domenica, who looked in the direction in which Pat was pointing, and inclined her head in affirmation.

"He appreciates a bit of a spectacle," Domenica said. "And why not? He's put on such wonderful shows in the gallery. Besides, art is theatre, is it not – and theatre art?"

5. All Downhill From Here

The sword was swallowed, and regurgitated, as had been expected. There were gasps, and then applause. Many of those present expressed the view that they would not like to try that – no thank you! – and Sir Timothy was heard to mutter something about Titian before he retreated into his gallery. Domenica, who had seen considerably more entertaining spectacles during her time in India, turned to Pat and said: "Such feats, without a religious dimension, are less impressive, I feel, than those that allude to the sacred. What's the point of swallowing a sword if one gives the process no spiritual significance?"

Pat was puzzled by this remark, and as they crossed Princes Street to begin the walk back down the hill, she asked Domenica to explain.

"In India, we used to see such things from time to time," Domenica said. "We lived in Kerala, in the Christian south, but Hindu holy men used to pop down from time to time to remind us of the old gods. Some of these were fakirs, who would walk across beds of hot coals or swallow fire, or whatever. They did this to show that spirituality could conquer the body – could overcome the material world. And you could offer the whole thing up to the glory of the gods, which gave it a religious point. But our sword swallower on the Mound won't have any of that in mind, I'm afraid. Mere spectacle."

Pat felt that she could add little to this. She had never been to India, and she knew nothing about Hinduism, or indeed about many of the other topics on which Domenica seemed to have a view. And yet she was open-minded enough to know that she did not know, and she was a listener. That was her gift.

The streets were crowded with Festival visitors, and their progress down Dundas Street was slow, interrupted by knots of people standing in the middle of the pavement, some, their eyes glazed, in a state of cultural indigestion, some consulting maps and programmes. Domenica gave directions to a puzzled Japanese couple and bowed politely at the end of her explanation, setting off a sequence of further bows and inclinations of the head.

"They find us so rude, in general," she said. "A few bows here and there serve to redress matters." She paused for a moment. "And we smell a little rancid to them, you know. They are so hygienic, with their steam baths and so on. However much we wash it seems we have this slight smell, I understand, even Edinburgh people, would you believe? Heaven knows what they think of those parts of the country where they aren't too attentive to bathing requirements."

Pat smiled. This was vintage Domenica. Nobody else of her acquaintance would speak like this, and she found it curiously refreshing. Her own generation was too timid – beaten into compliance with a set of imposed views.

She looked about her, almost furtively. "And which parts would those be?" she asked.

Domenica waved a hand in the air. "Oh, there are various parts of the country where people haven't washed a great deal. Probably because they didn't have enough taps and baths in the houses. It's all very well for the middle classes to go on about cleanliness, but people used to have a terrible battle.

"Mind you, I had an aunt who was an officer in the Wrens during the war. She used to tell me that some of the recruits were charming, just charming, but she could never get them to wash. She had to force them into the showers. But I suspect that she was exaggerating. She had a slight tendency to egg things up a bit.

"That aunt had wonderful stories, you know. When they sent her off to officer training school in 1940 she was in a batch of twenty women. They all slept in those long Nissen huts – you can still see some of them standing if you go up to Cultybraggen, near Comrie. Well, there they all were, all thrown together. And my aunt, who was from Argyll, was thrown in with people from all over the shop. The woman in the bed next to hers was terribly grand – her uncle was an admiral or something like that – and when she joined up she brought her lady's maid. Would you believe that? It sounds absolutely astonishing today, but that's what she did – and the Navy allowed it! The maid enlisted at the same time and was given a bed at the end of the hut. She cleaned her mistress's equipment, polished her shoes, made her bed, and all the rest. It was an absolute scream, but apparently nobody batted an eyelid. It was a different country then, you know.

"And apparently this grand person drank. Every night after lights were turned out in the hut, my aunt heard a bit of fiddling about in the next bed and then she heard 'glug, glug . . .' as she downed the gin. Every night! But there was a war on, I suppose, and people had to get by as best they could. Which they did, you know. They did just that and they very rarely complained. Can you imagine how we'd behave today if we had to knuckle down and deal with another fascist monster on our doorstep? We'd fold up in no time at all. We couldn't do it – we simply couldn't do it." She paused, and for a moment, just a moment, looked doubtful. "Or am I simply making that great mistake, which everyone of my age makes, I suspect, and which leads us to believe that things have got worse? Are they worse, Pat?"

Pat was glad to be given the chance to answer. "No, they aren't. If you look at it from the perspective of people of my age, things are much better now than they were then. Much better. Think of colonialism. Think of what was done to people at the receiving end of that. You couldn't do that today."

"That's true," said Domenica. "But since you mention these values – self-determination, human rights and the rest – my point is this: would we be able to defend them if push came to shove? Those young men who climbed into their Spitfires or whatever back then – many of them were your age, you know. Twenty. Some even younger. They knew the odds. They knew they were going to die. Would the boys you were at school with do the same thing, do you think? Would they do it now? Be honest. What do you think?"

Pat was silent. She was not sure. But then the thought occurred to her: some of the girls would do it. Maybe that was the difference. Yes!

6. Domenica Gets into Top Gear

Deep in conversation on the subject of the defence of values, and courage, Pat and her neighbour, Domenica Macdonald, had now reached the point where Heriot Row becomes Abercromby Place. Domenica glanced at the Open Eye Gallery on the corner; a private viewing was in full swing and for a moment she wondered whether they should drop in and look at the pictures.

"That's Tom Wilson's gallery," said Pat. "He's been very good to Matthew. He's given him advice and helped him. He's a very nice man. And he can draw, too."

"Well, that's something," said Domenica. "Very few artists can. They've stopped teaching people how to draw at the art colleges, with the result that very few of their graduates can represent the world they see about them. They can arrange it, of course – they can install the world – but they can't represent it. At least not in any recognisable form. Do you think Mr Damien Hirst knows how to draw?"

"I have no idea," said Pat, gazing at the knot of people who had spilled out on to the front steps of the gallery, glasses of wine in their hands. "He may – I don't know. But Tom draws very well. He does portraits of people by drawing the things

they have. Bits and pieces that say something about their lives. Letters. Books. A favourite place. Things like that."

"Very interesting," said Domenica. "I wonder how my life would be represented? Perhaps by the bed in Scotland Street in which I happened to be born, and in which I propose, in the fullness of time, to die."

"Or something from India? The house you lived in?"

Domenica thought for a moment. "Too sad. I have a picture of my late husband's electricity factory in Cochin. But I can't bring myself to look at it. I really can't."

"Do you miss him badly?" asked Pat.

"Not in the slightest," said Domenica. "I regret the hurt I caused him. And I regret his untimely electrocution – not that any elec- trocution, I suppose, can be considered timely. But I do feel a certain nostalgia for India itself, particularly for Kerala. For frangi- pani trees. For the sight of a man washing an elephant in the road. For the sight of a group of little boys sitting in an old Ambassador car, down on its springs, pretending to drive it. For overstated advertisements for hair products in lurid purple and green. For white-washed churches where they set off fireworks on saints' days. Little things like that." She looked at Pat. "Do you think Tom Wilson would be able to draw those things for me?"

"I'm sure he could," said Pat. "Ask him. There he is in the doorway. That's him."

"I can't intrude," said Domenica. "Perhaps later."

They crossed the road, having decided that the opening at the gallery was too crowded to allow them a view of the fishing boats and pagodas.

"We can stop over there for coffee," suggested Domenica, pointing to the café immediately opposite the gallery. "Do you go in there very much? I rather like it."

Pat explained that she usually frequented Big Lou's coffee house slightly further down the hill. It being a Saturday after- noon, Big Lou's, of course, was closed. And on a Saturday afternoon in the Festival it was very closed, as Big Lou did not approve, in general, of Festival visitors: "Gey pretentious," Pat had heard her muttering.

"One must stick to what one knows," observed Domenica. "I shall try Big Lou's one day, but this is highly convenient for me and they have a very good range of olive oils. And as for their staff – well, you'll see what I mean."

They found a table at the back – the café was very crowded – and Domenica glanced round at the other customers. A woman at a nearby table inclined her head slightly, and the man she was with nodded curtly in her direction.

"That couple over there," whispered Domenica, returning the greeting. "They're very friendly with that awful woman downstairs, Bertie's mother. I think that they go to the floatarium together, or at least *she* does. I bumped into her on the stair one day and then I overheard their conversation while I was looking for my key – you known how sound travels on that stair. It was exactly what you would expect. Exactly. All about some plan to start an orchestra for five-year-olds. To be called the Edinburgh Junior Symphony. Can you believe it?

"And then, curiously enough, I met him when the two of them went to a talk at Ottakar's Bookshop. Willy Dalrymple had just written a new book about India and was talking about it. It was wonderful stuff, and he told a marvellously funny story about a misunderstanding he had had with an official somewhere in India or Pakistan about the pronunciation of the name of that English cricketer, Mr Botham. The official pronounced this 'bottom', and this led to difficulties. Terribly funny."

Domenica stopped, and for a moment there was a silence. Then she leaned forward and whispered to Pat. "I mentioned the staff here. Look at them. Look at this young man who's coming to serve us. Look at him. Doesn't he look like Rupert Brooke? They're all so tall – so willowy. But shh! Here he is."

Pat felt embarrassed – the young man might so easily have heard what Domenica was saying; not, Pat thought, that Domenica would care too much about that. But she – Pat – did.

The waiter leaned forward to take their order, and Domenica smiled up at him.

"We're probably going to be really rather unadventurous and

just order a couple of coffees," she said. "Although some of those quiches over there look very tempting. Do you make them yourselves?"

The young man smiled. He glanced at Pat. "I don't. I just work here part-time. Someone else makes them in the kitchen back there."

"You're a student?" asked Domenica brightly. "No, let me guess! You're a student of . . . No, you defeat me! You're going to have to help me. What are you a student of?"

The young man laughed. "English," he said.

"I see," said Domenica. "I should have guessed that. You see, I thought that you bore an uncanny resemblance to Rupert Brooke, the poet. I don't suppose anybody studies him any more. Too light. You've heard of him, of course?"

"Yes," said the young man. "I've heard of him. I've not read him, though."

"Well, let me lend you one of his books," said Domenica quickly. "Come round and have dinner with us some time and I'll give you one. We live just round the corner – Scotland Street. You know it?"

For a moment the young man hesitated. He looked quickly at Pat, who lowered her eyes, and blushed.

"Yes, I know it. I live in Cumberland Street, you see."

"Perfect!" said Domenica. "Well, if you give me your name, I'll leave a message for you here and we can arrange something. I'll get the book out to give to you."

7. *Anger and Apology*

When Pat eventually got back to her flat in Scotland Street, she still felt angry over what Domenica had done. Their cups of coffee in Glass and Thompson's delicatessen and café had been drunk largely in silence.

"I've done something to upset you, haven't I?" said Domenica, after the silence became too obvious to remain unremarked upon. "Is it to do with what I said to that young man – what was his name again?"

"Peter."

"Yes, Peter. A nice name, isn't it?"

Pat said nothing. Domenica looked at her, and frowned. "I'm sorry. I really am. I had no idea that you would be so . . . well, so embarrassed by all that. I did it for *you*, you know."

Pat looked up sharply. "You asked him to dinner, out of the blue, just like that – for *me?*"

Domenica seemed surprised by this. "But of course I did! You don't think that I go around picking up young men for my own sake, do you? Good heavens! I do have a sense of the appropriate, you know."

"And it's appropriate to go and ask perfect strangers to dinner to meet me? Do you consider that appropriate? How did you know that I wanted to meet him anyway? Just because he looks like some ridiculous poet you've read . . ."

Domenica put down her coffee cup – firmly. "Now wait a moment! I'm sorry if you think I've overstepped the mark, but I will not stand by while you refer to Rupert Brooke as a ridiculous poet. Have you read him? You have not! He wrote wonderful pastoral, allusive verse, and the story of his brief life – yes, his brief life – is really rather a moving one. So don't call him a ridiculous poet. Please don't. There are lots of ridiculous poets, but he wasn't one of them. No."

There was a further silence. Then Pat rose to her feet. "I think we should go. I'm sorry if I got upset – and I'm sorry if I offended you. It's just that . . ."

They walked out of the delicatessen, passing Peter, working at the counter, as they did so. Pat looked away, but Domenica smiled at him, and he smiled back at her, although weakly, as one smiles at a new acquaintance of whom one is unsure.

"Look, it's not such a terrible thing I've done," said Domenica, as they went out into the street. "And if it embarrasses you, I suggest that we just forget the whole thing."

She looked at Pat, who turned to her, frowning. "No," she said. "Don't do that."

Domenica raised an eyebrow. "Oh? So you'd like me to invite him after all? Do I detect . . . do I detect a slight mellowing?"

Pat looked down at the ground. Her feelings were confused. She was irritated by the assumptions that Domenica had made, but there was something about Peter that interested her, and she had seen that he had looked at her too, that he had noticed her. There was something that her friends called "the look", that glance, that second take, which gives everything away. One could not mistake the look when one received it; it was unambiguous.

Peter had given her the look. Had she been by herself, she would have not known what to do about it. They might have exchanged further glances, but it was difficult to take matters further when you were working, as he was. You could hardly say: "Here's your coffee, and what are you doing afterwards?" Perhaps people did say that, but it was not the most sophisticated of approaches and he would not have done that. And for much the same reason, she could hardly have said: "Thanks for the coffee, and what are you doing afterwards?" One did not say that to waiters, whatever the temptation.

So the fact of the matter was that Domenica must have intuitively worked out that there was potential in that casual encounter and had acted with swiftness and ingenuity. She had set up a meeting which would enable nature to take its course – if that was the course that nature intended to take. They would meet for dinner at Domenica's flat and if the look were given again, then they could take it further. No doubt Domenica would ease the way, perhaps by suggesting that they go out after dinner to the Cumberland Bar and then she would herself decline on the grounds of tiredness, leaving the field open for the two of them.

I should be grateful to her, Pat thought, and now, back in her flat, she realised that she had been churlish. She wondered whether to cross the landing and apologise there and then, but she decided against that. An apology would lead to a conversation and she did not feel in the mood for further discussions. She felt slightly light-headed, in fact, as if she had drunk a glass of champagne on an empty stomach. She went through to her bedroom, lay down on her bed, and closed her eyes, imagining herself back in the café with Peter standing beside the table, staring at her. She remembered the way he stooped – like the other tall employees – and he put the coffee down in front of her and then looked up. What had he been wearing? She had hardly noticed, but it was a white shirt, was it not? And jeans, like everybody else. If one could not remember somebody's trousers, then jeans were the safe default. Indeed, "defaults" was a good name for jeans. I put on my *defaults*. It sounded quite right.

She got up off her bed and picked up her key from the table. Bruce was in the flat – she had noticed that his door was closed, which inevitably meant that he was in – but she had no desire to talk to him. Bruce was history in every sense of the word. He was history at the firm of Macauley Holmes Richardson Black, where he had lost his job as a surveyor after being found having an intimate lunch in the Café St Honoré with the wife of his boss – an intimate *and* innocent lunch, but not so to the outside observer, unfortunately in this case his boss himself.

And he was history in Pat's eyes, too, as she had quite recovered from her brief infatuation with him. How could I? she had asked herself, in agonising self-reproach. To which a Latinist, if there were one about, might have answered *amor furor brevis est* – love (like anger) is a brief madness. The most prosaic of observations, but, like many such observations, acutely true. And one might add: if love is a brief madness, then it is often also sadness, and sometimes, alas, badness.

She left the flat and walked down to Henderson Row, where she bought a small bunch of flowers. This she subsequently placed outside Domenica's door, where she might pick it up when next she opened it.

8. An Exchange of Cruel Insults

It was not that there was an atmosphere between Bruce and Pat; relations, in fact, were quite cordial. Bruce was indifferent to the fact that she had rejected his advances ("her loss," he told himself, "silly girl"). He knew, of course, that she had been besotted by him – any man would have realised that – and for Bruce it was nothing in the least unusual for a woman to feel like that about him. Indeed, it was the normal way of things, and Bruce would have been surprised if Pat had not found herself in this position, sharing the flat, as they did, when she had every opportunity to be in close proximity to him. Poor girl! It must have been hard for her, he thought; rather like living with a full fridge or store-cupboard when one is on a strict diet. One may look, but not touch. What a pity!

There had been a brief period during which Pat had seemed to avoid him – and he had noticed that. However, he had been tolerant. If it helped her to stay out of his way for a few days, then that was her way of dealing with the situation and he would not force his company upon her. And after a while that awkwardness passed, and there seemed to be no tension in the air when they coincided in the kitchen, or when they passed on telephone messages to one another.

Bruce was pleased that things had not become more fraught. His life over the past couple of months had not been particularly easy, and he would not have enjoyed having to deal with domestic difficulties on top of what he had been experiencing elsewhere. To begin with, there had been the problem with the job. He had been planning to leave the firm and to move on to something more satisfying even before the show-down with his employer, Raeburn Todd, joint senior partner with his brother, Jock Todd, of Macauley Holmes Richardson Black, Chartered Surveyors and Factors. But it was unfortunate, from Bruce's point of view, that this departure should have been on Todd's terms rather than on his own. That had been extremely irritating.

What annoyed Bruce in particular about that episode was that when he was asked by Todd's wife, Sasha, to lunch with her in the Café St Honoré, he had agreed to do this only out of charity. He had no particular interest in her, and he had certainly not been planning any involvement with her, although it had been perfectly obvious to him at the South Edinburgh Conservative Ball that she found him attractive. That was understandable, of course, but he had not expected her to do anything about this, and indeed that fatal lunch was hardly a romantic encounter at all. It was true that when Todd walked into the Café St Honoré unexpectedly, he had found his wife holding Bruce's hand in hers, over the table, but that had been purely in the context of their discussion about tennis prowess and the importance of having a strong wrist. If he were going to hold hands with a married woman in an Edinburgh restaurant, then he would do so under the table, not above.

And of course Todd had behaved in exactly the way one would have expected of him. He had fired him on the spot, right there in the Café St Honoré, using as his pretext the fact that he had put in a false report on a roof-space inspection some time back. That was typical of the man, in Bruce's view – to keep a little thing like that up his sleeve, waiting for his chance to use it. No harm had been done by that slight cutting of the corner. The client had been perfectly happy with the purchase, he had heard, and the seller was happy too. Everybody was happy, apart from Todd, who parroted on about professional standards and integrity. Blah, blah, blah, thought Bruce. If everybody behaved in such a retentive way, he reflected, then would anything in this world ever get done? It would not. The world needed people of spirit – people of decisiveness; people who were prepared to see beyond the narrow rules, as long as they kept to the general spirit of things. That's me, Bruce said to himself.

Bruce remembered very clearly each detail of that fatal afternoon. Todd had stormed out, closely followed by Sasha, who had run after him up the narrow cobbled lane outside the restaurant. From his table near the window, Bruce had seen the two of them standing on the corner of Thistle Street, yelling at one another, although he could hear nothing of what was said. Presumably she was explaining to her husband that things were not as he imagined, and indeed after a few minutes Todd appeared to calm down. They began to talk more calmly, and Sasha then leant forward and planted a kiss on her husband's cheek.

The sight of this brought relief to Bruce, who concluded that the matter had been sorted out and that Sasha would return to the rest of her lunch and he would in due course return to his job. However, this did not happen, as Sasha merely walked off in the opposite direction, leaving Bruce to pay for his ruined lunch. This outraged him. She had invited him, after all, having recently inherited four hundred thousand pounds, and she very specifically said that the lunch was on her. Now Bruce had to pay for both of them, as well as the wine, which he had offered to pay for anyway, but which was largely untouched. Still, at least he would get his job back, until the time arrived for him to resign on his own terms.

But that was not to be. He returned to the office half an hour or so later to find a note from Todd awaiting him on his desk. He could speak to the cashier about his final cheque, the note said (he would be paid up to the end of that month), and would he please ensure that all personal effects were removed from his desk by four o'clock that afternoon? He should also return the mobile telephone which the firm had bought him and duly account for any personal calls that he had made on it during the period since the last bill.

Bruce stood there, quite still, the note in his hand. Several minutes passed before he let the piece of paper fall from his hand and he walked out of his office and made his way to the end of the corridor and pushed open Todd's door.

"You should always knock," said Todd. "What if I had a client in here with me? What then?"

"I'm going to take you to a tribunal," said Bruce.

"Go ahead," said Todd. "I'd already spoken to the lawyers about getting rid of you and they assured me that the making of a fraudulent survey report constitutes perfectly good grounds for dismissal. So by all means take me to a tribunal."

Bruce opened his mouth to speak, and then closed it again. It was difficult to know what to say. Then the words came to him. "You have a ridiculous name, you know, Mr Todd. Raeburn! That's the name of a gas cooker, you know. That's what you are, Mr Todd – you're just a gas cooker."

Raeburn Todd appeared undisturbed by the insult. "A gas cooker, am I?" he said quietly. "Well, I've just cooked your goose for you, young man, would you not say?"

9. Sally's Thoughts

After he had lost his job – or resigned, as he put it – Bruce went home to Crieff for several days to lick his wounds. His parents had been concerned over his resignation, and they had quizzed him as to what lay behind it.

"It's not much of a firm," Bruce had explained airily. "I found myself – how shall I put it? – a bit thwarted. The job didn't stretch me enough."

His mother had nodded. "You thrive on new challenges, Brucie," she said. "As a little boy you were like that. You were a very creative child."

Bruce's father had looked at him over the top of his spectacles. He was an accountant who specialised in the winding-up of companies, and he had a strong nose for lies and obfuscation. The trouble with my son, he thought, is that he's vain. He's lost this job of his and he can't bring himself to tell us. Poor boy. I suppose I can't blame him for that, but I wish he wouldn't lie to us.

"What are you going to do?" asked his father. "How are things in surveying at the moment? Are they tight?"

Bruce shrugged, and looked out of the window of "Lochnagar", the family's two-storey granite house in Crieff. One thing one has to say about the parental house, he thought, is that it has a good view, down into the strath, over all that good farming land. I should marry the daughter of one of those farmers down there – those comfortable farmers (minor lairds, really, some of them) – and then things would be all right. I could raise Blackface sheep, in a small way, and some cattle, some arable. It would be an easy life.

But then there was the problem of the farmer's daughter – whoever she turned out to be. Some of them were all right, it had to be said, but then the ones he might find worth looking at tended to move to Edinburgh, or even to London, where they had jobs in public relations or possibly at Christie's. At Christie's, they were the ones who were sometimes allowed to hold up the vases and paintings at the auctions (provided, of course, that they had studied history of art at university, although sometimes a declared intention to study history of art was sufficient qualification). That was the problem; they had no desire to remain in Perthshire. That was until they became broody; things changed then, and the idea of living in the country with dogs (labradors, usually, the dog of choice for such persons) and children suddenly became an attractive one. Bruce sighed. Life seemed very predictable, whatever choice one made.

He looked back at his father, and held his gaze for a few moments. Then he looked away again. He knows, he thought. He knows exactly what has happened. "I think I'll try something different," he replied quietly. "The wine business is interesting. I might try that."

"You always had a good nose for wine, Brucie," said his mother. "And for sniffing things out in general." She cast a glance at her son's hair. "Is that cloves, I smell, by the way? I love the scent of cloves. I think it's marvellous that boys have all those different things to choose from at the chemist's these days. Hair things and shaving things, that is."

Over the next few days, he was looked after by his mother, and felt reassured. It still riled him to think of Todd and the injustice that had been done him, but after three days in Crieff the pain seemed to ease – unconditional maternal affirmation had its effect – and he found himself in a position to make decisions. He would return to Edinburgh, plan a holiday – a month or two perhaps, since he had the opportunity – and then he could start seriously to look for a job in the wine trade. He had some leads there. Will Lyons had more or less guaranteed that he would find something, and so, with any luck, he would be fixed up by, say, late September. That would be a good time to start in the wine trade, with Christmas and New Year sales coming up.

Bruce felt positively buoyed by the thought of a couple of months off, and spent the first few days after returning to Scotland Street in deciding where he would go. He had never been in the Far East, and he spoke to one or two people in the Cumberland Bar who had been to Thailand.

"Terrific country," one of them said. "Just terrific. South – terrific. North – terrific. Unconditionally terrific."

That helped Bruce a bit, but gave him very little concrete information. What about Vietnam?

"Not quite as terrific as Thailand," said the same person. "But terrific in its own way."

Bruce was still seeing Sally, the American girl he had met in the Cumberland Bar. The relationship had not progressed as far as he had imagined it might, and he had decided that he most definitely would not ask her to marry him, but it was a convenient arrangement for both of them and they met one another once or twice a week, usually in the Cumberland Bar, and thereafter they went to 44 Scotland Street, where they were able to continue their conversation.

"I find him a bit of a drag," Sally had written in an e-mail sent to her friend, Jane, who lived in Nantucket. "You don't know Scotsmen, do you? Well, I'll tell you a bit about them. They're usually quite pale, as if they've spent too much time indoors, which they often have (although I must say that Bruce is really good-looking, and a few months in Arizona or some-where like that could really improve him). They like drinking, and they go on and on – and I really mean on and on – about soccer, even the relatively civilised ones (the ones you meet in the Cumberland Bar – and you should just see the rest!). Bruce doesn't talk about soccer, but he makes up for it with rugby. You won't have even heard about rugby, Jane. It's this really weird game, a bit like football – the proper football, the one we play – but without the shoulders. It's very tribal. They run up and down a soggy pitch and bring one another down in hugs. I don't think that's the word they use for it – I think there's some other term – but that's what they are – hugs. And so it goes on.

"Bruce is all right, I suppose, for a couple of months. (So, OK, I've been bored. You can't blame a girl who's feeling bored.) But I would love – just love – to meet some nice, normal boy over here – you know what I mean? – somebody like that guy you met at Dartmouth (what was his name again? Remember him?!) But they just don't exist. So I'll make do with Bruce a little longer before I give him his pink slip and then it's back home and we can meet up and you can introduce me to some-body. Agree?"

And Jane had written back: "Don't worry. I've met the cutest guy at a party at the Martinsons and I'm saving him just for you! I've told him all about you and he's really interested. So come home soon. You won't believe your luck when you meet him. His name's Billy, by the way. Isn't that cute? Yale."

10. Bruce's Plan

When Sally revealed to Bruce that she was intending to return to the United States at the beginning of September, and that she would only come back to Scotland in November, for her graduation, and for no more than a week at that, she was surprised that he took the news so calmly. There was a reason for his unruffled demeanour in the face of this impending separation: Bruce was, in fact, more than a little relieved that she would be going, as he was beginning to find her company slightly irksome. She's neurotic, he thought; always probing into his reasons for doing and saying things, as American girls tended to do. Scottish girls were almost always more straightforward and less demanding; they did not ask you to explain yourself at every step, but accepted you for what you were, a man – and let you get on with it.

The roots of the difference lay in the very nature of the two societies: whatever Scotland was, it was not a matriarchy; whereas the United States was a profoundly matriarchal society – and much more feminine than would be suggested by all that male bravado. That was a front, and a misleading one at that; underneath the male swagger lay a passive acceptance of female dominance – a fact not always appreciated by outsiders. And as a result, such people often fundamentally misread American society and assume that decisions articulated by men are male decisions – a serious mistake.

Although he had not reflected on the general issue of why American women behaved the way they did, Bruce found it very difficult to adjust to the independence which Sally showed in her relationship with him. In his view, it was only natural that the male should take the lead in most matters ("That's the whole point of being a male," he had once remarked to a friend who had consulted him about a fraying relationship). Women who did not accept this were, in Bruce's view, self-evidently unhappy in their gender. They made very unstable girlfriends and were best avoided, even if they were sometimes every bit as enthusiastic as other women were in flinging themselves at him. Bruce knew that he was attractive even to women who were not interested in men at all, although they often fought so hard against it and felt so bad about their feelings towards him. Go with the flow, he might have said. That is how Bruce thought.

The impending departure of Sally, rather curiously, added a zest to the relationship. Although neither would have thought of it in these terms, this was probably owing to the fact that neither now felt trapped, and a sense of freedom in a friendship – or in a love affair – often adds a certain lightness to what might otherwise weigh heavily. It is not hard to be considerate, or even enthusiastic, towards those who are going away; in fact, they often appear much more attractive and desirable as friends than they did before they announced their intention to go. Now, after the decision to go is taken, the obligation of those who are staying behind is finite; we do not have to be nice to them for much longer – the smile need not be maintained into some distant and unknowable future.

For her part, knowledge of the fact that Bruce was about to be dropped made Sally feel slightly guilty, which caused her to be particularly affectionate towards him. She gave him several small and unexpected presents – a set of cufflinks from Jenners, and a silk tie which she bought from Stewart Christie in Queen Street. And Bruce reciprocated with a box of Callard and Bowser nougat and a book of Edinburgh views taken by a well-known soft-focus photographer. "So that you can remember how happy you've been in Edinburgh," he wrote on the title page of the book. "And to remind you of me."

Sally was touched by this, but when she began to analyse the wording of his inscription, her irritation with Bruce resurfaced. Was he implying that her happiness in Edinburgh was directly attributable to her having met him? If so, that was nonsense. She had been perfectly happy before she had met him; indeed she had even been slightly happier then. So the inscription might more accurately have read: "To remind you of how happy you've been in Edinburgh, in spite of memories of me." But people never wrote that sort of brutally honest thing in books, largely because people very rarely have a clear idea of the effect that they have on other people, or can bring themselves to admit it. And Bruce, as Sally had discovered, lacked both insight into himself and an understanding of how somebody like her might feel about somebody like him. I really am wasting my time with him, she said to herself; I may as well bring the whole thing to an end right now. And yet there was something compelling about him, something fascinating that drew her to him. Something to do with the way he looked, she thought; the lowest common denominator of such dalliances. The conclusion depressed her, but there it was: some relationships are a matter of the physical, try as we might to ennoble them. Ultimately, the reason why one person may stay with another may be as small a thing as the shape of the other's nose.

Unaware of Sally's doubts, Bruce assumed that she would find the separation difficult, and that she might wish to prolong their affair at a distance. So when the idea occurred to him of how he might spend a month or two before he started his new job in the autumn, he imagined that Sally would welcome the suggestion.

"I've got some good news for you," he said casually, as they sat in the garden at the Cumberland Bar, enjoying some late Saturday afternoon sunshine.

She looked at him and smiled. The sun was in his hair, melting the gel. Poor Bruce!

"I can come to Nantucket with you," said Bruce. "You've made me curious about it. We could spend a few weeks there maybe, at your place, and then do some travelling. I've always wanted to see New Orleans. We could go down there maybe."

Sally stared at him. The moment had come, unexpected just then, but it had definitely arrived.

11. A Bus for Bertie

"We have to reach a decision," said Irene Pollock, mother of Bertie, and neighbour, one floor down, of Pat, Bruce and Domenica. She looked at her husband and waited for him to speak.

He was sitting in the chair which he liked to occupy near one of the windows of the sitting room, immediately under the small reproduction Warhol which Irene had bought for him at the Museum of Modern Art in New York. He had not been listening closely to what Irene was saying, as he had been thinking about a row which had blown up at the office – Stuart was a statistician in the Scottish Executive – and there had been an intense discussion in an internal meeting of how figures might be presented. The optimists had been pitted against the pessimists, and Stuart was not sure exactly into which camp he fitted. He believed that there were sometimes grounds for optimism and sometimes grounds for pessimism, and that one might on occasion choose between them at the level of subtle, and permissible, nuances but in general should stick to the truth, which was often uncomfortable.

All of this was some distance away from the matter which Irene was talking about, which was the issue of how their son, Bertie, the remarkably talented five-and-three-quarter-year-old, should get from Scotland Street, where they lived, to the school in Merchiston, in which he had now been enrolled.

"Obviously I shall go with him for the first year or so," said Irene. "And I'll pick him up at three in the afternoon or whenever it is that he finishes. But before we know where we are he'll be big enough to go by himself, and we'll have to make a decision."

"About what?" Stuart asked, distractedly.

Irene felt vaguely irritated. There were times when Stuart's mind seemed to be less focused than it might. And these occasions, she had noticed, were increasingly occurring when she was talking about something important to do with Bertie. Was he fully committed to the Bertie project? She would have to talk to him some time about that. One did not raise a little boy like Bertie without full commitment from both parents, and that meant a full commitment to all aspects of the project: educational, social and psychological.

"About which bus he takes," she said, the irritation creeping into her voice. "There are several possibilities, as you know. The

23 or the 27. And there's also the number 10 to be thought about."

Stuart shrugged. "Which goes closer to the school?" he asked.

"The 27," said Irene. "Both the 23 and the 27 go up Dundas Street and on to Tollcross. Then the 23 carries on up to Morningside, whereas the 27 turns right at the King's Theatre and goes along Gilmore Place to Polwarth."

"Oh," said Stuart.

Irene looked out of the window, staring, while she spoke, at a window on the other side of the street. A woman stood at this window, brushing her hair. "If he took the 23," Irene went on, "he would get off in Bruntsfield and then walk along Merchiston Crescent and down Spylaw Road. It would take him about ten minutes to reach the school gate. Alternatively, if he took the 27, he would have a walk of about four minutes from a stop on Polwarth Terrace."

"And the 10?"

"The number 10 is a different proposition," said Irene. "That bus goes along Princes Street and ends up on Leith Walk. If he took that, he would have to walk along London Street and then up to the top of Leith Walk. It's a slightly longer route, but there's another factor involved there."

Stuart raised an eyebrow. The ethics of statistical presentation seemed simple in comparison with the complexities of Edinburgh bus routes. "And this factor? What is it?"

"Going along London Street would remind him of the walk to the nursery school," she said quietly. "That's the route which I took him to that . . . that place." She shuddered involuntarily, remembering her last confrontation with the nursery-school teacher, and that awful morning when Bertie had finally been suspended for writing graffiti, in Italian, in the children's toilets. That had been so unfair, so cruel. It was entirely natural for small boys to explore their environment in this way and to seek to express themselves. If there were any fault involved, then surely it was that of the nursery itself, which had failed to provide adequate stimulation for him; not that that woman who ran the place would even begin to understand that.

"I don't want Bertie to be reminded of his suspension," she said firmly. "So that rules out the number 10."

"Fine," said Stuart. "And if the 27 involves a shorter walk, then shouldn't we opt for that? Is there much else to be discussed?"

"There is a difference between a 27 bus and a 23 bus," said Irene. "It's not just a question of which bus goes where."

Stuart smiled. "The Morningside factor?"

Irene nodded. "Yes," she said. "You could refer to it as that. The 23 bus is probably the most middle-class bus there is. It's the archetypical Edinburgh bus, if one uses the word Edinburgh in its pejorative sense. Do we want Bertie to become part of that whole Edinburgh scene? Is this not the reason why we're sending him to a less-stuffy school? To get him away from that whole, tight Edinburgh attitude, that whole middle-class, Merchant Company view of the world?"

"Then why don't we send him to the school round the corner?" asked Stuart.

Irene shook her head. "Impossible. It's a question of music lessons. It's not their fault, but many schools don't have the resources. It's society's fault. We let this happen. We've starved the schools of resources."

Stuart was silent. There was a sense in which his wife was right. We had allowed state education to decline because we had not been prepared to make the sacrifices needed to support the schools. But it went deeper than that in places like Edinburgh, where the middle classes – or a large part of the middle classes – had developed a parallel world for their children. But they would reply that all that they were doing was paying for that which the state did not provide. And this might be countered with the argument that their lack of commitment perpetuated this state failure. And so the debate went on.

"I don't think that it matters too much," he said calmly. "And, anyway, it looks as if the 27 is the solution. Unless . . ."

Irene hesitated. "The 27 can get a bit rough sometimes," she said, almost apologetically. "There are some bits of Oxgangs . . ."

"Then it's the 23," said Stuart.

Irene hesitated for a moment, but only a moment. "Yes," she said. "The 23."

12. *A Thin Summer*

Bertie had not enjoyed a particularly good summer. It had seemed to him – as it seems to all small boys – that the months of summer would be endless, a long, hazy succession of days of adventure and excitement. But that was not how the summer had actually turned out.

To begin with, they had barely left the city in spite of his repeated requests that they go somewhere – anywhere. Even the Pentland Hills would have done. He had heard that there were lochs there in which you could catch trout. A boy who lived in Fettes Row had told Bertie that he went there with his father and they had both caught two trout. It was easy, said the boy; you put the fly in the water and the trout jumped out and ate it. "Even somebody like you could do it," the boy went on.

"Can I go fishing in the Pentlands?" Bertie asked his mother. "That boy who lives in Fettes Row went fishing with his dad and caught two trout. You like trout, Mummy. I could catch some for you. And I could catch some almonds to put on top of the trout."

"If that's a joke, Bertie," said Irene severely, "then it's not very funny. Fishing is cruel. Think of the poor trout swimming around in the loch and then some unkind boy from Fettes Row comes and howks them out of the water and that's the end of the trout. Would you want to do that sort of thing? I'm sure you wouldn't. Anyway, we couldn't get out to the Pentlands. Your father has parked the car somewhere and we're going to have to find it. I just don't have the time to look for it right now."

Bertie thought for a moment. "But you eat trout, don't you?

You and Daddy both eat trout. I've seen you. Isn't it just as cruel to eat trout as to catch them? What's the difference?"

"There's an important difference," said Irene. "I'll explain it to you some time, but not at the moment." She paused. "Bertie, you know that Mummy does her best for you, don't you? You know that I love you very much and only want you to be happy?"

Bertie looked down at the floor. "Yes," he said quietly. "It's just that I don't seem to have much fun. I want to have a bit more fun. That boy in Fettes Row has more fun than I do."

"Oh, Bertie, you can't say that! Look at all the fun you have! There's your saxophone – you love playing that. I bet that boy wouldn't know how to play the saxophone, or anything for that matter. Anybody can fish – very few boys can play the saxophone. And then there's your Italian lessons, and your yoga, and . . ." Irene was about to say "and your psychotherapy" but stopped. She was not sure if Bertie was enjoying that as much as she was, and it was best, perhaps, not to mention it in this particular conversation.

Bertie was certainly not enjoying his psychotherapy. It was not that he actively disliked Dr Fairbairn, the prominent psychotherapist and author of the seminal study on that three-year-old tyrant, Wee Fraser; no, it was not that he disliked him, it was more a question of finding Dr Fairbairn quite impenetrably odd. In fact, Bertie was convinced that Dr Fairbairn was mad, and that the only viable strategy was for him to humour him, hoping thereby to avoid becoming the target of Dr Fairbairn's unpredictable wrath.

This strategy of humouring had produced the desired effect on the psychotherapist. He found Bertie increasingly co-operative and indeed felt that there were depths to the boy's psyche that would repay very serious study. There was even the possibility of a paper there – something for the *British Journal of Child Psychotherapy* or *Studia Kleinia* perhaps. But that was a long-term goal; the more immediate task, in Dr Fairbairn's view, was to discover what dynamics were operating in Bertie's developing ego structure and to work out what blockages were preventing him from developing a more integrated personality.

Dr Fairbaim was something of a pioneer, and one of the techniques that he had advanced was what he called "Fairbairn's List Approach". In this, the child patient was invited to write a list of those matters which were most distressing and to rank these in order of seriousness. This was nothing new in psychotherapy; indeed, some perfectly ordinary parents, untutored in the techniques of Freud and Klein, had used just such a system in dealing with their unhappy or difficult children. "Tell me what's worrying you – write it down and then we'll have a look."

That was all very well, and in many cases it helped to identify the conflict points in the parent/child relationship. But what made Dr Fairbairn's technique so advanced was that in addition to writing down the matter that was troubling or unsatisfactory, the child was invited to write down, in a separate column, who he thought was responsible for the state of affairs in question. In Dr Fairbairn's opinion, this gave a direct and useful insight into the child's view of the problem-producing dynamic.

Bertie had been asked to do this. "I want you to make a list," said Dr Fairbairn, giving Bertie a piece of paper. "I want you to write a list of things that make you unhappy – things you don't like to do or would like to change. Then draw an arrow from each thing on the list – a nice long arrow, with feathers if you like – and at the end of the arrow you should put down whose fault that particular thing is. Do you want me to show you how to do it, Bertie?"

"Yes please," said Bertie. "You make your list, Dr Fairbairn, and then I'll make mine."

Dr Fairbairn laughed. "I'll not make a full list. You're not my therapist, Bertie! Remember that! No, I'll just make a little list just to give you the idea – here, pass me that pencil – a list of two or three things."

The distinguished psychotherapist took the pencil handed to him by Bertie and quickly wrote a few lines on a piece of paper.

"There," he said. "You see how it's done."

Bertie looked at Dr Fairbairn's list. What on earth did this mean? And what was that word? – he had never encountered that word before. He would have to look it up when he had the chance.

Now it was his turn. Dr Fairbairn passed him a fresh piece of paper. Bertie took the pencil and looked up at the ceiling.

There was so much wrong with his life that it was difficult to know where to start. Ranking would be the difficult part; the blaming would be much, much easier.

13. Bertie's List

It took Bertie no more than ten minutes to write down his list of things that distressed him and to assign an order of magnitude to each. But after a certain amount of crossing out and rewriting, he handed the paper over to Dr Fairbairn, who had been paging through a journal while Bertie worked.

"Now then," said Dr Fairbairn cheerfully. "Let's see what's troubling you. Do you mind if I read it out, Bertie?"

"No," said Bertie. "But don't show it to anybody else. Will you burn it after you've read it?"

"Heavens no!" exclaimed Dr Fairbairn. "I'll put it in this file where nobody else can see it. This list will be too important to burn."

"I don't want Mummy to see it," said Bertie anxiously.

"She won't," said Dr Fairbairn. "You can trust me."

"But you've already told her some of the things I told you," said Bertie.

Dr Fairbairn looked out of the window. "Have I? Well, perhaps a few little things. And surely you wouldn't want to keep secrets from Mummy, would you?"

"Yes I would," said Bertie.

"Very well," said Dr Fairbairn. "This list remains absolutely secret. Nobody else – not even Mummy – will see it. You have my word on that."

But Bertie did not trust Dr Fairbairn, and even as the

psychotherapist started to read, he had begun to regret ever having committed these thoughts to paper.

"Number 1," read Dr Fairbairn. "People making me do things I don't want to do. I hate this. I hate this. Every day I have to do things that other people want me to do and it leaves me no time to do any of the things I want to do. And nobody asks me what I want to do, anyway." And then there was an arrow, rather like an ornate arrow of the sort used by Red Indian braves, pointing at the word Mummy, which was written in capitals.

Dr Fairbairn looked up from the paper and stared at Bertie for a moment over his spectacles. "Number 2," he read on. "Not being allowed to go fishing or go to Waverley station to see the trains. This makes me very sad. Other boys do these things – why can't I? It would make me so happy to be able to do this." And then the arrow, pointing again to the word Mummy.

"Number 3. Not having a friend. I hate not having a friend. All I want to do is to play with other boys and do the things they do. I want to go fishing with a friend. I want to go camping with him and make a fire and cook sausages. I've never been allowed to do any of these things." The arrow of blame pointed off to the right, to the word Mummy.

Dr Fairbairn frowned. All the blame seemed to be focused on his mother. It was not unusual for mothers to be blamed for many misfortunes, but to be the sole blame figure was exceptional – and worrying.

He looked at the last item on the list. "Number 4," he read out. "Having a pink bedroom. What if other boys saw this? What would they do? What if it gets out at school that I have a pink bedroom? What then?" And the blame, again, was laid fairly and squarely at Irene's door.

There was silence for a moment after the list had been read out. What puzzled Dr Fairbairn was that all this hostility was being directed towards the mother and none appeared to be directed against the father. This was unusual, because at this stage of his development Bertie might have been expected to be experiencing an Oedipal rejection of his father, whom, quite naturally, he would see as a rival for the affection of the mother. Yet Bertie in no sense appeared to be resenting his father's share of his mother; indeed, it would seem that Bertie took the view that his father was welcome to his mother, if that's what he wanted.

Dr Fairbairn looked at Bertie. This was a highly intelligent child – the most intelligent he had ever encountered, in fact – and perhaps the psychic drama was playing itself out in a rather different way in his case. The underlying dynamics, of course, must be the same, but it was possible that Bertie's understanding of adult feelings had enabled him to bypass some of the normal stages. So if Bertie had detected some fundamental pathology in the relationship between Stuart and Irene – a pathology which meant that maternal affections were in no danger of being diverted from Bertie to his father – then he might have decided that Oedipal feelings were simply unnecessary and a waste of energy. Why bother to view your father as a rival when he was clearly no competition?

Another possibility was that Bertie felt intense Oedipal jeal-ousies, but was clever enough to conceal them. If this were the case, then he would have to try to winkle them out through dream analysis, as they would certainly turn up there. But before that, there were questions that could be asked.

"Bertie," began Dr Fairbairn. "This list of yours is very inter-esting. Poor Mummy! Is she that bad?"

"Yes," said Bertie.

"I'm sure she isn't," said Dr Fairbairn. He paused. The next question, and its answer, would be vital. Oedipus would be lurking somewhere, and it would require no more than a tiny cue to get him to display himself in all his darkness. "If Mummy were that wicked, then would Daddy love her? Surely not. And yet he does love her, doesn't he? Mummy and Daddy must love one another, and you must know that."

Bertie narrowed his eyes. This was obviously a trap and he must be very careful. He could tell that Mummy liked Dr Fairbairn, and possibly liked him even more than she liked Daddy. So this was Dr Fairbairn trying to find out whether he had a chance of seeing more of Mummy. And that would mean more psychotherapy, because that was how they saw one another, at the beginning and end of the psychotherapy session. At all costs he must discourage Dr Fairbairn from thinking that.

"Mummy and Daddy are very happy," said Bertie firmly. "They like to hold hands all the time."

Dr Fairbairn raised an eyebrow, but barely noticeably. It was clear to him that Bertie was in denial of matrimonial disharmony. He had to be made to express this.

"I'm going to give you a little notebook, Bertie," he said. "And I want you to write down your dreams for me. Will you do that?"

Bertie sighed.

14. Pat and Bruce Work It Out

"So you're staying?" asked Bruce. They were standing in the kitchen, the two of them. Pat was waiting for the kettle to boil so that she could make herself a cup of coffee. Bruce had come in to make toast: he liked to eat toast when he was feeling insecure, and now he needed toast.

"If that's all right with you," said Pat. "I've given up my place at St Andrews and transferred to Edinburgh. I'll need somewhere to live, and I'd like to stay on here if you don't mind."

Bruce shrugged. "That's fine by me," he said. "My first test of a good tenant is whether the rent is paid. You've always paid."

"And your other tests?" asked Pat.

"Noise," said Bruce. "And tidiness. You're fine on both of those. I never hear you and you don't mess up the kitchen. You'll do just fine."

"Thanks," said Pat.

A silence then followed. Bruce raised himself up and sat on one of the surfaces, his legs dangling down over the edge. Pat looked at the kettle, which was slow to boil. She had to talk to him, of course, but she still felt slightly ill at ease in his presence. It was hard for things to be completely easy, she thought, after what she had once felt for him.

At last she broke the silence. "There's something I've been meaning to ask you, Bruce," she said. "Those other rooms. Is anybody ever going to live in them? Those two – those people who went to Greece – are they ever going to come back?"

Bruce laughed. "They paid until the beginning of August," he said. "It was their choice. They wanted to keep the rooms while they went travelling. I was expecting to have heard from them by now, but I haven't. I suppose I'll give them a month's grace and then clear the rooms and get somebody else." He paused. "Why do you ask? Do you know somebody who's looking for somewhere to live?"

"No," said Pat. "I just thought . . . Well, I suppose I thought that it might be easier for us to have somebody else staying here."

Bruce smiled. "A bit crowded with just the two of us? Is that what you mean?"

Pat drew in her breath. It was exactly what she had meant – and why should she not feel this? It was perfectly reasonable to suggest that the presence of a couple of other people should make life in a communal flat a little easier.

Everybody who had ever shared a flat knew that two was more difficult than three, and three was more difficult than five. Bruce must know this too, and was being deliberately perverse in pretending not to.

"All right," said Bruce. "I know what you mean. I'll give them two weeks to get in touch and then I'll move their stuff into the cupboard and we can get somebody else. What do you want? Boy or girl?"

Pat thought for a moment. The presence of another girl would be useful, as they could support one another in the face of Bruce. But what if this girl behaved as she had done and fell for Bruce? That would be very difficult. A boy would be simpler.

"Let's get a boy," she said. "Maybe you'll meet somebody at work . . ." She stopped, realising the tactlessness of her remark.

She had quickly guessed that Bruce had lost his job, rather than resigned, as he claimed.

"I wouldn't have anybody from that place," said Bruce quickly.

"Of course not," said Pat. "What about Sally? Would she know anybody? Maybe an American student at the university. She must meet people like that who are looking for somewhere to live."

Bruce was silent for a moment. He looked at Pat resentfully. "Sally's history," he muttered. "Since last night."

Pat caught her breath. That was two tactless remarks in the space of one minute. Could she manage a third? So Sally was history? Well, that meant that she had got rid of Bruce, and that he was the one who was history! She wanted to say to him: So you're history – again! But did not, of course. One never told people who were history that they were history. They knew it all right; there was no need to rub it in.

"I'm sorry to hear that," she said. "What happened?"

Bruce slipped down off the surface and moved over to the toaster. He put two slices of bread into the slot and depressed the lever. Toast would make him feel better; it always did.

"Oh, she became a bit too clingy," he said casually. "You know how it is. You're getting on fine with somebody and then all of a sudden they want more and more of you. It just gets too much. So I gave her her freedom."

Pat listened to this with interest. It was as if he was Gavin Maxwell talking about an otter, or Joy Adamson talking about a lioness. *I gave her her freedom.*

"You let her go?" she asked, trying to conceal her amusement.

"You could say that," said Bruce.

"I see," said Pat. "And where did she want to go? Back to America?"

"She would have stayed here to be with me," said Bruce. "But I didn't want to be selfish. I didn't want to put her in a position where she had to choose between me and . . ."

"And the United States?" prompted Pat.

"Something like that," said Bruce.

"Poor girl," said Pat. "It must have been so hard for her."

Bruce nodded. "I think it was." His toast popped up and he reached for the butter. "But water under the bridge, as they say. Let's not talk about it any more. Let's look to the future. Plenty of other girls – know what I mean?"

"Of course there are," said Pat. "And you've got a lot in your life as it is."

Bruce looked at her. "Are you winding me up?" he asked.

"Yes," said Pat. "Sorry. I couldn't help it. You see, wouldn't it be easier to tell the truth? Wouldn't it be easier to admit that you've lost your job and your girlfriend? Then I could tell you how sorry I am and that might help a little, just a bit. Instead of which you stand there and spin a story about resigning and giving people their freedom and all the rest. It's all a lie, isn't it, Bruce?"

Bruce, who had been buttering the toast as he spoke, stopped what he was doing. He looked down at the plate, and moved the toast slowly to one side, putting down the knife. Then his shoulders began to heave and he turned and walked out of the room, leaving Pat in the kitchen, alone with her sudden guilt.

"I feel terrible," said Pat to Domenica. "I could have stopped myself, but I didn't. And then, suddenly, he seemed to crumple."

"Crumple?" asked Domenica, taking a sip of her sherry. It was a lovely thought. "Deflate?"

"Yes," said Pat. "And that was it. He left the kitchen – and I felt terribly guilty. After all, he's lost his job and now he's lost his girlfriend. I suppose he just felt a bit vulnerable – and I made it all the worse for him by crowing."

Domenica shook her head. "You didn't crow. You just told him a few truths about himself. I suspect that you did him a good turn."

Pat thought about this. Perhaps it was time for Bruce to be deflated, and perhaps she was the person who had to do it. And yet it had not been easy and she had felt bad about it; so bad that she had come straight through to speak to Domenica.

"Not that your good turn will have much effect," Domenica went on. "I don't think that a few painful moments will have much long-term impact on that young man. Yes, he's feeling miserable, and he might do a little bit of thinking as a result of what you said. But people don't change all that radically on the basis of a few remarks made to them. It takes much more than that. In fact, there's the view that people don't change at all. I think that's a bit extreme. But don't expect too much change."

Pat frowned. Surely people did change. They changed as they matured. She remembered herself at fourteen. She was a different person now. "People grow up, though," she said. "They change as they grow up. We all do."

Domenica waved a hand in the air. "Oh, we all grow up. But once the personality is formed, I don't think that you get a great deal of change. Bruce is a narcissist, as we've all agreed. Do you see him becoming something different? Can you imagine him not looking in mirrors and worrying about his hair? Can you imagine him thinking that people don't fancy him? I can't. Not for the moment." She put her glass down on the table and looked at Pat. "How old is Bruce, by the way?"

"He's twenty-five," said Pat. "Or just twenty-six. Somewhere around there."

Domenica looked thoughtful. "Well, that's rather interesting. Men are slower, you know. They mature rather later than we do. We get there in our early twenties, but they take rather longer than that. Indeed, I believe that there's a school of psychology that holds that men are not fully responsible until they reach the age of twenty-eight."

Pat thought this was rather late. And what did it mean to say that men were not fully responsible until that age? Could they not be blamed for what they did? "Isn't that a bit late?" she asked. "I thought that we were held responsible from . . ." From what age were we held responsible? Was it sixteen? Or eighteen? Young people ended up in court, did they not, and were held to account for what they had done? But at what age did all that start?

Domenica noticed Pat's surprise. "Twenty-eight does seem a bit late," she said. "But there's at least something to it. If you look at the crime figures they seem to bear this out. Young men commit crimes – ones that get noticed – between seventeen and twenty-four, twenty-five. Then they stop." She thought for a moment and smiled at some recollection. "I knew a fiscal," she went on. "He spent his time prosecuting young men up in Dunfermline. Day in, day out. The same things. Assault. Theft. So on. And he said that he saw the same people, from the same families, all the time. Then he said something very funny, which I shall always remember. He said that the fiscals saw the same young men regularly between the age of seventeen and twenty-six, and then the next time they saw them was when they were forty-five and they had hit somebody at their daughter's wedding! What a comment!"

"But probably true?"

"Undoubtedly true," agreed Domenica. "On two counts. Weddings can be violent affairs, and everything runs in families. You've heard me on genetic determinism before, haven't you? But that's another topic. Let's get back to excuses, and change, and Bruce. If you think that twenty-eight is a bit late for responsibility – true responsibility – to appear, then what would you say to forty?"

"Very late."

Domenica laughed. "Yes, maybe. But again, if you ask people to describe how they've behaved over the years, you will often find that they say they've looked at it very differently, according to the stage of life that they're at. Here I am, for example, sitting here with all the wisdom of my sixty years – what a thought, sixty! – and I can definitely see how I've looked at things differently after forty. I'm less tolerant of bad behaviour, I think, than I used to be. And why do you think that is?"

Pat shrugged. "You get a bit more set in your ways? You become more judgmental?"

"And what is wrong with being judgmental?" Domenica asked indignantly. "It drives me mad to hear people say: 'Don't be judgmental.' That's moral philosophy at the level of an Australian soap opera. If people weren't judgmental, how could we possibly have a moral viewpoint in society? We wouldn't have the first clue where we were. All rational discourse about what we should do would grind to a halt. No, whatever you do, don't fall for that weak-minded nonsense about not being judgmental. Don't be excessively judgmental, if you like, but always – always – be prepared to make a judgment. Otherwise you'll go through life not really knowing what you mean."

Pat was silent. She had not come to see Domenica to discuss developmental psychology. She had come to talk about Bruce, and, specifically, to ask what she should do.

"Very interesting," she said quietly. "But what should I do? Do you think I should apologise to Bruce?"

"Nothing to apologise about," snapped Domenica.

"I feel so sorry for him," said Pat. "I feel . . ."

"Don't," interrupted Domenica. "Be judgmental. He told you a series of lies. And even if he isn't quite twenty-eight yet, he should know better."

"More judgmentalism?"

"Absolutely," said Domenica. "Silly young man. What a waste of space!"

16. Bertie Goes to School Eventually

Irene would have liked to have driven Bertie to his first day at the Steiner School, but there was the issue of the location of their car and she was obliged to begin as she intended to continue – by catching the 23 bus as it laboured up the hill from Canonmills.

"It would be nice to be able to run Bertie to school," she had remarked to Stuart the previous evening, "but not knowing exactly where the car is makes it somewhat difficult, would you not agree?"

"Don't look at me," said Stuart. "You were the last to use it. You parked it. You find it."

Irene pursed her lips. "Excuse me," she said. "I very rarely use that car, and I certainly was not the last one to drive it. You drove it when you went through to Glasgow for that meeting a couple of months ago. Remember? It was that meeting when you bumped into that person who used to live next to your parents in Dunoon. I distinctly remember your telling me that. And that was the last time the car was used. So you parked it – not me."

Stuart was silent. Irene glanced at him with satisfaction. "Try to remember the journey back," she said. "You would have come in on the Corstorphine Road, would you not, and driven back through Murrayfield? Did you turn off at the West End? Did you come along Queen Street? Try to remember."

Stuart remained silent, looking up at the ceiling. Then he looked down at the floor.

"Well?" pressed Irene. "Did you come back that way?"

Stuart turned to her. "I came back by train," he said quietly. "I remember it because I saw the Minister on the train, eating a banana muffin, and he said hello to me and I was impressed that he had remembered me. I remember thinking how nice it was of him to make the effort. He sees so many civil servants."

"Yes, yes," said Irene. "The Minister. Banana muffins. But the car. What about the car?"

"Are you sure that I drove there?" asked Stuart weakly,

although he knew the answer even as he asked the question. Irene would remember exactly; she always did.

For a few moments there was complete silence. Then Irene spoke. "I saw you get into it," she said. "You waved goodbye and drove off. So what does this mean?"

When Stuart replied his voice was barely audible. "Then it's still in Glasgow," he said. He waved a hand in a westerly direction. "Somewhere over there."

Irene's tone was icy. "You mean that you have left the car – our car – in Glasgow? That it's been there for several months? And you completely forgot about it?"

"So it would appear," said Stuart. He sounded wretched. He was in awe of Irene, and he hated to be the object of her scorn. "I must have caught the train without thinking."

"Well, that's just fine, then," said Irene. "That's the end of our car. It'll be stripped bare by now. Or stolen."

Stuart attempted to defend himself. "I'm sure that I parked it legally," he said. "Which means that it's probably still there. Perhaps the battery will be flat, but that may be all."

Irene failed to respond to his optimism. "When you say it will still be there," she said evenly, "what exactly do you mean by there? Where precisely is there?"

"Glasgow," said Stuart.

"Where in Glasgow? Glasgow's a big city."

"Near the Dumbarton Road," said Stuart. "Somewhere . . . somewhere there. That's where my meeting was. Just off the Dumbarton Road."

"Well, I suggest that you go and find it as soon as possible," said Irene, adding: "If you can."

Stuart nodded miserably. He would go through to Glasgow next weekend, by train, and take a taxi out to the Dumbarton Road. He had a vague recollection of where he might have parked, in a quiet cul-de-sac, and there was no reason why the car should not still be there. People left their cars for months at the roadside, and the cars survived. It was different, of course, if one had a fashionable or tempting car, like the car that Domenica Macdonald drove – that sort of car would be bound to attract the attention of joy-riders or vandals – but their car, an old Volvo estate, would be unlikely to catch anybody's eye.

And then it occurred to him that when he made the trip over to Glasgow, he would take Bertie with him. He would take him away from whatever classes Irene had planned for him – Saturday was saxophone in the morning, if he remembered correctly, and junior life-drawing in the afternoon – and he would take him with him on the train. Bertie would love that. He had hardly ever been on a train before, Stuart realised, and yet that was exactly the sort of thing that a father should do with his son. He felt a momentary pang. I've been a bad father, he thought. I've left the fathering to Irene. I've failed my son.

No more was said about the car that evening and the next morning Irene was too busy getting Bertie ready for school to talk to Stuart about cars, or anything else. She had awoken Bertie early and dressed him in his best Oshkosh dungarees.

"Such smart dungarees," said Irene.

Bertie looked doubtful. "Do other boys wear them?" he asked.

"Dungarees? Of course they do," Irene reassured him. "Go down to Stockbridge and see all those boys in dungarees."

"But theirs aren't pink."

"Nor are yours, Bertie," scolded Irene. "These are crushed strawberry. They are not pink." She looked at her watch. "And we don't have the time to sit around and talk about dungarees. Look at the time. You're going to have to get used to being in time for school. It's not like . . ."

She was about to say "nursery school", but stopped herself. In time, Bertie would forget about nursery school and the ignominy of his suspension. His psychotherapy would help – she knew that – but ultimately it was time; simple, old-fashioned time that was the healer.

They ate a quick breakfast and set off for Dundas Street. Irene noticed that Bertie avoided treading on the lines in the pavement, and sighed. There were definite signs of neurosis there, she thought; Dr Fairbairn must be informed. As she thought this, she pictured Dr Fairbairn in his consulting room, wearing that rather natty jacket that he liked to wear. He was such a sympathetic man, and so attuned to the feelings of others, just as one could expect. It would be wonderful to be married to a man like that, rather than to a statistician in the Scottish Executive. She glanced down at Bertie, as if afraid that he might read her disloyal thoughts, and he looked up at her.

"It's all right, Mummy," he said quietly. "I know what you're thinking."

17. *Down Among the Innocents*

Sitting at his new desk, with his name printed out in large letters in front of him, Bertie stared at his new classmates. There were fifteen of them, eight boys and seven girls, none of whom he knew. He at least had the advantage over them; he could read the names of all the others, whereas most of them could not. He looked at the placards: Luke, Marcus, Merlin, Tofu, Larch, Christoph, Hiawatha and Kim (boys); and Jocasta, Angel, Lakshmi, Skye, Pansy, Jade and Olive (girls).

He looked in vain for Jock, the boy he had met at his interview and who he wanted so much to be his friend, but there was no sign of him. So he had gone to Watson's, Bertie concluded; it was just as I thought. Jock would be at Watson's that very morning, playing rugby perhaps, rather than sitting in a circle with Tofu and the rest.

There was a short talk from Miss Harmony, the teacher, a tall woman with an encouraging smile, who explained what fun going to school was. They would learn so much, she said, and enjoy themselves in the process. There would be music, too, and they would shortly start on the recorder.

"It's like a whistle," said the teacher. "You blow it and – *peep* – out comes some music. Such fun!"

"And very well suited to early music," said Bertie brightly.

There was a silence, and the teacher spun round. "What was that, Bertie? Did you say something, Liebling?"

"I said that the recorder is very well suited to playing Renaissance music," he said. "Italian music, for example. *The Lamento di Tristan*. That sort of thing."

"She said it goes *peep*," said Tofu, looking accusingly at Bertie. "Or does it go *poop*? Hah!"

All the children thought this was extremely funny, and laughed loudly. Tofu smiled modestly.

The teacher sighed. "We don't laugh at things like that," she said softly. "We must learn that such things just aren't funny. Tofu, darling, remember that we're quite grown-up now. And you, Bertie, what an interesting thing to say. Can you play the recorder already?"

"A bit," said Bertie. "The fingering isn't all that hard. It's easier than playing the saxophone."

"Sexophone?" said Tofu, smiling at the resultant giggles.

The teacher glared at him. "Bertie said 'saxophone', Tofu. Perhaps you did not hear him correctly." She turned to Bertie. "And do you play the saxophone, Bertie?"

"Yes," said Bertie. "But I don't have it with me."

"No," said the teacher. "So I see. Well, I'm sure that we shall all have the chance to hear you playing the saxophone some time soon. The saxophone, boys and girls, was invented by a man called Arthur Sax, a Frenchman. He made many beautiful brass instruments."

"Adolf Sax," corrected Bertie politely. "And he was Belgian."

The teacher looked at Bertie, and then at Tofu, who had started to tickle the girl sitting next to him.

"Tofu, dear," she said firmly. "Girls don't like being tickled."

"Oh don't they?" said Tofu. "I know lots of girls who like being tickled. They like it a lot."

The teacher was silent. It was time for some diversion, she felt. She crossed the room to the cupboard and opened the door. The children watched closely as she took out a pile of old copies of the *Guardian* and handed a folded copy to each child.

"Now you'll know what this is," she said.

A forest of hands shot up. "It's the *Guardian*," the innocents cried out.

"Well done," she said. "And can anybody name another news-paper for me?"

There was complete silence. The children looked at one another in puzzlement. Then Bertie spoke. There were plenty of other newspapers, and he had read a number of them. There was the *Scotsman* and the *Herald* and a newspaper called the *Daily Telegraph*.

"The *Daily Telegraph*," he said.

The teacher looked at him. "Perhaps," she said. Then, turning to the class in general she gave them their instructions. They were to fold the *Guardian* up, she said, and then they were to try to cut out the shape of a man. Then, when they unfolded it, they would have lots of little men, all joined together in a chain.

Picking up a copy herself, she demonstrated the folding and the cutting. "There," she said, holding up the result. "Look at that long line of little men, all holding hands."

"Gays," said Tofu.

The teacher put down her paper cut-out. "Tofu, dear, if you wouldn't mind just going and standing outside the door for five minutes. And while you're there, you can think about the things that you say."

"Shall I hit him for you?" asked Larch, a burly boy with a very short hair-cut.

"No," said the teacher quickly, and then, under her breath so that nobody might hear, she muttered: "Not just yet."

When the time came for the morning interval, Bertie went out into the playground by himself. He was aware of the fact that he alone was wearing dungarees and he smarted with embarrassment. Tofu, for example, had electric sneakers that sent out small pulses of light each time he took a step, and even Merlin, who was wearing obviously home-made sandals and a rainbow-coloured jacket, at least had normal trousers. Bertie felt miserable: everybody else seemed to have made a friend already, or even more than one friend. Tofu had a knot of four or five others around him, even including somebody from one of the classes above. Bertie had nobody, so when

Tofu came up to him a few minutes later, he had nobody to defend him.

"Dungarees!" the other boy said contemptuously. "Or are they pyjamas?"

"It's not my fault," said Bertie. "It's my mother."

Tofu looked at him and sneered. "Dungarees are good for falling over in," he said suddenly. "Like this." And with that he gave Bertie a push, causing him to fall to the ground. There was laughter, and Tofu walked off.

Bertie picked himself up off the ground and dusted his dungarees. There was a large brown patch on one of the knees. As he attended to this, he became aware of the fact that a girl was standing beside him. It was Olive.

"Poor Bertie," she said. "It's not your fault that you look so silly. It really isn't. And that Tofu is a horrid boy. Everybody knows he's horrid." She paused. "But I suppose we should feel sorry for him."

"Why?" asked Bertie. "Why should we feel sorry for him?"

"Because he doesn't have a mummy," explained Olive. "She was a vegan and she starved to death. My dad told me all about it."

Bertie was horrified. "And what about his daddy?" he asked. "Has he got a daddy?"

"Yes," said Olive. "But he's a vegan too, so he won't last long either."

"And Tofu himself?" whispered Bertie.

"He's very hungry," Olive replied. "We were at nursery together, and I saw him stealing ham sandwiches from the others' lunch boxes. Yes, he's very hungry. In fact, he's not going to last too long himself. So cheer up, Bertie! Cheer up!"

18. On the Way Home

For the first few days, they went home early. Irene was there at the school gate, in good time, along with all the other parents, waiting for the children to be released. She looked about her, seeing whether she recognised anybody: she knew that the parents of the other children would see a lot of one another over the years ahead, and she was interested to find out what they were like. Most of the faces were unfamiliar, although there was one woman whom she had met somewhere or other and who nodded in her direction. Where had it been? Yoga? The floatarium? Edinburgh was like that; there were so many familiar faces but they were often difficult to place exactly.

Her gaze moved discreetly over the other parental faces. They were much as she expected; ordinary, reasonable people, just like herself. Irene felt comfortable.

"Warm, isn't it?" said a voice just behind her.

She turned and looked at the speaker. He was a tall man, with a rather thin face, and dark hair swept back over his head. He was wearing a pair of bottle-green slacks and a thin, denim jacket.

"I'm Barnabas Miller," he said, reaching out to shake her hand. "I'm Tofu's father. And you're . . ."

"Bertie's mother," said Irene. And then, laughing, she added: "I have a name as well, I suppose. Irene Pollock."

Barnabas nodded. "No doubt we'll all meet at the parents' evenings," he said. "They're very good with that sort of occasion. This is a very happy school."

"Yes," said Irene. "No doubt we will." She paused. "And Tofu – it was Tofu, wasn't it? – was he at nursery here?"

"Yes," said Barnabas. "We took him out for a while – minor behavioural issues – and then he went back. He's a very expressive child. I looked after him at home while I was writing my book. My wife is often away. She lectures on diet." (Note: *Olive was wrong, of course; Tofu's mother may have been thin, but she was still quick – in the old-fashioned sense of the word.*)

Irene was interested. "Your book? What do you write?"

"I've just had a new one come out," said Barnabas. "*The sorrow of the nuts*. I don't imagine that you've read it."

"Sorry," said Irene. "What is it? Fiction?"

Barnabas shook his head. "No. It's a holistic nutrition book. It examines the proposition that nuts have energy fields – and some form of morphic resonance. You'll have heard of Rupert Sheldrake, I take it?"

Irene had, but only just. "The man who wrote *The New Science of Life*?"

"Yes," said Barnabas. "He's the one who pointed out that there are resonant energy fields that contain biologically significant information. He proved it with the milk-top hypothesis."

Irene frowned. "I'm sorry," she said. "I did look at that book, ages ago, and I've forgotten . . ."

"No need to apologise," said Barnabas. "Sheldrake reminds us that before the war birds had worked out how to peck away at the foil tops of milk bottles and drink the top of the milk on the doorstep. It took them some time to learn this, but eventually they did. Then along came the war and they stopped using those foil tops – metal had to be kept for other uses. And so several generations of birds never saw those milk tops. Then, after the war they were able to introduce those tops again and, lo and behold, the birds knew immediately what to do."

"And Sheldrake says?"

"That the only way in which the birds could have picked up that knowledge would be if there had been some sort of energy field which contained that information for them. He calls it morphic resonance."

Irene reflected on this. It was challenging stuff. "And your book?" she asked.

"It explores the possibility that nuts have feelings," said Barnabas solemnly. "And it concludes that they do. Not feelings in the sense that we might use the term about ourselves, but feelings in the sense of some form of quasi-conscious response to the world." He paused. "Not everyone would agree with me, of course. But it does have major dietary implications."

"It means that eating nuts is cruel?" prompted Irene.

"Not exactly," said Barnabas. "But it might be thought inconsiderate."

"Do you eat them yourself?" asked Irene. "Not that I mean to be personal. I hope you don't mind my asking."

"I'm in the process of giving them up," said Barnabas. "After all, I feel that I should practise at least some of what I preach."

Irene was about to say something when there was a sudden noise of shouting and laughing and the children streamed out of the building. When Bertie saw Irene, he seemed to hesitate for a few seconds, but then came forward to her.

"Well, Bertie," asked Irene. "How was it? How was your first day of school? Did you learn anything."

"I learned a little about life," said Bertie.

"Good," said Irene. "Now let's go home. We'll get the 23 from up the road."

They walked back up Spylaw Road and on towards Bruntsfield. They were just in time for a 23 bus as it came up the road from Holy Corner.

"We shall sit on the top, Bertie," said Irene. "We can look out and see what's happening on the pavement."

They found seats and sat down on the upper deck. Bertie was silent as the bus started its journey back. He looked down at the dirt stain on the knee of his trousers, the stain caused by the assault perpetrated on him by the poor, doomed Tofu. Could Olive be right that he was starving to death? Were people allowed to starve to death these days, now that the Labour Party was in power? Surely not.

Irene was lost in her thoughts too. The bus had stopped near a bank cash machine, and she noticed a young man, blanket around his legs, sitting on the pavement right next to the machine. As people came to draw their money, he looked up at them and asked for change. The sight made her angry. He was able-bodied, was he not? He was young enough to work, or draw benefit if he could not: what right did he have to importune people in this way? People had the right to draw money, she felt, without being subjected to any pressure. And where were the police? Did they stand by and tolerate this? It appeared that they did.

She stopped herself. Should I be thinking like this? she wondered. Like what? She supplied her own answer: like a Conservative. The problem was that whenever the Conservatives made a policy statement these days she found herself agreeing with it. That was awkward, in her book, and she put the thought out of her mind. But then the thought occurred to her: perhaps I'm a Conservative leftist. That sounded much more respectable than being a leftist Conservative. But what exactly was the difference?

19. Matthew's Situation

Matthew, proprietor of the Something Special Gallery, and Pat's employer of four months' standing, opened the gallery that morning rather earlier than usual. Pat often arrived well before he did. She came in shortly after nine, at a time when all the other galleries in the area were still firmly closed. And what would have been the point of their opening that early? People did not buy paintings at that hour, and indeed the sort of people who bought paintings were still enjoying a leisurely breakfast then or were hard at work in their offices.

Matthew had tried to work out exactly who his customers were. He had read few business books, but had eventually picked one more or less at random from the business section of a bookshop, that section so distinguished by such titles as *Cut out the Competition!* and *The New Executive You*. His choice was called *Retail Success: Ten Secrets Revealed*. Matthew thought the title absurd but had found the book more interesting than he had imagined it would be. Retail, it appeared, was a complicated process, in which people who were unwilling, for entirely understandable reasons, to hand over their money to others, were persuaded by those very others to do just that. That was secret number one: nobody really wanted to buy anything. It was then revealed that the second secret, closely allied to the first, was that even if people were persuaded to hand over their money, they wished to minimise the extent to which they did so. This led the authors of the book to counsel the reader to encourage unanticipated overspend.

Matthew's business career had not been conspicuously successful. Indeed, it had been a dismal failure: each time his father had set him up in a new enterprise it had not lasted long. If, then, there were secrets to business success, he was not party to them. His last business before the gallery had been a travel agency, which had failed as well, largely due to the incompetence of the two members of staff whom Matthew had employed and whom he had not had the courage, nor the business acumen, to dismiss. One of these employees had made a series of bad mistakes, usually of a geographical nature, but also, occasionally, of a linguistic one. One client had been sold a package holiday to Turkey, in the belief that it was Greece, and another who was travelling to Strasbourg and who wished to be booked into the Hotel de Paris there, had unfortunately been booked into the Hotel de Strasbourg in Paris. This sort of thing happened all the time.

Matthew had, in fact, tackled the young man about his geographical ignorance.

"Did they teach you geography at school?" he had asked, after one particularly awkward geographical mix-up (involving a confusion between British Columbia in Canada and the Republic of Colombia).

"What?" asked the young man.

"Geography," said Matthew. "You know – the world. Maps. Where things are."

The young man shook his head. "Dunno," he said. "Don't think so."

"Clearly not," said Matthew. "Tell me: which do you think is further south – India or Australia?"

The young man shook his head. "Difficult," he said. "Not sure."

Matthew had sighed, and left it at that. And the travel agency had limped on, and then collapsed, and he had gone back to his father apologetically and reported the failure.

Matthew's father had not been surprised. "You've got to be tougher, son," he had said. "You have to have a clear business plan and then stick to it. Set targets. Beat them. Look for ways of cutting costs. Businesses can't be left just to tick over. They go under if you do that."

Matthew had nodded. The problem was that he was not very good with people. He was too soft. He paid them too much and he could never bring himself to criticise their performance. He was not cut out for business. And that was well understood by his father, who had come to the realisation that even if the best thing for his son was to find him a business, that was no more than a facade – a sinecure, in other words. So when he heard that one of the tenants in a building he owned in Edinburgh, a gallery, was going to close, it seemed the perfect opportunity. Matthew could run that. He need not make any money, as long as he did not make too much of a loss. Perhaps a loss of fifteen to twenty thousand pounds a year would be about right, although he could carry much more than that, if need be. To Matthew's astonishment, at the end of the first quarter's trading, the gallery appeared to have made a modest profit. He had arranged an appointment with his accountant, a man who acted for one of his father's companies, and they had gone over the accounts together.

"I must say that is amazing," said the accountant, pointing to the balance sheet which he had prepared for Matthew. "I'm quite astonished. You're showing a profit." He said this, and then immediately felt embarrassed. It was tantamount to saying that he expected Matthew to fail – which of course he did.

Matthew had not noticed the slight; he looked at the figures. "According to this, I've made eleven thousand pounds in three months. Are you sure there's no mistake?"

The accountant smiled. "We're very careful about that. And I've checked the spread-sheets. You've made just over eleven thousand, as it says there. Profit. But remember, trading goes in cycles. A good quarter doesn't make a good year."

"But even if I made no more this year, that's still a respectable profit . . ." he tailed off, and then added, "for me."

The accountant nodded. "I've told your old man. I hope you don't mind. He's been quite chirpy over the last few weeks, I think. This news cheered him up even more."

Matthew barely took in this news about his father, so ecstatic was he over the gallery's success. And the news from Pat, that she was going to stay in Edinburgh and could continue to work part-time while at university, had boosted Matthew's spirits. In fact, he realised that Pat had had a great deal to do with this profit. She was good at sales. She knew the ten secrets of retail, even if she did not know that she knew them. He must talk to her about that.

Having opened the gallery that morning, and having switched on the lights that illuminated the paintings, Matthew sat back in his chair and browsed through an auction catalogue that had arrived the previous day. There was to be a sale of Scottish art at Hopetoun House, and it occurred to him that now was the time for him to start buying. With that eleven thousand pounds profit behind him he could go to the bank and get a line of credit for the expansion of his stock. Not little, frippery things, but big paintings. A Hornel perhaps.

He was thinking of this when he heard the bell which sounded as the front door opened. It would be Pat. He looked up. It was not. It was his father.

20. Second Flowering

Matthew greeted his father warmly. Although they had not always been on the easiest of terms, particularly in the days of Matthew's earlier business failures, they had come to understand one another, and with that understanding had come a comfortable and undemanding relationship. Matthew's father, Gordon, came to appreciate the fact that even if his son was a bad businessman, he was honest and well-meaning, and would not disgrace him in any way. And for his part, Matthew had reached that stage in life when one accepts parents for what they are. His father's world – the world of Rotary clubs and business lunches – would never be his own world, but did that matter?

Matthew did not know it, but Gordon felt strongly guilty about him. He felt this guilt because he believed that he had been a failure as a father. While other fathers had made time to spend with their sons, he had not. He had gone to none of the school plays which Matthew had appeared in, and had even missed the school production of *Carousel*, in which Matthew had played Billy Bigelow and his friend, Mark, had played Mr Snow. He had been too busy with business affairs and with the social life that went with that. Then Matthew had grown up and left home and he had tried to make it up to him by setting him up in businesses and putting money in his bank account. And now it was too late.

Matthew rose to greet his father. "A nice surprise," he said. "Want to buy a painting?"

Gordon smiled. "I have simple tastes in art," he said. "Highland scenes. Seascapes."

"We have both of those," said Matthew. "And a very rare Vettriano abstract."

"I came to say hello," said Gordon. "I was on my way to the lawyers in Charlotte Square. They look after me very well, those people. I'm seeing them at eleven, and I thought I'd drop in and see how things were going. I gather you're turning in a profit."

Matthew sat back in his chair and smiled. "Yes," he said. "Surprised?"

Gordon looked down. My son knows what I think of him, he thought. He expects me to be surprised if he does anything well. And that's my fault; nobody else's – mine.

"I wanted to congratulate you," he said. "Yes, I was a little bit surprised. But perhaps . . . perhaps you've found your niche. And good for you."

Matthew looked at his father. There was something about him which was slightly different. He had had a haircut, yes, and he was losing a bit of weight. But there was something else. Were his clothes slightly younger in style?

"You look in good shape," he said. "Have you started going to the gym?"

Gordon blushed. "As a matter of fact, I have. Nothing too strenuous, of course. A bit of weight training and those running machines – you know, the ones which make you sweat. I do about two hours a week."

Matthew raised an eyebrow. "Do you go by yourself?"

Gordon hesitated before he answered. "Actually," he began, "I have somebody who goes with me. She does aerobics and I do my running and pushing weights."

Matthew said nothing for a moment. She. That would explain the change. He had found a girlfriend. "Good," he said, after a while. "It's nice to have company. Who is she, by the way?"

Gordon moved across the room. He continued the conversation as he leaned forward to examine a painting.

"Nice landscape this," he said. "She's called Janis. I met her a few months ago at the Barbours. Remember them? They send their regards. Anyway, Janis was at a dinner party there and . . . and, well, we hit it off. I'd like you to meet her."

Matthew looked across the room. Why was it so hard to imagine one's parents having an emotional life? There was no reason why this should be so, but it just was. And his father, of all people! What could any woman possibly see in him . . . apart from money, of course?

"What does . . . what does Janis do?" he asked.

"She owns a flower shop," said Gordon. "It's a nice little business. People still buy flowers, you know. She says that flowers are all about guilt. Men buy flowers because they feel guilty about something. About neglecting their wives, about all that sort of thing . . ." He tailed off. And what about neglect of sons? he thought. What about that?

Matthew listened to this information. A woman who owned a flower shop? There was nothing wrong with that, of course, but he could picture her – alone in her flower shop, amidst all those carnations and bunches of red roses, waiting for her chance. And along comes his father, with his GBP 11.2 million (or that was the figure that Matthew had last heard) and, well, it would be infinitely better, would it not, than selling flowers to guilty husbands. *Gold-digger,* he thought.

Gordon turned round from the painting he had been examining. "I'd like you to meet her," he said. "How about dinner in the club this Friday? Would that suit?"

There was something almost pathetically eager in his tone that made Matthew regret what he had been thinking; more guilt, but this time the son's rather than the father's. There was so much guilt in Edinburgh, everywhere one turned. Everyone felt guilty about something. Guilt. Guilt.

"Yes," said Matthew, guiltily. "I could be free. What time?"

"Seven-guilty," said Gordon, and then rapidly correcting himself, "I mean seven-thirty."

"Fine," said Matthew. "I look forward to meeting . . ."

"Janis," supplied his father. "With an *is,* not an *ice.*"

Matthew wondered whether this made a difference. He had a very clear idea of what she would be like, however she spelled her name. Blonde hair. And sharp features. And a nose for money.

They moved on to other subjects. Gordon had recently sold off one of his businesses and told Matthew about what had happened to it in its new hands. Then he related developments at the golf club, where a new secretary had been appointed and had upset some of the members by unilaterally changing the date of the annual dinner dance, a small thing perhaps, but a big thing for some.

And there was more of that sort of news, although Matthew paid even less attention to it than usual. He was wondering: what if I didn't have my father behind me? What if somebody came along and took all that support away from me? How would I react to being done out of my inheritance? Badly, he thought.

21. *Demographic Discussions*

Pat came into the gallery to find Matthew at his desk, sunk in thought. She looked at her watch. "You're in early," she said brightly. Matthew looked up at her and mumbled a good-morning.

Since his father had left ten minutes earlier, he had been sitting at his desk thinking of the implications of Janis. It was possible – just possible – that she had no ulterior intent, that her interest in his father was emotional rather than pecuniary. But was that likely? Matthew could not imagine that anybody could find his father attractive; indeed, he was a most un-romantic figure, with his thoughts of balance-sheets and the Watsonian Club and Rotary lunches. Could any woman find any of that interesting? Surely not. And yet, and yet . . . It was one of the constant surprises of this life, Matthew had found, that women found men attractive, against all the odds, and irrespective of the sort of man involved. The most appalling men had their partners, did they not, and these women often appeared to *like* them. There were so many examples of that, including people in the public eye. It was well-known, for instance, that psychopaths took rather well to the world of business and that modern business culture encouraged precisely that sort of personality. Some of these business moguls were often much sought after by women. Why? Because such men were cave-men, without their physical clubs, perhaps, but with the modern equivalent, and there were some women who simply found such men interesting.

And of course one had to remember – and Matthew did – that there were many women whose condition was one of quiet desperation. There were many women who wanted a man and who simply could not find one, for demographic or other reasons. Such women will accept anybody who comes along and shows the remotest interest, even my father, thought Matthew.

He looked up at Pat. "Why are there so few men, do you think, Pat?"

He asked the question without thinking, and was immediately embarrassed. But Pat smiled at him, apparently unsurprised to be greeted this early in the morning with such a query.

"Well," she said. "Are there so few men? Aren't there roughly the same number – to begin with – and only a little bit later, when the men die off, does the number of women go up? Isn't that the way it works?"

Matthew frowned. "That may be true," he said. "That may be true in terms of strict numbers, but why is that even before the point at which men start to die off, there do not seem to be enough men to . . . to go round. Isn't that what women find?"

Pat thought about this for a moment. Matthew was probably right; there never seemed to be enough men to satisfy women. Now that sounded odd; she would not put it quite that way. There never seemed enough men to provide each woman who was looking for a man with a man. That was it. Yes, Matthew was right. "Yes," she said. "It's not easy to find a boyfriend these days. I know plenty of people who would love to find a man, but can't find one. We don't know where they've gone. Disappeared."

Matthew thought: you could look under your nose, you know. What about me? But said nothing. Somehow, he suspected, he did not count in this particular reckoning.

"Why is it?" he said. "What's happened?"

Pat thought that he must know; but Matthew had always struck her as being unworldly. Perhaps he was unaware.

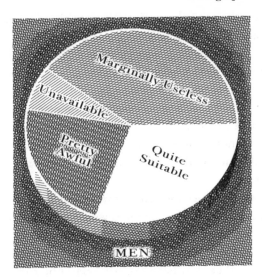

"Some men aren't interested, Matthew," she said. "You do realise that, don't you?"

"Oh, I know about all that," said Matthew. "But how many men are like that?"

Pat looked out of the window, as if to assess the passers-by. "Quite a lot," she said. "It depends where you are, of course. Edinburgh's more like that than Auchtermuchty, you know. And San Francisco is more like that than Kansas City. Ten per cent?"

"Well, that leaves ninety per cent."

Pat shook her head. There had been a major change in social possibilities for men. They had been trapped, too, by the very structures that had trapped women, and now they had been freed of those and were enjoying that freedom. "No, it doesn't," she said. "Of those ninety per cent, a very large percentage now aren't interested not because they're not interested – so to speak – but because they're perfectly happy by themselves. Women clutter their lives. They don't need women any more. There are maybe . . ." She plucked a figure out of the air . . . "Twenty per cent of men who think that they're better off by themselves. So if you add the ten per cent who aren't available anyway, that means thirty per cent who are out of it, so to speak."

Matthew thought about this. "But surely there will be the same number of women who drop out too? There'll be women who don't like men and women who may like men but who don't want any involvement with them. So surely these two cancel one another out, and you end up with two equal groups?"

Pat was sure that this was wrong. The objection to Matthew's theory, at least from her point of view, was that she had not met many women who would prefer to be by themselves rather than with a man, if a suitable man came along. But that, of course, meant nothing – and she was intelligent enough to see it. One should not generalise from one's own experience, because one's own experience was coloured by one's own initial assumptions and perspective. If you like men, then you'll end up in the company of those who like men too, and then you reach the conclusion that the whole world likes men. And that clearly was not true.

She sat down, facing Matthew. She was puzzled. "Why are you asking about all this?"

"It's because my father seems to have found a girlfriend," he said glumly. "And I don't know what she sees in him."

Pat had met Matthew's father on a previous visit he had paid to the gallery. "But your father's very nice," she said. She paused, before adding: "And tremendously rich."

22. *Chow*

"Now tell me, Bertie," said Dr Fairbairn, straightening the crease of his trousers as he crossed his knees. "Tell me: have you written your dreams down in that little notebook I gave you?" Bertie did not cross his legs. He was unsure about Dr Fairbairn, and he wanted to be ready to leap to his feet if the psychotherapist became more than usually bizarre in his statements. The best escape route, Bertie had decided, would be to dart round the side of his desk, leap over the psychotherapist's leather-padded couch, and burst through the door that led into the waiting room. From there he could launch himself down the stairs, sliding down the banister, if needs be, and run out into the safety of the street. No doubt somebody would call the police and Dr Fairbairn would be led off to Carstairs, which Bertie understood to be the place where people of this sort sometimes ended up. They would take good care of him there, as the doctors would all be friends of his and would perhaps allow him to play golf in the hospital grounds while he was getting better.

He looked at Dr Fairbairn. He noticed that the tie which the psychotherapist frequently wore – the one with the teddy-bear motif – was missing, and that in its place there was a dark silk tie with a question-mark motif. Why would Dr Fairbairn have a question-mark on his tie? Bertie was intrigued.

"Yes, I've written down my dreams," said Bertie. "But can you tell me, Dr Fairbairn: why have you got those question-marks on your tie?"

Dr Fairbairn laughed. "You're always very observant about what I'm wearing, Bertie. Why do you think this is?"

"Because I can see your tie," said Bertie. "I have to look at you when I talk to you and I see what you're wearing."

Dr Fairbairn stared at Bertie. "You're not jealous, are you Bertie? You're not jealous of my tie, are you?"

Bertie drew a deep breath. Why should he think that he should be jealous, when he already had a tie at home? "No, I'm not jealous," he said. "I just wondered."

Dr Fairbairn nodded. "You wouldn't by any chance have thought of cutting my tie off? Have you thought that about your father's ties?"

Bertie's eyes narrowed. Would they let Dr Fairbairn wear a tie in Carstairs? he wondered. Or would they take it away from him? Would they cut if off? Dr Fairbairn was always going on about other people's anxieties that things would be cut off; well, it would teach him a lesson if somebody came and cut his own tie off. That would serve him right.

"I've never wanted to do that," he said quietly. "I like Daddy's ties. He's a got a tartan one that he sometimes wears with his kilt."

The mention of a kilt seemed to interest Dr Fairbairn, who wrote something down on his pad of paper. The psychotherapist opened his mouth to speak, but Bertie was too quick for him. "My dream," he said, fishing into his pocket for the notebook he had been given. "We mustn't forget my dream."

Dr Fairbairn smiled. "Of course," he said. "Why don't you tell me all about it? I'm very interested in your dreams, Bertie. Dreams are very important, you know."

Bertie opened the notebook. He did not think that dreams were important. In fact, he thought that dreams were silly, and hardly worth remembering at all. Indeed, he had been quite unable to remember many dreams recently and had been obliged to resort to a dream he had experienced some months ago, so as to humour Dr Fairbairn.

Dr Fairbairn stared at Bertie. What a strange little boy this was – only six years old, and how determined, how astonishingly determined he was to suppress the Oedipal urge. It would come out, of course, but it might take some time, and dream analysis could help. All would be revealed. There would be father figures galore in this dream; just wait and see!

"I was on a train," read Bertie. "I was on a train and the train was going through the countryside. There were fields on either side of it and there were people standing in the fields waving to us as we went past."

"Were these people men or women?" asked Dr Fairbairn gently, his pencil moving quickly across the paper. They would be men, of course: fathers . . . watching, scrutinising.

"Girls," said Bertie. "Girls with wide-brimmed hats. All of them were girls."

Dr Fairbairn nodded. "I see," he said. "Girls." Waving goodbye to girls? To mother, of course; that was mother in the field, being left behind by the masculine train.

"Yes," said Bertie. "Should I go on, Dr Fairbairn?"

"Of course."

"I looked out of the window of the train and then I went back into the compartment. It was an old train, and there were separate compartments, with wood panels on the walls. I sat there for a while, and then I got up and went out into the corridor. It was a long corridor and I began to walk down it, looking into the other compartments as I went along."

"And who was in the compartments?" asked Dr Fairbairn. "Was your father there?"

"No," said Bertie. "I did not see my father. He must have been in his office – at the Scottish Executive. No, I did not recognise anybody on the train. They were all strangers. Strangers and dogs."

"Dogs?" interrupted Dr Fairbairn. "How interesting!"

"One of the dogs was a big furry dog. He looked at me and barked."

Bertie looked at Dr Fairbairn, who had stopped writing when he mentioned the dog and who was staring at him in a very strange way. He wondered whether the time had come to make his escape, but the psychotherapist did not move. Dr Fairbairn was thinking about the dog. A large furry dog could only be one thing . . . a chow. And that, as every follower of Vienna was only too aware, *was precisely the breed of dog owned by Sigmund Freud*. Already the title of a paper was forming in his mind: *Echoes of the Freudian Chow: nocturnal symbols and a six-year-old boy*.

"Chow," said Dr Fairbairn quietly.

Bertie looked up sharply. This must be a signal.

"Ciao," he said quickly, and rose to his feet.

For a moment, Dr Fairbairn looked puzzled, but then he glanced at his watch and nodded to Bertie. He wanted to speak to Irene, and there would be ten minutes or so before his next patient arrived.

"Ask Mummy to come in for a moment," he said to Bertie. "You don't mind waiting in the waiting room, do you?"

Bertie did, but did not say it. There was no point. There was nothing he could do to make his life more as he wanted it to be. His life was so limited, so small in its room. Waiting. Listening. Being lectured to. Told to write his dreams down. Taken to the floatarium. Forced to learn Italian. And there were years of this ahead of him – year upon endless year.

23. *An Astonishing Revelation is Almost Made*

Bertie sat quietly in the waiting room, paging through a magazine. He hated it when his mother went in for what she described as her "few quick words" with Dr Fairbairn. To begin with, it would be more than a few words, and they were never quick – she would be ages, he thought – and then he knew that they were discussing him, and he resented that.

Dr Fairbairn had promised him that he would not tell his mother about that list he had made him write down, but Bertie was sure that he would do just that, and would in all probability show it to her too. Dr Fairbairn was simply too unstable to be trusted, Bertie thought, and it astonished him that nobody had yet noticed just how dangerous he was. They would find out one of these days, of course, when Dr Fairbairn finally attacked one of his patients, and then he would be able to say that he had seen it all along. But until then nobody would listen to him.

Bertie turned the pages of his magazine, an old copy of *Scottish Field*. He liked this magazine, because it had pictures of people fishing and advertisements for waterproof clothing, for fishing tackle, and for multi-bladed penknives. Bertie had seen an article on how to tie a fly, and had been fascinated by what he had read. He could try that, perhaps, if only somebody would teach him – which of course they never would. He imagined that that was the sort of thing one learned at Watson's, with boys like Jock; and what fun it would be to cut up the little bits of feather and then tie them together to resemble a fly. That would be far more fun than cutting up old copies of the *Guardian* to make chains of paper men.

Bertie found himself perusing the social section, at the end of the magazine. He studied the pictures carefully. The life depicted there looked such fun. There had been a vintage-car rally, and a party afterwards, and the people were standing about their old cars, drinking a glass of champagne, their motoring glasses pushed over the brow of their heads. They were handsome, exciting-looking people, and the cars were so beautiful;

unlike our car, thought Bertie – and we don't even know where our car is parked.

He stared at the people in the photograph. A tall man was smiling at the camera – that was Mr Roddy Martine, it said underneath. It would be wonderful to be as tall as that, thought Bertie. Nobody would try to push Mr Roddy Martine over, thought Bertie; they wouldn't dare. And next to him was a kind-looking man with a moustache – Mr Charlie Maclean, it said. He was holding a fishing rod and smiling. What fun they were all having, thought Bertie. At least there are some people in Scotland who can have some fun. Perhaps Mr Charlie Maclean had a son, he thought, and I could meet him and he could be my friend, as Jock so nearly was. There was no photograph of Dr Fairbairn, Bertie observed, nor one of anybody he knew. Even Mr Dalyell, that nice man he had met in Valvona and Crolla, was not pictured here. Bertie sighed.

Inside the consulting room, Irene sat in the chair so recently vacated by Bertie. She looked at Dr Fairbairn and noticed his tie. She always noticed his clothes – the lightweight blue linen jacket, perfectly pressed in spite of linen being such a difficult material. And the tie, with its enigmatic decoration; of course that was just right: life was a quest, and why should ties not reflect the fact?

"Linen's so difficult," she said. "How on earth do you manage to keep your jacket so uncrumpled? Linen defeats me."

Dr Fairbairn smiled; a modest smile, thought Irene. There was nothing triumphalist about Dr Fairbairn, even if he had the insights.

"This is a mixture, actually," said the psychotherapist. "It's mostly linen, but they've added an artificial fibre – just a little. It makes all the difference. I hardly have to iron this jacket."

"I must get the details," said Irene. "I have a linen top which looks just like Auden's face."

"After the geological catastrophe?" asked Dr Fairbairn. "Or before?"

This was a very clever reference – in fact, both of these were very clever references, and they both allowed themselves a small

smile of satisfaction. Auden had referred to the sudden deep lining
of his features – caused by a skin condition – as a geological
catastrophe. Few people knew this, of course, but *they* did.

"He might have written *In Praise of Linen*," went on Dr
Fairbairn. "If it form the one material . . ."

"Which we, the inconstant ones . . ." supplied Irene.

"It is chiefly because it is difficult to iron," ended Dr Fairbairn,
with a flourish.

They both giggled. Irene looked down at Dr Fairbairn's
houndstooth trousers – such a discreet check, she thought – and
at his highly-polished shoes.

"You take such trouble with your clothing," she said. "So few
Scotsmen do." She paused. "But I suppose we should talk about
Bertie."

"Yes," said Dr Fairbairn, frowning slightly. "We did a bit of
dream work today. Made a start on it at least."

"He never says anything about his dreams," said Irene. "He's
gone quite silent on me, in fact. It's almost as if my little boy
has become a stranger."

Dr Fairbairn nodded. "You must expect that." He paused.
"Any signs of further obsessional behaviour?"

Irene looked up at the ceiling. There had been nothing quite
as bad as the setting fire to Stuart's *Guardian*, but there certainly
had been little things. There had been deliberate mistakes with
Italian verbs (a mixing up of past participles, for example), and
there had been reluctance, marked reluctance, to practise his
scales for his grade seven saxophone examination. But apart from
that, there had been very little one could put one's finger on.

Dr Fairbairn waited for Irene to say something, but she was
silent. "Of course, Bertie could be affected by tensions within
the home – if there are any. Do you mind if I ask you about
that? Do you mind?"

Irene looked down at the floor. "Of course, you can ask," she
said. "And the answer that I'd give you would be this. Yes. There
are tensions, but they're not my fault. It's not my fault that I'm
bored. Yes, I'm bored. I feel like a wretched Madame Bovary.
I'm trapped, and my only way out, my only way out to a life

that is bigger, and more exciting, is through my little boy. My little boy who will grow up to be everything that his father is not. I am determined on that, Dr Fairbairn, I really am."

Dr Fairbairn waited for her to finish. Her voice had risen; now it subsided, and she sat quite mute, as though exhausted by the dangerous intimacy of the confession.

"I'm trapped too," he said very quietly. "And you know, I've got something to confess to you."

Irene looked up sharply. "What is that?" she whispered.

"The time's not right," said Dr Fairbairn. "Perhaps later."

24. Bruce Meets a Friend

Now that he had time on his hands, Bruce tended to stay in bed until well after eleven in the morning. He had never been keen on getting up early, in spite of having been brought up in an early-rising household, and now that he did not have to get in by nine to the offices of Macauley Holmes Richardson Black he was making the most of the opportunity to lie in bed, drifting between sleep and a delicious state of semi-wakefulness.

It was a time to think, or, rather, to dream; to luxuriate in fantasy – with thoughts of the ideal date, for example; or the car one would purchase if money were no object. The ideal date would be something like Sally – no, he would not think of her again, that stuck-up American girl who had the gall (and bad judgment) to tell him that she did not want to see him again. How dare she! Who did she think she was, telling him that she didn't want him to go over to Nantucket with her? And as for Nantucket – who had even heard of the place; some remote island with a thin beach and cold water? What made her think for even a moment that he really wanted to go there, rather than being prepared to accompany her as a gesture to her sense of disappointment over their impending separation?

It hardly did to think of all this, and Bruce, turning over crossly in his bed, tried to think of something else. There were plenty of other girls waiting for him, positively counting the minutes before he would say something to them, give them some sign of favour.

That morning he stayed in bed until twelve. Then, lazily swinging his legs over the side of the bed, allowing himself just the quickest of glances at the full-length mirror at the other end of the room, he dressed himself slowly – a pair of jeans, a rugby shirt, slip-on brown shoes. Then there was hair gel to apply and a quick shave in front of another mirror, one that enlarged the face. He stroked his chin, applying a small amount of sandalwood cologne. There was no sign of ageing, he thought; no wrinkles – yet – no sagging. Some people began to age in their twenties, or even before; not me, thought Bruce. I do not sag. Pas moi!

He left the flat, bounding down the common stairway two steps at a time, his footsteps echoing against the walls. Then out on to the street and a quick walk uphill and around the corner to the Cumberland Bar, where George Salter was waiting for him.

They shook hands. "Long time," said George.

Bruce nodded. He liked George, whom he had known since Crieff days. They were an unlikely pair, in many respects; George, who was much shorter than Bruce, with fair, close-cropped hair and a slight chubbiness, lacked Bruce's dress sense and feeling for the cool. His clothes, which always seemed slightly too tight for him, would never have been worn by Bruce; poor George, thought Bruce, with amusement; he really doesn't get it.

For all his failure to keep up with Bruce, George admired his old friend immensely. At school, he had worshipped him, to be rewarded with the occasional invitation and the general sense of privilege that went with being associated with somebody such as Bruce. He would have liked to have been as confident as Bruce was; to have had his flair; to have been able to talk like him – which I shall never be able to do, he concluded miserably, simply because I'm not clever enough. Bruce is clever.

George bought Bruce a drink and they made their way to a table.

"I hear you've resigned," said George. "Fed up?"

Bruce looked carelessly at the door. "Absolutely," he said. "I was bored out of my skin. It was the same thing every day, that job. Sheer tedium." He paused, and took a sip of his pint of Guinness. "Of course, they begged me to stay."

"Offered more money?"

"That sort of thing," said Bruce. "But no deal."

George smiled ruefully. "I admire your determination," he said. "Last time I was offered more money to stay, I accepted it like a shot."

Bruce looked at his friend. Would anybody seriously have offered George money to stay? It seemed a somewhat unlikely claim.

"So what now?" asked George. "Are you looking around?"

"I've got a few irons in the fire," Bruce said casually. "One, in particular. The wine business."

George's expression revealed that he was impressed. Bruce would be an ideal wine dealer in his view. He looked the part.

Bruce inspected his fingernails. "Yes," he went on. "It's an interesting business, one way and another. You have to know what you're doing, but I've got the basics and can pick up the rest as I go along. I thought that I might do the MW course."

George was enthusiastic. "Great idea. You'd have no difficulty with that. You'd walk it. Remember how easy you found Higher Physics."

"Maybe," said Bruce. "It's not in the bag yet, though."

There was a silence, during which Bruce glanced at George once or twice. An idea was forming in his mind. It was strange, he thought, that it had not occurred to him before, but it was really very obvious once one began to think of it. George, for all his shortcomings, had one major asset. He had capital.

"Are you interested in wine?" Bruce asked.

"Very," said George. "I don't know as much about it as you do, of course. But I like it. Sure."

Bruce thought quickly. If he had some capital at his disposal, then he would not have to look for a job in the wine trade: he could make his own job. He could take a lease on a shop somewhere in the New Town and start from there. Wine was expensive, and one would need . . . what? One hundred thousand to start with?

He picked up his glass and tipped it back to drain the dregs of the Guinness.

"Let me buy you a drink," he said to George. "And then I want to tell you about a scheme I've just thought up. And it involves you!"

George looked up at his friend with frank admiration. He had always wanted to be Bruce, but never could be; a silly, irrational desire.

"Great," he said. "Me? Great."

25. *Agreement Is Reached*

"All right," said Bruce. "This is the deal."

George smiled at him. "Go ahead."

"You've got some capital, haven't you?" Bruce said. "I don't know what you've done with it, of course. But I assume that it's reasonably intact."

George shrugged. "Reasonably," he said. "The market's taken a hit, but I was never very keen on those dot-coms, and so I'm all right. Fairly safe stuff, I think."

Bruce lowered his voice. "Do you mind my asking: who manages it?"

"Most of it is with a stockbroker over in Glasgow," said George. "He moves it around."

"Bonds?"

"Some," said George. "Equities. A property fund. They say that you should spread the risk."

Bruce laughed. "And they're right," he said, adding: "Except sometimes they're so careful that you have no risk at all. They let things stagnate."

George frowned. "Do you think . . . ?" He tailed off.

"Yes," said Bruce. "I'm prepared to bet that you're safe as the proverbial Banque d'Angleterre, but just as dull. Nothing's ever going to happen to your capital. Pure stagnation, George, my friend."

George looked at Bruce with his small, pale eyes. "But . . ."

"But if you look to see who's really making money," said Bruce, "who's really coining it in: it's the venture capital people, that's who."

George took a sip of his beer. "I thought that they didn't necessarily do so well. There's risk there, isn't there?"

Bruce exploded into laughter. "Didn't do too well? Have you seen the return they get? Twenty, thirty per cent. Easy." He paused. "Of course, some of their projects don't come up with the readies when the time's come to offload, but those are the exceptions. Believe me, I've seen it."

George smiled weakly. "You make me seem very unadventurous."

Bruce patted him on the shoulder. "Just a bit, George. Just a bit." He paused. The moment was right, he judged, and he was confident that George would agree. "But listen, here's the plan. I'm prepared to cut you in on my wine business in return for an investment from you. We'll split the profits down the middle, but you needn't lift a finger. I'll run the business. I'll do the work. You . . . you're the venture capitalist. This is your chance to get a piece of the action."

He watched for George's reaction, which was slow in coming. For a moment he wondered if he had been too quick to bring up the proposition, in which case he could merely give him time to think. George was not particularly quick on his feet – he had never been – and perhaps he would need time. But he would surely come round in the end, which should be in no more than an hour or so. In Bruce's experience, George always came round to his suggestions.

George looked down at the table. "How much are you thinking of?" he asked.

Bruce looked his friend in the eye. "We don't want to be under-capitalised," he said. "There's nothing worse than starting a business at half-cock. If you do that, then you give the opposition a head start. I've seen under-capitalised businesses go under time and time again."

ANDERSON ET SALTER

VINOTHEQUE

"Have you?" asked George. "Which ones?"

"Too many to mention," Bruce replied quickly. "Believe me."

"So how much?" asked George.

"One . . ." Bruce faltered, and stopped. "Fifty thousand," he said. "Fifty thousand will set us up as long as the lease is not too expensive. Do you think you could manage that?"

George puckered his lips. It was a weak, fleshy gesture, thought Bruce, but he controlled his irritation and smiled encouragingly at his friend.

"I suppose I could," said George, hesitantly. "I could sell some bonds and switch the funds. It wouldn't break the bank."

Bruce chuckled with delight, leaning forward to pat his friend on the back. "You've just made the best decision of your financial life," he said. "We're going to be going places together, you and me."

George moved his lips in a hesitant smile. "I hope so."

Over the next hour, Bruce outlined his plans. They were still in an incipient state, but they gathered flesh as he went along. He knew of a suitable shop, as it happened. He had surveyed it for the firm and the lease had then fallen through. He would be able to get it from the landlord for a reasonable rate if they moved quickly. And then there was the stock. That he could get from the wholesalers, although he would probably have to go and buy some of it himself from the growers. That would be fun, and he could take George along too, although . . . perhaps not. George was slightly heavy-going – although very generous, it had to be admitted, and a most loyal friend – and a trip to Bordeaux would hardly be improved by his tagging along.

George suddenly smiled. "We could go and buy the wine together," he said brightly. "You and me. We could fly to Bordeaux and then hire a car and drive round the vineyards, sampling the product. That would be great."

"Yes," said Bruce. "We might do that. Although we wouldn't be able to leave the business too long, you know. Maybe it would be best to order from wholesalers."

"You're the expert," said George.

Later, back in the flat, Bruce sat in his chair and contemplated what he had done. After George's agreement, which had really been given remarkably promptly, it had occurred to him that he should perhaps have given his friend some time to mull over his proposal – perhaps a day or two. He also wondered whether it was quite right to spring the suggestion on him in the Cumberland Bar, in a social setting. But he quickly disposed of these objections. George was a responsible adult – even if a slightly malleable one – and he had given his agreement voluntarily. And the proposition itself was not a bad one. It was not as if he were asking him to invest in some highly speculative mining shares; quite the contrary. He was offering him a stake in a business, with stock, and premises, and, what was most important of all, expertise. There was no substitute for expertise; that was the real capital of a business and their venture would have it in abundance.

And then there was the question of the name. Anderson would have to come into it, of course, and Salter too, in recognition of the source of the capital. Anderson and Salter, Vintners. That sounded good. But Bruce had a better idea, and the mere thought of it thrilled him: Anderson et Salter, Vinotheque. Brilliant! thought Bruce. World beating!

26. Bertie's Idea

While Bruce and George were having their meeting in the Cumberland Bar, during which they sealed the terms of their forthcoming partnership agreement, Bertie and his mother were in a George Street clothing shop. Bertie needed new socks, Irene had decided, as did Stuart. It was extraordinary how male socks migrated; virtually every wash produced a deficit of socks, but never of shirts or towels or indeed anything else. She had tried the expedient of securing each sock to its partner with a twist of thread, but this had simply resulted in the loss of two socks rather than one. It defied belief.

"Perhaps socks dissolve," Bertie had suggested. "Or go down the plug hole."

"Possibly," said Irene. "But we must be rational, Bertie. These socks cannot disappear in the washing machine – they must get lost at some other stage in proceedings."

"But then they'd turn up," said Bertie. "And they don't, do they?"

"We shall have to leave the issue for the time being," Irene said firmly. "There is a rational explanation for everything, as you well know."

"Except missing socks," muttered Bertie.

Irene chose to ignore this last comment. One had to combat irrational, magical thinking in children, but there were times and places to do this, and this was neither. One also had to choose one's issue, and the problem with missing socks was that the rational interpretation seemed quite inadequate. It was the sort of issue on which Arthur Koestler might have expressed a view, and perhaps had even done so, for all she knew.

Now, standing in a corner of Aitken and Niven in George Street, she surveyed the available socks. Stuart would get grey socks, as usual, as they seemed to suit him so well, while Bertie would get a couple of pairs of dark green ones – if they had them in his size. She picked up the socks and began to examine them. Bertie, seeing his mother occupied, drifted off. He had spied a rugby ball which was displayed on the top of a low cabinet. It had been signed by several players and behind it, on a stretch frame, was a rugby shirt. "All Blacks", the legend on the shirt said, and Bertie's heart gave a leap. They were very famous, those All Blacks, and they performed a frightening ritual dance before they played. Bertie had seen that on television and had been struck by the fierceness of it all. It must be very intimidating to face the All Blacks at Murrayfield and see them dancing this frightening dance right in front of you. Would he be brave enough to stand up to it, he wondered, or would he run off the field and back into the dressing room? It would be entirely understandable if one did that, although the crowd would not like it at all. They would boo and jeer, Bertie thought, if half the Scottish rugby team ran off the field in the face of the war dance of the All Blacks.

Bertie's gaze moved on from the rugby shirt. There was a framed photograph behind it, propped up against a stack of drawers in which various rugby garments were stored. He moved towards the photograph and stared more closely at it. It was a photograph of a smiling man, and it was signed. Bertie read the signature: Gavin Hastings. He stood back and looked at the picture. He liked the look of Mr Hastings, who seemed to be gazing out at him in a kind way. It would be nice to know somebody like Mr Hastings, who might invite him to watch rugby with him or who might even toss a ball to him for him to catch. What fun it would be to play rugby with Mr Hastings.

Bertie turned away. His mother was still looking at socks, examining the labels in order to exclude any which contained nylon. It would take her a long time, thought Bertie; Irene was a slow shopper and liked to scrutinise everything very carefully before she bought it. This could have its difficulties. There had been more than one unseemly row with the local greengrocer when he had asked her to stop squeezing the avocado pears to determine their ripeness. And the fishmonger had also objected when Irene had so shamelessly picked up his fish from the slab and smelled it very carefully, wrinkling her nose with disgust as she did so. Both of these occasions had embarrassed Bertie, in spite of his being used to her behaving in this fashion. It would be nice to have a normal mother, he had thought; but even normal mothers could be embarrassing to their children.

Bertie looked about him. He usually found shops rather boring, but this one, he decided, was fairly interesting. He looked at a rack of dinner suits, reaching out to feel the velvet, and behind that – what was that? – a row of kilt jackets in green tweed with buttons made of horn. Then Bertie saw a sign pointing into the next room, and stopped. *School blazers*, it said.

Glancing over his shoulder at his mother, Bertie made his way over to the few steps that led down into the next room. He moved forward slowly, and peered in the direction indicated by the sign. Yes, there they were! A whole row of Watson's plum-coloured blazers, in all the sizes. Bertie approached the rack. He reached out to touch the sleeve of one of the blazers – one that would be about his size – and then, in a sudden rush of excitement, he slipped it off its hanger and began to put it on. He could hardly believe that he was doing this, and his breath came to him in short, excited gasps.

There was a full-length mirror nearby and Bertie turned sideways-on to get a glimpse of how he looked. He saw the reflection of the badge, that wonderful crest, and he smelled the new-wool smell of the fabric. It was a perfect fit, just perfect, and he looked so good in it – just like a real Watson's boy. And it was while he was standing there, looking at himself in the mirror, that Bertie's idea came to him. It was an idea that was quite simple, when one came to think of it, but of immense significance for Bertie. It was a bold plan, an astonishing plan, but there was no reason why it would not work. All one had to do was to be brave.

And then, from behind him, so unexpected as to make him start, a voice: "Well, young man. Well?"

27. Socks

Bertie looked up at the man who was standing behind him. It was one of the assistants, smartly dressed in a dark suit. He was peering at Bertie through half-moon glasses and his expression was bemused.

"Well, young man," he said again. "Is that a good fit, do you think?"

Bertie glanced in the mirror again. "Yes," he said nervously. "I was just trying it on. I wasn't going to steal it."

The man laughed. "I didn't for one moment think you were going to steal it," he said. "Good heavens, no. I assumed that you were trying it on for size. And you say that it fits?"

Bertie unbuttoned the blazer and began to take it off. "It fits very well," he said. "It's very nice."

"It's a good brand, that one," said the man, taking the blazer from Bertie and dusting it down before replacing it on the rack. "Tell me, do you enjoy Watson's?"

Bertie looked down at the floor. "I don't go there," he said sheepishly.

The man raised an eyebrow. "You don't go there? But you were trying on the blazer . . ."

"I'd like to go there," said Bertie. "I thought that I would see what it was like to wear a Watson's blazer."

The man adjusted his glasses. "I see," he said. "Well, I suppose that's fair enough. Where do you go to school?"

"Steiner's," said Bertie.

"A very good school," said the man. "You're lucky. We hear very good reports of it."

"I know," said Bertie. "It is very nice. But there's no rugby . . ."

The man nodded. "I suppose if one wants rugby then one would need to find somewhere else. Are you very keen?"

Bertie nodded enthusiastically. "Very," he said. "I've never had the chance to play, but I'd love to." He paused. "Does Mr Hastings come in here?" he asked.

The man nodded. "Quite often. Do you know him?"

Bertie hesitated for a moment before replying. "Yes," he said. "I know him."

He did not know why he said this. It was something to do with wanting to be something that he was not; something to do with wish-fulfilment; something to do with freedom.

"I'll tell him about you next time he comes in," said the man. "What's your name?"

Bertie hesitated again, and then replied: "Jock."

"Well, Jock. Perhaps you'd better go over there to see your mother. Look, she must be wondering where you are."

Bertie saw Irene picking up a sock and scrutinising it. She caught his eye and beckoned him over. The man came with him.

"Can I advise you on those?" he asked. "Are they for Jock?"

Bertie froze. Then, leaning forward very quickly, he snatched the sock from his mother.

"I like this sock," he blustered. "I like it very much."

"Don't be ridiculous," said Irene. "That sock is Daddy's size. You need something much smaller."

The man indicated to a drawer. "We have a good selection of boys' socks here," he said. "We should be able to find something suitable for Jock."

Irene looked puzzled. "For Jock?" she asked.

"Yes," said the man, pointing to Bertie.

Again Bertie acted quickly. "He said for sock," he said to his mother. "Sock, not Jock."

The man smiled. "Does Jock need socks or not?" he asked patiently.

"I have no idea," said Irene. "I would, however, like socks for Bertie here, if you have something suitable."

The man looked at Bertie. "I thought you said your name was Jock," he said.

Irene frowned, and looked down at Bertie. "Did you, Bertie? Why did you say you were called Jock?"

Bertie looked down at the floor. "It was a mistake," he said.

Irene turned to the man. "I'm sorry," she said. "Young boys can be very fanciful."

"No matter," said the man. "Perhaps he'd like to be called

Jock. I remember wanting to be called Joe when I was a little boy. I wrote the name Joe in all my books."

Irene appeared to lose interest in this conversation and returned to the subject of socks. Bertie, feeling miserable, stood by while the adults talked. The blazer had been wonderful; such a smart garment, and it fitted him so well. His plan depended on that blazer, but it would not be easy to get hold of it. When he had tried it on, he had looked at the price ticket and had made a mental note of what it cost. It was a lot of money, of course, but Bertie had been prudent. Every birthday, when he had received a present from his aunt in Jedburgh, he had put the money into his savings account at the bank. This sum now stood at over one hundred and eighty pounds, and it would easily cover the cost of the blazer. But how would he be able to buy it? He was never allowed to come into town on his own, and his mother would surely notice it if, on their next visit to George Street, Bertie darted into Aitken and Niven and came out with a large parcel. No, he would have to get somebody else to draw the money from his account and then go up to George Street and buy it for him. But who?

On the way back down the hill, Bertie was deep in thought, as was Irene. She was wondering why Bertie should have chosen to call himself Jock. It was such a strange thing to do, and she would have to report it to Dr Fairbairn in advance of Bertie's next psychotherapy session. The thought occurred to her that Bertie was possibly suffering from a dissociative condition in which multiple personalities were beginning to manifest their presence. Jock could be one of these personae. She looked down at Bertie, who was staring at the pavement as he walked along. Was he avoiding the lines again? she wondered.

Bertie looked up and smiled, as if he had suddenly worked out the answer to a recalcitrant problem. And indeed he had. He had remembered the boy round the corner, Paddy, the one who lived on Fettes Row and who went fishing in the Pentlands. He was allowed to walk around the streets in freedom with his friends. Bertie would ask him. He would give him his card and ask him to withdraw the money from the bank machine. Then

Paddy could go up to George Street, buy the blazer for Bertie, and deliver it in secret.

Irene noticed Bertie's expression and frowned. "What are you thinking about, Bertie dear?" she asked.

And Bertie gave that answer with which all parents are so wearily familiar. "Nothing," he said.

28. Lonely Tonight

At the end of work that day, Matthew had asked Pat whether she would be interested in going to a film at the Film Theatre in Lothian Road.

"The crowd's going," he said.

Pat had heard of the crowd, and was vaguely interested in meeting them. The fact that the invitation was from Matthew was potentially problematic, as there was no possibility of a romantic association between them and she did not want to encourage any false hopes on his part. And yet there was no reason to avoid all social contact with him, particularly if there were to be other people there. So she agreed.

"What's the film?" she asked.

"Something Italian," Matthew said. "Do you like Italian films?"

"It depends," said Pat. "I like Fellini."

"This might be by Fellini," said Matthew. "But it might not."

"Or Pasolini," added Pat. Matthew nodded vaguely. "I think I've seen some of his films too," he said. "But I forget the names of directors."

They made arrangements to meet at the Film Theatre itself and then, after helping Matthew to close the gallery, Pat made her way back to Scotland Street to get ready for the evening. She let herself in at the bottom of the stairs and began the climb up to the top floor. As she turned the corner on the first landing, she heard a voice drifting down from above her.

"So it's you."

Domenica, who must have entered the building just a few moments before her, had reached the top landing and was looking down on her. Pat looked up and saw her neighbour staring down. She waved, and continued her journey to their landing. Domenica was standing in her doorway, the full bag of groceries that she had been carrying laid down on the floor beside her.

"I hate doing this sort of shopping," Domenica said, with feeling. "I find the whole process of buying apples and things like that so disheartening. But one has to do it, I suppose. Apples don't grow on trees."

Pat smiled. She was not sure whether she wanted to engage in a conversation with Domenica, as she had relatively little time to prepare herself for the Film Theatre.

"You left me some flowers," said Domenica. "And I haven't thanked you yet. You're a sweet girl. You really are."

"I felt rather bad about being so . . . so cross with you," said Pat. "Especially when you were only trying to help me."

"You had every right to be cross with me," said Domenica. "But I take it that you would like me to carry on with the planned invitation of that young man to dinner."

Pat shrugged. "I don't mind."

"Which means you want me to do so," said Domenica. "And I shall. Of course, if you don't want to come along, you needn't. You could leave that nice young man to me."

Pat stared at her in astonishment. Did Domenica really mean that?

Domenica, seeing Pat's reaction, smiled coyly. "Why not, may I ask? Isn't it fashionable these days for a . . . how shall we put it? – a more mature woman to have a somewhat younger man friend? Stranger things have happened."

Pat wanted to laugh. It was absurd to think of Domenica as having a younger man; it was inconceivable. And what made Domenica imagine that Peter would even look at her for one moment? It was quite ridiculous.

"He's a bit young for you, isn't he?" she said. "You could have a younger boyfriend, I suppose, but not that young."

"What you mean," said Domenica, "is that in your opinion I'm too old. That's what you mean, isn't it?"

Pat wanted to say yes, it was, but refrained. The whole discussion was becoming embarrassing. She looked at her watch. She had forty minutes to get ready if she was to arrive at the Film Theatre in time. "I have to hurry," she said. "I'm going to see a film."

Domenica picked up her bag and reached for her hallway light switch. "I might just surprise you one of these days," she said. "I could get a man if I wanted one, you know."

"Of course you could," said Pat hurriedly. "You're an attractive woman. Men like you. Look at Angus Lordie."

Domenica let out a shriek. "Oh, not Angus! For heaven's sake! He would be desperation stakes – complete desperation stakes. No, I'm thinking of somebody a bit more romantic than that."

Pat giggled, and gestured towards her own doorway. "Bruce?"

Domenica laughed. "There are limits," she said. "But wait and see. I think I'm going to surprise you."

Back inside the flat, Pat took out a fresh blouse and ran a bath for herself. She reflected on her conversation with Domenica, realising that she had made so many assumptions in it. She had assumed that somebody of sixty could not fall in love; that was ridiculous – it was ageist of her, she decided; very ageist. People said that you could fall in love at any stage in life – at eight, at eighteen, at eighty. And why not? The capacity to experience the other emotions did not wither; you could still feel anger, jealousy, distress and all the rest, however old you were. Love was in the same spectrum as these. And you could love anything, and anyone, whether or not the passion were returned. When she was very young, she had loved a knitted doll, a sailor in a blue suit. She had called him Pedro, for some inexplicable reason, and had carried him with her wherever she went. She had loved Pedro with all her heart, and she had been sure that he had loved her from the depths of his woolly being. The object of affection did not matter; the feeling did.

What did she have to love now? Pedro was no more, or, at

the most, he was a few scraps of wool in the bottom of a drawer. He would have to be replaced; and Pedro . . . was Peter.

She reached out and turned off the taps. She was tired of being by herself. She did not want to have to go to the Film Theatre with the crowd; she wanted to go with somebody who would give all his attention to her, and her alone; who would take her out for dinner afterwards, or for a drink at the bar, and who would exchange confidences with her. And that, presumably, was the sort of thing that poor Domenica wanted for herself too. They were two lonely women wanting the same thing. And there was Bruce wanting it too, but going about the getting of it in quite the wrong way. Companionship. Tender friendship. Love. None of them had it at present, and time was leaking away, especially for Domenica.

29. *At the Film Theatre*

Matthew's crowd, it transpired, consisted of five people, including Matthew himself. With Pat present, there were six of them, all sitting in a row in the half-empty film theatre. This Italian film was an obscure one, made by an obscure director and starring obscure actors, and although the programme notes referred to it as a key example of the Milanese Emptiness School, this distinction was not sufficient to draw the Edinburgh crowds. And to add to the general air of participation in an obscure event, the print was dark and scratchy, as if not enough light could penetrate it, or as if it had been made at dusk, on a cloudy day. The action took place in a small village between Milan and Parma, in the early 1950s. The village was closing, it seemed, through lack of support. The local priest, played by a man with a pronounced limp, had despaired of saving his congregation, which was now reduced to a few aged widows and a young girl who appeared to be developing stigmata. The stigmata which, if genuine, would have revived the village's fortunes, turned out to be no more than a rash.

All the village men were in Bologna, where they were on strike. The strike had no cause and had no apparent ending. There was nobody to negotiate with, as the bosses had gone to Rome and declined to return. There was a profound crisis.

At the end of the film, the crowd had arisen from its seats and made its way through to the bar. Some people remained seated in the theatre, as if waiting for further explanation. Pat walked through with Matthew, and asked him what he thought of the film.

"Well," he began, and then tailed off. He looked at her; she would have views perhaps; for his part, he had no idea what to say.

"Exactly," whispered Pat. "And what did the crowd think?"

"The crowd's not fussy," said Matthew.

As they entered the bar, Pat looked at the individual members of the crowd. Matthew had introduced them to her before they had gone into the theatre, and now she recalled their names. Ed was the tall one in the black tee-shirt; Jim was the one with the earring; Philly was a blonde with rat's-tail hair; and Rose had a curious pair of sixties-style glasses. Pat found herself staring at Rose, who caught her eye and smiled at her, hesitantly, Pat thought.

When they reached a table and sat down, Pat sat next to Rose, Ed on her other side. Matthew, who was several places away looked inquiringly at Pat. He wanted her to move, thought Pat, but she would not: she was with the crowd, not with Matthew.

"You work for Matthew, don't you?" asked Rose. Her voice was strange; rather high-pitched; not a confident voice.

"Yes," said Pat. "I'm his assistant."

Rose looked at her and said: "Lucky."

"To work for Matthew? Lucky?"

"Yes," said Rose. "I would love that." She paused. It seemed to Pat as if she was preparing to ask something awkward, and indeed she was.

"Do you go out with him a lot?" Rose asked. "Or are you just . . . well, I suppose one should say, are you just . . . ?"

"An employee," Pat supplied. "I work for him, you see."

This information seemed to please Rose, who glanced over at Matthew and then looked back at Pat. "I've known him a long time," she said. "We used to go to a tennis club together. Not that my tennis is any good – it's hopeless. Did you know that Matthew played tennis?"

Pat shook her head. She had always thought of Matthew as being slightly lazy; surely tennis would be too strenuous for him.

"And then," Rose continued, "we went – the whole crowd, that is, minus Ed, who was having his appendix out – we went off to Portugal last year. For two weeks. That was such good fun." She closed her eyes, as if to remember.

Pat looked at her. It was perfectly apparent that Rose had her eye on Matthew, but would her interest be reciprocated? She feared it would not. Rose was reasonably attractive, and appeared likeable enough, but that was not the point in these matters. What counted was chemistry, and when Matthew had introduced her to Rose he had done so in a way which did not suggest that there was anything special between them. Rose, no doubt, was trying too hard. Men did not like to be pursued – as a general rule – and Matthew would have picked up her interest – and retreated. There was no chance for Rose, Pat thought, unless she changed tactics – and people did not generally change tactics.

Ed now addressed a remark to Rose. Pat looked around her. The film in one of the other cinemas had come to an end and had discharged its patrons into the bar. They looked animated, and amused; no Milanese emptiness. She watched a couple of young men walk up to the bar. One of them was tall and was wearing a dark-green shirt. He stopped short of the bar to say something to his companion, who leaned forward to catch the remark. As he spoke, the tall young man looked out across the bar, directly at Pat. He paused, and the person with him looked back too.

He tried to place her. He had met her somewhere – at the café? Yes. At the café. With that woman who went on about that book. He nodded, and waved.

Pat thought: *I want him to come over to me. That's what I want.* And he did, muttering something to his friend, who went on to order a drink.

"You," he said, smiling.

"Yes," she said. "Me."

He bent down to speak to her. Rose looked up, glanced at him, and then at Pat. She thought: this is what happens to girls like that. They only have to walk into a room and they get men like that flocking round them. Bees to honey. And I can't even get Matthew to notice me. Not even that.

"Were you in that Italian film?" Pat asked. "*The Crisis*?"

Peter shook his head. "No. We went to an Australian comedy. About an airline pilot and a nurse who get stuck in the Outback with a couple of Shakespearean actors."

"I think I've heard about that one," said Pat. "It's a great idea for a film."

She waited for Peter to say something, but for a few moments there was a silence. Then he said: "Do you want to come round some time? To Cumberland Street?"

"Yes," said Pat. "That would be great."

"Tomorrow evening?"

Pat nodded. She sensed that Rose had been listening.

30. At Big Lou's

Big Lou stood in front of her new coffee-making machine, polishing its gleaming stainless-steel spouts, and admiring the fine Italian lines of the reservoir and high-pressure steam chamber. Only the Italians could produce a machine of this beauty; only the Italians would care enough to do so.

But she had more to think about than aesthetics; over the late summer, several major developments had taken place at Big Lou's coffee bar. The purchase of this expensive new machine was one of the most important, and satisfying, and had attracted a great deal of attention from her regular customers, especially from Matthew, who had fallen in love with it the moment he had seen it. To gaze at the machine was pleasure enough; to turn the levers and control the outflow of steam – as Matthew was occasionally permitted to do – was a positive joy.

Another of these developments was the removal of the expensive newspaper rack. In its place she had installed a small table, which she had acquired from a saleroom on Leith Walk. On this table she stacked copies of the day's papers and any magazines which were left behind by customers, provided, of course, Big Lou approved of them. The *Scots Magazine* was always there, and was popular, curiously enough, with some of the most intellectual customers, who read it with what seemed suspiciously close to a condescending smile. Why they should affect this expression was not clear to her. The *Scots Magazine* was popular in Arbroath, Big Lou's home town, and she saw no reason why it should not be equally popular in Edinburgh. Or did Edinburgh, for some unfathomable reason, feel itself superior to Arbroath?

A further development was an important change in the mid-morning coffee regulars. Matthew still came every morning, of course, and stayed longer than anybody else, but the two furniture restorers had disappeared entirely. It was almost as if they had been written out of a story, thought Lou; simply no longer on the page. They had disappeared, and had taken their world with them. But just as they had gone, others had arrived. Mrs Constance, for instance, with her curious unkempt hair, had appeared one morning and had announced herself as "the woman from upstairs" – her flat being more or less immediately above the coffee bar. She was silent, for the most part, but occasionally joined in the conversation with observations that were remarkably acute.

Then there was Angus Lordie, the portrait painter from Drummond Place, and occasional poet. He had ventured into the coffee bar one morning and had found Matthew, whom he knew, engaged in conversation with Big Lou. Big Lou had been unsure about Angus Lordie to begin with, but had accepted his presence after she had taken to Cyril, his dog.

"There's something strange about that creature," she had remarked to Matthew. "He keeps looking at me and I could swear that he winks from time to time."

"Yes, he does wink," said Matthew. "Pat says that he winks at her all the time – as if they were sharing a secret. And he has a gold tooth, you know. It's most peculiar. But then Angus is peculiar too. They suit one another."

"Aye, well, he gives Cyril coffee," Big Lou went on. "He thinks I don't notice, but I do. He slips a saucer under the table and Cyril drinks it. The other day he ordered two cups of cappuccino. He assumed I would think they were both for him, but one was for Cyril. I saw him drink it – from the cup. He had the foam from the milk all around his jaws afterwards."

Matthew nodded. "Cyril drinks beer too," he said. "He's a regular at the Cumberland Bar. Quite an intelligent dog, I think. And a good friend to Angus."

She had thought about that over the following days. Big Lou was a sympathetic person and aware of loneliness. She had been by herself since she had come down to live in Edinburgh. Her solution had been to immerse herself in the books which she had inherited from the bookshop which had previously occupied the coffee-bar premises. These books were on a wide range of subjects – philosophy, topography, literature, and even dogs – and Big Lou was patiently making her way through all of these, one by one, completing an education which had been cut short at the age of sixteen.

That morning, nobody had come in before Matthew, and for a few minutes he and Big Lou were alone together.

"Are your parents alive, Lou?" Matthew suddenly asked. "You've never mentioned them, you know."

Big Lou shook her head. "My father left us when I was eleven," she said. "He died a bit later. Drink, I was told. My mother died when I was nineteen."

"I'm sorry," said Matthew.

Big Lou said nothing. She looked down at the counter. What was there to be said about the loss of parents? She could barely remember her father now, and her mother's memory was fading. All she could recall was kindness, and love, like a surrounding mist.

"And you?" she asked. "You've just got your father, haven't you?"

Matthew nodded. "He's found himself a girlfriend, by the way," he said quietly. "Some woman called Janis."

Big Lou smiled. "That's nice. That's nice for him."

Matthew took a sip of coffee. "I suppose so."

Big Lou watched him. She was about to say something to him, but the door opened and Angus Lordie arrived, closely followed by Cyril. He nodded to Lou and made his way over to take his seat next to Matthew. Cyril sat down beneath the table and stared at Matthew's ankles. He would have loved to bite them, but would not. He understood the rules.

"I've been reading the paper for the last hour," Angus remarked breezily. "And the state of the world – my goodness! Everywhere one looks – ghastly. And of course we, you may recall, Matthew, are actively engaged in hostilities, together with our friends, the Americans. Not exactly on our doorstep, but hostilities nonetheless. Were you aware of that? Does it feel like wartime to you? What about you, Lou? Do you feel as if you're at war?"

"No," said Lou. "I don't. Nobody consulted *me* about it."

"Ah," said Angus Lordie. "But nobody is ever consulted about a war, are they? It's still our war, though."

Matthew interrupted. The war was not Big Lou's fault, as far as he was concerned – nor his, for that matter.

"There's nothing that Big Lou can do about it," he said. "I don't think it's anything to do with her."

Big Lou had been busying herself with the cup of foamed coffee she was preparing for Angus. She had been listening too, of course, and now she turned round. She had something to say on this subject.

31. Act and Omission

Big Lou leaned over the counter. "Yes," she said. "That's very interesting, what you say, Matthew. You say that there's often nothing we can do, but I'm not sure that that's quite right. I'm not just talking about this war, now. I'm talking about things in general. Can you really say that there's nothing that we can do about things that we disapprove of, when they're done by the government? Are you sure about that?"

"You can vote," said Angus. "Get people out." He thought for a moment before adding: "Mind you, have you ever tried getting the Labour Party out in Scotland? Ever tried that?"

"That might be because people want them in," said Big Lou. "I do, at least. Anyway, you can vote. But how often do we get the chance to do that? And even then, we might not have much of a choice."

"But at least you've done what you can," joined in Matthew, who had never voted, never; from lethargy, and indecision. "Once you've voted, that is."

Big Lou agreed with this, but there was more to the issue than simple voting. There were many other things one could do, she thought. One could write to politicians. One could give money to causes. One could protest in the street. There were options. She pointed this out to Matthew and Angus, but then she added: "But the real question, boys, is this: do we have a duty to do anything to stop things we may not like? Is it all right just to do nothing, provided that we don't do anything that makes matters worse?"

Angus exchanged a glance with Matthew. He was not yet used to Big Lou's philosophical reflections, and his attitude was slightly condescending. Matthew sensed this and wanted to say something to him about it, but had not yet had the chance. He would speak to him, though, later.

"I would have thought," said Angus, "that we are more responsible for what we do rather than for what we don't do. If I didn't start something, then I'm not sure that it's my duty to stop it."

"Oh yes?" asked Big Lou. "Oh yes?"

Cyril looked at Big Lou and then at his master. Like all dogs, he was attempting to understand what was happening in the human world, but this was difficult to read, and he looked away. His was a world of floors and low things, and smells; a whole room, a world of smells, waiting for dogs to locate them and file away for future use.

Angus met Big Lou's challenge. "Yes," he said. "I'm pretty sure about that. Don't blame me for what I haven't done. Simple. I didn't start the Cuban missile crisis. I was around at the time, I suppose. But I didn't start it."

Big Lou smiled. "That may be so, but let me tell you about something I've just read." She paused, looking directly at Angus Lordie. "Do you want to hear about it?"

Angus nodded graciously. "You are constantly entertaining, most excellent Lou," he said. "We are all ears, aren't we Matthew?"

"Well," said Lou. "What I've been reading about is this. It's a chapter in a book by a philosopher, and it's called *The Case of the Two Wicked Uncles*. That's what it's called."

She leant forward on the bar as she continued. "There's Uncle A and Uncle B, you see. Both of these uncles have a nephew, who's just a wee boy, about eight maybe. If this bairn dies before they do, then each stands to come into a lot of money.

"Uncle A goes to see his nephew one day. He arrives at the house and finds that the parents have gone out for some reason, leaving the boy alone in the house."

"Somewhat unlikely," said Angus, smiling at Matthew. "Parents don't leave eight-year-olds in the house. Not these days."

Lou sighed. "It's a story, remember. Philosophers like to tell stories. They don't have to be true. Anyway, Uncle A goes upstairs and finds that the nephew has decided to take a bath. The door to the bathroom is open and he goes in, sees the boy in the water, and decides, on the spur of the moment, to drown the poor bairn. Which he does, knowing that he will come into all that money."

"Good God!" said Angus Lordie.

"Yes," said Big Lou. "Not a nice uncle. Now here's what Uncle B does. He goes off the same day to see his particular nephew and finds exactly the same situation there. When Uncle B goes upstairs in that other house, he sees the bathroom door open and goes in to see what's happening. There's his nephew, in the bath, but with his head under the water. He realises that the poor boy has slipped, knocked himself unconscious, and is submerged. He realises that if he doesn't drag him out of the water – which will be a very simple thing to do – the boy will soon drown. He also realises that if this happens, then he will come into all the money. He does nothing."

"He stands there?" asked Matthew.

"Aye," said Big Lou. "He stands there. That's Uncle B for you. Standing there, doing nothing."

For a few moments there was silence. The story had touched both Matthew and Angus Lordie in a curious way. It was almost as if it had been true; that they had been hearing something shocking that was reported in the newspaper. Cyril, disturbed by the silence, looked up from the floor and stared at his master. Then he looked at Matthew's ankles again, scratched at an ear, and closed his eyes again.

"So," said Big Lou, breaking the silence. "What you have to decide is this. Is Uncle A, who does something, worse than Uncle B, who does nothing? You just said to me, Angus, that we are only responsible for the things we do and not for the things we don't do. Yes, you did. Don't deny it. So are you going to say that Uncle B did nothing wrong? Is that what you're going to say?" She paused. "But also, you tell me this: is Uncle A worse than Uncle B, or is there no difference between them? Well? Come on. You tell me."

Angus looked down at the table.

"Let me think," he said.

32. The Two Wicked Uncles: Possible Solutions

While Angus Lordie thought, Big Lou, lips pursed in an almost undetectable smile, made him another cup of coffee. She knew what Angus Lordie thought of her – that she was just a woman who made coffee for people. Big Lou was used to this. Back home in Arbroath, they had thought that she was just a girl – she had heard one of her male relatives say just that – and that somebody who was just a girl had nothing really important to say about anything. And in Aberdeen, where she had worked for years in the Granite Nursing Home, she had been just one of the assistants, somebody who helped, who cleaned up, who made the beds. And nobody had ever suggested to her that she might be something other than this.

Matthew, in silence, stared up at the ceiling, thinking of uncles. He might so easily have been drowned by one of his uncles when he was eight, he thought. But which of his two uncles would have been most likely to drown him? His Uncle Willy in Dunblane, the one who farmed and who used to take him up the hillside on his all-terrain tractor to look at the sheep? Or his Uncle Malcolm in the West, who ran a marina and was a keen sailor? Uncle Willy might have drowned him in sheep dip, up at the high fank, and nobody would have been there to see it. It would have been a lonely death, under those wide Perthshire skies, and he would have closed his eyes to the sight of the heather and the mottled grey of the stones that made the fank. But Uncle Willy was an elder of the Kirk and would never have drowned anybody, let alone his nephew. No. It would not have been Uncle Willy.

Would Uncle Malcolm have pushed him overboard from his yacht, he wondered? Hardly. And yet, now that he came to think of it, Uncle Malcolm had a temper and might, just might, have drowned him in a rage. Matthew remembered crewing for him off Colonsay when he was much younger and clearing away the breakfast things from the galley. He had tossed the dregs from a couple of tea cups into the sea and had done the same with the contents of a mug beside the sink. Unfortunately, that had contained his uncle's false teeth in their sterilising solution, and the teeth had been lost at sea. His uncle had shouted at him then – strange, gummy shouts which had frightened him. Yes, Uncle Malcolm was the suspect in his case.

Suddenly, Angus Lordie clapped his hands together, causing Cyril to start and leap to his feet. "Uncle A," he said. "Uncle B is off the hook. He did nothing, yes? And even if he hadn't been there the boy would have drowned. So he didn't cause the drowning. Whereas Uncle A caused it to happen."

Big Lou listened intently. "Oh," she said. "So it's all down to causing things? Is that it?"

"Absolutely, most cogitative Lou," said Angus. "That's your answer for you."

"Maybe if Uncle B were to . . ." Matthew began, but was interrupted by Big Lou.

"So it's cause then," she said. "But the problem is this. I could say to you, surely, that Uncle B's omission to act was a cause of the drowning just as much as Uncle A's positive act was. Ken what I mean?"

Angus Lordie looked momentarily confused. Serves him right, thought Matthew. It was a bad mistake to condescend to Big Lou, as Angus was about to find out.

Big Lou reached for her cloth and gave the counter a wipe. "You see, there's no reason why we should not see omissions to act as being as causally potent as positive actions. It's simply wrong to think that failures to act can't cause things – they do. It's just that our ordinary idea of how things are caused is too tied to ideas of physical causation, of pushing and shoving. But it's more subtle than that."

"So there's no difference between Uncle A and Uncle B then?" asked Matthew.

"Not really," said Big Lou. "The book I'm reading says that ordinary people – the man in the street – would always say that Uncle A was worse, while the philosopher would say that there was no real difference." She finished her sentence, and then looked at Angus Lordie.

Angus Lordie picked up his coffee cup and drained the last few drops. "Well, Lou," he said. "That's pretty impressive. I'll have to think about what you said. You could be right."

"I am right," said Big Lou.

"Could be," said Angus, looking for support from Matthew, but getting none. He looked at Cyril, who returned his gaze directly, but gave no further sign.

Matthew now spoke. "There could be a difference, though. There could be a difference between things we do on the spur of the moment and things we do after a bit of thought."

Big Lou looked at him with interest. "Maybe," she said.

"So in this case," Matthew went on, "Uncle A had a bit of time – maybe only a minute or so to think about it. Then he acted. Whereas Uncle B acted – or failed to act – spontaneously."

Angus Lordie snorted dismissively. "Doesn't work," he said. "They have had exactly the same amount of time to think about it. Uncle A thinks about it while he's holding the boy's head under the water. Uncle B thinks about it while he stands there and watches the poor boy drown. No difference, in my view."

Big Lou wanted to side with Matthew, but could not. "Yes," she conceded, a note of reluctance in her voice. "Angus is probably right – in this case. But you're right, too, Matthew, when it comes to most of the things we do. There must be a difference between the things you do on a sudden urge and the things you do after you've thought about them for a long time."

"So what do you think, Lou?" asked Angus. "Is there a difference between Uncle A and Uncle B as far as you're concerned? What did that book of yours say?"

"It hinted at an answer," said Big Lou. "But mostly it just raised the question. Books don't always give the answers, you know. Sometimes they just raise the questions."

Angus smiled. "So nothing's certain, then?"

"That's right," said Big Lou.

"Except death and taxes," interjected Matthew. "Isn't that how the saying goes?"

"They don't pay taxes in Italy," observed Angus. "I knew a painter in Naples who never paid taxes – ever. Very good painter too."

"What happened to him?" asked Matthew.

"He died," said Angus.

33. *Bertie Makes a Move*

In the days that followed his visit to George Street with his mother, Bertie had been preoccupied with his plan. The purchase of the Watson's blazer from Aitken and Niven was feasible only with the co-operation of the boy from round the corner.

Unfortunately, there was a difficulty with this as he was not sure exactly where this new friend lived. He had met him only on the one occasion and although the other boy had given him his name – he was called Paddy – he had not been specific as to where he lived. He had pointed in the direction of the far end of Fettes Row, which was just round the corner, when

Bertie had asked him, but he had given no number.

Nor had he given Bertie his surname, which would have allowed the telephone directory to be consulted. So all that Bertie could do if he wanted to contact him was to wait in the street in the hope that he might appear.

And there was a difficulty with doing even that. Bertie was now allowed out alone in Scotland Street and Drummond Place, provided that he did not cross any busy roads and provided that he told Irene exactly where he was going. This allowed him to sit on the steps outside No 44 and watch people going in and out of their houses. It also allowed him to stand at the end of Scotland Street Lane in the hope of seeing one of the motor-cycles that occasionally roared out of the vintage-motorcycle garage (out of bounds).

Bertie liked the motorcyclists, who sometimes waved or nodded to him. He would like to have a motorcycle like that, which he could ride to rugby matches, and he would do so, he thought, when he was bigger.

His mother would not like it, of course – she said that motor-cycles were noisy things – worse than cars – and that if she were the Lord Provost of Edinburgh she would ban them from the streets. But even if he got hold of a motorcycle, she would still try to spoil it for him, thought Bertie. Motorcyclists wore leather outfits, sometimes with badges on them; she would force him to wear leather dungarees, he thought, and all the other motor-cyclists would laugh at him.

If Paddy lived on Fettes Row, then he would have to go and seek him there. But again there were obstacles. Although one section of Fettes Row was accessible, the other section, where Paddy lived, lay beyond Dundas Street, and the crossing of Dundas Street was definitely forbidden.

Bertie wrestled with this. He could not tell his mother that he was going to the other side of Fettes Row because she would forbid him outright. And if he lied, which he did not want to do – for he was a truthful boy (apart from his habit of occasionally giving a false name) – then he would surely give himself away with his blushes. So he would have to develop a form of words which allowed for the crossing of Dundas Street.

"Can I go down to Royal Crescent?" he asked one afternoon.

Irene glanced up from the book she was reading, a new biography of Melanie Klein. For a moment she wondered how Melanie Klein would have answered had anybody asked her permission to go to Royal Crescent. It would have been too simple just to say yes. Perhaps she would have said: Why do you want to go to Royal Crescent?

"Why?" she said.

Bertie shrugged. "I want to play."

Irene looked back at the book. The biographer had reached a point where Kleinian theories of play were on the point of being discussed at an important meeting in London. Melanie was anxious about the implications of a possible attack from Freudian loyalists who believed she had strayed too far from the fold. The pace of the account, with all its intrigue, was building up.

"That's fine, Bertie. You play. And then maybe we can talk about how you played. Would that be all right? You could tell Mummy about your little games?"

Bertie pursed his lips. It was none of her business how he played. He wanted to play Chase the Dentist, but she said that it was too violent, and he could never find anybody to play it with him. But he did not want to argue about that now; bland acceptance was a better policy.

"And then I'll go round to the end of the street and then come back," he said.

Every word of the sentence had been rehearsed, and he delivered his line faultlessly. It was true, after all, and there was no need to feel ashamed or to blush over what he had said. Royal Crescent and Fettes Row were, strictly speaking, separate streets, but in a broad sense they were the same street, as Fettes Row was a continuation of Royal Crescent. And the section of Fettes Row which lay on the far side of Dundas Street could, of course, be described as the same street as the bit that lay on the near side. So he felt that it was quite reasonable for him to say that he was going to the end of the street, even if he knew that Irene might misinterpret what he said. A boy was not responsible for the misinterpretations of his mother, he thought. That was carrying things far too far.

Irene nodded. "Be careful," she said. "And don't be too long." She paused, and looked up again from her book. "And have you done your Italian today, Bertie?"

Bertie had taken the precaution of doing his Italian exercises to prevent their being used as a way of thwarting his plan.

"Si, si," he said. "Ciao, Mama!"

"Ciao, ciao, bambino!" Irene muttered, and returned to her Melanie Klein. It was typical, she thought, that institutional forces should have sought to discredit truly innovative developments in the international psychoanalytical movement. It was absolutely typical.

For a moment she allowed her mind to wander. Dr Fairbairn had been something of a pioneer himself – a recent pioneer – with his theory of the juvenile tantrum. But he must have encountered opposition to his theories when he first published his study of Wee Fraser.

Presumably there were those who were envious of his success, who wanted to bring him down because they hated the fact that he had done something. There were always people like that, she thought. They are unsettled by the good fortune, or the happiness, of others. They allowed envy, that most corrosive of human emotions, to prompt them to make sneering remarks.

And all they achieved in this way was an increase in the sum total of the world's unhappiness and a contraction, a deformation, of their own hearts.

34. Bertie Prepares to Cross Dundas Street

Bertie left the front door of 44 Scotland Street in that state of heightened excitement of mind and senses that goes with the performance of the dangerous, or the plainly forbidden. He had not lied to his mother – he was certain of that – but at the same time what he was proposing to do was clearly outside the understanding that existed between them.

He thought for a moment: I am going to cross Dundas Street, alone, and the enormity of his adventure came home to him. In such a state of anticipation might Adam have reached up to pick the fruit, thought Bertie, although as all boys, and men, knew, that was really Eve's fault. If he was breaking the rules, then, it was obviously his mother's fault for making them in the first place.

This thought encouraged him, and he smiled as he began to walk along Royal Crescent and then to Fettes Row, with its fateful conjunction with Dundas Street. He knew that this mission might prove futile, that there might be no trace of Paddy, and that he would return with nothing accomplished. But it was at least a first step in the execution of his plan, and he was confident that sooner or later he would meet up with Paddy and put his proposal to him. And Paddy would accept, of course; he was that sort of boy. He went fishing in the Pentland Hills and caught trout. For a boy who did that, the task which Bertie had planned for him would be simplicity itself.

Bertie had decided that he would walk up and down Fettes Row for half an hour or so in the hope that Paddy might emerge. It was a warm afternoon, part of an Indian summer in which Edinburgh was basking, and Paddy might well come out on to the street to play. But even if he did not, then Bertie had brought with him a small piece of blackboard chalk, and with this he would leave a message for Paddy on some of the stairs that led up to the front doors on Fettes Row. PADDY, he would write, MEET ME IN SCOTLAND STREET SOON. URGENT. SECRET. BERTIE.

That would draw him out, thought Bertie. No boy could resist a message like that. And then Bertie thought: will Paddy know how to read? If he did not – and that was perfectly likely – then there would be no point in writing the message. This conclusion slightly dampened his spirits; it was not easy, he realised, being more advanced than others. And again this was not his fault, he thought with irritation; it all came back to his mother. She's the one who has ruined my life. She's the one.

Royal Crescent, a terrace of high, classical buildings, was quiet as Bertie made his way along it. A cat watched him from the top of a car, its eyes narrowing as it assessed the threat which he presented to its peace of mind and safety. But Bertie was no threat and the cat closed its eyes again. And then a woman came out of a front door and stood for a moment at the top of her steps as Bertie walked past. Bertie looked up, and she smiled.

"Going somewhere?" she asked in a friendly tone.

Bertie stopped in his tracks. "Yes," he said.

The woman continued to smile. "Don't get up to any mischief," she said.

Bertie stood quite still. How could she tell? Did something give it away, just as Pinocchio's face gave away his lies? Could adults just tell?

"I won't," he muttered.

"Good," she said, and turned away, fumbling with her key. Bertie continued on his way, more slowly, more circumspectly. Now the end of the first section of Fettes Row was in sight and there was Dundas Street, with its traffic. A bus went past on its way up to town, its engine straining against the hill. Behind it, a blue van waited its chance to overtake. The traffic seemed heavy.

As he came to the corner, the shadows of the buildings gave way to a burst of sunlight. Bertie stopped at the edge of the pavement and looked across the busy thoroughfare of Dundas Street. For a moment, out of ancient habit, he looked up beside him, expecting to find the familiar adult, his mother or his father, at his side. That is how one crossed the street – beside an adult – with one's hand in the adult hand, safe and guided. But there was no adult now; no mother, no teacher, no psychotherapist. Bertie was alone. He swallowed hard, and closed his eyes for a moment. Nobody had taught him the principles of crossing a busy street. Should he wait until there were no cars in sight and then walk slowly across? The problem with that was that he would stand there forever: there were always cars in sight on this busy road.

He looked up the hill. The traffic came down more quickly than it went up. This meant that if he could find a break in the traffic coming down, it would not matter so much if there was something coming up the hill – such traffic would always take longer to reach him. But how long would he need? It was difficult to judge the precise speed of the traffic, and although the buses seemed to be moving very slowly, some of the cars were doing anything but that. Indeed, as he stood there, a small red car shot past him so quickly that he would have missed it, he felt, had he blinked. That car would most certainly have run him over if he had been crossing the street when it had roared round the corner of Henderson Row.

For a few moments, Bertie considered abandoning his mission. It would be simple to turn round and retrace his steps – as yet innocent steps – back to Scotland Street and home. If he did that he would have done nothing wrong at all and could face his mother and tell her exactly what he had done. He had gone to the end of the safe part of Fettes Row – that was all. But to do this was a complete capitulation. If he did not even have the courage to cross Dundas Street, then would he have the courage to do anything at all? And what of Gavin Hastings? he thought. Would he have been afraid to cross Dundas Street at the age of six? He would not. He imagined that Gavin Hastings had run across Dundas Street on many occasions as a boy; run and jumped and kicked his heels so that anyone watching would have nodded their heads wisely and said: Look at that boy! That's a boy who's bound to play rugby for Scotland! Bertie took a deep breath. He decided to run.

35. Halfway Across

Peter Backhouse, musician and aficionado of old railways, happened to be walking down Dundas Street that afternoon. He had spent a very satisfactory hour practising on the St Giles' organ and was pleased with the Olivier Messiaen and Herbert Howells which he planned to perform at a "St Giles' at Six" concert the following Sunday. There was such quiet in the music, such calm; it was the perfect antidote to the frenzied pace of modern life. Now, returning to the Academy for afternoon chamber-choir practice, he thought of what lay ahead of him. No Messiaen or Howells for the choir – at least not today – but a quick run through of *Stand by Me* and *So it Goes*, which the chamber choir had sung before and would respond to well; tear-jerkers, both of those pieces, if one were in a sentimental mood – which parents often were at school concerts.

He had reached the point at which Cumberland Street meets

Dundas Street when he realised that something was happening. He had glanced at his watch – a quick check to see that he was still in good time for choir practice – and for some reason, perhaps through an unconscious prompting of things seen but unseen, he looked over to his right and saw a small boy, wearing strawberry-coloured dungarees, suddenly run out into the street. For a moment, Peter Backhouse thought that the boy had kicked a ball into the road and was rushing out to retrieve it – it was that sort of purposeful, darting movement – but then the boy hesitated, took a few more steps, and stopped again.

Oliver Sacks has pointed out that those who are involved in moments of extreme peril often report a slowing-down of time. They see the danger, they may even see impending annihilation, but they often feel that they have plenty of time to react. The quick seconds of peril are slowed, become minutes in the minds of those involved. This is how it seemed that afternoon. For Peter Backhouse, the boy seemed to be standing still for an inordinately long time, quite enough time to step from the path of the bus that was approaching him as he stood, momentarily frozen, in the middle of the road. The bus lumbered past, some faces at least peering out from the window at the sight of the small boy, statue-like, in the middle of the traffic. Then there were cars, one of which slowed down and swerved, avoiding a small movement that the boy had made.

Peter Backhouse shouted out to the boy, "Don't move!" He looked up the road at the approaching traffic; a red light on the corner of Great King Street had changed and a stream of vehicles seemed to be hurtling down towards the boy while at the same time more cars came from the other direction. He looked behind him and decided that he should step out into the traffic and hold it up, hoping that it would heed him and allow the boy to complete his journey. But a car had already reached the point where he was standing and had shot past the stationary boy. Perhaps they could not see him; perhaps they thought that he was waiting to cross and knew exactly what he was doing.

And then, quite suddenly, a car careered round the corner

behind him and launched itself down the road, going far too fast, the driver, distracted perhaps, unaware of the boy in the middle of the road – the boy who now seemed on the verge of overcoming his panicky indecision and launching himself into the rest of his interrupted crossing of the road. Peter Backhouse shouted, and began to leap forward, but he had been anticipated by another, a man on the other side of the road. This man, who had been walking up Dundas Street, had also seen what was happening and had acted. With a quick glance behind him, he darted forward, narrowly avoiding a passing van, and ran into the middle of the road. There, he seized the frightened boy and lifted him up bodily, right out of the path of the oncoming car. Then, still holding him in his arms, he strode back to the edge of the road and to safety. A car squealed to a halt and a motorist shouted something out – a compliment, an expression of relief, an offer to help – but the rescuer indicated that all was well and the car drove off. On the other side of the road, Peter Backhouse shook his head, but breathed a deep sigh of relief. Then he strode off to choir practice. *Stand by Me* indeed! How very appropriate.

Bertie, quivering with fright and on the point of tears, stood abjectly on the pavement, his rescuer beside him.

"That was rather too close for comfort," the man said. "You should stick to the crossings, you know. That's what the green man's for."

His tone was not unkind, and Bertie looked up at him for a moment. His face looked familiar, but Bertie was not quite sure. The man smiled. "Where do you stay?" he asked.

Bertie pointed in the direction of Scotland Street.

"Well, I think you should get back home," said the man. "Will you be all right, do you think?"

Bertie nodded. He had always been taught to thank people, and now he remembered. "Thank you very much," he said. "Thank you for saving me."

"That's all right," said the man, smiling. "I'm sure that you would have done the same for me if that had been me stuck out there!"

"I don't know," said Bertie.

"I'm sure you would."

Bertie returned the smile. Then he began to walk back along Cumberland Street, turning once to wave to the man, who was watching him set off safely on his way. It had been a dreadful, humiliating experience – and a terrifying one, too. And had he not been saved by that kind man, whoever he was, he would be crushed by now; perhaps in a wailing ambulance, being carried off to hospital. Or would they take him to Dr Fairbairn's office first, where he would be asked at great length why he wanted to cross Dundas Street in the first place? That was possible, thought Bertie. Nothing was ever simple.

In Dundas Street, things had quickly returned to normal, as they do in cities when something untoward occurs. Few people had seen what had happened; Peter Backhouse had, but he had missed one detail. That detail had been spotted by an elderly woman who happened to be looking out of her window more or less immediately above the point where the incident had taken place. She had seen it all, and she now telephoned her friend in Trinity.

"Effie," she said breathlessly, "Effie, you simply won't believe what I've just seen, right outside my window. A wee boy panicked in the middle of Dundas Street and froze. Then he was rescued, snatched from the jaws of death by . . . Now, you won't believe who it was, Betty, you really won't. Jack McConnell, First Minister of Scotland. Yes! Yes! What a to-do! But he slipped away, and so I don't think he'll want this to get into the papers. So not a word, Effie. We don't want it to get into the *Scotsman*, do we?"

36. Ramsey Dunbarton

High above the city, on the bracing slopes of the Braids, Ramsey Dunbarton stood before the window of his study, looking out over the rooftops and to the hills of Fife beyond. It was a view that he had lived with for almost forty years and he knew it in every mood. In winter, when the light was thin, the distant hills became shapes of pale grey, hardly distinguishable from the scuddering clouds above them. In summer and in autumn, the hills would stand out, sharply delineated mounds of green and purple, folds of earth that seemed, so misleadingly, to be just a short distance away. And always there was that wide, unpredictable northern sky, with its constantly changing clouds that shifted and parted with the wind.

Ramsey was a northerner by temperament. He felt ill at ease whenever he travelled south, to England or to France, feeling inside him that things were just too bright, and dusty – almost as if the sun had taken something out of the countryside and blanched it. And the air was stale in such latitudes, he thought; stale and stagnant. Ramsey liked Scottish light, pure and clean, and sharp. He liked long, cool evenings in summer and the comfortable darkness of winter days. He liked Scotland exactly as it was: unfussy, cold, and sometimes only half-visible. "I am not a Mediterranean type," he had once remarked to his wife, Betty. And she had looked at him, and sighed. He was not. And nor, she reflected, was she.

Standing before his window, Ramsey thought of the day that lay ahead. It was ten-thirty in the morning and he had already dealt with the newspaper and the morning mail. Since there had been little news of any consequence, he had not taken long to finish the newspaper, and the mail had not been much better. There had been a rose catalogue from Aberdeen – it was his policy always to order roses from Aberdeen, as northern roses would always be the hardiest and would do well in Edinburgh. Buy north, plant south, Ramsey had often said, and the success of his roses spoke to the wisdom of this policy. It could equally apply to people, he had sometimes thought: Aberdonians did well wherever they went in the south.

Then there had been a newsletter from the secretary of the local Conservative Association in which plans for several social events had been revealed to members. The ball a few months earlier, of course, had been most enjoyable, although the attendance, it was pointed out – six people – had been a little disappointing. The secretary, who had been unable to attend herself, exhorted the members to make next year's ball an even greater success, and noted that an attempt would be made to secure the services of a different band. "We had some very critical comments about the performance of the band," she wrote, "and these have been forwarded to the ball committee (convened by Sasha and Raeburn Todd). One member has raised with me the question of whether it is proper for bands to allow their socialist convictions to interfere with the performance of their duties at paid functions. This is a very pertinent point and I believe that we should take action. If anybody knows of a Conservative ceilidh band, please contact us as soon as possible so that we can book them for next year. So far, no suggestions of possible bands have been received."

Ramsey Dunbarton read this with interest. He was the member who had raised the question of the band's performance and he was pleased to see that his complaint had been taken up. There had been a lot wrong with the organisation of the ball, in his view. To begin with, somebody had tried to put him and Betty at a separate table from the other four guests. This was a ridiculous idea, and he had soon dealt with it by the simple expedient of moving the tables together. Then there was the question of the raffle, about which he still felt moderately vexed. There had been some very generous prizes donated by the members, and it was imperative that any raffle for these should have been carried out fairly. He was not convinced that this had happened; in fact, he was sure that Sasha Todd, who had arranged the whole thing, had actually fixed the lottery so that she and her family should get the most desirable prizes. In particular, Ramsey had noted that she had made sure that she would win the lunch with Malcolm Rifkind and Lord James, which was the prize that he would most have liked to win. It can hardly have been much fun for the two politicians to have to sit through a lunch and listen to her going on about the sort of things that she tended to talk about. She was a very superficial woman, in his view, and she would have had no conversation of any interest.

He, by contrast, could have talked to them about things they understood and appreciated.

Ramsey's thoughts on the newsletter were interrupted by the arrival of Betty in his study.

"Coffee, dear," she said, handing him his cup with its small piece of shortbread perched on the edge of the saucer.

"Bless you, Betty," Ramsey said, taking the cup from his wife.

"Deep in thought?" Betty asked. "As always."

Ramsey smiled. "Politics," he said. "I was reading the newsletter. That made me think about politics."

Betty nodded. "You would have made a wonderful politician, Ramsey," she said. "I often wonder what would have happened had you entered Parliament. I'm sure that you would have reached the top, or close enough to the top."

"I don't know, Betty," said Ramsey. "Politics are dirty. I'm not sure whether I would have had the stomach for it. They are very rude to one another, you know. And the moment they get the chance, they stab you in the back."

Betty nodded. "Of course, if you had gone into politics, you'd now be sitting down writing your memoirs. That's what they all seem to do these days."

Ramsey spun round and looked at his wife. "Memoirs?" he asked.

"Yes," said Betty. "Your political memoirs."

Ramsey put down his cup. "Betty," he said. "There's something that I've been meaning to talk to you about. The question of memoirs."

Betty looked at him inquiringly. "Yes?"

Ramsey lowered his gaze, as if in modesty. "It's funny you should have mentioned memoirs," he said quietly. "I've actually been writing them. I've got quite a bit down on paper already."

For a moment, Betty said nothing. Then she clapped her hands together. "That's wonderful, my dear. Wonderful!"

Ramsey smiled. "And I thought that you might like to hear a few excerpts. I was plucking up courage to offer to read them to you."

"I can't wait," said Betty. "Let's hear something right now. I'll fetch more coffee and then we can sit down."

"It's not going to set the heather on fire," said Ramsey modestly. "But I think that my story is every bit as interesting as the next man's."

"Even more so," said Betty. "Even more so."

37. *The Ramsey Dunbarton Story: Part 1 – Early Days*

Ramsey Dunbarton, having shuffled through a sheaf of papers, looked at his wife over the top of his reading glasses. "I shan't bore you with the early stuff," he said. "School and all that. I had a pretty uneventful time at school, and nothing much happened; it's hardly worth recording. So I'll start off when I was a young man. Twenty-five. Can you imagine me at twenty-five, Betty?"

Betty smiled coyly. "How could I forget? The year we met."

Ramsey frowned. "No, sorry, my dear. Not the year we met. We met when I was twenty-six, not twenty-five. I remember it very well. I had just finished my apprenticeship with Shepherd and Wedderburn and had been engaged by another office. I remember it very well."

Betty took a sip of her coffee. "And I remember it very well too, my darling. You were twenty-five because I remember – very clearly indeed in my case – going to your twenty-sixth birthday party, and I couldn't have done that if I hadn't already met you. You don't normally go to the birthday parties of people you have yet to meet, do you?"

Ramsey laid down the sheaf of papers. "That party – and I was going to say something about it in the memoirs – was not my twenty-sixth. It was my twenty-fifth. I did not cele-brate my twenty-sixth because – if you cast your mind back – I had tonsillitis and was having my tonsils removed in the Royal Infirmary! I remember getting a card from the office wishing me a speedy recovery, and a happy birthday too. It was signed by the senior partner, and I kept it. I was very pleased to have received it."

Betty pursed her lips. For a moment it seemed as if she was about to speak, but then she did not.

"I suggest that we stop arguing," said Ramsey. "If you're going to find fault with my memoirs on matters of detail, then I'm not sure if it will be at all productive to read them to you."

Betty sprang to her own defence. "I was not finding fault, as you put it. I was merely wanting to keep the historical record straight. These things are important. Imagine what the world would be like if memoirs were misleading. You have to be accurate."

"And I am being accurate," retorted Ramsey. "I'm checking every single fact that I commit to paper. I've been consulting my diaries, and they are very full, I'll have you know. I've gone down to George IV Bridge to make sure that everything I say about contemporary events is true. I am being very historical in all this." He paused, and then added peevishly: "I don't want to mislead posterity, Betty."

Betty thought for a moment. She was certain that she was right about the birthday being the twenty-sixth rather than the twenty-fifth, but she felt that she should let it be, even if it was a serious mistake on her husband's part. "Of course you don't want to mislead, Ramsey," she said placatingly. "Let's not discuss it any further. Twenty-five, twenty-six – it's very much the same thing. You carry on, dear. I'm listening."

Ramsey Dunbarton picked up the sheaf of papers again and cleared his throat. "I was now twenty . . . somewhere in my mid-twenties. I had recently finished my years as an apprentice lawyer and had been admitted to the Society of Writers to Her Majesty's Signet. This was a great honour for me, as this entitled me to put the letters WS after my name. I lost no time, I must admit, in having new notepaper printed and cards too. I was proud of the new letters, and I must admit that I became very impatient with people who affected not to know what WS stood for. (One of these people even had the gall to ask whether I was a water surveyor!) 'If you live in Edinburgh,' I would point out, 'you should know these things. Wouldn't you expect a Roman to know what the Swiss Guard is?'

"This question often silenced people, and I hope that they were sufficiently chastened to go home and look the abbreviation up. I did not want to embarrass anybody, of course, and one should be slow to point out to others their ignorance. But there are limits, and I think that ignorance of the meaning of WS is one of them.

"One very important feature of the WS Society is that it's always mainly been for lawyers working in Edinburgh firms, and not every Edinburgh firm at that. There may be some members who have their practices elsewhere – even in places like Pitlochry – but in such cases it is perfectly obvious that they are really Edinburgh types. This is as it should be, as the Society has its premises here in Edinburgh and was founded by Edinburgh lawyers for themselves and nobody else. Lawyers from Glasgow have their own societies and are welcome to join those, if they wish – and I'm sure that some of these societies are perfectly respectable and worthwhile organisations, although I do not know for certain. So I have usually had very little time for those who question our important institutions, such as the WS Society or the Royal Company of Archers, for that matter. These people are usually jealous and would soon change their tune if they were to be admitted to membership of one of these bodies.

"I was now working as an assistant in the firm of Ptarmigan Monboddo, which was a very highly-regarded Edinburgh legal firm. There were eight partners and three assistants, of whom I was one. I was told by my principal, the late Mr Fergus Monboddo, that if I played my cards right I could expect to be assumed into the partnership within five years. It was possible, he said, to become a partner rather earlier than that, but if I wanted to achieve that I would have to marry one of the senior partner's daughters, and that, he said, was asking too much. I think that this was meant to be a joke, but I thought that it was in very bad taste, and I was surprised that a partner in an Edinburgh firm would speak in this way. I later discovered that Mr Monboddo only said things like that when he had had a small glass of sherry, and so I learned to distinguish between those things that were said in all seriousness and those that were not. I have always taken the view that one should never hold against a man anything that he says after twelve o'clock at night or after a glass or two of something.

"I had no desire to marry the senior partner's daughter, as it happened, because I had just met the woman whose hand I was determined to obtain. This was my dear wife, Betty, to whom I have been married for many happy years. Although it is a long time ago now, I remember very vividly the day we met, which was in the Brown Derby tea room on Princes Street. That was the most important day of my life, I think, and I hardly dare contemplate what might have happened had I not gone there on a whim and met the person who was to transform my life."

Betty smiled at this. It was so kind of him, so gallant. And yet he was wrong again, she feared. It had not been the Brown Derby, it had been Crawford's. But she did not have the heart to correct him again, and so she nodded brightly and urged him to continue. Their courtship had been a passionate one, and she wondered whether he was going to say anything about that!

38. The Ramsey Dunbarton Story:
Part 2 – Courting Days

"Those were very special days," read Ramsey Dunbarton. "I knew almost immediately that this was the girl I wished to marry, but in those days one had to go through a good deal of courting before one felt it right to pop the question. Of course I knew some people who got engaged very quickly, but they were usually rather fast types, and although I considered myself adventurous, I would not have described myself as fast.

"We used to go to the cinema, to the Dominion in Church Hill, and sometimes to the Playhouse, where there was a splendid cinema organ. This rose out from under the floor with the organist sitting at the keyboard, playing for all he was worth. It was a splendid sight, and I think that it contributed in no little way to the romance of those occasions. They had newsreels then, of course, and we would come away from the cinema not only entertained but also informed about current affairs. It would be no bad thing if they reintroduced newsreels in the cinemas, but I suspect that people would just laugh or pay no attention. Nobody is serious about these things any more.

"Another favourite outing of ours was to Cramond, where we went for walks when the weather was fine. It was very romantic down at Cramond in those days and there were many courting couples who went there in search of a place to be alone and to talk about the future. Betty and I used to like walking along the shore, watching the oyster catchers and other sea-birds. We would also watch ships in the Forth, heading out from Rosyth or from Leith. In those days there was a passenger ship that came down from Kirkwall and Aberdeen, the *St Rognvald*. It was owned by the North of Scotland Orkney and Shetland Shipping Company and I once had the privilege of making a trip on that vessel. It had a beautiful panelled dining room. We also counted ourselves lucky if we saw the *Pharos*, which was the ship that the Northern Lighthouse Commissioners used to inspect their lighthouses. That was a beautiful ship. I myself would have loved to have been a Commissioner of the Northern

Lighthouses, but I was never invited. That's the problem with Edinburgh: to be a member of anything really worthwhile and important – such as the Royal Company of Archers or the Northern Lighthouse Board (not to mention the Knights of the Thistle!) – one has to be invited. Why can one not apply? I ask. Of course they would get all sorts of applications from undesirables, but these could be weeded out by the civil servants who, in my experience, have a pretty good idea of who's desirable and who isn't!

"There was also the *Gardyloo*, of course. That was the vessel that took the sewage sludge out from Edinburgh and dumped it in the Firth. It went out every day and came back a few hours later, somewhat lighter. Once, many years later – in the late nineteen-seventies, I think it was, we were back down walking at Cramond and we saw this ship. Betty pointed it out to me and asked me one day what I thought that strange boat was carrying. I replied that I thought that it brought in gravel from a quarry down near North Berwick. I knew that this was not true, but I could not tell her what was really going on. That is the only occasion on which I lied to Betty, and I later admitted it to her. She said that I had done the right thing, as it would undoubtedly have spoiled the romance of our walk if she had known what the real business of the *Gardyloo* was.

"Our romance blossomed, as I knew it would, and eventually Betty invited me to accompany her to Broughty Ferry, where her parents lived. We agreed to motor up there on a Sunday, have lunch with them and then travel back in time for dinner.

"I shall never forget that first meeting with Betty's parents. It was daunting for any young man, of course, to have to meet the parents of his intended, and I felt pretty nervous as we went up to the front door of their house. Betty must have sensed my nervousness, because she patted me on the forearm and assured me that I was bound to like them. 'Everybody likes them,' she said. 'They are very kind people.'

"And she was absolutely right. They made me feel immediately at home and seemed to know all about me and my career.

Her father said that he liked lawyers and that he would have become a lawyer himself if he had not been required to take over the family business. This was a marmalade factory in Dundee – a business which his own father had set up on his return from Calcutta, where he had been an agent for a cousin's jute firm.

"After lunch, the ladies withdrew and left Betty's father and me in the dining room. We had talked about all sorts of things over the meal, but now the conversation seemed to dry up. I looked out of the window, hoping to see something on which I could pass comment, but there was nothing unusual to be seen. It was a large garden, full of rhododendra, but I could not think of anything to say about rhododendra. So I remained silent.

"Eventually, Betty's father spoke. He looked at me for a moment, as if assessing me, and then he said: 'What are your views on marmalade?'

"At first I was not sure how to reply. I liked marmalade, but I was not sure whether that was the nature of the question I had been asked.

"He must have sensed my confusion, as he fairly quickly explained his question. 'What I mean,' he said, 'is this. Do you think that you could work in the marmalade business? That is, if anybody were to offer you a post in such a business.'

"I had not been prepared for this question. It seemed to me that he was sounding me out about my willingness to commit myself to their family business; this seemed a little bit premature, as I had not yet announced my intention of proposing to Betty. But I supposed that it was a wise move on his part. If he wanted to marry Betty off, then perhaps he thought that an early offer of a partnership in the business would prompt me to make a proposal. The more I thought of it, in fact, the more convinced I became that this is what he had in mind.

"Of course I had to be honest. I had nothing against the marmalade business, but I did not think I would wish to make my life in it. It is undoubtedly the sort of business that suits many people very well, but I liked the law and had worked hard to become a solicitor. I did not want to throw that all away just for the sake of marmalade.

"I explained to him that I thought that I would continue to practise law. He nodded, rather sadly, I thought, and told me that this was the answer he had expected. 'We're not the most exciting business in the world,' he said. 'But, you know something? I love it. I love every moment of it. Marmalade has been my life. It really has.'"

39. The Ramsey Dunbarton Story: Part 3 – Further Highlights

"Betty and I were married in St Giles', where my father was an elder. We then moved into our first matrimonial home, which was a terraced house at the end of Craiglea Drive, in Morningside. It was not a large house, but it suited us very well, as we were on the sunny side of the street and got the morning sunlight through our drawing-room windows. That meant, of course, that the garden, which was on the other side, did not get quite as much sun as I would have wished, and I think that is the real reason why we were to move six years later. I know that some people have suggested that it was because we thought that that end of Craiglea Drive was not quite 'grand' enough for us, but that really was not the case and I'm happy to have this opportunity to scotch those rumours.

"One of the main attractions of that house was the many pleasant walks which one could have in the vicinity. If one went to the end of the road and then turned right, and then left after that, one came quite quickly to the gates of Craig House. This was a splendid building which had been built as a hospital but which was more like a large country house. It had a splendid hall in which the patients could take formal meals on occasion, and very extensive grounds. Like many of the neighbours, I enjoyed the privilege of walking in those grounds, admiring the fine views. Betty and I spent many happy hours walking in those grounds when we lived in Craiglea Drive and when I drive past it today and reflect on those days I cannot help but feel a little bit sad. I think of those poor people who stayed there, and of all their unhappiness, and of how we used to look after people with rather greater dignity than we do today. In those days, if you were ill you were welcomed in the hospitals. You were made to feel comfortable and you were addressed by your full name. Today, the first thing they think of is how quickly they can get you out of there and then they put you in a ward with men and women all mixed up together, as if privacy did not matter. I sometimes reflect on what we have lost in our society and how it all happened. But then if I speak about this, people simply sneer and call me old-fashioned and conservative. Well, they are welcome to do that, but at least I can console myself with the knowledge that I always, always called people Mr so-and so or Miss so-and-so and never presumed a familiarity with them to which they had not admitted me.

"When we left Craiglea Drive we came to the Braids, to the house in which we were to remain for many years, and where we still live. I am not a rolling stone; I like to gather moss. It suited us very well to live up here, with its good air and its fine views, and over the years we have established a remarkable garden. In fact, we once considered volunteering our garden for public admission under Scotland's Gardens Scheme, but I hesitated to do something which some people around here might consider pushy, or pretentious. Most of the gardens opened to the public are fairly large ones, attached to substantial country houses, but there is still a place for the small, intimate garden which can be a real jewel if planned and tended with care and good taste.

"Betty was keen enough to open the garden to the public, but I eventually decided that it would not be wise. 'One has to keep one's head below the parapet,' I said to her. 'Put it above the parapet and people will take a pot shot at you.'

"She seemed surprised at this, and suggested that I was rather exaggerating the situation. Her nature is so sweet, I suppose, that she couldn't imagine people behaving in a nasty way. But I had seen a lot of human nature and knew very well that there were people in the street who would be only too happy to have some excuse to pass hostile comments on me. I had already encountered it when I had proposed myself for membership of the local amenity association and had suggested that my legal expertise might be useful in dealing with any controversial planning applications that came up. It came back to me that one or two neighbours were saying that this offer on my part meant that I thought I knew more about bureaucratic procedures than they did. This was very unfair. I would never have implied that, and I had only put myself forward in order to be of use to the community.

"But some people are not interested in the public good; they are consumed by envy of anybody who might be just a little bit more enterprising than they are. I don't wish to point any fingers politically, but I think that there might be one or two Scottish politicians who are perhaps a tiny bit guilty of harbouring such sentiments in their otherwise generous bosoms. But political sniping is not to my taste, and I shall say no more about that!

"Time passed remarkably quickly. Betty and I had no family, which was a disappointment to us, I know, and I would wish that it could have been otherwise. But we have been blessed in so many other ways that I do not wish to dwell on what we might have missed. We have had a fortunate life, Betty and I, and it has been packed with more than its fair share of excitement. I should like to share some of that with you, and tell you, in particular of some of my exciting legal cases, of how I played the Duke of Plaza-Toro in *The Gondoliers* at the Church Hill Theatre, of my racy friend Johnny Auchtermuchty, and of the occasion that I played bridge with no less a person than Angus, late Duke of Atholl."

40. Bertie's Plan is Launched

As he made his way back to Scotland Street after his unfortunate experience in Dundas Street – unfortunate in the sense of having been stranded so ignominiously and terrifyingly in the middle of the traffic, yet fortunate in the sense of having been rescued by a well-known politician who happened to be walking up the hill at the time – Bertie felt utterly despondent. He had not hatched many plans in his brief life – his mother did his planning for him – and this scheme, with which he had been so pleased, had not even got off the ground. As he walked home, fingering the piece of chalk which he had in his pocket and which he had planned to use to leave a message for his proposed collaborator, Paddy, he decided that perhaps it was useless to rebel. It seemed to him that his mother would always outsmart him, whatever he tried to do, and she also had that powerful ally in the person of Dr Fairbairn. It was hopeless, thought Bertie, to attempt to take control of his life in the face of two such calculating opponents. Like a prisoner-of-war, he should perhaps just keep his head down and wait for the moment of liberation to come. That would be when he was eighteen, when Bertie understood that one became an adult and could leave home and behave as one wished. Once one was eighteen, then one could abandon crushed strawberry-coloured dungarees if one wished and wear whatever one liked. Bertie could hardly wait, and there were only twelve years to go.

Bertie was thinking along these lines when he turned the corner into Drummond Place. As he did so, he heard a sound coming from his right, from the gardens in the middle of the square. It was a strange sound, something between a whistle and a hoot, and he wondered for a moment if it was some unusual bird that had lost its way and had settled in one of the trees.

Bertie stopped, and stared into the bushes. Again the sound came, and this time it was followed by a parting of the undergrowth. Revealed within, half crouching, half standing, was Paddy, the boy whom Bertie had hoped to see in Fettes Row.

"Bertie!" Paddy called. "Quick! Over here!"

Barely waiting to see if any cars were coming, but nonetheless being careful not to tread on any lines, Bertie ran across the pavement and over the road. In a moment he was through the half-open gate to the gardens. Paddy called out again, and held back the branches of the large bush under which he was hiding.

"Hello," said Paddy, as Bertie joined him under the bush. "This is my special observation post. You can come here any time you like. You can see everything that's going on. And nobody can see you!"

"Great," said Bertie. "Magnifico . . ." And then, correcting himself very quickly, he said: "Magnificent!"

"Yes," said Paddy. "But don't tell anybody. I don't want anyone else coming in here."

"Of course not," said Bertie. "Just you and me. Like one of those Masonic lodges."

Paddy looked puzzled. "Masonic lodges?"

"Yes," explained Bertie. "That's where men go – grown-up men. They get dressed up and go to these secret club houses."

"How strange," said Paddy. "What do they do there?"

"I'm not sure," said Bertie. "They don't let anybody else have a look. And there are no girls allowed."

"Good," said Paddy. "Girls spoil things."

Bertie thought about this for a moment. He did not know many girls – in fact the only girl he knew was that girl called Olive at school. She was rather nice, he thought, and he was not at all sure that she spoiled things. It was Olive who had helped him up after Tofu had pushed him over, and it was she who had comforted him with the thought that Tofu would eventually fade away through enforced veganism.

"There are some nice girls," said Bertie. "There's a girl called Olive . . ."

"Never heard of her," said Paddy. "Anyway, let's not talk about girls. Let's talk about something else."

Bertie saw his opportunity. "I've had a very good idea," he said quickly. "I need your help for a plan that I've made. Are you allowed to go wherever you like?"

"Yes," said Paddy. "I'm allowed to go anywhere, as long as I'm back by six. I'm completely free."

"And what about your . . . your mother? Doesn't she . . . ?" It was so difficult for Bertie to say this, but it seemed so extraordinary to him, so impossible, that a boy could be free of his mother, that he needed to seek confirmation.

"My mother's cool," said Paddy, with a shrug. "She says that boys need to have fun. She likes to have fun herself. Everybody says that she's full of fun."

Bertie's eyes widened. "And your dad? What about him?"

"He's cool too," said Paddy. "He takes me fishing in the Pentlands. I told you that, didn't I? And he likes to drink too. He has lots of fun."

Bertie looked at Paddy with admiration, and envy. This is what it must be like to be eighteen, he thought. But there was no point wallowing in regret for what was not; there was a plan to be explained to Paddy, and over the next few minutes he told him exactly what he wanted him to do. Paddy listened intently and then nodded enthusiastically. "Piece of cake," he said. "I'll get the money for you and I'll buy the blazer – and the tie. Then I'll bring it down here and leave it under the bushes – in our place. You can pick it up any time. Easy."

"I'll give you a present for doing all this," said Bertie. "You can keep ten pounds."

"How about twenty?" said Paddy.

Bertie thought for a moment. Twenty pounds was a great deal of money, but he was sure that Paddy would do everything he said he would and this was an important plan after all. "All right," Bertie said. "You can keep twenty pounds."

"Good," said Paddy. "Give me the card then, and tell me your number."

Bertie reached into his pocket and took out his bank card. "You'll be able to remember the number easily," Bertie said. "It's the date of Mozart's birth."

Paddy stared at Bertie. "Who?"

"Mozart."

Paddy continued to stare. "Who did he play for?" he asked.

Bertie laughed. That was very funny. Then he stopped. Perhaps Paddy did not get the joke.

41. *Irene's Plan for Bertie*

Paddy was as good as his word. The day after the fortuitous encounter of the two boys in their newly-established meeting place in Drummond Place Gardens, Bertie found a neatly-wrapped parcel in Aitken and Niven livery waiting for him under the appointed bush. He had obtained leave from Irene to go out and play in the gardens for fifteen minutes or so prior to his yoga class in Stockbridge, and had used the time to locate the parcel. Fumbling with the string which Paddy had tied about the package, he tore it open and gazed in wonder at the contents. There before him was a pristine, plum-coloured Watson's blazer, complete with tie and, tucked neatly into the top pocket of the blazer, his now somewhat depleted junior saver bank card.

Since it was going to be very important to ensure that Irene did not see the blazer, Bertie had to be careful in smuggling it back into the flat. This proved to be easier than he had expected; Irene was on the telephone when he let himself in and he was able to slip along the corridor, into his room, and bundle the blazer under the bed. It was easy, but it was dangerous nonetheless, and he felt his heart beating loud within him as he stood at his door and listened for a few moments to his mother's conversation. No, she had not heard; she suspected nothing.

Irene's voice drifted down from the other end of the flat. "Of course there's no question but that he can manage," she said. "He's very advanced, you know."

Bertie winced. She was talking about him – again. And what was this that he was advanced enough to do? Certainly not rugby.

There was a silence as the voice on the other end of the telephone said something. Then Irene spoke again. "His age? What's his age got to do with it?"

Again a silence. Then Irene's response: "Well, that's a completely absurd rule. Bertie happens to be not quite six yet, but he has the intellectual ability of a boy way, way beyond that. There are many eighteen-year-olds who are quite a bit behind him, you know. Bertie could go to university if he wanted to."

Bertie felt a cold knot of fear grow within him, an emptiness in his stomach. She was going to send him off to university now before he even had the chance to go to primary school! It was so unfair. He would have to leave home and live in a hall of residence and make his own meals. And there would be no boys of his own age at university; everybody would be eighteen, or even older. And the other students would laugh at his dungarees – he knew they would. He would be the only person at university made to wear dungarees.

"Yes," said Irene. "I really mean that. He could easily manage a degree. His Italian, for example, is already fluent. No, I am not hot-housing him, as you put it – and that's a ridiculous term anyway. There is such a thing as natural intellectual curiosity, you know."

The voice at the other end must have spoken at some length, as Irene was silent for several minutes. Then, somewhat abruptly, she said goodbye and rang off.

Bertie withdrew into his room and closed the door. He lay down on his bed and stared at the ceiling. It was the one white surface in his otherwise pink room, as his mother had been unwilling to stand on a ladder to paint it when she had painted the rest of the room. He stared at his walls. He was sure that Paddy did not have a pink room, nor Jock, the friend he had almost made and who would have been his blood brother had his mother not intervened. They lived in normal rooms, with model cars and footballs and objects of that sort. They did not have mothers like his, who called his room his space.

Suddenly, the door opened, and Irene stood in the doorway. Bertie wished that she would knock before she came into his room, and had once asked her to do this, but she had just laughed. "Now, now Bertie! Do you seriously want me to knock before I come into your space? Why would you want that?"

"Because it's polite," said Bertie. "That's what you should do before you go into another person's space. You should knock."

"But remember: I'm Mummy," said Irene. "And you're Bertissimo. You have no secrets from Mummy, do you Bertie?"

Bertie had looked down at the floor and thought about his secrets. Yes, he did have secrets, and he would like to have more. His mother did not know about his secret thoughts, his thoughts of freedom. She did not know about his plan, which was now getting so close to fruition. And it was good that she did not know any of this. She thought that she knew everything about him, but she did not know as much as she imagined. That gave him great satisfaction. Ignorant Mummy, he thought, with relish. Mummy in the Dark!

Now, standing in the doorway, Irene looked down at Bertie and smiled. "It's time for yoga," she said brightly. "If we hurry, we might be able to have a latte on the way down there."

Bertie took a deep breath. He did not want to go to yoga. He did not like to lie with his stomach on the ground and his back arched and pretend to greet the morning sun. Nor did he want to take a deep breath and hold it while the yoga teacher counted up to twenty-five. He did not see the point of that at all.

"I don't really like yoga," he said quietly. "Couldn't I give it up and stay at home?"

Irene looked at him sharply. "Of course you like yoga, Bertie. Of course you like it."

"I don't," he said. "I hate it."

"Nonsense," she said. "You can't hate yoga. One doesn't hate yoga. And you had better hurry up. At this rate we're never going to get there."

Bertie sighed, and pulled himself up off his bed.

"Are you sending me somewhere, Mummy?" he asked.

Irene raised an eyebrow. "Why do you ask, Bertie?"

"Because I want to know," said Bertie. "I want to know what's going to happen to me."

"Well, I do have a little plan for you, Bertie," said Irene. "But this is not the time to discuss it."

Bertie looked at her. And I have my own little plan, he said to himself. You don't know about it, you horrible old . . .

He stopped. He did not want to think that way about his mother. He wanted to love her; he really wanted to. But it was proving difficult.

42. *Bertie Escapes!*

Bertie carried the Watson's blazer to school folded up and stuffed into the bottom of his rucksack. He was ready with an explanation for his mother, if she asked him why his bag looked so bulky, but Irene seemed preoccupied with something else that morning and paid little attention to Bertie as they boarded the bus together.

"Is something making you feel sad, Mummy?" he asked, as the bus toiled up the Mound.

Irene, who had been looking out of the window, turned to Bertie and smiled. "No, Bertie, Mummy's not sad. Mummy's thinking."

"Thinking of what?" asked Bertie. "Of Dr Fairbairn?"

Irene caught her breath. "Why on earth should I be thinking of Dr Fairbairn?" she snapped. She had been thinking of him, of course, of his blue linen jacket to be exact, but she had not expected Bertie to guess this. Perhaps this was that extraordinary familial telepathy that she had read about somewhere. Could Bertie be psychic? she wondered. Not that such matters were anything more than a lot of weak-minded mumbo-jumbo. He had just guessed – that was all. He had been thinking of Dr Fairbairn himself – by sheer coincidence – and that had led him to attribute the thought to her – it was a common phenomenon, she reminded herself, the transfer of our states of mind to others.

Bertie said nothing. He wanted his mother to be happy, but it seemed to him that she herself was the obstacle to that. If only she would stop worrying about him; if only she would stop thinking about why people do things; if only she would accept people and things as they were. But he knew that it was hopeless to expect her to do this. If Irene stopped forcing him to do things, then what life would she have? She had very few friends, as far as Bertie could work out. There were some other women at the Floatarium whom she liked to talk to, but she never saw them anywhere else and they never came to their flat in Scotland Street. In fact, nobody came to the flat in Scotland Street, apart from one of his father's friends from the office, who came to play chess once a month. It was possible that his father had other friends at the office, but Bertie was not sure. He had asked him once, and had received a rather strange reply. "Friends, Bertie? Friends? Mummy and I are friends, aren't we? Do I need more friends than that?"

Bertie thought he did, but did not say so. One thing he was certain of was that he was not going to grow up to be like his parents. Once he was eighteen he would not go to a psychotherapist; he would not go floating; his room would have white walls, or even black perhaps, but certainly not pink; and he would never talk Italian. There were a great deal of changes in store, he thought.

Irene walked Bertie from Bruntsfield to the school gate. Then she kissed him goodbye and Bertie watched for a few moments while she walked back up the street. Now it was time for action. Glancing about to see that he was not being watched, Bertie darted down the first part of the school drive and then suddenly turned and ran into the school garden, making straight for a small shed which was propped up against the high stone wall that enclosed the school grounds. This was a shed which the gardener used for the storage of rakes and forks and other bits and pieces of equipment. Bertie had done his reconnaissance well, and knew that it was not kept locked. Now he opened it and slipped inside.

It took no more than a few minutes for Bertie to be transformed. In place of the crushed strawberry dungarees and check shirt he was now regaled in a neat white shirt and tie, shorts that were just about the right colour, and the splendid new Watson's blazer. His old clothes were bundled into his bag and tucked away underneath a rusty bucket which was sitting, inverted, on the ground. Then, glancing out of the cobweb-covered window to check that it was safe to go out, Bertie opened the door of the shed and ran the short distance to the school gate.

It was now time to bring the first stage of the plan to completion. From the pocket of his new blazer, Bertie extracted a neatly written note which he had forged the previous evening. Looking around for a familiar face, he found Merlin, one of the boys in his class.

"Please give this note to Miss Harmony," Bertie said, thrusting the envelope into Merlin's hands. "Don't say it was me who gave it to you. Just leave it on her desk."

Merlin looked at the envelope and then at Bertie. "Why are you wearing that funny outfit?" he asked.

"I just am," said Bertie.

Merlin shrugged, brushing a speck of dust off the shoulder of his rainbow-coloured jacket. "I suppose you've got the right to be weird," he said.

Bertie thanked him and then quickly went out of the gate and began to make his way round the corner to George Watson's College. As he walked, he thought of the contents of the letter which he had just entrusted to Merlin. He was good at imitating his mother's writing, and he thought that he had made a good job of it. "Dear Miss Harmony," he had written. "Unfortunately my son, Bertie, has contracted an infectious disease and will have to be away from school for some time. I would have come to speak to you about this personally, but I was concerned about passing the disease on to you, in case I have it myself. Please do not worry about Bertie, as he is perfectly happy and will surely be returned to good health in due course. He is being treated with steroids, as are my husband and I, as a precaution. Yours sincerely, Irene Pollock."

Bertie had been very pleased with this wording and thought that it might work, particularly in view of the medical detail at the end. The mention of an infectious disease, he reasoned, would surely keep the school from contacting his mother, as schools have to be very careful about infections. So if all went according to plan he could simply keep his Watson's uniform in the shed and change every morning. There were so many children milling about that nobody would notice anything, and Watson's, he understood, was a very large school. In a large school like that none of the teachers would notice one extra boy, he felt, and there was no reason why he could not get his entire education there.

He arrived at the Watson's gate. Now, he thought, I must just act as if I belong. I must not act suspiciously. I must be confident.

Bertie swaggered up the drive to the school.

43. *Rugby!*

Once he had entered the portals of George Watson's College, it was simple matter to find a suitable class. Prominently displayed on the walls were signs indicating which class was which, and Bertie merely followed one that pointed in the direction of Primary One. Once there, he slipped into the classroom with a couple of other boys.

"Is there a spare desk?" he whispered to one of them. "I'm new here."

The other boy pointed towards the back of the classroom. "That's one's empty," he said. "Somebody was sitting there, but he went away after only one day. I think he got lost in the corridor."

Bertie glanced at the desk. It was ideal for his purposes, as he did not want to draw undue attention to himself. Thanking his new classmate, he made his way to the back of the room and sat himself down at the desk. After a short while the teacher arrived and the class settled down to the task of copying out letters along a straight line. While the pupils were engaged in this, the teacher moved between the rows of desks, stopping to comment on the work of each child. Bertie sat quite still, staring down at the piece of paper on his desk and hoping that the teacher would stop before she reached him. But she did not, and he looked up to see her staring down at him, a surprised expression on her face.

"Are you in the right room, dear?" she asked kindly. "Have you got a little bit mixed up?"

Bertie looked up at her and swallowed. "I've been transferred," he said. "I was over there, and now I'm here." He pointed vaguely in the direction of the corridor.

"Surely not," said the teacher. "Tell me: what's your name?"

"Bertie," he whispered. "Bertie Pollock."

"Well, I think that there must be a bit of a mix-up," said the teacher. "I'll check with the office later on. Perhaps they've just forgotten to tell me."

"Yes," said Bertie quickly. "That's probably what's happened. This is such a big school. It must be difficult to keep track."

The teacher looked at Bertie with curiosity. "Well, yes, I suppose it is a big school. But people usually end up in the right place. I'm sure that we'll sort it all out. Don't you worry about it!"

When playtime came, Bertie made his way out of the room as quickly as he could. He was not sure whether he would go back into that particular class, as the teacher would presumably discover quite soon that he was not meant to be there. It might be better, he thought, to try another class, perhaps one with a less nosy teacher, if there was one.

He went out and stood at the side, watching the games that were developing around him. Children were dashing about, shouting at one another, enjoying themselves, but nobody asked Bertie to join in. Bertie looked down at the ground; there did not seem to be much difference between Watson's and Steiner's so far; perhaps the whole plan was not such a good idea after all. But then he saw him, and his heart gave a leap. Yes, there was Jock; brave Jock, the boy whom he had met before, the boy who would be his friend.

"Jock!" shouted Bertie. "Jock! Here I am!"

Jock, who was running towards the gate, a bag of some sort in his hand, stopped in his tracks and looked at Bertie. He looked puzzled.

"Yes," he said. "There you are."

Bertie took a few steps towards his friend. "It's me," he said. "Bertie. Remember?"

Jock still looked puzzled. "Not really," he said.

Bertie felt a stab of disappointment, but did not show it. He gestured to the bag that Jock was carrying. "What are you doing with that?"

"Rugby," said Jock. "Over there." He pointed to a playing field, where a group of boys was beginning to form round a teacher wearing a red tracksuit. "Are you coming too?"

Bertie lost no time in replying. "Of course," he said. Then he paused, and added: "I've got no kit. I can't play in my blazer."

"Changing rooms," said Jock casually. "There's always stuff lying around. Just wear that."

Bertie followed Jock to the changing rooms, where he soon found a pair of discarded rugby shorts, a torn and muddy jersey, and a pair of boots that, although several sizes too large, at least did not pinch his toes. Then, trotting along beside Jock, he made his way on to the field, to join the knot of other small players in the middle. His anxieties over the possibility of detection had now faded, and he felt immensely happy. Here he was at last, on the rugby field, in rugby kit, about to play a game with his rediscovered friend, Jock. Mr Gavin Hastings must have started like this, he thought, although he probably wore boots that fitted his feet and wore a jersey that did not have a tear across the right shoulder. But these were small things; the important matter was that he was about to play rugby, on real grass, with real boys, and with a real ball.

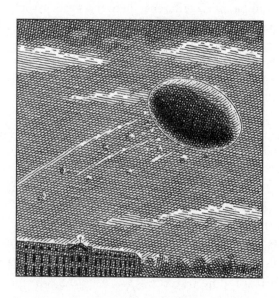

The teacher divided the boys into two teams. Bertie had hoped that Jock would be on his side, but he was not. He waved to Jock, though, but Jock did not return the greeting. Perhaps he did not see me, thought Bertie. Perhaps his mind is on the game already.

The whistle blew and the ball was in play. Bertie was not quite sure what to do, but he ran enthusiastically in the direction of play. The ball was passed, and Bertie's side had possession. Bertie cried out: "Over here!" and, rather to his surprise, the boy who had the ball passed it over to him. Now, the ball in his arms, Bertie started to run towards the posts in the distance. He knew that one had to score a try if at all possible, and that all one had to do was to run fast and touch the ball down on the other side of the line.

He ran as fast he could. There were boys coming towards him, but he ran on. Then one of the boys – and it was Jock – stepped in front of him and neatly inserted a foot and ankle between Bertie's feet.

Bertie fell to the ground, the ball beneath him. Jock, standing above him, now kicked Bertie in the ribs and, as the effect of this kick made him writhe in agony, Bertie felt the ball being snatched from beneath him. There was no whistle blown; there was no shout of objection; the game simply passed Bertie by.

Bertie picked himself up and looked at the game, now at the other end of the field. He tried to control himself, but he could not, and the tears ran down his cheeks; bitter tears, that were for everything, really – for the failure of his plan, for the end of his friendship with Jock, for the sheer humiliation of being who he was.

44. *Going Back*

Bertie ran out of the gate of George Watson's College, hesitated at the edge of the street, and then launched himself across Colinton Road. The traffic was light and he felt none of the panic that had paralysed him during his recent foiled attempt to cross Dundas Street. Now, the ill-fitting rugby boots chafing against his lower ankles, he made his way blindly back towards Spylaw Road and the sanctuary of the Steiner School. It had been a terrible mistake, his break for freedom; he did not belong at Watson's and he never would. And rugby, which he had so looked forward to playing, was a violent nightmare; a game in which even one's friends would think nothing of tripping one up and kicking one in the ribs. There was none of that at Steiner's, where aggressive ball games were not encouraged.

By the time he reached the Steiner's gate he was exhausted. Running all the way from Watson's had given him a stitch, and the nagging pain from Jock's kick was still present. He had hurt his wrist, too, in his fall, perhaps from clutching the ball as he went down. That was a sharp pain, that seemed to come and go, but which made him catch his breath and wince each time it made itself felt.

He slipped through the gate and walked slowly to the shed at the edge of the garden. He did not bother about being seen now; there was no secret any more – or no secret worth keeping. Entering the shed, he kicked over the bucket under which his clothes were stuffed. There were his familiar dungarees and his checked shirt. But there were no shoes, of course, as he had left those in the changing room at Watson's. Those were gone forever, then, as was his new plum-coloured blazer and his tie. Those at least he had no use for; it was different with his shoes – the loss of these would have to be explained to his mother.

The rugby kit abandoned on the floor of the shed, Bertie made his way to his classroom. The door was closed, but through the glass panel he could make out the figures of his classmates, all seated in a circle. He took a deep breath and entered the room.

Miss Harmony looked up as Bertie came in. She smiled, and indicated to the empty place which awaited him.

"You're a little late today, Bertie," she said. "But no matter.

We're doing some drawing and I know you're good at that!"

Bertie sat down and sank his head in his hands. He was aware of the interest of his fellow pupils – of Tofu's stare, of Olive's more discreet, and concerned, glance. They would have noticed his rugby boots, he thought, or heard them at least, as the studs had made a loud clicking noise on the floor. They would also be laughing at his dungarees, of course, once they had finished laughing at his boots.

After a few minutes, he became aware of Miss Harmony crouching beside his table. She had bent down and was whispering in his ear: "We were very worried, Bertie. That funny note you sent me – that was very odd, you know."

Bertie looked up at her. She was smiling, and had placed a hand upon his shoulder. "Don't worry about it," she whispered. "I won't show it to anybody. I'm on your side, you know."

Bertie stared fixedly at the table surface. He had not expected this. He had thought there would be recriminations and a summons to the office. He had not expected sympathy.

"You see," went on Miss Harmony, quietly so that even the neighbouring tables could not hear, "this school is based on love and respect. We love one another and look after one another. So we all love you, Bertie, because you are one of us. And if there is anything wrong, then you can tell us about it, and we will try to help – because we love you."

"My mother . . ." Bertie began. But he did not know what to say, and so he stopped. And as he stopped, he felt the pressure of Miss Harmony's hand tighten upon his shoulder.

"I know," she said. "Sometimes mothers make it difficult for their boys. They don't mean to, you know. The trick is not to let it worry you."

"She makes me wear dungarees," said Bertie. "And I feel so silly."

Miss Harmony nodded. "Would you like me to talk to her about that?" she asked.

"Yes," said Bertie. "But she won't listen."

"Well, I can try," said Miss Harmony. "There's no harm in trying." She paused, and looked down at Bertie's boots. "We have some spare shoes in a cupboard downstairs," she said. "Should we go and have a look for a pair that fits you?"

They left the classroom together and went downstairs, Bertie hobbling now from the pain in his chafed ankles. "Poor Bertie," said Miss Harmony. "Here – take my arm. Lean on me."

There was a pair of shiny brown shoes in the cupboard that fitted Bertie exactly, and once he was thus clad he began to feel somewhat more cheerful. He looked up at Miss Harmony and smiled.

"I'm sorry I wrote you that letter," he said. "I haven't got an infectious disease, you know."

"Don't worry," she said. "I didn't think for one moment that you had. The important thing is that you should be happy. And you've said sorry to me, which is very important." She paused. "You will be happy here, you know, Bertie. It's a very happy school."

Bertie thought for a moment. She was right. He did feel happier here than in the din and rush of Watson's, with all those hundreds of boys and girls with names he would never remember. Rugby was not for him, he decided, and it was a good thing that there was no rugby at Steiner's. It was fine for Mr Gavin Hastings to play it, he thought, but he, Bertie, would find something else to do. Even learning Italian was better than rugby.

Later that day, as he waited for his mother at the school gate, Tofu came up to him and asked him where he had found those boots. "Great boots," he said.

"Would you like them?" said Bertie nonchalantly. "You can have them if you like."

Tofu accepted gratefully. "Thanks, Bertie," he said. "You're a real pal."

"And would you like me to bring a ham sandwich in tomorrow?" asked Bertie.

"Yes, yes," said Tofu quickly. "Two, even. If you can spare them."

"Fine," said Bertie.

Tofu slapped him on the back in a friendly manner and went on his way.

Bertie watched him walk away and thought about the events of the day. There had been several discoveries. One was that rugby was a rough game and another was that Jock was a false friend. But there were other things to reflect upon. Tofu was no longer a threat – and could even become a friend. And he suspected, too, that he might be happy at this nice school, which was a good place – even if it had been his mother's choice. After all, there were some things which she might just get right.

45. *Dinner with Father*

If Bertie's problem was with his mother, Irene – and that would seem to be the case – then Matthew's problem was with his father, Gordon. Irene and Gordon would not have seen eye to eye on anything very much, but, in their own ways, they had each succeeded in bringing unhappiness into the lives of their offspring. So, while Bertie was trapped by a mother who was relentlessly ambitious for him, Matthew was aware that his father nursed no ambitions for him whatsoever. Gordon had decided that his son was a failure, and had come to accept this. The gallery in which he had set him up was not intended to be anything but a sinecure, a place to sit during the day while the rest of the world went to work. And if this was an expensive arrangement – for Gordon – then it was an expense which he could easily afford to bear.

Matthew had accepted his father's offer simply because it was the only one on hand. He understood that he was not a good businessman, but one had to do something, and running the gallery had proved rather more interesting than he had anticipated. This interest had made up for the discomfort that he felt over his father's writing him off. It is not easy to accept another's low opinion of oneself, and there were times when Matthew longed to show his father that he was made of sterner and more successful stuff. The problem, though, was that if he tried to do this, he thought it highly likely that he would fail.

Now Matthew was preparing for an evening with his father. Gordon had called in at the gallery unannounced and invited his son to dinner to meet his new friend, Janis, who owned a flower shop. As he stood before the mirror and tied his tie, Matthew thought of what he might say to this woman, whose motives were, in his view, perfectly clear. It would be good to indicate to her that he understood exactly what was going on, and that no gold-digger could fool him. But how to do this? One could not say anything direct, especially since the dinner was taking place at the New Club – where one could hardly speak directly about anything – and it would be necessary then to give a mere indication – to allow her to read between the lines. But would a woman like that – a "challenged blonde" as Matthew imagined her – be able to read between these lines? Some such people had difficulty enough in reading the lines themselves, let alone what lay between them. "She'll move her lips when she reads the menu," Matthew thought, and smiled at himself in the mirror. "Like this," he thought, and he mouthed the word *money*.

Matthew stared into the mirror at the tie he had chosen. It had linked red squares on a blue background. It was wrong. He reached for another one, a blue one with a slight jagged pattern in the background. These jagged lines looked vaguely like lightning, Matthew thought. That would be appropriate. If Janis looked at his tie she would receive a subliminal message: back off. Yes, he thought; that would be just the right note to strike. He would be distant and cool, which would send to her exactly the message he wanted to convey: *I know what you're about; it doesn't really matter to me, of course, but I know.*

Satisfied with his appearance, he moved away from the mirror and fetched his coat from the hall. Matthew lived in India Street, in a flat bought for him by his father, and the walk up to Princes Street and the New Club would take no more than fifteen minutes. As he left the front door and made his way up the hill, he realised that it was not going to be easy to be distant and cool. Indeed, he already felt hot and edgy. It was not going to be simple: this woman is taking my father away from me, he thought. It's as simple as that. She's taking him away from me – and he's mine.

He stopped at a corner and composed himself, telling himself that it did not mean that much to him. How often did he see his father? Less than once a month, and yet here he was persuading himself that he felt possessive. I shall be mature about this, he told himself. I shall see the whole thing in perspective. Janis is a passing phase – an entertainment. She was no more than that. And as a passing phase she could be tolerated.

He arrived at the New Club, making his way up the sombre, cavernous staircase that led into the lobby. Everything was very quiet and measured – a world away from the bustle outside, and the chewing-gum-encrusted mess that had been made of Princes Street. As Matthew stood at the window of the drawing room, looking out across the dark of the gardens to the illuminated rock of the Castle, he thought for a moment of how his father would be feeling about this meeting. He would be feeling anxious, no doubt, because it was always awkward for a parent to introduce a lover to a child. It was all wrong. Parents did not have lovers as far as their children were concerned.

Matthew turned round. His father was approaching him from the doorway, walking round the imposing leather sofas that stood between his son and himself. They shook hands.

"Janis will be through in a moment," said Gordon. He dabbed at his nose. "Powdering . . . you know."

It was intended to be a moment of shared understanding between men, but it did not set Matthew at his ease. He did not smile.

Gordon looked at his son, and frowned. "This is important to me, Matthew," he said, his voice lowered. "I'm . . . I'm very fond of Janis, you know. Very fond."

Matthew closed his eyes, and swallowed.

"You're going to be all right about this?" his father continued.

"Of course," said Matthew, quietly. "Why should I not be all right about this?"

Gordon tried to hold his son's gaze, but Matthew looked away, down to the floor.

"You're all tensed up," said Gordon. "Look at yourself. All tensed up. She's not going to bite you, you know."

"I never said . . ."

Gordon raised a hand. "Here she is."

46. The Language of Flowers

Matthew felt the satisfaction that comes with knowing that one has been right about somebody, at least in anticipating appearance. He had imagined Janis to be blonde, and she was certainly that. He had thought of her as petite, and again he was right. It was true that he had not envisaged her mock endangered-species shoes, but that was simply because when picturing her he had not got as far as the feet. Had he done so, then he would perhaps have thought of faux snakeskin, or so he told himself as he watched her arranging herself demurely on the chair opposite him. He tried not to make his stare too obvious – he was, after all, striving for an effect of coolness and distance – but he took in the details nonetheless.

Gordon glanced at his son, but only briefly. He was smiling at Janis in a way which Matthew thought revealed just how smitten he was. This was not his guarded, cautious father, this was a man in thrall to another.

Janis commented on the view of the Castle. "That castle has so many moods," she said. "But it's always there, isn't it?"

Matthew looked at her, resisting the sudden temptation to laugh. What an absurd thing to say. Of course the Castle was always there. What did she expect?

"Yes," he said. "It would be odd to wake up one morning and discover that the Castle wasn't there any more. I wonder how long it would take before people noticed."

Gordon turned slightly and looked at his son, as if he had heard something slightly disagreeable. Then he turned back to face Janis. "Yes, it's a marvellous view, isn't it? Edinburgh at its best."

No, thought Matthew. Edinburgh is far more than that. The Castle was the cliché; nothing more.

"I don't really like the Castle," he said airily. "I wouldn't mind if they replaced it."

Gordon made a sound which might have been a laugh. "Replaced it with what?"

"Oh, one of these large stores," said Matthew. "The sort that you get in Princes Street. A chain store of some sort. People could park on the Esplanade and then go shopping inside."

Janis was watching Matthew as he spoke. "I'm not sure . . ."

"You'd approve of that, Dad," Matthew interrupted. "You could invest in it."

Gordon drummed his fingers on the low table in front of him. "Matthew runs a gallery," he said to Janis. "You should drop in and see it sometime."

Janis looked at Matthew and smiled, as if waiting for the invitation.

"Of course," said Matthew. "Sometime."

"Thank you," said Janis. "I like art."

"Oh?" said Matthew. "Any particular painters? Jack Vettriano?"

Gordon turned to his son. "Why do you say that?" he asked. "Why do you mention Vettriano?"

Matthew eye's did not meet his father's gaze. He continued to look at Janis. "Vettriano's very popular. Lots of people like his work."

"But you don't?" asked his father. "I take it you don't?"

Matthew looked up at the ceiling, but said nothing.

Gordon addressed Janis. "You see, there's an awful lot of snobbery in the art world. Look at the people who win that prize, what's it called – the Turner. Pretentious rubbish. Empty rooms. Piles of rocks. That sort of thing. And then along comes a man who can actually paint and, oh dear me, they don't like that. That's what's happened to Vettriano. I certainly like him."

Janis nodded politely. "I'm sure he's very good," she said.

"Anyway," said Gordon, "it's time for dinner." He shot a glance at Matthew, who had risen to his feet with alacrity.

They made their way into the dining room and took their seats under a picture of a highly-plumaged Victorian worthy.

"Such beautiful portraits," said Janis brightly, as she unfolded her table napkin.

"In their own grim way, perhaps," said Matthew. "They don't look terribly light-hearted, do they?"

"Maybe they weren't," said Gordon. "The Victorians were serious people."

"Undoubtedly," said Matthew. "But I wouldn't care to sit underneath one of these scowling old horrors for too long."

Gordon ignored this remark. "Busy today?" he asked Janis.

"Yes," she said. "We ran out of roses by midday. A good sign."

"Oh?" said Matthew. "Of what?"

Janis took a sip of water. "Oh, that romance is in the air."

Matthew saw his father react to this. He saw him look down and finger the edge of his plate, as if slightly embarrassed, but pleased, by what Janis had said. And she had looked at him as she spoke, Matthew noted. How corny! How . . . well, there was a certain distastefulness to the whole performance – late-flowering love, so inappropriate for these two middle-aged people, although she was far younger than he was, hardly middle-aged. What was she? Late thirties? Who did she think she was? A coquettish twenty-year-old on a first date? And did his father not see how ridiculous it was for a man of his age to be interested in . . . the carnal. It wasn't even sex. It was *carnality*.

"Of course there's the whole language of flowers, isn't there?" asked Gordon. "Each flower has a meaning, you know, Matthew. Janis knows them all."

Excuse me, Matthew said to himself. I feel nauseated. The language of flowers! Is this really my father speaking? The pillar of the Watsonian Rugby Club? The Rotarian? He listened as Janis began to say something about the symbolism of variegated tulips. He had the opportunity to study her more closely while she talked, and he began to stare at her eyes and then at her chin and neck. For a few moments he was unsure, and then he became convinced that it was true. Janis had undergone plastic surgery.

Matthew looked at the skin about the edge of the eyes. It was tighter than it should be, he thought, and the smooth, rather stretched appearance of the skin carried on down to the side of the nose itself. It was as if it had been pulled back somewhere, tightened, and then polished in some way. He saw, too, the make-up that she had applied there; heavier on one side than on the other, but insufficient to fool the close observer, which he now was. She suddenly stopped talking about lilies. She had noticed his stare. Well, what can she expect? thought Matthew. If one gives in to vanity, then one can only expect others to notice. Mutton dressed up as lamb.

Janis looked at him. "Did your father tell you I had an accident?" she asked.

47. *Information*

Some evenings are just not a success, and Matthew's dinner with his father and his father's new friend, Janis, undoubtedly fell into that category. The conversation limped on until the arrival of the cheese, when it faltered altogether and the three of them sat energetically eating their Stilton, not wishing to put off any longer the moment when they could leave the table and go through to the morning room for coffee. The drinking of coffee, as it happened, did not take long.

"I have an early start tomorrow," Gordon said, looking at his watch. "It's been most enjoyable."

"Yes," said Janis. "I enjoyed that."

They looked at Matthew, who nodded. "Me too," he said. "Very enjoyable."

There was silence for a moment. Then Matthew rose to his feet. "I'm going to get my coat," he said. "I'll see you in the lobby."

He made his way to the cloakroom, noticing as he left the morning room that his father and Janis had immediately huddled in conversation; discussing me, he thought. Well, it had been a disaster, the whole thing, but what could his father expect? Did he expect him to welcome this woman, with her transparent motives? Is that what he expected? He went into the cloakroom and took his coat off the hook. A sleeve had become turned in upon itself and he busied himself for a few moments disentangling it. As he did so, he heard a voice from the basin area round the corner.

"Dramatic results, you know. Quite dramatic."

A tap was turned on and something was said that he did not quite catch. Then the first voice spoke again.

"They're desperately short of cash, so they're having to go back to the market for a couple of million. But they'll have to do this before the results of this research are confirmed. So they'll still seem pretty shaky when they go for the cash."

The other man spoke. "AIM? They're still on the AIM market, aren't they?"

"Yes."

"So the new shares will be pretty low until . . ."

"Until the research results get the stamp of approval and then . . . well, it's a major breakthrough. The shares will go through the roof. Of course, we're advising them on the whole business and so keep this under your hat, of course. I only mentioned it because you know Tommy, of course, and you'll be pleased for him."

"Of course. He's still chairman?"

"Yes. But they're moving from that place of theirs out of town. They've taken one of those new buildings down near the West Approach Road."

"Oh." A tap was turned off. "You know, I must have a word with Charles about this soap . . ."

Matthew took his coat and left the cloakroom, silently. His father was waiting for him in the middle of the lobby, Janis at his side. She looked at him encouragingly and he tried to return her smile. But it was difficult.

As they walked down the stairs together, Matthew turned to his father and stopped him. "I've just heard a very interesting conversation."

Gordon smiled. "In the gents? Suitable for mixed company?"

"Yes," said Matthew. "A commercial conversation."

As Matthew had suspected, this attracted his father's attention. "Oh? What was it?"

Matthew described what he had heard. For the first time that evening, he thought, my father is really listening to me.

"Very interesting indeed!" said Gordon after Matthew had finished. "I can very easily find out who they're talking about. It's very simple to find out which Scottish companies have their shares traded on the AIM market. Very simple. In fact . . . you said the chairman was referred to as Tommy?"

"Yes."

"I think I know exactly who they are then." Gordon smiled at Matthew and patted him on the shoulder playfully. "I'll get in touch with you about this, Matt."

Matthew winced. He did not like being called Matt, and his father was the only one who did it. "Why?" asked Matthew.

Gordon smiled at him. "Information can be put to good use, Matt. The market's all about information, and that sounds like a very useful bit of information. If it's the company that I'm thinking about, then they're a biotech company. The results must be a clinical trial or something of that sort. That can mean a great deal if it enables them to sell something on to one of the big pharmaceutical companies, for instance. Major profits all round."

"But why couldn't they – the people who were talking – buy the shares and make the profits themselves?"

Gordon shook a finger in admonition. "Tut, tut!" he said. "Insider dealing. Those chaps were obviously lawyers. They can't use their private knowledge to make a quick buck on the market. Very bad! The powers that be take a dim view of that sort of thing."

"But can we . . . ?"

Gordon made a dismissive gesture, and indicated that they

should continue to make their way downstairs. "Oh, we're all right. We just happen to have heard a little snippet, that's all. We can buy their shares. Nobody would associate us with insider information. Why should they? We're perfectly safe."

Matthew was not sure about this. "But wouldn't we also be taking unfair advantage of the people we buy the shares from? After all, we know something they don't."

Gordon looked at his son, who saw in his father's gaze something akin to pity, and resented it. "Life is hardly fair, Matt," he said. "If I had scruples about this sort of thing, do you think for a moment that I would have got anywhere in business? Do you really think that?"

Matthew did not reply. They had almost reached the front door now, and he could hear the low hum of the traffic outside. He glanced sideways at Janis, and for a moment their eyes met. Then she looked away. Matthew reached out and took his father's hand, and shook it.

"Thanks for dinner."

Gordon nodded. "Thank you for coming. And I'll let you know about those shares. I may have a little flutter on them. Can't do any harm."

Matthew opened the door and they stepped outside on to Princes Street, disturbing a thin-faced man who was standing near the doorway. He looked at them in surprise, as he had evidently not expected anybody to emerge from the unmarked door. The man looked tired; as if worn out by life. He had a cold sore, or something that looked like a cold sore, above his lip.

Matthew felt ashamed. How did he look in the eyes of this man? And what would this man have thought had he known the nature of their conversation of a few moments ago? Matthew wanted to say: "Not me, not me."

48. Private Papers

Pat hesitated at the door of Peter's flat in Cumberland Street. It would be easy to turn back now, to return to Scotland Street and to call him from there. Something could have arisen to prevent her from seeing him as planned – there were so many excuses to stand somebody up: a friend in need, a headache, a deadline to meet. If she did that, of course, then she would not see him again, and she was not sure whether that was what she wanted. She was undecided. Men complicated one's life; that was obvious. They made demands. They changed everything. In short, the question was whether they were worth it. And what was it anyway? The pleasure of their company? – women were far more companionable than men. The excitement of male presence? – how long did that last, and did she want that anyway? She thought not, and was about to turn away when she remembered his face, and the way he had stooped to talk to her at that first meeting, and how physically perfect he had seemed to her then and was still, in the imagining of him.

She tugged at the old-fashioned brass bell-pull. There was a lot of give in the wire, but eventually there was a tinkling sound inside. Then there was silence. She tugged at the bell again and as she did so the door opened and Peter stood there. For a moment he looked puzzled, and then he raised a hand to his brow in a gesture of self-mockery over some stupidity.

"I forgot," he said. "I totally forgot."

Pat had not expected this. He had issued the invitation, after all; she was not self-invited. "I'm sorry," she said lamely. "I'm sorry. We'd arranged . . ."

Peter shook his head. "Of course, of course. We'd arranged it. I'm so damn stupid. Come in."

"If it's inconvenient . . ."

He reached out and gripped her forearm, pulling her in. "Don't be silly. I was doing nothing anyway. Just come in."

She entered a hall, a large square room of similar proportions to the hall of the flat in Scotland Street. This was in markedly worse order, though, with scuffed paintwork on the doors and skirting boards. The floor, which was sanded, was made of broad Canadian pine boards, covered in part by frayed oriental rugs; the planks were uneven, and caused the rugs to rise in small ridges, like tiny mountain ranges.

"This flat belongs to somebody who works in Hong Kong," said Peter, waving a hand behind him. "An accountant, or something like that. He's mean. He never fixes anything, but the rent isn't too bad and it suits us. I've been here over a year."

"How many do you share with?" asked Pat.

"There are three of us," said Peter, pointing to a half-open door off the hall. "That's the biggest room. Joe and Fergus live in that. And that's my room over here. We've got a sort of sitting room, but it's a tip and we hardly ever use it."

Pat looked at the half-open door. Joe and Fergus. Then she remembered. When she had seen Peter at the Film Theatre he had been with another young man, a boy who had stared at her while Peter had whispered something to him. I'm naive, she said to herself. I've missed the obvious.

Peter gestured towards the door of his room. "Are you easily shocked?" he asked, smiling as he spoke.

Pat thought quickly. She was not sure what to expect, but who could admit to being shocked these days? "Of course not," she said.

"Good," said Peter. "Because it's a bit of a mess. If I'd remembered, I would have tidied it up before you came."

Pat laughed. "I'm a bit untidy myself."

"Well," said Peter. "That may be, but . . ."

They went into the room, which was dimly lit by a single reading lamp on the desk near the window. The curtains, made of a heavy red brocaded material, were drawn closed, but did not quite meet in the middle. A thin line of orange light from the street lights outside shone through the crack.

Pat glanced about her. There was a bed in the corner, covered with a white counterpane, made, at least, unlike Bruce's bed, which was usually in a state of dishevelment. Then there were two easy chairs with brown corduroy slip covers; the seat of one of these was covered with a pile of abandoned clothing – a shirt, a couple of pairs of socks, some unidentified underclothes and a pair of jeans. Peter reached down, bundled the clothing up and stuffed it in a drawer.

"This isn't a mess," said Pat. "Bruce – my flatmate – has a far messier room."

Peter shrugged. "Every so often I have a blitz on it. But the vacuum cleaner's bust and it's difficult."

"You could borrow ours," said Pat. She spoke quickly, and immediately wondered whether this was the right thing to say. It was as if she was offering to clean up for him, which was not what she intended.

"We're all right," said Peter, pointing to one of the chairs and inviting her to sit down. "We get by."

Pat sat down and looked at the walls. There could be clues there, just to confirm. A picture of . . . who were the appropriate icons? She realised that she was not sure. There was a poster above the bed, a film poster of some sort; but it was for a Japanese film and she had no idea what that signified.

And above her head, behind the chair, was a framed print of *American Gothic*, the mid-West farmer, pitchfork in hand, and his wife, standing grimly in front of a barn. Again, that conveyed nothing, except some sense of irony perhaps.

Peter rubbed his hands together. "I'll go and make coffee," he said. "How do you like it?"

Pat told him, and he went off to the kitchen, leaving her alone in his room. Once he had gone, she looked at his desk. There was a pile of books – a Jane Austen novel, a book of critical essays, the *Notebooks* of Robert Lowell, a dictionary. Behind the books was an open file into which what looked like lecture notes had been inserted. She rose to her feet and went over to the desk. Yes, they were his lecture notes. He had written the title of a lecture at the top: *Social expectations and artistic freedom in Austen's England: Tuesday.* There was a pile of papers on the edge of the desk – a couple of opened letters and what looked like an electricity bill.

She moved the letters slightly; of course she would not read them, she was just looking; a foreign stamp: Germany. And underneath the letters, two or three photographs, turned face downwards. She hesitated. She should mind her own business; one did not go into another person's room and look at his photographs. But at least she could examine the writing on the back of one of them, the photograph on top of the pile. It was not very distinct, as the ink had smudged, but she could just make it out. *Skinny dipping, Greece, with T.*

Pat looked over her shoulder. She should not look at his private papers – they were nothing to do with her. But then, he had invited her into his room and the photographs were lying around and how could anybody resist the temptation to look at a photograph with that inscription written on the back? If you left photographs lying about then you were more or less giving permission for people to look at them. It was the same as sending postcards: the postman was entitled to read them. And Pat was human. So she turned the photograph over and looked.

Holding two cups of steaming coffee, Peter came back into his room. "I don't have anything else to offer you," he said. "Not even a biscuit. We often run out of food altogether. And I find that when I buy some, Joe and Fergus eat it. I'm not sure if they know what they're doing. They just eat it."

Pat was not hungry, and did not mind. Peter had made real coffee, she noticed, and it smelled good, like strong . . . strong what? Coffee was complicated now, with all those americanos and mochas and double skinny lattes with vanilla. This was a bitter coffee, which Pat liked, and made for herself in the flat, although Bruce always turned his nose up at it. Shortly after she had moved in, Bruce, uninvited, had taken a cup of coffee from her cafetière and had spat it out after the first mouthful. But Bruce was Peter's polar opposite – unsubtle, uninterested in literature (he had once asked if Jane Austen was an actress), and quite without that willowy charm that Peter had in such abundance. She reflected briefly on this, and ruefully too, because she was now sure that Peter had nothing more in mind than casual friendship. How naive she had been to imagine otherwise: he was far too handsome to be interested in girls. There was that quality of sensitivity, that look in his eyes that told her, and everybody else who cared to look for it, that he *understood*, but, at the same time, that he was elsewhere.

Peter sat on the bed; she sat on the chair from which the pile of clothes had been moved. He sat there, with his bare feet on the counterpane, his cup of coffee cradled in his hands; she sat with both feet on the ground, her cup of coffee sitting on the table beside her. For a few moments they looked at one another. Then Peter smiled, and she noticed his teeth, which were perfectly straight, either by nature, or through the efforts of orthodontists. There was something familiar about these teeth and she struggled to recall what it was; then she remembered – Pedro, the doll whom she had loved so much, had had teeth painted on the fabric of his face, and these teeth were just like Peter's. Had Pedro, the doll, been interested in girl dolls, or did he prefer the company of other boy dolls? As a girl, she had thought that Pedro had loved only her, but that might have been a mistake. Pedro might have wished for something else altogether but had been obliged all his woolly life to be with, like the captive he was. Such a ridiculous thought, and she smiled involuntarily at the thinking of it. Peter smiled back.

They both began to speak at that same time.

"I . . ." said Pat.

And he said, "I . . ." and then, laughing, "You go ahead."

"No, you go," she said. "Go on."

"What do you do? I suppose that's what I was going to ask you."

Pat explained that she was a student, or almost a student. "I've had a couple of years off," she said. "I went to . . ." She paused, and he watched her expectantly. "To Australia, actually."

He nodded. "So did I. Where were you?"

She could not bring herself to speak about Western Australia, although she knew that she would have to do so sooner or later. So she mentioned Queensland and New South Wales, and Peter replied that he had been in both of those places. "I picked fruit," he said. "And I worked in a bar in Sydney, down in that old part near the harbour bridge. I did all sorts of things. Then I went travelling with somebody I met there. We had a great time. Two months of travelling."

"Where was he from?" asked Pat.

"She," said Peter. "She was Canadian. She came from somewhere near Winnipeg."

Of course she was probably just a friend, thought Pat. She had travelled in Thailand with a boy who was no more than a friend; it protected one from all sorts of dangers. And of course if she had been with somebody in Western Australia, then she would not have ended up in that plight in the first place.

"I had some pretty strange jobs in Australia," Peter went on. "I spent a month on a sheep station, looking after the owner, who was ancient. He couldn't walk very far and so they had made him a sort of trolley which he put a chair on. It had bike wheels, front and back, and I had to push him around the garden and down to the edge of the river. He was doing a correspondence course in history and I had to help him with that."

Pat laughed. She had taken peculiar jobs too, and none more peculiar than that job in Western Australia; but she did not feel like talking about that.

Peter looked thoughtful. "I miss Australia, you know. I miss the place. Those wide plains. The eucalyptus forests and the noise of the screeching birds. Remember that? The galahs? And the people, too. That friendliness. I miss all that a lot."

She felt his gaze upon her, a quizzical, slightly bemused look, and she wondered what it meant. It was as if he was sounding her out, determining whether she could respond to those images of Australia, that evocation of atmosphere. And she could, of course, and was about to say something herself about the Australian countryside and the effect it had wrought upon her when there was a knock at the door. He looked away, the spell broken, and answered.

The door half opened and a head appeared. It was a young woman, of about Pat's age, or a year or two older. The young woman looked briefly at Peter and then at Pat. "Sorry to inter-rupt," she said. "The thermostat on the hot water has stuck again. Can you fiddle with it like you did last time?"

Peter put down his coffee cup and rose from the bed. "Of course," he said. Then, half-turning to Pat, he said: "By the way, this is Joe."

Pat nodded a greeting, which Joe returned with a cheerful wave. Then, while Peter and Joe were out of the room, Pat looked up at the ceiling and smiled. Josephine and Fergus: rather a different picture from the one she had imagined. And this meant that Peter was quite possible now, although there was still the question of T. Who was T and did she (or he) take the photograph of the skinny-dipping in Greece? She could always ask Peter directly, but then that would reveal that she had sneaked a look at the photograph, which was none of her business. Unless, of course, she were to place her coffee cup on the table and inadvertently cause the books and photographs to fall on to the floor . . . just like this.

50. A Trip to Glasgow in the Offing

Sitting at the breakfast table, her single piece of toast on her plate, Irene said to Stuart: "When you go through to Glasgow on Saturday, you may take Bertie with you, but . . ." Stuart interrupted her. "Thank you. I'm sure that he'd like the train ride. You know how he feels about trains. Little boys . . ."

Irene nodded impatiently. "Yes, yes," she said, buttering her toast. She knew how little boys – or some of them – felt about trains, but that was no reason to encourage them. Little boys felt that way about trains because they were socially encouraged to do so – and she was sure that it was Stuart who had brought trains into the picture; she certainly had not. There was nothing inherent in the make-up of boys that attracted them to trains. Boys and girls were genetically indistinguishable, in her view (apart from the odd chromosome), and it was social conditioning that produced interests such as trains, in the case of boys, and, quite appallingly, dolls in the case of girls. Irene had never played with dolls, but had Stuart played with trains as a boy? They had never discussed the matter, but she had a good idea as to what the answer would be.

"Don't spend more time in Glasgow than you have to," she said. "Bertie's going to miss his yoga class as it is, and I don't want him to miss his saxophone lesson as well."

"It would be nice to take him down to Gourock or somewhere like that," Stuart ventured. "He would probably like to see the ferries. We could even pick up some fish and chips."

Irene laughed ominously. "And a deep-fried Mars Bar while you're about it?"

Stuart thought that Bertie would probably rather enjoy that, but had the good sense not to say it. He was looking forward to the outing and he did not want to provoke Irene into offering to accompany them. It was good to be going off alone with his son – as a father should do from time to time. Bertie hardly spoke to him these days; he seemed to have withdrawn into a world from which he, Stuart, was excluded, and this was worrying. Yet Stuart found it difficult to know what to say to Bertie, or to anybody else for that matter. He was a naturally quiet man, and throughout his marriage to Irene, whom he admired for her strength of character and her intellectual vision, he had left it to her to do the talking. She had always been in charge of what she called the Bertie project, and he had left it to her to make the decisions about the little boy. But beneath this acceptance there was a vague unease on his part that he was not much of a father to Bertie, and Bertie's distance from him had fuelled this unease. And when that dreadful incident had occurred and Bertie had set fire to his copy of the *Guardian* he had done nothing; a real father would have remonstrated with his son and punished him – for his own good. He had done nothing, and it had been left to Irene to arrange a psychotherapeutic response.

For his part, Bertie was fond enough of his father, but he wished that he would be somewhat less passive. It seemed to him that his father led a very dull life, with his daily journey to the Scottish Executive and all those statistics. Bertie was good at mathematics, and had absorbed the basic principles of calculus, but did not think that it would be very satisfying to do mathematics all day, as his father did. And what did the Scottish Executive need all those statistics for in the first place? Bertie wondered. Surely there was a limit to the number of statistics one needed.

When Bertie was told that he was going to Glasgow with his father, and on a train to boot, he let out a yelp of delight.

"That means we'll go to Waverley Station?" he asked. He had seen pictures of Waverley Station but he had never been there, as far as he could remember.

"Yes," said Stuart. "And we'll get on the Glasgow train and

go all the way to Queen Street Station. You'll like Queen Street Station, Bertie."

Bertie was sure that he would, and gave vent to his pleasure with a further yelp.

"Now remember to wear your duffel coat over your dungarees," his mother said. "And wash your hands before you eat anything. Glasgow is not a very salubrious place, and I don't want you catching anything there."

Bertie listened but said nothing. He would not wash his hands in Glasgow, as his mother would not be there to make him. Being in Glasgow, in fact, would be like being eighteen, the age which Bertie yearned for above anything else. After you were eighteen you never had to listen to your mother again, and that, thought, Bertie, would be nirvana indeed.

"Glasgow's not all that bad," said Stuart mildly. "They've got the Burrell and then there's . . ."

Irene cut him off. "And the mortality statistics?" she snapped. "The smoking? The drinking? The heart disease?"

Bertie looked at his father. He would defend Glasgow, he hoped, in the face of this attack.

"They have their problems," Stuart conceded. "But not everybody's like that."

"Close enough," said Irene. "But let's not think too much of Glasgow. It's time for some Italian, Bertie, especially if tomorrow is going to be so disrupted by your little trip."

Bertie complied, and busied himself with a page of his Italian grammar. His heart was not in it, though, and he could think only of what lay ahead of him. The Glasgow train! He would get a window seat, he hoped, and watch the countryside flashing past. He would see the signals and hear the squeal of the brakes as they neared a station. And then there would be Glasgow itself, which he thought sounded very exciting, with all its noise and germs. They would find their car and he would help his father to get it started. And perhaps on the way back, he might be able to do some fishing with his father, if they went anywhere near the Pentlands. There was always a chance of that.

Bertie reflected on his lot. He felt much happier with his life now. He had settled in to Steiner's, and he found that he liked it. He had made a tentative friendship with Tofu, and now he was being taken to Glasgow by his father. If this good fortune continued, then he would be able to put up with all the other things that made his life so trying: his psychotherapy with Dr Fairbairn, and, of course, his mother. He had only another twelve years of his mother, he thought, which might be just bearable. Unless, of course, they went over to Glasgow, his father and he, and stayed there . . .

51. On the Glasgow Train, a Heart is Opened

Bertie sat with his face pressed to the window, his father in the seat beside him, on the ten o'clock train from Waverley Station. It had been a morning of excitement at a level quite unparalleled in his young life. It had begun with the walk up from Scotland Street with Stuart, during which they had seen two mounted policemen riding their horses down Dundas Street; one of the policemen had waved to Bertie, and he had waved back. And then they had arrived at Waverley Station itself, nestling in its hollow with the buildings of the Old Town towering above it, flags fluttering in the morning breeze; all of this was perfect background for a soaring of spirits. In the booking hall, they had stood together in the ticket queue and Bertie had heard his father utter those potent words: "One and a half returns to Glasgow," and had realised that he was the half that was going to Glasgow, and back; oh happy, happy prospect!

Bertie had thrilled at the sound of the conductor's whistle, which had set the train off on its journey, and almost immediately they had entered the tunnel under the National Gallery of Scotland, and were out again so soon, with the Castle Rock soaring above the track, before another tunnel enveloped them in its darkness. After a couple of minutes, they emerged from this tunnel into a station.

"Is this Glasgow?" Bertie asked, rising from his seat.

Stuart laughed. "Haymarket, Bertie. We're still in Edinburgh. Glasgow's forty-five minutes away."

Bertie sank back into his seat, delighted at the prolongation of the journey. Forty-five minutes seemed like a wonderfully long time to him – more or less the length of time he spent in a session with Dr Fairbairn, and those sessions lasted forever, he thought. With nose pressed to the window glass he watched the great shape of a stadium draw near, and he tapped his father's shoulder and pointed.

"Murrayfield," said Stuart. "That's the rugby stadium."

Bertie stared in wonder. Although he had decided that rugby

was perhaps not for him – a conclusion which he had reached after that unfortunate experience at Watson's when Jock, his false friend, had kicked him in the ribs – he would still like to watch Scotland play rugby against the All Blacks, or even England. That would be a thrilling thing to do, and perhaps he would find himself sitting next to Mr Gavin Hastings and would be able to listen to his view of the game they were watching. That would be a fine thing to do, Bertie thought.

"Have you ever been there, Daddy?" he asked. "Did you ever go to Murrayfield?"

Stuart nodded. "Yes," he said. "I used to go there when I was a student. I went with . . ." He paused, and then continued. "I went there with the boys, I suppose."

Bertie looked puzzled. "Small boys? Boys like me?"

Stuart smiled. "No, not boys like you. Friends of mine. I used to call them the boys. We used to go to see rugby matches and we would also go to pubs."

"To get drunk?" asked Bertie politely.

On the other side of the compartment a woman overheard this question and smiled. She had noticed this small boy in his dungarees and had been amused by his excitement over the trip.

Stuart caught the woman's eye and raised an eyebrow. "Not really, Bertie. Well . . . well, maybe some of the boys had a little bit too much to drink. But usually they didn't."

Bertie digested this answer. He was intrigued by the thought that his father had had another life altogether different from the one which he led in Scotland Street. "What was it like before you met Mummy?" he asked suddenly. "Was it fun?"

Stuart looked at his son, and then out of the window. They were now leaving the outer suburbs of Edinburgh and the fields and hills were all about them. An expanse of earth, ploughed in readiness for the winter crop, rich earth, shot past on one side of the track. A crow flew up from a tree, and was left behind. Stuart looked back at Bertie.

"It was fun," he said quietly. "Yes. I had a lot of fun." He paused. "And you'll have fun too, Bertie. I'm sure you will."

Bertie said nothing for a few moments. He was pulling at a

loose thread on the seam of his dungarees. "You need to have friends to have fun," he said at last. "I have no friends."

Stuart frowned. "You must have some friends, Bertie. What about this boy you mentioned to me. Paddy? What about him?"

"I don't really know him very well," said Bertie. "I hardly ever see him. I have to go to psychotherapy and yoga all the time."

Stuart reached out and took his son's hand. It felt so small; dry and small. "Friends are very important, aren't they?"

Bertie nodded. Stuart continued: "I had a best friend, you know. That's very important, too. To have a best friend."

"What was he called?" asked Bertie.

"He was called Mike," said Stuart. "He was very kind to me."

"That's nice," said Bertie. "Kind friends are the best sort, aren't they?"

Stuart nodded his assent to this and they both looked out of the window, Bertie's hand still resting in his. I shall not fail this little boy, he thought. My God, how close I've come to doing that. What is that corny line from that musical? *I let my golden chances pass me by.* Yes, that was it; sentimental, but absolutely true. We all let our golden chances pass us by – all the time.

The woman who had overheard this conversation had been staring at the page of her book – staring but not reading. She had heard every word and now she looked very discreetly in their direction and saw the two of them quite still, quite silent, sunk in their thoughts. She transferred her gaze back to the words on the page before her, but she could no longer concentrate. It had nothing to do with her, of course – the business of others. But now she willed with all her heart that this stranger into whose life she had unwittingly strayed should listen to every word that the little boy had said. And when she glanced again, and saw the expression on the man's face, she knew that he would.

52. *Arriving in Glasgow*

As the Edinburgh train neared Glasgow, the light with which the passing countryside had been suffused became subtly attenuated. The clear skies of the east of Scotland yielded place to a lowered ceiling of grey and purple rain clouds. And above the train, rising on each side of the railway line, reared up the shapes of high flats, great dispiriting slabs of grey. Bertie watched the changing landscape, his mouth open in awe; so this was Glasgow, this was the place of which his mother had spoken so ominously. Perhaps she was right. Perhaps it was a dark and dangerous place after all. And to think that such a place existed less than an hour away from Edinburgh! That was the extraordinary thing. One could be in Edinburgh, with its floataria and coffee houses, and then, in the space of a short train journey, one could be in this place, under these purple clouds, facing heaven knows what perils.

They left their railway carriage and stepped out on to the platform. Bertie looked down at his feet and thought: "I'm standing on Glasgow!" The stone of the platform, a special, highly-polished stone, chosen by the railway authorities as the surface most likely to become dangerously slippery if wet, was very similar to the slippery stone floors he had seen at Waverley Station. And the people waiting at the barrier were not all that different from the people he had seen at Waverley Station, he thought.

"This way, Bertie," said Stuart, pointing in the direction of a large glass door. "We'll get a taxi out there."

Bertie hurried along behind his father, his duffel coat buttoned up to the top to disguise the fact that he was wearing crushed-strawberry dungarees. He had not noticed any crushed-strawberry trousers in Glasgow yet, and he was sure that they did not wear them here.

"Where are we going?" he asked his father, as they took their place in the short queue for taxis. "Do you remember where you left the car?"

"More or less," said Stuart, waving a hand in the general

direction of the Dumbarton Road. "I'll recognise the place . . .
I think."

Their turn came to get into a taxi. Stuart opened the door
and Bertie climbed in. This was far better than the No 23 bus,
he thought: comfortable seats, small glowing red lights, and a
taxi driver who looked at them in his rear-view mirror and smiled
cheerily.

"Whauryousesgaahn?" the driver asked.

"Dumbarton Road, please," said Stuart.

The driver looked back up at the mirror. "Radumbartonroad?
Butwhitpartoradumbartonroadyouseswantinanthat?
Radumbartonroadizzaroadanahafwhaurabit?"

Stuart explained that he was not sure exactly which part of
the Dumbarton Road they wanted, but that he would let the
driver know when they neared it. The driver nodded; people
who got off the Edinburgh train were often a bit vague, he had
found, but they very rarely tried to jump out of the taxi without
paying. Nor did they try to walk half the way in order to save
money. You had to watch the Aberdeen train for that.

"Now, Bertie," said Stuart. "Look over there. That's . . . well,
I'm not sure what that is, but look over there anyway."

Bertie looked out at Glasgow. It seemed busier than
Edinburgh, he thought, and the buses were a different colour.
But everybody seemed to know where they were going, and
seemed happy enough to be going there. He was going to like
Glasgow, he thought, and perhaps he would even come to live
here when he was eighteen. If he did that, then he would even
start to learn the language. It sounded quite like Italian in some
respects, and was possibly even easier to learn.

They made their way to St George's Cross and then down
below Glasgow University. Stuart pointed in the direction of
the University and drew Bertie's attention to the fact that his
own father, Bertie's grandfather, had studied medicine there.

"It's a very great medical school," said Stuart. "Many famous
doctors have trained there, Bertie. You could even go there
yourself."

"That would be nice," said Bertie. The thought had occurred

to him that perhaps Dr Fairbairn had trained there, but then that would have been a long time ago. Glasgow did not seem like a good place for psychotherapists, Bertie thought. It was difficult to say exactly why this should be so, but Bertie certainly felt it. Edinburgh was better territory for that sort of thing. And he had not seen a single floatarium during the taxi drive, not one; a large number of Indian restaurants, of course, but no floataria.

Once they reached the Dumbarton Road, Stuart began to sit forward in his seat and peer out at the roads going off to either side.

"It's pretty near here," he said to the driver.

"Ayeitspruttybutwhauryuzwantintogetaff?" the driver replied genially.

Stuart stared at a road-end which was approaching them on their right. Yes, this was it. There had been a church at the end of the street because he had remembered its odd-shaped tower. "Right here," he said to the driver. "This is where we want to get aff."

The driver nodded and drew into the side of the road. Stuart paid the bill, and then he and Bertie strode across the busy Dumbarton Road and began to walk slowly down the quiet residential street to the right.

"It was along here," said Stuart. "Further along on this side."

Bertie skipped ahead of his father, looking for the familiar shape of their red Volvo station wagon. It was not a long street, and before he had gone very far he realised that he had cast his eyes down the line of cars parked along the street and there was no sign of a red Volvo. He turned to face his father.

"Are you sure, Daddy?" he asked. "Are you sure that this is the right road."

Stuart looked down towards the end of the road. He was sure that this was it. He closed his eyes and imagined that afternoon. He had taken his files from the back of the car and had locked the door. And then he had begun to walk towards the Dumbarton Road and the place where the meeting was to be held. And there had been a dog crossing the road and a motorist had braked sharply. There was no doubt about it; this was the place.

"This is it, Bertie," he said quietly. "This is where the car was. Right here."

Stuart pointed to a place now occupied by a large green Mercedes-Benz. Bertie stepped forward and stared into the car, as if expecting to find some clue to the disappearance of their Volvo. And as he did so, they heard a door open in the house directly behind them and a voice call out:

"Yous! Whit chu doin lookin at Mr O'Connor's motor?"

53. Lard O'Connor

Bertie sprang back guiltily from the green Mercedes-Benz. He had not so much as touched the glittering car, but the voice from behind him, more of a growl really, would have been enough to frighten anybody, let alone a six-year-old boy on his first trip to Glasgow.

Stuart was taken aback, too, by the accusatory tone of the voice. "My son hasn't done anything," he said. "We were just looking."

The man who had appeared at the door of the house had strode down the path and was now facing Stuart, staring at him belligerently. "Looking for what?" he asked. "Yous never seen a Merc before, eh?"

"I've seen one," said Bertie brightly. "Mrs Macdonald, who lives at the top of the stair, has got a custard-coloured one. She offered to take me for a ride in it."

The man looked down at Bertie. "Whit you talking aboot, son?"

"He's just saying . . ." began Stuart.

"Shut your gob, Jim," said the man. "Whit's this aboot custard?"

"Oh really!" said Stuart in exasperation. "This is quite ridiculous. Come, Bertie, let's go."

The man suddenly leaned forward and grabbed Stuart by the arm. "Not so fast, pal. You're coming in to have a word with Mr O'Connor. He disnae like people hanging aboot his street. You can come in and explain yourself to the man hissel."

The man's grip on Stuart's arm was too powerful to resist, and Stuart found himself being frog-marched up the garden path, followed by an anxious Bertie, his duffel coat flapping about his crushed-strawberry dungarees. Propelled by his captor, Stuart found himself in a sparsely-furnished hallway. "Through there," said the man, nodding in the direction of a half-open door. "Mr O'Connor will see you now."

Stuart glared at the man, but decided that the situation was too fragile for him to do anything but comply. He was concerned for the safety of Bertie, who was standing at his side, and he thought that the best thing to do would be to speak to this Mr O'Connor, whoever he was, and explain that they had had no intentions in relation to his car. Perhaps they had experienced vandalism in the past and had, quite unjustifiably, thought that he and Bertie were vandals.

They entered a large living room. The floor was covered with a tartan carpet and the walls were papered with red wallpaper. The room was dominated by a large television set, which was displaying a football game, but with the sound turned down. On a chair in front of the television set was an extremely overweight man, the sleeves of his shirt rolled up to reveal fleshy, tattooed forearms. As they entered the room, this man half turned round, glanced at them, and then flicked the remote controls of the television set. The football match died in a fading of light.

"So," said the fat man. "So you've been looking at my motor. You fancy it?"

"Not at all," said Stuart. "We had no designs on it at all."

The man smiled. "I should introduce myself," he said, glancing at Bertie briefly and then returning his gaze to Stuart. "I'm Aloysius O'Connor. But you may call me Lard O'Connor. Everybody else does, don't they Gerry?"

Gerry, the man who had brought Stuart into the room,

nodded. "Aye, they do, Lard. Nae respect these days. People have nae respect."

Lard O'Connor raised an eyebrow. Turning to Bertie, he said: "And you, young man. What's your name?"

"I'm called Bertie," said Bertie. "Bertie Pollock. I live in Edinburgh and I go to the Steiner School. And this is my Daddy. We live in Scotland Street. Do you know where that is, Mr O'Connor?"

"Could do," said Lard. "Is that a nice street?"

"It's very nice," said Bertie. "It's not far from where Mr Compton Mackenzie used to live. He wrote books, you know."

Lard smiled. "You don't say? Compton Mackenzie?"

"Yes," said Bertie. "He wrote a book called *Whisky Galore* about some people who find a lot of whisky on the beach."

"That sounds like a good story," said Lard. He turned to Gerry. "You hear that, Gerry? Some people find whisky on the beach. Fallen aff a ferry mebbe!"

Gerry laughed politely. Lard then turned to Bertie again. "I must say I like your style, young man. I like a wean who speaks clearly and shows some respect. I like that." He paused, and looked inquisitively at Stuart. "So what are you doing in these parts? Why have you come all the way from, where is it, Scotland Street, all the way over here? You sightseeing?"

"I left my car here," said Stuart quickly. "I left it some time ago and now it seems to be gone."

"Oh," said Lard. "Walked?"

"So it would seem," said Stuart dryly.

"Well, well," said Lard, stroking the side of his chair. "Can you tell me what this motor of yours looked like? Model and all the rest. And the registration number."

Stuart told him, and Lard signalled to Gerry, who wrote it down laboriously in a small notebook which he had picked up from the top of a display cabinet.

"Gerry," said Lard. "You go and make inquiries about this matter and see what you can come up with. Know what I mean?" He turned towards Bertie. "And you, young man, how about a game of cards while we're waiting for Gerry? You and your Dad might like a game of cards. I'm very partial to a game of cards myself, you know. But I don't always have company of the right intellectual level, know what I mean?" He nodded in the direction of Gerry, who was now leaving the room. "Good man, Gerry," Lard went on. "But not exactly one of your Edinburgh intellectuals."

"I like playing cards," said Bertie. "What game would you like to play, Mr O'Connor?"

They decided on rummy, and Lard rose slowly from his chair to fetch a pack of cards from a drawer.

"You're very big, Mr O'Connor," said Bertie brightly, not seeing a frantic sign from his father. "Do you eat deep-fried Mars Bars like other people in Glasgow?"

Lard stopped in his tracks. Without turning, he said: "Deep-fried Mars Bars?"

Stuart looked frantically about the room. It would be possible to make a run for it now, he thought. Lard would be unable to run after them, with that bulk of his, but he had heard sounds out in the hall and he had assumed that there were other men, apart from Gerry, in the house. These gangsters rarely had just one side-kick, he remembered.

Then Lard spoke again. "Oh jings!" he said. "What I wouldn't do for one of those right now!"

54. A Game of Cards and a Cultural Trip

It was an interesting game of cards. Lard had started off making every concession to Bertie's age, offering friendly advice on tactics and making one or two deliberate mistakes in order to give Bertie an advantage. But it soon became apparent that such gestures were entirely misplaced as Bertie succeeded in playing even his more mediocre hands with consummate skill. Lard had suggested playing for money, a proposition to which Stuart had agreed only because he felt that it would be impolitic to antagonise their host. He had given Bertie five pounds to start him off and had explained that that would be his limit. But after an hour's play, Bertie had won sixty-two pounds from Lard O'Connor and was now sitting behind a high pile of one-pound and two-pound coins.

"I'll give it back to you, Mr O'Connor," Bertie said generously. "I don't want to take all your money."

Lard O'Connor shook his head. "Not a chance, Bertie," he said. "You won that fair and square. Just as I earned that money fair and square in the first place."

Stuart threw Lard a glance, and then looked away again quickly.

"What do you do for a living, Mr O'Connor?" Bertie asked politely as he dealt a fresh hand of cards.

"I'm a businessman," said Lard. "I have a business. But it's pretty difficult for us small businessmen under this government, you know. So I vote for the Liberal Democrats. That's what I do. That Ming Campbell. He's the man. And David Steel, too."

"I'm sure they're very glad of your support," said Stuart dryly.

"Aye, I'm sure they are," agreed Lard.

The game of cards continued for a further half hour, and then Gerry returned. He stood at the door, smiling broadly. "Mission accomplished, Lard," he said.

Lard looked round and stared at his assistant. "You found the car?"

Gerry nodded. "I did. It had been removed withoot authority, as we say. Some boys had been using it for their own purposes. So I spoke to them aboot it and explained this is not the way tae treat an Edinburgh car."

Lard smiled. "And they agreed with you, Gerry?"

"They took a bit of persuading, Boss," said Gerry. "You know how ill-mannered some of these boys can be. Nae manners."

Lard sighed. "Yes," he said. "You're right there, so you are. But the important thing is that you've got your car back, Stewie. How about that then?"

Stuart reached forward and shook Lard's hand enthusiastically. "You've been very kind, Mr O'Connor," he said. "I really am very indebted to you." Lard shrugged off the thanks. "It was nothing," he said. "I'm only sorry that youses were inconvenienced. It gives people the wrong impression of Glasgow when they come over here and their car is taken aff them. Very unfriendly."

"Well," said Stuart, looking at his watch. "No harm done. Now that we have our car back we can get back to Edinburgh. You've been very kind to us, Mr O'Connor."

Lard made an expansive gesture with his right hand. "No bother. No bother at all." He paused. "But it would be a pity if you were to rush off so quickly. Young Bertie here has hardly had the chance to see Glasgow, have you, Bertie? There's plenty of time to get back to Edinburgh later on, especially as you now have your car back. A leisurely drive at your own convenience."

Stuart began to explain that they really should get back as Bertie had a saxophone lesson, but was cut short by Lard.

"What do you think, Bertie?" asked Lard. "What would you like to see while you're over here?"

Bertie was ready with an answer. He had decided that he liked Glasgow and that there was a great deal that he wished to see. He would like to go to a fish and chip shop and get a . . . No, he could never do that. His mother would be sure to hear about it and there would be a terrible row. And so he said: "The Burrell Gallery, Mr O'Connor." And then he added: "If that's convenient to you."

Lard frowned and looked at Gerry. "You know where that is, Gerry? The Burrell? You heard of it?"

Gerry shook his head. "I've got a map, Boss. I can get you there."

"In that case we should be on our way," said Lard. "We can go in my motor, and then you can pick yours up when we finish and you can drive back to Edinburgh. How about that, Stewie?"

Stuart realised that he had little option but to agree. But a visit to the Burrell was a good idea, anyway, as it would enable him to say to Irene that they had spent their time in Glasgow well. He could clearly not tell her that he and Bertie had played cards, for money, with a Glasgow gangster, but he could tell her that they had gone to the Burrell with two charming Glaswegians who had helped them locate the car.

They set off in Lard O'Connor's green Mercedes-Benz. Gerry drove, with Stuart beside him in the front passenger seat, while Bertie sat in the back with Lard.

"It's a very nice car, Mr O'Connor," said Bertie, running his hands over the soft leather of the seats.

"It is that," said Lard. "You work hard, Bertie, just like me, and one day you'll be able to get yourself one of these."

"But what does your business actually do, Mr O'Connor?" asked Bertie.

"Distribution," said Lard. "We circulate things We make sure that things don't just stay in one place forever. We encourage changes of ownership."

"What things?" asked Bertie.

"Bertie," interrupted Stuart from the front seat. "Don't keep asking Mr O'Connor questions. He's very busy thinking. Leave him be."

They travelled on in silence. Then Bertie said: "Mr O'Connor, have you heard of Rangers Football Club?"

Lard O'Connor smiled. "I've heard of them. Aye, I've heard of them."

Bertie looked out of the window. There was much about Glasgow that he still had to find out. "Everybody says that they're very good," he said. "They say that they're the best football team in the country."

"I'm not so sure about that," said Lard, catching Gerry's eye in the rear mirror. "There's a team called Celtic. Have you heard of them?"

"Yes," said Bertie. "But I've heard they're not so good."

Lard O'Connor said nothing. Then he began to smile. "You know, Bertie, you're a clever wee boy. Very good sense of humour. Very good. You and I have got a brilliant future together – I can tell." Then he tapped Stuart on the shoulder. "What do you think, Stewie? What say you that we get together a bit more regularly. You. Me. Bertie. What do you think?"

55. At the Burrell

They drew into the grounds of Pollok House, and drove up the drive towards the building that housed the Burrell Collection. Lard O'Connor, sitting in the back of his green Mercedes-Benz, with Bertie at his side, was impressed by the sylvan setting.

"Crivvens!" he exclaimed. "Who would have guessed that we had this in Glasgow! Right under our noses! You'd think we were in Edinburgh, wouldn't you?"

"You have some fine museums over here," said Stuart. "Very fine."

Lard listened carefully. "Fine museums, you say, Stewie? Well, that's good to hear."

Gerry parked the car and they walked over to the entrance to the Burrell. Guidebooks were bought – Stuart insisted on paying, as a thank-you for the finding of his car – and Lard and Gerry graciously accepted. Then they made their way into the first of the exhibition halls. There, hung on a wall was a giant Flemish tapestry depicting a hunting scene, complete with dogs.

"Jeez," said Lard. "Look at those dugs on that carpet."

"It's a tapestry, actually," said Stuart.

Lard looked at him. "That's what I said," he muttered. "You trying to show me up, Stewie?"

Stuart paled. "Certainly not. I was just . . ."

"Because some people think," Lard continued, "that just because you haven't had much formal education, then you don't know anything. You wouldn't be one of those, would you, Stewie?"

"Of course not," said Stuart. "There are a lot of educated people who know very little about the world."

"You hear that, Gerry?" asked Lard. "Stewie here says that there lots of folk in Edinburgh who don't know anything about anything. That's what he said."

Stuart laughed. "I wouldn't go that far," he said.

"Well I would," said Lard.

They moved on to look at a small series of bronze figures in a glass display case. Lard signalled to Gerry and the two of them bent down to look at the display. As they did so, Lard ran his fingers over the lock which prevented the glass doors from being opened. He threw an inquiring glance at Gerry, who smiled.

"Easy," he said. "Dead easy."

Lard nodded and straightened up. "A very interesting little collection of . . . of . . ." he said. "Very nice taste this Wally Burrell had. Shipping man, you said he was, Stewie?"

Stuart nodded. "He was a great collector," he said. "He kept very good records of what he bought. And he searched all over the world for objects for his collection."

Bertie was studying his guidebook closely, checking each object they saw against its entry. They moved into the Hutton Castle Drawing Room, the room which Burrell had used as his principal place of display and which had been recreated in the gallery. They stopped in front of a French stained-glass Annunciation scene. Lard nodded to Gerry and the two men crossed themselves quickly.

"I'm glad to see that Wally Burrell was a Celtic supporter," said Lard.

Stuart smiled. "Sometimes the fact that one has a stained-glass representation of the Virgin does not necessarily mean . . ."

He tailed off, having intercepted a warning glance from Lard, who now moved over to a small window and appeared to be taking a close interest in the catch. "Bertie," he called. "Come over here a wee minute."

Bertie joined Lard at the window and looked outside. "This is a nice wee window, Bertie," said Lard. "I wonder whether a boy your size, you even, would be able to squeeze through it? Not now, of course. Just wondering."

Bertie studied the window. "I think so, Mr O'Connor," he said.

Lard smiled. "That's good to know. Mebbe some time we could come in and have a look at this place in the evening when there are no crowds. It would be more fun that, don't you think? We could take a better look at Wally Burrell's things. What do you think, Bertie?"

"That would be very nice, Mr O'Connor," said Bertie.

"Good," said Lard. "But that's just between you and me. Understand?"

Bertie nodded, and the party then moved on. There was much more to see – great urns, Greek antiquities, paintings – all of it much appreciated by Lard and, although to a lesser extent, by Gerry.

"Do you think they have anything by your man Vettriano?" Lard asked at one point.

Stuart thought not. "Sir William Burrell died in 1958," he said. "Jack Vettriano is our own contemporary."

Lard fixed Stuart with a glare. "You trying to tell me something, Stewie?" he said. "You think I don't know all that?"

Stuart made a placatory remark and then looked at his watch. "I wonder if we shouldn't be getting back to Edinburgh now," he said. "Bertie's mother will be wondering what's keeping us."

"Well, we wouldn't want that, would we, Bertie?" said Lard. Bertie was silent. It was exactly what he wanted, but he thought it best not to say it to Lard. So they left the gallery and returned to the car. A short time later they were back outside Lard's house, where their own car, the shabby red Volvo, was ready to be driven back to Edinburgh. Farewells were said and telephone numbers exchanged. Then, waved to by Lard and Gerry, who stood at the gate to see them off, Bertie and Stuart drove back down the road, back in the direction of the motorway that would bring them home to Edinburgh.

"It feels great to be back in one's own car again," said Stuart as they left the outskirts of Glasgow behind them.

"Yes," said Bertie. "I wonder how Gerry managed to find our car so quickly."

Stuart smiled. He would not disabuse Bertie of his touching faith in humanity. He would not spell it out to him that strong-arm tactics had undoubtedly been used to wrest their car back from the people who had stolen it. He would let him believe in the goodness of Gerry and Lard. But what a bunch of rogues!

"Daddy," said Bertie suddenly. "This isn't our car."

Stuart looked down at Bertie, who had been examining something on the door panel.

"Nonsense, Bertie," he said. "I looked at the number plate."

"Yes," said Bertie. "But look at the door handles. Ours had round bits at the end. These are straight. And look at the radio. It's a different make."

Stuart glanced quickly, fearfully, in the direction indicated by Bertie. Then he swallowed. "Don't tell Mummy, Bertie," he said. "Please don't tell Mummy."

56. Domenica meets Pat

It was a time to take stock – not that any of those who lived under the same roof at 44 Scotland Street knew that it was such a time. But had they been considering their position, then they might have realised that there were metaphorical crossroads ahead.

Irene and Stuart Pollock, parents of that gifted six-year-old, Bertie, might have realised, but did not, that their marriage was going nowhere – if marriages are meant to go anywhere, of course; there are many people who are very happy in marriages that show no sign of movement in any direction, neither forwards, backwards, nor indeed sideways. Such people are often contented, not realising, perhaps, that they are going in that direction in which we all go – downwards.

Irene and Stuart, though, were about to face a fundamental trial of strength, in which Irene, who thought that she made all the decisions in the marriage – and did – would have to deal with Stuart's new determination to do something about the way in which Bertie was treated. Stuart had realised that he had not been a good father to Bertie, and had resolved, in the course of those luminous moments on the Glasgow train, those moments when he had held his son's hand and discussed friendship, that he would play a much greater role in Bertie's upbringing. And if this meant a clash with the iron-willed Irene, armed as she was with a great body of knowledge and doctrine on the subject of child-raising, and supported to the rear by her ally, Dr Fairbairn, the renowned psychotherapist, author of the seminal volume on the analysis of Wee Fraser, the three-year-old tyrant, then so be it. Or rather, to reflect Stuart's weakness, then so might it be. (Wee Fraser, incidentally, now almost fourteen, had been spotted recently crossing the road at the end of Princes Street, heading in the direction of South Bridge. He had been seen by Dr Fairbairn himself, who had stopped in his tracks, as Captain Ahab might have sighted Moby Dick and stood rooted to the deck of his whaler. In this case, though, there had been no pursuit.)

Even if his parents were not consciously taking stock of their position, Bertie still reviewed his plight from time to time, with a degree of insight which was quite remarkable for a six-year-old boy. He was quite pleased with the way things were going. There had been setbacks, of course, his ill-fated attempt to enrol at George Watson's College being one, but that was compensated for by his discovery that Steiner's was where he wanted to be.

Friendship had been an area fraught with difficulties. Adults sometimes glimpse only in the dimmest way the intensity of the child's need for friends; this need is profound, something that seems to the child to be more powerful and pressing than any other need. And Bertie felt this. Jock, brave Jock, with whom his first meeting had been so very promising, had proved to be callous and disloyal. That had been very hard for Bertie. But then he had almost made a friend, in the shape of Tofu, although it was sometimes difficult to get Tofu's attention, engaged as that boy was in a constant attempt to secure the notice of all around him through displays of bravado and scatological comment. But the few scraps of attention that he did obtain were worth it for Bertie, and made it easier for him to bear his psychotherapy sessions with Dr Fairbairn, his yoga in Stockbridge, his advanced Italian, and his preparation for his Grade Seven saxophone examinations.

Pat's life was one in which there were no such significant saliences. She was about to begin her course at university, and was looking forward to the student life. It would have been marginally better, she thought, if she were sharing a flat with other students, rather than with Bruce, but Scotland Street was convenient and she had become fond of it. And now, of course, she had met Peter, the part-time waiter from Glass and Thompson, who was also a student of English literature and given, she had surreptitiously learned, to skinny-dipping.

She was not sure what to make of Peter, and wanted to discuss him with Domenica, whom she had not seen for some time, but whom she now encountered while turning the corner from Drummond Place into Scotland Street. There was the custard-coloured Mercedes-Benz being manoeuvred laboriously into a parking place which was almost, but not quite, too small for it. Pat waited while her neighbour extracted herself from her impressive vehicle.

"Everything," began Domenica, as she locked the door behind her, "is getting smaller and smaller. Have you tried to sit in an aeroplane seat recently? Legs, it would appear, are to be left behind, or carried, separately, in the hold. Houses are getting smaller, ceilings are being lowered. Offices too. Everything. Not just parking spaces."

Pat smiled. Domenica had an endearing way of launching straight into controversy. There was never any warming up with remarks about the weather or inquiries after health. "I suppose you're right," she said.

"Thank you," said Domenica. "Not that I wish to complain. There is nothing worse, in my view, than people of my age – which is not unduly advanced, I hasten to point out – nothing worse than such people complaining all the time. *O tempora, O mores*! That sort of thing. That comes from seeing the world changing and not liking it simply because it's different. We must embrace change, we're told. And I suppose that's a sensible thing to do if the change is worthwhile and for the better. But why should we embrace change for its own sake? I see absolutely no reason to do that. Do you?"

Pat did not, and said as much as she accompanied Domenica down the street.

"The problem," said Domenica, "is that the cost-cutters are in control. They are the ones who are setting the tone of our age. They are the ones who are insisting that everything be cheap and built to the barest specifications. Nobody can do anything which is large and generous-spirited any more, because a cost-cutter will come along and say: Stop. Make everything smaller."

Pat said nothing. She had been thinking about Peter. Perhaps it would be an idea to discuss him with Domenica. "I'm thinking about a boy," she said suddenly.

"How interesting," said Domenica. "Interesting, but often a terrible waste of time. Still, come up with me, my dear, and we shall talk about boys in the comfort of my study. How delicious!"

57. *The Natural Approach*

"Well," said Domenica, perching on the edge of her chair. "Tell me, then. You went to see him? That rather handsome young man whom we jointly encountered? You went to see him?"

Pat thought the question rather pointed. She had forgiven Domenica her tactless attempt to introduce the two of them, through the transparent device of offering to lend Peter a book of Rupert Brooke's verse. She had even laughed, in retrospect, over the obviousness of the ploy. But in view of her neighbour's somewhat heavy-handed, not to say socially clumsy, behaviour, she did not think that she was in a position to criticise her going to Peter's flat. "He did ask me," she said, defensively, and went on to explain to Domenica about the meeting at the film theatre and the invitation which Peter had extended to her. He had meant it, she said, even if by the time she went to see him he had forgotten that he had invited her.

"And did it go as planned?" asked Domenica.

"I had no plan," said Pat. She frowned. What did Domenica imagine she had intended to do once she got to Peter's flat? Sometimes people of Domenica's generation, in an attempt to be modern, missed the point. Young people no longer bothered about engineering seduction. It happened if they wanted it. And if they did not, it did not. People were less coy about all that now.

Domenica provided the answer. "But you must have gone hoping to find something out – to learn a bit more about him? Did you?"

Pat nodded. "I learned a bit," she said. "But I'm not sure about him. I'm just not . . ."

Domenica waved a hand. "The most important thing these days, is whether he . . . whether he's interested. There are so many young men who just aren't interested these days. It never ceases to surprise me."

Pat studied her neighbour. It embarrassed her slightly to have this conversation with a woman so many years her elder – even if circumlocution was employed. *Interested* was such an old-fashioned way of putting it; laughably so, she thought. And yet Domenica was a woman of the world; she had lived abroad, lost a husband, done anthropological field work in South America. She was no innocent. Why did she need circumlocutions?

"Of course, the terminology has changed," Domenica went on, waving a hand airily. "In my day we used to refer to men as being musical. That was a code word. The other words came in, and now, of course, everybody spells it out. Is he, do you think?"

"Is he what?"

"You know. Cheerful?"

"You mean gay?"

Domenica blushed. "Yes."

"I don't know," said Pat. "I really don't."

Domenica laughed. "But you must. Any woman can tell. We can just tell."

"I'm not so sure," said Pat. "Do you think men can tell when a woman isn't interested in men?"

Domenica did not hesitate. "Of course they can't," she said. "But that's because men aren't as perceptive as woman. Men don't pick these things up. They just don't notice the obvious."

"And the obvious is?"

Domenica picked her glass up off the table beside her chair. "Trousers," she said. "Big, baggy trousers, and boots. Certain tattoos. Subtle clues like that." She paused. "But tell me – is he available, so to speak?"

"I think so," said Pat. "I get the impression that he is, but . . ."

Domenica's eyes widened. "There was something?"

Pat looked down at the floor. She would not emerge very well from this story, but she wanted to tell it to Domenica, and so she continued. "There was a photograph," she said. "It had something written on the back – *skinny-dipping in Greece with T.* And I had a quick look at it when he was out of the room. I couldn't help myself."

"Entirely understandable," said Domenica. "Anybody would have done the same. Anybody."

"Well, I did. And it was a picture of him, of Peter, standing in the sea. It looked as if it had been taken on a Greek island somewhere. He was a little bit off the shore and so the water came up almost to his chest. It was a perfectly respectable photograph."

Domenica sighed. "How disappointing."

Pat was not sure what to make of that. There was something racy about Domenica, something liberated. And yet at the same time, she was in no sense coarse. There was no scatological language of the sort that is so casually pumped out by the foul-mouthed, for whom the obscene, predictable expletive is an obsessive utterance. And yet there was a complete lack of prudery. It was contradictory – and puzzling.

"T must have taken it," said Pat. "But I didn't know who T is."

Domenica shrugged. "Does it matter?"

"Well, I think it may," said Pat. "If T is Tom, for example, then perhaps Peter wants me just to be a friend. But if T is Theresa or Tessa, then, well, it could be different."

"You should have asked him," said Domenica.

"I tried to. I made the photograph fall on to the floor and when he came back in I picked it up and said: "Oh! Who's T?"

"And?"

"And he said, 'Oh, that! That was on Mykonos.' And then he said – and this is the bit that really surprised me – he said: 'I'm a nudist, you know.'"

For a moment there was complete silence. Pat watched Domenica's reaction. In all the time she had known her, she had not seen her at a loss for words. Now she was. She looked beyond Domenica, to the bookshelf behind her. Margaret Mead, *Coming of Age in Samoa*; that was all about nakedness and the innocently carnal, was it not?

And then there were the books on feral children that rubbed spines with Mead and Pitt-Rivers. Feral children wore no clothes. More nakedness. Why should her neighbour be surprised by nakedness in Edinburgh?

Domenica herself supplied the answer to the unspoken question. "A nudist? In Edinburgh? Does he realise what parallel we're on?"

Pat smiled at that. This was vintage Domenica. Then she told her what Peter had said.

"And then he invited me to something," she said, dropping her voice as if others might somehow hear.

"To?"

"To a nudist picnic in Moray Place Gardens," she said. "Next Saturday night." And then added: "Subject to confirmation."

58. Moray Place

Domenica had just opened her mouth to speak when the doorbell sounded. She looked towards the door with evident irritation. She had been on the point of responding to the extraordinary disclosure that Pat had made of her invitation to a nudist picnic in Moray Place Gardens, and now, with a visitor, her comments on that would have to be delayed.

"Nobody is expected," she muttered, as she rose to go to the door. "Please stay. We must discuss that invitation."

As she approached the door a loud bark could be heard outside. "Angus," Domenica said. "Announced by Cyril."

She opened the door. Angus Lordie, wearing a white linen jacket and with a red bandana tied round his neck, was standing on the doorstep, his dog Cyril sitting at his feet. Cyril looked up at Domenica and smiled, exposing the single gold tooth in his lower jaw.

"Well," said Domenica. "This is a rare pleasure. Is this a visit from Cyril, with you in attendance, Angus, or a visit by you, with Cyril in attendance?"

"The latter," said Angus. "At least from my point of view. It's possible, of course, that the canine point of view on the matter is different."

He came in and was led through to Domenica's study, where he greeted Pat warmly. Cyril licked Pat's hand and then lay down at her feet, watching her through half-closed eyes. She thought that he winked at her, but she could not be sure. There was something deeply disconcerting about Cyril, but it was difficult to say exactly what it was. While Domenica fetched Angus a drink, Angus engaged Pat in conversation.

"The reason why I'm here," he said, "is artistic frustration. I've just been working on a portrait of an Edinburgh financier. I mustn't give you his name, but suffice it to say that his expression speaks of one thing, and one thing alone – money. But that, oddly enough, is a difficult thing for me to get across on canvas. You see it in the flesh, but how to capture it in oils?" He paused. "Can you tell when somebody is rich, Pat? Can you tell it just by looking at them?"

"I can," said Domenica, as she came back into the room. "I find it easy enough. The signals are usually there."

"Such as?" asked Angus.

"Self-assurance," said Domenica, handing him a glass of wine. "People with money carry themselves in a different way from the rest of us. They have a certain confidence that comes with having money in the bank. A certain languor, perhaps."

"And their clothes?" suggested Pat.

"Look at their shoes," said Domenica. "The expression well-heeled says it all. Expensive shoes have that a look about them." She turned to Angus and smiled. "Speaking of clothing, Angus," she said. "Pat has had a very interesting invitation. Do tell our visitor about it, Pat."

Pat was not sure whether she wanted to discuss Peter's invitation with Angus, but could hardly refuse now. "I've been invited to a nudist picnic," she said quietly.

Angus stared at her. "And are you going to go?" he asked.

Pat shrugged her shoulders. "I don't know. I'm not sure whether . . ."

Domenica interrupted. "It's not just any nudist picnic, Angus," she said. "It's to be held in Moray Place Gardens. Would you believe that, Angus? Isn't that rich? Can you believe it?"

Angus did not appear to be surprised. "Of course I can," he said. "Moray Place has quite a few of them."

"Who?" Domenica demanded.

"Nudists," said Angus. "Moray Place may think itself very grand. It may be a frightfully smart address. But there are more nudists living there than any other part of the New Town! It's always been like that. They meet in Lord Moray's Pleasure Grounds."

Domenica gave a snort of disbelief. "I find that very difficult to swallow, Angus. Nudists in Moray Place? All those Georgian drawing rooms and grand dinner parties. Nudists? Certainly not!"

Angus raised an eyebrow. "Of course I'm not saying that everybody in Moray Place goes in for naturism, but there are some of them who do. I believe they have some sort of association, the Moray Place Nudists' Association. It doesn't advertise, of course, but that's because it's Moray Place and advertising would be a bit, well, a bit beneath them."

For a moment there was silence. Then Domenica turned to Pat. "You do know, don't you, to take whatever Angus says *cum grano salis*?"

Pat said nothing. It seemed unlikely that there would be any nudists at all in Edinburgh, given the temperature for most of the year, but perhaps there might be in summer, when it could get reasonably warm, sometimes. Perhaps that brought them out. And, of course, Peter had declared himself to be one, and he had seemed to be serious when he issued the invitation.

Angus frowned. "You may not believe me, my dear Pat, but this old trout here," and at this he gestured towards Domenica, "is somewhat out of touch, if I may say so. No offence, of course, Domenica carissima, but I'm not sure whether you understand just how deep is the Deacon Brodie streak in this dear city of ours."

Pat glanced at Domenica. She wondered whether she would take offence at being referred to as an old trout, but her neighbour simply smiled. "You may call me a old trout," Domenica said. "But if there's anybody fishy around here, Angus, it surely is you. And let me tell you that I do understand the whole issue of social concealment and its place in the Scottish psyche. But let's not waste our time in idle banter. My question to you, Angus, is this: how do you know that there are nudists in Moray Place? Have you seen them? Or is it just gossip that you've picked up in the Cumberland Bar?"

Angus took a sip of his wine. His expression, thought Pat, was that of one who was about to produce the clinching argument.

"I'd like it to be true," he said. "Moray Place and nudists. Can't you just see it?"

"No," said Domenica. "I can't."

"Bob Sutherland would have loved it," mused Angus. "My goodness, he would have loved it."

Domenica looked puzzled. "Bob Sutherland?" she asked.

"Robert Garioch," said Angus. "A great makar. And one of our neighbours, you know. He lived in Nelson Street. Lived. Dead now, alas."

"Garioch," mused Domenica. "*At Robert Fergusson's Grave?*"

"You'll make me weep," said Angus quietly.

59. *Robert Garioch*

"Yes," said Angus. "*At Robert Fergusson's Grave.* Such a wonderful poem. I could recite it to you, you know, all fourteen, heart-breaking lines. But I won't do that." He paused. "Tell me, Pat . . . and Domenica, for that matter, how important is poetry to you?"

Pat thought for a moment. She had read some poets, but now that she came to think of it, who had they been? Chaucer had been forced on her at school – the respectable parts, of course – and there had been Tennyson too, and MacDiarmid, although she could not remember which bits. And then Yeats: something about an Irish airman, and towers, and wild swans. But how important had that been to her? She had stopped reading it after she had left school, and had not gone back to it. "Not very important," she said. "Although . . ."

Angus nodded. "I'm afraid I expected that answer," he said. He looked at Domenica.

"I find comfort in it," she said. "But why bring up Garioch? And why would he have been so amused by nudists in Moray Place?"

Angus laughed. "Because he had a fine sense of the contrast between grandeur on the one hand (not that I'm suggesting for a moment that Moray Place is overly grand) and the ordinary man in the street on the other. He's the heir to Fergusson, you know. Just as Burns was. An awful lot of Burns is pure Fergusson, you know."

"What a tragedy," said Domenica. "Do you know how old Robert Fergusson was when he died, Pat? No, of course you don't. Well, he was just a little bit older than you. Just a few years. Twenty-four."

"And he died alone in his cell in the Bedlam," said Angus. "That bonny youth."

"That seems to be the lot of so many poets," said Domenica. "To die young, that is. Rupert Brooke." She glanced at Pat. *The Collected Poems of Rupert Brooke* had been the ploy to bring Pat and Peter together – and where had that led? To an invitation to a nudist picnic in Moray Place.

"Don't talk to me about Brooke," said Angus dismissively. "Or at least don't talk to me about Brooke in the same breath as Fergusson. What a pain that young man was. Have you read his letters to Strachey? Ghastly egotistic diatribes. Full of upper-middle-class swooning and posturing. The Cambridge Apostles! What a bunch of twerps – and so pleased with themselves. All deeply damaged by the English boarding school system, of course, but still . . ."

Domenica was more tolerant. "They were gilded youth," she said. "One must allow gilded youth a certain leeway . . . And, anyway, they were all doomed, weren't they? They knew that once they were sent to France they didn't stand much of a chance."

"Fergusson was the real thing," Angus interrupted. "He had a real feeling for what was going on in the streets and taverns of Edinburgh. And he suffered. Brooke and his like are all too douce. That's why their poetry is so bland."

Domenica rose to her feet to refresh the glass which Angus was holding out to her. "I'm not sure where this is going," she said mildly. "But then I never am with you, Angus. Your thoughts . . . well, they do seem to drift a bit."

"Along a very clear path," said Angus. "I was speaking about Garioch and how he would have appreciated the contrast between the outward respectability of Moray Place and the desire of at least some of the inhabitants to practise nudism. That's just the sort of thing that he liked to write about.

"He wrote a wonderful poem, you know, called 'Glisk of the Great'. The narrator sees a group of people coming out of the North British Grill, 'lauchan fit to kill'. Then the party climbs into a 'muckle big municipal Rolls Royce' and disappears off towards the Calton Hill. The narrator thinks how grand this is, although the rest of us can't join in. It gives the town some tone, you see."

He paused. Pat and Domenica were looking at him expectantly. Cyril, who had raised his head, appeared to be listening too, one ear cocked towards his master. Cyril had no idea what was going on – which is the lot of dogs for most of the time. But he did know that he had been enjoying a pleasant dream before his master's voice disturbed him. In this dream he had been biting Matthew's ankle, something he had wanted to do for a long time. And he was getting away with it too.

"Well," said Domenica, after a few moments, "be that as it may. Robert Garioch is not here to write about this invitation of Pat's. We have to decide – or, rather, Pat has to decide – whether to go. And I would say certainly not."

"Oh, I don't know," said Angus. "They'll all be perfectly respectable. These nudists are a very tame lot, you know. They don't practise nudism for any lascivious reasons. It's all very pure and above board."

"That may be so," said Domenica. "But doesn't it strike you as a bit strange that this young man should have invited Pat, who is not currently a practising nudist, to join them?"

"They have to recruit somehow," said Angus. "It's like people inviting you to come along to a church service or an amateur orchestra. They're hoping that you'll join. People are recruiters at heart, you know. It makes them feel more comfortable to see the ranks of their particular enthusiasm swelling."

Pat listened to this with interest. She had been intrigued by what Angus had to say, but felt at heart that any advice he gave was bound to be wrong. Angus was harmless enough, she thought, but his view of things was such a strange one – almost a poetical turning upside-down of the world. Domenica, by contrast, seemed to understand things as they were, and if she were to listen to anybody, she should listen to her. Of course, there were other people she could ask. There was Matthew, but she sensed that he would be jealous and resentful if she even told him about Peter's existence, let alone his bizarre invitation. Then there was her father. He had a profound understanding of the world, but it would embarrass her to talk to him about something like this. Finally, she could make her mind up for herself; she could follow her instincts. But what were her instincts? She thought for a moment. She closed her eyes, trying to imagine the scene in the Moray Place Gardens. Then she opened them again. She wanted to go.

60. The Ramsey Dunbarton Story: Part IV – Legal Matters

High above the city, in their house in the Braids, Ramsey Dunbarton was embarking on a second reading of excerpts from his memoirs to his wife Betty. They had finished with his account of their courtship and early years in Craiglea Drive before they moved to the Braids. Betty had enjoyed the reading, although she had detected a number of inaccuracies in her husband's recollection of events. He had confused the place of their first meeting and had got his age at the time quite wrong. He had also mixed up the name of the late Duke of Atholl, whom he had described as Angus, but who had actually been called Iain. These were little things, of course, although the cumulative effect of a number of errors of that nature could make for a narrative which was perhaps less than reliable, but she had refrained from correcting him. Ramsey had many virtues, but he also had a slight tendency to become peevish when it was pointed out to him that he was wrong about something. So Betty had remained silent in the face of these mistakes and had confined her reaction to nods of agreement and small exclamations of appreciation. And she reflected on the fact that nobody was ever likely to read Ramsey's memoirs, even if he found somebody prepared to publish them. That was not because they were intrinsically irrelevant, but because these days people seemed to be interested only in reading about vulgar matters and violence. And there was no vulgarity or violence in Ramsey's memoirs . . . at least so far. Betty sighed.

"I shall now move on to some legal reminiscences," said Ramsey, looking down at his wife in her comfortable chair. He preferred to read while standing, as this gave freedom to the diaphragm and allowed the voice to be projected.

"Legal things," muttered Betty. "That's nice, dear."

"I have been a lawyer for my entire working life," Ramsey began. "And I have never regretted, not for one single moment, my choice of the law. Had I decided differently at that fateful lunch with my prospective father-in-law in Broughty Ferry, I might have ended up in the marmalade business, but I did not. I stuck to the law.

"Now that should not be taken to mean that I have anything but the highest regard for those in the marmalade business. I know that there are some who think it in some sense undignified to be involved in that sort of trade, but I have never understood that view. In my view, it is neither the bed you are born in, nor the trade you follow, that determines your value. It is what you are as a man. That's what counts. And I believe that Robert Burns, our national poet, expressed that philosophy perfectly when he wrote *A man's a man for a' that*. It does not matter who you are or what you do; the ultimate question is this: have you led a good life, a decent life? And I believe, although I do not wish to be immodest, that I can answer these questions in the affirmative.

"I have, as it happens, had a strong interest in Burns since the age of ten. That was when I started to learn his works off by heart, starting with *To a Mouse*. I always recommend that poem to parents who want their children to learn to love poetry. Start with that and then move on to *Tam O'Shanter* when the child is slightly older and will not get too nervous over all those references to bogles and the like.

"But I digress. I knew from my very first day as a law student that the law was the mistress for me. I remember very clearly my first lecture in Roman Law when the professor told us all about the *Corpus Iuris Civilis* of Justinian and of how it had been transmitted, through the agency of Italian and Dutch scholars, to Scotland. That was romance for you! And it got better and better as we went on to topics such as the Scots law of succession and the principles of the law of delict. Succession was full of human interest, and I still remember the roar of appreciative laughter that rose up in the lecture theatre when Dr George Campbell Paton told us about the case of Mr Aitken of Musselburgh who instructed his executors to erect in his memory a bronze equestrian statue in Musselburgh High Street. And then there was the man in Dundee who left his money to his dog. That was very funny indeed, and it was only through the firmness of the House of Lords that the instruction was held to be *contra bonos mores*. I shudder to think, incidentally, what would have happened had the courts decided otherwise. It's not that I have anything against dogs – anything but – it's just that all sort of ridiculous misuse of money would have to be sanctioned in the name of testamentary freedom. I have very strong views on that.

"One never forgets cases like that. And there were many of them, including the famous case of Donoghue v. Stevenson, which was concerned with the unfortunate experience of a Mrs May Donoghue who went into the Wellmeadow Café in Paisley and was served a bottle of ginger beer in which there was a decaying snail. Mrs Donoghue was quite ill as a result, and so we should not laugh at the facts of the case. But it must certainly be very disconcerting indeed to find a snail in one's ginger beer! And there were other very good Scots cases, such as the case of Bourhill v. Young, which dealt with the claim of Mrs Euphemia Bourhill, a fishwife, who saw a motorcyclist suffer

an unfortunate accident very close to the bus in which she was travelling. There is a remarkable, but little known fact about that case. The former professor of jurisprudence at the University of Edinburgh, the late Professor Archie Campbell, employed a housekeeper whose nephew was involved in the accident! I happen to know that, but not many others do. And there is a further co-incidence. Archie Campbell used to live in one of those streets behind the Braid Hills Hotel, which is not far from the house occupied by me and my wife, Betty. Edinburgh is a bit like that."

Ramsey Dunbarton paused after these disclosures, and looked at his wife. She had gone to sleep.

61. *The Ramsey Dunbarton Story:*
Part V – Johnny Auchtermuchty

"I do think it's a bit rude of you to nod off like that," said Ramsey Dunbarton. "Here I am going to the trouble of reading you my memoirs and I look up and see you fast asleep. Really, Betty, I expect a bit more of you!"

Betty rubbed at her eyes. "I'm terribly sorry, dear. I was only away for a moment or two. I think that you had got to the point where somebody was building a statue of a dog in Dundee."

"Oh really!" Ramsey said peevishly. "You've got it all mixed up. It was Musselburgh that the bronze equestrian statue . . ."

"Of a dog?" interrupted Betty. "Surely not. Surely one couldn't have an equestrian statue of a dog? Wouldn't that look a bit odd, even in Musselburgh?"

Ramsey sighed. "My dear, if you had been listening, instead of sleeping, you would have understood that the dog was in Dundee, and there was never any question of erecting a statue to it, equestrian or otherwise. But, look, do you want me to go on reading or do you want me to stop?"

"Oh, you must carry on reading, Ramsey," said Betty enthusiastically. "Why don't we do this: you read and then, every so often, take a look in my direction and see if my eyes are closed. If they are, give me a gentle nudge."

Ramsey agreed, reluctantly, and took up his manuscript again.

"Well, after all that legal training and whatnot I was duly admitted as a solicitor and found myself as an assistant in the Edinburgh firm of Ptarmigan Monboddo. It was a very good firm, with eight partners, headed by Mr Hamish Ptarmigan. I liked him, and he was always very good to me. If ever I needed advice, I would go straight to him and he would tell me exactly what to do. And he was never wrong.

"'Always remember,' he said, 'that although you have a duty to do what your client wishes, you need never do anything that offends your conscience. If a client asks you to do that, you can simply decline to accept his instructions. And if you do this, you will never get into any trouble with either the Law Society of Scotland, or God.'

"And I remembered this advice when a client came to me and said that he wished to transfer all his assets into immoveable property – or land, as laymen call it – and in this way to defeat the right of his son, whom he did not like, to claim his legal rights to a share of the property on his father's death. I was appalled by this, because I knew the son, and knew him to be a perfectly decent man. So I said to the client that I did not think that this was the right thing to do, especially as the person who stood to benefit from the arrangement was his mistress, a sleazy woman who drank a lot and had a real roving eye.

"The client became very agitated by this and said: 'If that's the way you feel, then I can always go to another firm.' So I said to him, 'You do just that! I would remind you that I am a professional man and not some paid lackey you can order to do this, that and the next thing.'

"He took his business away from the firm and I had to report this to Mr Ptarmigan. I shall never forget his reaction. He said: 'Dunbarton, you have done the right thing, even if this is going to cost the firm a lot of money, for which I must express a slight regret. But well done, nonetheless.'

"Later, I am happy to say, the son, whose interests I had sought to protect, and who had heard of my stand, became very successful and brought his business to us. Mr Ptarmigan noted that fact and pointed out that virtue was not always its own reward, in the sense that it sometimes brought additional benefits of a material nature. We both had a good laugh over that!

"Of course that particular client was an important one, but I never got to know him particularly well. I knew other clients rather better, and one or two of them even became friends. Johnny Auchtermuchty was one of these.

"Johnny had an estate up near Comrie. His father, Ginger Auchtermuchty, had been a well-known golfer, but had not been particularly good at keeping the estate in good order. In fact, he was rather bad at that, and by the time that Johnny had left the South East Scotland Agricultural College everybody thought that it would probably be too late to do much with the farms that they had in hand. The fencing was in a pretty awful state and a lot of work needed to be done on the steadings. In fact, when Ginger handed over to Johnny and went to live in Gullane, we were very much expecting to have to sell off a large parcel of land just to keep the place from folding up altogether.

"I first met Johnny when he came in to discuss the possibility of raising some money to do essential repairs. I prepared a deed which gave security for the loan and I remember thinking that he would never be able to repay even part of what he had to borrow. How wrong I was! Johnny proved to have a real nose for the managing of shooting and fishing and within a few years the estate was one of the most successful in Perthshire. And Johnny was also one of the most socially successful people of his day. Everybody liked him and invited him to stay with them. He used to make people laugh and told the most wonderful stories.

"I had heard about his house parties, which were legendary, but I had never received an invitation to one of them. This slightly distressed me, and I began to wonder whether Johnny thought of me as just his lawyer and not worth having anything to do with socially. That would have been very unjust. I enjoyed a party in exactly the same way as the rest of them did and even if I was not a particularly experienced shot I saw no reason why I shouldn't be invited to join in now and then.

"And then at last the invitation came. Would I care to come up to Mucklemeikle to shoot? Friday to Sunday? I replied that I would be delighted to do this. I did not ask what it was that we were going to shoot. Betty, who did not treat the invitation with the same enthusiasm as I did, suggested that it might be fish in a barrel. That was meant to be a joke, but I must admit that I did not find it very funny at the time. Indeed, I don't find it funny now. In fact, it has remained as unfunny as it was when she first uttered it – it really has."

62. The Ramsey Dunbarton Story: Part VI – a Perthshire Weekend

"Now," said Ramsey Dunbarton to his wife, Betty, as he read his memoirs to her. "Now things get really interesting."

"Johnny Auchtermuchty!" mused Betty. "What a card he was,

Ramsey! And such a good-looking man with that moustache of his."

"A great man," agreed Ramsey.

They were both silent for a moment. Then Betty asked: "And they found no trace of him?" she said. "Not even a few scraps?"

"Not a trace," said Ramsey sadly. "But let's not slip into melancholy. I'll resume with my memoirs, Betty." He looked at his watch. "This will have to be the last reading for the time being, my dear. People will just have to wait for the rest."

"And we haven't even got to the part where you played the Duke of Plaza-Toro at the Church Hill Theatre," said Betty.

"Time enough for that in the future," said Ramsey. "Now back to Johnny Auchtermuchty and the invitation up to Comrie.

"I was delighted, of course, to receive this invitation to shoot, even though, quite frankly, I had not done a great deal of shooting before. In fact, if the truth be told, I had hardly ever handled a shotgun, although I had done a bit of clay-pigeon shooting when I was much younger. I don't hold with shooting really: I'm rather fond of birds and I think that the whole idea of blasting them out of the sky is a bit cruel. But it was not really for me to criticise my clients and certainly Johnny Auchtermuchty would have been very surprised if I had taken a stand on the matter. There are plenty of Edinburgh solicitors who would have jumped at the chance of a day's shooting with Johnny and some of them would not have been above a bit of subtle persuasion that he should perhaps take his legal business to them rather than to Ptarmigan Monboddo. Now I am not going to mention any names, but I'm sure that if any of them are reading this they will know that I mean them.

"Betty decided that she would not come after all, and so I motored up to Comrie by myself on the Friday afternoon. I had borrowed a friend's Rolls Royce for the occasion and I enjoyed the drive very much, taking the road past Stirling and then up across the hills behind Glenartney. Johnny was standing outside the Big Hoose, as we called it, when I arrived and he said to me: 'Nice Rolls there, Dunbarton! You chaps must be charging us pretty handsomely to afford a car like that!' I was a bit embarrassed by this and started to explain to him that it really belonged to a solicitor from another firm but he paid no attention. 'That's right,' he said. 'Blame the other chaps! Old trick that, Dunbarton!'

"We all had dinner that night and had a very good time too. There were a couple of people from Ayrshire and somebody from Fife. Johnny's wife was a splendid cook and had prepared a very fine set of dishes for us. I asked her if she could give me the recipes to take home to Betty, but she said no. I thought that this was rather rude of her, but I fear that she had long been nursing a grudge against me, at least since she unfortunately had overheard me, some years before, telling somebody that I thought that Johnny had married beneath him. That was most unfortunate, but I was absolutely right. He had, and I think she knew it. I also noted that I was given the smallest bedroom in the house – one at the end of the corridor and that the sheets on the bed did not quite reach the end. And the water in the flask beside my bed did not taste very nice at all, and so I decided not to drink it.

"In the morning we went out to shoot. Johnny had a keeper who I think was hostile to me from the start, although he was polite to the others. He looked at my shoes and asked me whether I thought they were sufficiently robust for the occasion – I thought that was a cheek and I decided there and then that he could expect no tip from me, and told him as much. He was a Highlander, of course, and these people can be quite resentful when they get some sort of notion.

"We took our places alongside several pegs which the keeper had inserted in the ground. I was right at the end, which I suspected was the worst place to be, as there was a clump of whin bush immediately to my right which kept scratching me. Then they started to drive the birds out of their cover and suddenly people started to point their shotguns up in the air and blast away. I did my best, but unfortunately I did not seem to get any birds going in my direction and so I got nothing. Then quite

suddenly a bird flew up immediately in front of me and I jerked up my shotgun and pulled the trigger.

"I only heard the keeper shout when it was too late, and by then the bird, which I noticed was quite black, had gone down into the heather. I realised then that I had shot a blackbird and I felt very apologetic about it.

"'I'm awfully sorry,' I shouted. 'I seem to have shot a black-bird.'

"The keeper came storming over. 'That's no blackbird, sir,' he hissed. 'That was a black grouse.' Then he added: 'And you gentlemen were very specifically told that you were not to shoot any black game. Perhaps you forgot yourself, sir.'

"In the meantime, Johnny Auchtermuchty had wandered over. He had a word with the keeper and I overheard what he said. He told him to bite his tongue as he wouldn't have him being rude to any of his guests. Then he said something about how Mr Dunbarton was from Edinburgh and one shouldn't expect something or other. I didn't really hear the rest of it.

"I must say that I was very embarrassed about all this, although I very much enjoyed Johnny Auchtermuchty's company and the rest of the shoot were very decent to me and said nothing about what had happened. I left the next morning after breakfast, although my departure didn't go all that well. The Rolls would not start for some reason and they had to push me down the drive to start it that way.

"Poor Johnny Auchtermuchty – I miss him very much. He was the life and soul of the party and the most exciting friend I am ever likely to have in this life. I think that it's an awful pity what happened and I wish they had found at least some bit of him that we could have given a decent send-off to. But they didn't. Not even his moustache."

63. *Bertie Receives an Invitation*

The invitation from Tofu was solemnly handed to Bertie in the grounds of the Steiner School. "Don't flash it around," said Tofu, glancing over his shoulder. "I can't invite everybody. So I've just invited you, Merlin and Hiawatha. And don't show it to Olive. I really hate her."

Bertie looked briefly at the invitation before tucking it into the pocket of his dungarees. It was the first invitation that he had ever received – from anybody – and he was understandably excited. Tofu, the card announced, was about to turn seven and would be celebrating this event with a trip to the bowling alley in Fountainbridge. Bertie was invited.

"Can you come?" asked Tofu, as they went back into the class-room.

"Of course," said Bertie. "And thanks, Tofu."

Tofu shrugged his shoulders. "Don't forget to bring a present," he said.

"Of course I won't," said Bertie. "What would you like, Tofu?"

"Money," said Tofu. "Ten quid, if you can manage it."

"I'll do my best," said Bertie.

"Better had," Tofu muttered.

Back in the classroom, while Miss Harmony read the class

a story, Bertie fingered the invitation concealed in his pocket. He felt warm with pleasure: he, Bertie, had been invited to a party, and in his own right too! He was not being taken there by his mother; it was not a party of her choosing; this was something to which he had been invited in friendship! And bowling too – Bertie had never been near a bowling alley, but had seen pictures of people bowling and thought that it looked tremendous fun. It would certainly be more fun than his yoga class in Stockbridge.

Seated beside him, Olive watched Bertie's fingers go to the shape in his pocket and move delicately over the folded card.

"What's that you've got?" she whispered.

"What?" asked Bertie, guiltily moving his hand away.

"That thing in there?" insisted Olive. "It's something important, isn't it?"

"No," said Bertie quickly. "It's nothing."

"Yes it is," said Olive. "You should tell me, you know. You shouldn't keep secrets from your girlfriend."

Bertie turned to look at her in horror. "Girlfriend? Who says you're my girlfriend?"

"I do, for one," said Olive, with the air of explaining something obvious to one who has been slow to realise it. "And ask any of the other girls. Ask Pansy. Ask Skye. They'll tell you. All the girls know it. I've told them."

Bertie opened his mouth to speak, but no words came.

"So," said Olive. "Tell me. What's that in your pocket?"

"I'm not your boyfriend," Bertie muttered. "I like you, but I never asked you to be my girlfriend."

"It's an invitation, isn't it?" Olive whispered. "It's an invitation to Tofu's party. I bet that's what it is."

Bertie decided that he might as well admit it. It was no business of Olive's that he was going to Tofu's party. In fact, it was no business of hers how he spent his time. Why did girls – and mothers – think that they could order boys around all the time?

"So what if it's an invitation?" Bertie said. "Tofu told me not to talk about it."

"Ha!" crowed Olive. "I knew that's what it was. He invited

me to his sixth birthday party last year. I refused. So did all the other girls he invited. He tried to get us to pay ten pounds to come. Did you know that? He tried to sell tickets to his own party."

Bertie said nothing, and Olive continued. "I heard that the party was pretty awful anyway," she said. "Vegan parties are always very dull. You get sweetened bean sprouts and water. That's all. Certainly not worth ten pounds."

Bertie felt that he had to defend his friend in the face of this onslaught. "We're going bowling," he said. "Merlin and Hiawatha are coming too."

"Merlin and Hiawatha!" exclaimed Olive. "What wimps! I'm glad I'm not going to that party. I suppose Merlin will wear that stupid rainbow-coloured coat of his and Hiawatha will wear those horrid jungle boots he keeps going on about. They'll make him take those boots off, you know. They won't allow boots like that in the bowling alley. And then people will smell his socks, which always stink the place out. Pansy says that she was ill – actually threw up – the first time Hiawatha removed his boots for gym. Boy, is it going to be a stinky party that one!"

It was clear to Bertie that Olive was jealous. It was a pity that Tofu had not invited her, as if he had then she would have been less keen to run the party down. But Bertie was not going to let her destroy his pleasure in the invitation and so he deliberately turned his back on her and concentrated on the story that was being read out.

"You're in denial," Olive whispered to him. "You know what happens to people in denial?"

Bertie turned round. "What?" he said. "What happens to people in denial?"

Olive looked at him in a superior way. She had clearly worried him and she was enjoying the power that this gave her. "They get lockjaw," she said. "It's well known. They get lockjaw and they can't open their mouth. The doctors have to knock their teeth out with a hammer to pour some soup in. That's what happens."

Bertie looked at Olive contemptuously. "You're the one who

should get lockjaw," he whispered. "That would stop you saying all these horrid things."

Olive stared at him. Her nostrils were flared and her eyes were wide with fury. Then she started to cry.

Miss Harmony looked up from the story. "What is the trouble, Olive?" she said. "What's wrong, dear?"

"It's this boy," Olive sobbed, pointing at Bertie. "He says that he hopes that I get lockjaw."

"Bertie?" said Miss Harmony. "Did you say that you hope that Olive got lockjaw?"

Bertie looked down at the floor. It was all so unfair. He had not started the conversation about lockjaw – it was all Olive's fault, and now he was getting the blame.

"I take it from your silence that it's true," said Miss Harmony, rising to her feet. "Now, Bertie, I'm very, very disappointed in you. It's a terrible thing to say to somebody that you hope they get lockjaw. You know that, don't you?"

"What if you got lockjaw while you were kissing somebody?" interjected Tofu. "Would you get stuck to their lips?"

Everybody laughed at this, and Tofu smirked with pleasure.

"That's not at all funny, Tofu, *Liebling*," said Miss Harmony.

"Then why did everybody laugh?" asked Tofu.

64. Bertie's Invitation is Considered

Irene Pollock was late in collecting Bertie from school that afternoon. She had been preparing for her Melanie Klein Reading Group, which would be meeting that evening, and she had become absorbed in a particularly fascinating account of the Kleinian attitude to the survival of the primitive. Irene was clear where she stood on this point: there was no doubt in her mind but that our primitive impulses remain with us throughout our life and that their influence cannot be overestimated. This view of human nature, as being envious and tormented, was in Irene's view obviously borne out by the inner psychic drama which we all experience if only we stop to think about it. Irene thought that it was quite clear that we are all confronted by primitive urges – even in Edinburgh – and these primitive urges and fears make for a turbulent inner life, marked by all sorts of destructive *phantasies*).

The topic for discussion at the reading group that evening was a problematic choice, suggested by one of the more reticent members of the group. Indeed, this member was probably a borderline-Kleinian, given her sympathy for the approach of Anna Freud, and Irene wondered whether this person might not be altogether happier out of the reading group altogether. Her ambivalence, she felt, was eloquently demonstrated by the topic she had suggested for discussion: *Was Melanie Klein a nice person?*

When Irene had first seen this topic she had expressed immediate doubt. What a naive question! Did she expect a genius of Melanie Klein's stamp to be a simpering optimist? Did she expect benignity rather than creative turbulence?

Of course she knew what sort of things would be said. She knew that somebody was bound to point to the facts of Melanie Klein's life, which were hardly edifying (to the bourgeois optimist). Somebody would point out that Melanie Klein started out life in a dysfunctional family and that from this inauspicious start everything went in a fairly negative direction. Indeed, she suffered that most serious of setbacks for those who took their inspiration from Vienna: her own analyst died. And then, when it came for Melanie herself to die, her daughter, Melitta, unreconciled to her mother because of differences of psychoanalytical interpretation between them, gave a lecture on the day of her mother's funeral and chose to wear a flamboyant pair of red boots for the occasion!

All of this would come out, of course, but Irene thought this was not the point. The real point was this: Melanie Klein was not a nice person *because nobody's nice*. That was the very essence of the Kleinian view. Whatever exterior was presented to the world, underneath that we are all profoundly unpleasant, precisely because we are tormented by Kleinian urges.

It was these complex thoughts that were in the forefront of

Irene's mind when she collected Bertie that afternoon and brought him back to Scotland Street. Bertie seemed silent on the 23 bus as they made their way home, and this silence continued as they walked back along Cumberland Street and round the corner into Drummond Place. Irene, however, still busy thinking about Kleinian matters, did not notice this and only became aware of the fact that something was on Bertie's mind when he came to her in her study and presented her with the crumpled piece of card that he had extracted from the pocket of his dungarees.

"What's this, Bertie?" said Irene, as she took the invitation from him.

"I've been invited to a party," Bertie said. "My friend, Tofu, has asked me."

Irene looked at the invitation. There was an expression of faint distaste on her face.

"Tofu?"

"Yes," said Bertie. "He's a boy in my class. You spoke to his Daddy once. He's the one who wrote that strange book. Do you remember him?"

"Vaguely," said Irene. "But what's this about Fountainbridge and bowling? What's that got to do with a birthday party?"

"Tofu's Daddy will take us bowling," said Bertie, a note of anxiety creeping into his voice. "It'll be Merlin, Hiawatha, Tofu and me. He's taking us bowling to celebrate Tofu's birthday." He paused, and then added: "It's a treat, you see. Bowling's fun."

"It may be considered fun by some," said Irene sharply. "But I'm not sure whether hanging about bowling places is the sort of thing that six-year-old boys should be doing. We have no idea what sort of people will be there. Not very salubrious people, if you ask me. And people will be smoking, no doubt, and drinking too."

Bertie's voice was small. "I won't be drinking and smoking, Mummy. I promise. Nor will the other boys."

Irene thought for a moment. Then she shook her head. "Sorry, Bertie, but no. It's for Saturday, I see, and that means that you would miss both Saturday yoga and your saxophone lesson with Lewis Morrison. You know that Mr Morrison is very impressed with your progress. You mustn't miss your lessons."

"But Mr Morrison's a kind man," said Bertie. "He won't mind if I have my lesson some other time."

"That's not the point," said Irene. "It's a question of commitment – and priorities. If you start going off to these things every Saturday then you'll end up missing far too much of the enriching things we've arranged for you. Surely you understand that, Bertie? Mummy's not being unkind here. She's thinking of you."

Bertie swallowed. Unknown to his mother, he was experiencing a Kleinian moment. He was imagining a bowling alley – probably the Fountainbridge one – with a set of skittles at the far end. And every skittle was painted to represent his mother! And Bertie, a large bowling ball in his small hand, was taking a run and letting go of the ball, and the ball rolled forward and was heading straight for the set of Irenes at the end of the alley and – BANG! – the ball knocked all the skittles over, every one of them, right out, into the Kleinian darkness.

65. Stuart Intervenes

When Stuart returned that evening from his office in the Scottish Executive (which Irene, provocatively, referred to as "the wee government"), he found Bertie in his bedroom, sitting at the end of his bed, greeting copiously. Dropping his briefcase, he rushed forward to his son and put an arm around the boy's shoulder.

An inquiry soon revealed the reason for Bertie's state of distress.

"I've been invited to a party," Bertie sobbed. "It's my friend Tofu's party."

Stuart was puzzled. "But why cry over that?" he asked. "Surely that's a nice thing – to be invited to a party?"

"Mummy says I can't go," said Bertie. "She says that there'll be smoking and drinking."

Stuart's eyes widened. "At Tofu's party? What age is this Tofu? Twenty-four?"

Bertie shook his head. "He's six at the moment," he said. "But he'll be seven soon."

"Then surely there won't be any drinking and smoking," he said. "Do you think that Mummy has got things mixed up?"

Bertie thought for a moment. His mother certainly did have everything mixed up, in his view, but not necessarily in relation to the party. It was more a case of her *Weltanschauung* being mixed up (in Bertie's view).

"It's going to be a bowling party, Daddy," Bertie explained, his voice still thick with tears. "At a place called Fountainbridge. She says that there will be people there who will be drinking and smoking."

Stuart hugged his son. "And you want to go to it, Bertie?"

Bertie nodded miserably. "Olive says that it won't be any fun, but that's just because she hasn't been invited. She wants to spoil it for me."

Stuart reflected on this. He did not know Olive, but he thought the type sounded familiar. Some girls took pleasure in spoiling it for boys. He could remember that. And it continued . . .

"I'll speak to Mummy," he said. "We'll fix it up for you. I'm sure that Mummy's just trying to be helpful, Bertie. Mummy loves you, you know, Bertie." And he thought: *she loves you too much*, but he did not say that.

He gave Bertie a final pat on the shoulder, rose to his feet and went through to the kitchen, where Irene was chopping vegetables.

"Bertie's in a state," he said. "I've just been talking to him through there. Poor wee boy. He was crying his eyes out."

Irene looked up from her vegetables. "I had to put my foot down, I'm afraid," she said. "I tried explaining things to him, but he wouldn't listen. He'll get over it."

"I don't think so," said Stuart quietly.

"You don't think what?" asked Irene.

"I don't think he'll get over this sort of thing all that easily," he said. "He had his heart set on going to that party, you know."

Irene put down her knife and looked Stuart in the eye. "You know what this so-called party consists of? Let me tell you. It's not a sit down round the table and have cake party. Oh no. It's a bowling alley, for God's sake! Some tawdry, smoke-filled den down in Gorgie or wherever! That's what it is."

"It's a perfectly clean and respectable bowling place," said Stuart. "I know it. I went to the opening of the whole complex, as it happens. The Minister was invited and a number of us went along."

"These places start off like that and then go downhill," said Irene quickly. "But that's not really the point. The point is that he would miss yoga and a saxophone lesson. He already missed yoga when you took him off on that jaunt to Glasgow."

Stuart struggled to control his anger. "That jaunt, as you call it, was the highlight of his little life. He loved it! He loved the train. He loved Glasgow. He loved the Burrell."

"And those dubious characters you bumped into?" asked Irene. "Oh yes, I heard all about that, you know. Bertie told me about Fatty O'Something, or whatever he was called."

"Lard O'Connor," Stuart said. "What about him? He was very helpful. Just because he's not middle class . . ."

Irene, eyes bright with anger, interrupted him. "Middle class!" she screamed. "Who are you calling middle class? Me? Is that it? Middle class? Me?"

"Calm down," said Stuart. "Nobody would call you middle class to your face."

He had not meant to add the words "to your face", but they somehow came out.

"Oh," shouted Irene. "So that's it. So you think I'm middle class, do you? Well, that's very nice, isn't it? I spend all my time, all my energy, on raising Bertie to be an integrated citizen, to make sure that he understands all about inclusiveness, and has the right attitudes, and then you come along and describe the whole enterprise as middle class. Thanks for your support, Stuart!"

Stuart sighed. "Look, I'm sorry," he said. "Let's not have a blazing row over this. The whole point is this: you have to give Bertie a bit more space, a bit more room to be himself, to be a little boy. And one way of doing that is to allow him to have his own social life. So let's allow him to go to this party. Let's allow him to go bowling. He'll have a whale of a time."

"No," said Irene. "We must be consistent parents. We can't say one thing one moment and another thing the next. Melanie Klein . . ."

She did not finish. "He's going," said Stuart. "That's it. He's going. And I'm going to go and tell him that."

"You'll do no such thing," said Irene, turning back to her vegetables.

She reached for a carrot and chopped it with her knife. Stuart could not help but think how symbolic this was. But the time had come to act, and he did. He remembered that conversation he had had with Bertie on the train, that moment when they had been so close and where he had vowed to be a better father. He would be that father, and he would be that father now. Not at some time in the future. Now.

He moved to the kitchen door. Irene reached for another

carrot and chopped it smartly with her knife.

"Bertie," shouted Stuart through the open door. "You can stop crying now. You're going bowling, my boy. The party's on!"

66. Tofu's Party

Stuart dropped Bertie off at the bowling alley, delivering him into the care and control of Tofu's father, Barnabas Miller.

"Well, well!" said Barnabas. "This is going to be fun, isn't it, Bertie? Have you ever bowled before? I'm sure you'll be good at it."

"I hope so," said Bertie. "Thank you for inviting me, Mr Miller."

"Tofu's suggestion," said Barnabas. "And my goodness, we're going to have fun, aren't we, Tofu?"

"Yes, Daddy," said Tofu.

"And I've brought some nice things for you to eat," said Barnabas, patting a bag slung over his shoulder.

A few minutes later, Hiawatha and Merlin arrived and then the four boys, together with Barnabas, made their way through the large glass-fronted building towards the bowling alley.

"Have you brought my presents?" Tofu asked his guests as they walked along.

Bertie's hand shot to his mouth. "Oh, Tofu, I'm very sorry. I meant to, but I forgot. I'll try and give it to you at school next week."

"Me too," said Hiawatha.

"And me as well," said Merlin. "And I'll only be able to give you three pounds, Tofu. I haven't got any more than that."

"You'd better not forget," said Tofu crossly. "Or else . . ."

He left the threat unfinished. They were now at the bowling alley and Barnabas led them to the lane which had been booked for them.

"I'll show you boys how it's done," he said, picking up one of the heavy balls. "You take a few paces to build up some impetus and then you let go."

The ball careered down the lane and collided with the skittles with a very creditable crash. The boys danced in their excitement. For Bertie, in particular, this was the most thrilling of moments. To send a ball off down a wooden lane like that to knock things over was the most splendid fulfilment of everything that a boy would wish to do. Noise. Action. Excitement. Destruction. As Melanie Klein would have pointed out . . .

After a half hour or so of bowling, they took a short break. The boys sat down and Tofu's father opened the bag that he had brought with him.

"Carrots," he said. "And delicious bean sprouts! Here we are."

The boys reluctantly took the proffered snacks and nibbled on them disconsolately.

"Have you got any money on you?" Tofu whispered to Bertie.

"Two pounds," said Bertie. "I keep it in my pocket for emergencies."

"This is an emergency," said Tofu. "Look over there. See that. That's where they sell hot-dogs. Can you smell them?"

"Yes," said Bertie, sniffing the air.

"Well," said Tofu, "if you buy me a hot-dog, I'll give you something in return."

"Such as?" asked Bertie.

Tofu looked at his friend. "You see those pink dungarees of yours . . ."

"Crushed strawberry," corrected Bertie.

"Whatever," said Tofu. "I know you don't like them. I'll swap you my jeans for your stupid dungarees if you buy me a hot-dog. I've got plenty of other jeans at home."

"Would you?" asked Bertie.

"Yes," said Tofu. He glanced at his father and lowered his voice still further. "Here's the plan. We say that we need to go to the bathroom. You go and get the hot-dog. Then you bring it to me in the bathroom and I give you my jeans in exchange for your stupid dungarees. How about that?"

Bertie thought for a moment. It seemed to him to be an unfair bargain – weighted in his favour – but it was irresistible. He had always wanted a pair of jeans and now here was an opportunity to acquire such a garment, at virtually no cost, and all within the next few minutes. It seemed to him to be a stroke of quite extraordinary good fortune.

"All right," he said.

"Good," said Tofu. "Now have you got everything straight? Good. Then let's synchronise our watches." He looked down at his wristwatch. "The big hand's on . . ."

Bertie interrupted him. "I haven't got a watch," he said. It was a further humiliation, but he was accustomed to humiliations and generally took them in his stride.

"Oh," said Tofu. "Well let's set off anyway."

Tofu informed his father that they needed to go to the bathroom, and off the two of them went. After a few paces, Bertie deviated, and ran across to the counter where hot-dogs were being sold. Ordering a large one, he paid for it and squeezed a lavish helping of tomato sauce on to the top of the frankfurter. Then, his precious warm cargo wrapped up, he ran off to make contact with Tofu.

They completed the transaction beside a washbasin. Tofu quickly removed his jeans and slipped into the crushed-strawberry dungarees vacated by Bertie. And Bertie, his breath coming in short bursts from the sheer excitement of it, donned the jeans handed to him by Tofu. Both garments were a perfect fit on their new owners. Then, the exchange completed, Tofu wolfed down the hot-dog, licking every last drop of tomato sauce off his fingers. Then he belched with satisfaction.

"Thanks, Bertie," he said. "That was really good. Now let's get back to my Dad."

"Won't he notice that I'm wearing your jeans?" asked Bertie.

"Never," said Tofu. "He doesn't care what I wear. He never notices. He's too busy thinking about nuts and carrots."

They rejoined the bowling group and enjoyed a further half hour of intensive bowling. Bertie did not do badly for one who had never bowled before, coming second to Tofu. Merlin came last, but said that this was because he had a sore wrist and he would probably have come first had he been uninjured. Hiawatha said nothing about the result.

Bertie was fetched and taken home by Irene, who remained tight-lipped about the outing and did not ask her son how it had gone. Bertie, realising that his presence at the party was a defeat for her and a victory for his father, tactfully made no mention of how much fun he had had, and talked instead of a saxophone piece he was preparing for his next music examination. Then, when they were driving back down Lothian Road, Irene suddenly said to Bertie: "This is very strange. I thought we had five gears on our car. This gear-lever seems to have only four."

Bertie felt a cold knot of fear within him. "Does it matter?" he asked. "Isn't four enough? Isn't it a bit selfish to want five?"

67. *Bruce's Enterprise*

Bruce took occupation of his newly-rented shop at nine o'clock on a Monday morning. His excitement over the move made him wake up at six, considerably earlier than he had been accustomed to waking up since the beginning of his enforced idleness.

He arose from his bed, opened the shutters, and looked out at the day. The sun was almost up, but not quite; autumn was round the corner and the days were starting to shorten. It was a good time of year to start a business, especially a wine dealership. He could expect a high volume of sales in November and December, as people stocked up for the frantic round of entertaining that marked the end of the year. Those were the months when people felt that they had to see their friends or somehow risk losing them. Nobody saw anybody in January and February, although Bruce thought by that time he would have built up a group of discerning customers who would appreciate his know-how and return for their normal requirements. So that would carry him through the dark months of the new year and then it would be spring, and time for large orders of New Zealand sparkling and light California whites!

He went through to the bathroom and looked at himself in the mirror. Is this the face of a surveyor, he asked himself, or is it the face of a wine merchant? Wine merchants were urbane, elegant, poised; all of which . . . well, false modesty aside, Bruce recognised all of those qualities in himself. He would fit the part admirably.

He showered, glanced in the full-length mirror, lingering a little perhaps, and then applied copious quantities of after-shower body-cooler skin-reviver, and, of course, a slick of clove gel to his hair. Ready, he thought. No: I must remember the clothes. So he got dressed.

He left Scotland Street at ten to nine and set off jauntily in the direction of St Stephen Street, in a basement of which his new business premises awaited him. Scotland Street was coming to life. There was the man who ran the historic motorcycle garage in the lane; Bruce nodded to him and received a wave in return; there was Mr Stephen Horrobin looking out of his window; there was Iseabail Macleod setting off to her work on the Scottish dictionary; such an interesting street, thought Bruce, and now a wine merchant to add to the mix!

He walked down Cumberland Street and crossed St Vincent Street. His shop was at the Stockbridge end of St Stephen Street, near the Bailie Bar, tucked under an antique dealer's and a shop that sold paste jewellery. It was not quite as large as he would have liked it to be, but it was big enough, and there was always the possibility of opening up an old under-street cellar that might do for the storage of wine. The rent, though, was bearable, and flush with the agreed injection of funds from his friend George, Bruce was confident that he would have no difficulty in acquiring an impressive stock list. And he was confident that in time the shop would become a place of pilgrimage for the discerning Edinburgh wine-buyer. After all, he asked himself: is there much competition? There were certainly a few fuddy-duddy people here and there, but they were so middle-aged, and nowadays people want youth, vigour and good looks. All of which I have, thought Bruce; that, together with a knowledge of wine and a good palate.

The agent from the letting solicitors was waiting for him at the door. He was a serious-looking young man with horn-rimmed glasses and a slightly-worried expression. "Oh no," Bruce said to himself. "Yawn, yawn." They shook hands, the young man wrinkling his nose slightly at the cloves.

"Essence of cloves," said Bruce. "Like it?"

They moved inside.

"You should find everything in order," said the agent. "We had a slight leak in the sink in the back room, but the plumber came in and fixed that. Everything seems in good order. Lights. Look." He moved to the switch and turned it on.

"Lumière!" said Bruce.

The agent stared at him. "And I gather that you don't need to do much to the fittings."

Bruce looked at the shelves. They were exactly the right size for the display of wine bottles.

"Perfect for bottles," said Bruce, taking the keys from the young man. "And will I have the pleasure of selling you wine in the near future? I'll have an excellent range."

"Thank you," said the young man. "But I don't drink."

"You could start," said Bruce cheerfully. "Cut your teeth on something fairly light – a German white maybe. The sort of thing women go for."

The young man pursed his lips. "No, thank you," he said.

"You sure?" asked Bruce. "It'll loosen you up a bit. You know what I mean?

"Have you everything you need?" asked the young man. "If you do, I'll be getting back to the office."

He left, and Bruce shook his head. What a wimp! But even with such unpromising material he thought that he had made a fairly good impression with his sales pitch and he looked forward to being able to try his salesman skills on other customers.

He looked about the shop. All he had to do now was to give the place a bit of a dusting, order the stock, and arrange for the various bits and pieces to be installed. Then he would be in business! He looked at his watch. He could work until just before noon, when he was due to meet the wholesaler whom he had contacted. They were to meet in the Bailie, and they could go over the list there. The wholesaler, who was somebody Bruce had met once or twice at the rugby club, had promised to give him substantial discounts.

"I cut my margins to the bone when I deal with chaps from the club," he had said. "You'll get the stuff virtually at cost." Then he had lowered his voice.

"And I've got some cases of Petrus, would you believe? Don't spread it around, whatever you do, because everyone will want some and I can't satisfy everybody. But I can get you a few cases at an unbelievably good price. Honestly, you'll pass out when you hear the discount."

Bruce had immediately gone to find out what Petrus was.

Then he had looked at the price. For a moment he thought he had misread the figures. But then he realised he had not: those noughts were meant to be there.

68. A Petrus Opportunity

Shortly before twelve, Bruce shut up the shop and made his way to the Bailie Bar at the end of the road. He was pleased with what he had achieved in the two hours or so that he had been working. He had dusted down all the shelves, swept the floor, and washed the front display window. That afternoon he would take delivery of furniture, including supplies of stationery and a filing cabinet. Then all he would need before he started selling would be the stock, which he was now about to arrange with Harry, his acquaintance from the rugby club and wholesaler of fine wines.

"Walked past your place," said Harry as he came and joined Bruce at the circular bar. "Nice position. You're going to clean up there, Bruce. No doubt about it."

"You think so?" asked Bruce. He was pleased to receive this verdict from somebody in the trade. Of course he never really doubted it, but it was good to have it confirmed.

"Yes, but you've got to have the right stock," said Harry. "You know what they say about retail? Position, position, position. Yes, that's right, but you could also say: stock, stock, stock."

Bruce listened carefully. "Could you?" he asked.

Harry reached out and punched him playfully on the arm. "That's where I come in, Bruce, my friend! I'll fix you up with deals that you just won't believe. I'm telling you." He paused. "But let me buy you a drink? What will you have?"

Bruce smiled. "A glass of Chateau Petrus 1982," said Bruce.

"Ha, ha," said Harry. "Very funny. But you obviously know what you're talking about. That 1982 vintage was amazing. Really amazing."

They were served their drinks and went to sit down at one of the tables. Harry had with him an attaché case, out of which he took a red folder. "Here's the list," he said. "It's arranged geographically. Shall we start with France?"

"I'm more of a New World man," said Bruce. "California. Oz. New Zealand."

"Very discerning of you," said Harry. "And I couldn't agree more. But you mustn't forget the Old World, you know. People still like French wine, and you'll have to sell it. That's where I come in. I can get you the stuff that sells. I know what people want."

Bruce liked Harry. He liked his directness and his confidence. He was the sort of man who let you know exactly where you stood. There would be no shadow-boxing with him over price – Harry would come right out with it, man to man, and you would know that the price he was asking was a fair one.

Harry began to page through his list. "France," he said. "Main choices: Bordeaux and Burgundy. I can do both for you at very good prices – including, since you mention it, Chateau Petrus. I did tell you about a Petrus opportunity, didn't I?"

Bruce nodded. "I must confess I've never had a bottle of that," he said.

"Bottle!" said Harry. "Most people would count themselves lucky to get a glass! But . . ." He lowered his voice, although the bar was quite empty. "But I have my sources, and I can get you three cases, yes, three cases of the 1990! It'll drink well in a few years, but it will keep for at least thirty. Not that it'll be keeping on your shelves, Bruce! You put that stuff on your shelf, word gets round, and in no time at all you'll have half of Scotland beating a path to your door."

"What makes it so great?" asked Bruce.

"Oh, please Louise! – as our non-rugby-playing friends would say. That stuff is perfection. Balanced just right. Subtle aromas. Deep purple. Bags of complexity. Everything, all in one bottle. You taste it, Bruce, and you'll think that you've died and gone to heaven. It's the stuff the Pope drinks. Fantastic!"

"So that's why it's expensive?"

Harry nodded. "Look at the wine auction records. That wine goes through the roof. Two thousand pounds a bottle – easy! – if it's the right vintage. The 1990 goes for eight hundred a bottle. That's not per case, Bruce, that's per bottle. So nine thousand quid a case, for starters. Unless . . ."

Bruce, who had been looking at the floor, now looked up. "Unless . . ."

Harry lowered his voice again. "Unless you have contacts. And I do. I have friends out there in Pomerol. Old friends. They see me right."

"You're very lucky," said Bruce. "Contacts are important."

"Well, you have contacts yourself, Bruce," said Harry. "You've got me. I'm a contact of yours. I've got contacts of my own. My contacts are your contacts. And that's how I can get you your three cases of Petrus. Simple."

Bruce looked doubtful. "I'm just starting," he said. "I'm not sure if I've got the money."

"Money's not a problem," said Harry quickly. "I'm going to sell you this at a price you won't belive. It'll be my gesture of support for your new business."

Bruce caught a glimpse of himself in a brewer's mirror on the other side of the room. The sight encouraged him.

"How much?" he asked.

"All right," said Harry. "Three cases of the 1990 at eight hundred quid a case. Three times eight hundred makes two thousand. No, it doesn't, ha, ha! Deliberate error! Two thousand four hundred. But . . . but there's an additional discount of four hundred since you're starting up. And then you take off the three hundred that I always take off when it's somebody from the rugby club on the other side. That makes seventeen hundred! Can you believe that? Seventeen hundred for three cases of 1900 Petrus!"

Bruce thought about it for a moment. He had hoped to keep his initial stock purchases as cheap as possible and then to branch out into more expensive wines later on, but this seemed to be too good an offer to turn down.

"When can I get them?" he asked.

"They're in the car," said Bruce. "Round the corner in Royal Circus."

Bruce hesitated. Harry looked at him.

"You're never going to get an offer like this again, Bruce," said Harry gravely. "You know that, don't you?"

"You're on," said Bruce.

69. The Best Laid Plans o' Mice and Men

Pleased beyond measure by the purchase of three cases of Chateau Petrus 1990 Pomerol at a price which could only be considered a steal, Bruce returned to the flat in Scotland Street that evening in high spirits. He saw that Pat's door was closed and knocked on it to offer to make her a cup of coffee. She was a strange girl, in his view, but she had proved to be a reasonably congenial flat-mate and a reliable tenant.

She opened the door in her stockinged feet.

"I'll make you coffee if you like," said Bruce generously. "Unless you've got any better plans."

Pat accepted his invitation and followed him into the kitchen. She asked him if he had started his new business.

"Today," said Bruce. "I collected the keys of the shop. And I bought some wine." He paused. The thought had suddenly occurred to him that he might need some help from time to time. Pat might well be interested. He would not have to pay her too much and she was at least a known quantity. "You wouldn't by any chance like a part-time job, Patty-girl?"

Pat was taken by surprise. She could imagine nothing worse than working for Bruce. "That's kind of you," she said. "But I think that I'm all right where I am. Matthew needs me."

Bruce's face took on a sneering expression. "He can't cope, can he? What a disaster area that guy is. If it weren't for his old man he'd go to the wall. Believe me."

Pat remained calm. "Actually, he made a profit in the first part of the year. Eleven thousand pounds."

Bruce raised an eyebrow. "Eleven grand? How did he do that?"

"Buying and selling," said Pat. "That's what galleries do, you know."

Bruce shrugged. "Running a gallery must be child's play – if Matthew can make a profit. Mind you, eleven grand is not all that much these days."

"You'll make much more?" asked Pat.

"Sure," said Bruce, spooning coffee into the cafetière. "Much more." He turned to Pat. "You want to hear what I bought today? Well, I'll tell you. Three cases of Chateau Petrus at just over fifty quid a bottle. Can you believe that?"

"Fifty?" exclaimed Pat.

"Yes," said Bruce, smirking. "Remember that this is not the

sort of stuff you take to parties. This is wine for the serious connoisseur. This will go down well in Charlotte Square and Moray Place."

The mention of Moray Place reminded Pat of her invitation. Should she tell Bruce about it? Would he merely laugh at her, or would he be able to give her advice?

"Moray Place?" said Pat.

"Yes," said Bruce. "That's what I said. Moray Place. It's a posh part of the New Town. Posh people live there. Toffs, you know. They like Chateau Petrus in Moray Place."

Pat decided to tell him about the invitation. "I've been invited to a nudist picnic in Moray Place Gardens," she said. "I'm not sure whether I should go."

Bruce stared at her in astonishment. "A nudist picnic in Moray Place Gardens? Oh, Patsy girl, that's really rich! Classic!"

Pat looked down at the floor. She might have known that he would not take it seriously. Now he started to let out strange whoops and began to take his shirt off, as if engaged in a strip-tease. "Moray Place!" he crooned. "Nickety, nackety, naked! Moray Place!" Dropping his shirt, he began to gyrate around the room, pausing to admire the reflection of his bare chest in the glass screen of the microwave.

Pat looked at him in disgust. "You're ridiculous," she said. "You're . . . very immature, you know."

"Moi? Immature?" crooned Bruce. "Who's the nudist, Patsy-Patsy? Who's the little blushing nudist? Hoop, hooop!"

Pat left the kitchen and stormed back into her room, slamming the door behind her. Bruce completed a few more steps of his dance and then completed his coffee preparations. Cradling his cup in his left hand, he sat down by the telephone and dialled his friend George.

"I've got the shop," he said. "And it's great. You must come and see it."

At the other end of the line, George sounded cautious. "And the rent?" Bruce told him the figure.

"That sounds a bit steep," said George. "For that size of place."

"Steep, George?" exclaimed Bruce. "Do you know what

Edinburgh commercial rents are like? Because I do, and I'm telling you that's nothing – nothing, compared with what some people have to pay. We're quids-in with that rent, I'm telling you."

George listened.

"And here's another thing, George," Bruce went on. "I've already got a very good deal on some stock. Have you heard of Chateau Petrus?"

"As it happens, I have," said George. "It's a very good French wine, isn't it? It sells for fancy prices."

"It certainly does," Bruce replied. "You can pay several thousand pounds for a bottle, if the vintage is right."

"And you've found some?" asked George.

Bruce laughed. "It was more a case of the Chateau Petrus finding me. Three cases at an amazingly low price."

There was a silence on the other end of the line. Then George spoke again. "There's usually a reason for low prices. You get what you paid for."

Bruce stiffened. George was an accountant, he thought, and they could be such pedants. "What do you mean by that, George?"

George sounded unusually assertive. "I meant just what I said, Bruce. I meant that if you get something at a knock-down price it's either stolen or it's not what it claims to be."

"I know that this stuff's not hot," said Bruce quickly. "The person I bought it from is in the rugby club. He doesn't go in for reset. And how could it not be what it claims to be? I've looked at it. The labels say Chateau Petrus – complete with a picture of the man himself, Saint Peter."

George let him finish. Then he said: "Have you heard of wine frauds, Bruce?"

For a moment, Bruce said nothing. He swallowed. Then, when he spoke again, his voice was quieter. "Wine frauds? Forgery?"

"Yes," said George. "Everybody knows about those fake watches and designer jeans. But not everybody knows that there are gallons of fake wine out there. There's been a big problem with it in the Far East. I've read all about it. There are gangs that make replica bottles and labels and slap them on bottles of

French plonk. Then they sell it to the victim. The patsy, they call him."

Bruce looked at his reflection in the microwave again. Do I look like a patsy? he asked himself. And then it occurred to him that he had just called Pat "patsy". And he was the real patsy all along.

70. Cyril Howls

Matthew was the first to arrive at Big Lou's that morning. Big Lou, standing at her coffee bar, wiping the surface with a cloth, nodded a greeting to him.

"You know, Big Lou," said Matthew, "you're a bit like Sisyphus with that cloth of yours. Wiping, wiping, wiping." He paused, and smiled at her. "Do you know who Sisyphus was?"

Big Lou bristled. "As it happens, I ken fine well who he was. He had to push a rock up a hill until it rolled down again and then he pushed it up. And so on." She gave the counter a furious wipe. "Do you know who Albert Camus was?"

Matthew shook his head. "Some Frenchman, I suppose."

"Well, before you start condescending to me, Matthew my friend, you might go and look him up. He wrote a book called *The Myth of Sisyphus*. Have you read it?"

Matthew held up his hands in surrender. "Nope. Never read it. But you have, Lou? You must have."

"Aye," said Big Lou. "I've read it. And it's all about finding meaning in life and getting through this world without committing suicide. Camus says that we can find meaning in a limited context and that is enough. He says we shall never be able to answer the really big questions."

"I never thought we could," said Matthew, taking his accustomed seat. "I've never even been able to find out what the really big questions are."

Big Lou tossed her cloth aside and began to prepare Matthew's cup of coffee. As she did so, the door opened and

Angus Lordie walked in, accompanied by his dog, Cyril.

"Lou, my love, make one for me too," said Angus. "Very strong. I have to paint a tricky sitter today, and I need my strength."

"And what's wrong with him?" asked Lou.

"Actually, it's a woman," said Angus. "And that's the problem. She's got three chins too many and I don't know what to do about them."

"Leave them out," said Lou. "No woman would object to that."

"I could do that," said Angus. "But then will it look like her at all? People expect one to get a fair likeness."

"You'll think of something," said Lou. "Here's your coffee. And don't let that dug of yours drink out of my saucer. I don't want any of his germs to end up on the crockery."

"There's nothing so healthy as a dog's mouth," said Angus Lordie defensively. "Cats' mouths are full of all sorts of dreadful beasties, but a dog's lick is positively antiseptic. That's well known."

Angus moved over to the table where Matthew was sitting and took the seat opposite him. Cyril, released from his leash, lay down at his master's feet, his tail curled about him, his nose tucked into the hair of his stomach, but one eye half-open, looking at Matthew's right ankle, which was just a few inches away.

"You went for that dinner with your father?" asked Angus. "Weren't you rather dreading it?"

"I was dreading it," said Matthew. "But I went along."

"And?"

"And it wasn't a roaring success. He brought his new . . ." It was an effort for him to say the word, but he said it nonetheless, ". . . mistress."

"How interesting!" said Angus.

Big Lou raised an eyebrow. "Mistress? What do you mean by that, Matthew?"

"Well, that's what she is," he said. "She's his mistress."

"But he's a widower, isn't he?" Big Lou persisted. "You shouldn't call her that! That's downright insulting."

Angus Lordie shook a finger at him. "Yes, Matthew! You should be ashamed of yourself! She's his *partner*, that's what she is. That's the approved term these days. Tut, tut!"

Matthew shrugged. "Whatever you say. But I think of her as his mistress."

"Well, you need to think again," said Big Lou. "What's she like, anyway?"

"A gold-digger," said Matthew.

Big Lou stared at him. "How do you know she's a gold-digger? Did she say or do anything that made you think that?"

"It's pretty obvious," said Matthew. "There she is, at least ten, maybe fifteen years younger than him, probably more, and she's all over him. She must know that he's not short of the readies."

"Maybe she likes him," said Big Lou. "Ten years isn't all that big a gap."

While this discussion was raging back and forth, Cyril had edged slightly closer to Matthew's ankles. He was now no longer curled up, but was lying flat on the ground, his front paws extended before him, his chin resting on the ground between his legs, his eyes fixed on the exposed flesh above the top of Matthew's socks.

Cyril was a good dog. Although he liked to drink beer in the Cumberland Bar and to wink at girls, he had few other vices, and in particular he was not aggressive. He liked people, in general, and was always happy to lick any hand which was extended to him in friendship. If people insisted on throwing sticks, Cyril would always fetch them, although he found this tedious and pointless. But he liked to oblige, and he knew that it was obliging to do the things that people expected dogs to do.

But there was something about Matthew's ankles that was just absurdly tempting. They were not fat ankles, they were average ankles. Nor were they any different in colour from most of the other ankles that dogs usually saw. In smell, they were neutral, and so there was no olfactory clue to their attractiveness. It's just that they were immensely attractive to a dog, and at that moment Cyril could think of nothing else that he would prefer to do than to bite them.

But he could not. He knew the consequences of succumbing to the temptation. There would be the most awful row and he would be beaten by his father, as he thought of Angus. There would be raised voices and words that frightened him. And worst of all there would be disgrace, and a feeling that the human world did not want him to be part of it. There would be rejection and exclusion in the most unambiguous sense.

Suddenly, Cyril stood up. He turned away from Matthew's ankles – put them beyond temptation – and began to howl. He lifted his head in the air and howled, pouring into the sound all the sadness of his world and of the canine condition. It was a howl of such regret and sorrow as to melt ilka heart, ilka heart.

And none of those present knew why he cried.

71. *Crushed Strawberry*

Trudging up Dundas Street with his mother, deep in thought, Bertie reflected on the dire course of events over the past few days. He had enjoyed Tofu's party immensely – and had decided that when he turned eighteen, and became free of his mother, he would go to as many parties as possible. He understood that when one was a student one did not even need to be invited to parties – one just went anyway. That prospect appealed to him greatly, as he doubted whether he would get many invitations. Indeed, the invitation to Tofu's party had been the only invitation he had ever received.

But if the party had been a conspicuous success, the same could not be said of its immediate aftermath. When Irene had picked him up in the car, Bertie had been worried that she would immediately notice the fact that he was wearing the pair of jeans which he had obtained from Tofu in exchange for his crushed-strawberry dungarees and a hot-dog. The jeans fitted him perfectly and they were just right in every respect. There were faded patches at the knees and the hems at the bottom of the leg were ragged. There were several pockets on each side, which were undoubtedly useful, although Bertie had nothing to put in them. He had always wanted a penknife, and had been consistently refused one by Irene; if he were ever to get one, then there was a place for that in the right pocket.

"What do you want a penknife for?" Irene had asked when Bertie had raised the subject some months earlier.

"They're useful for cutting things," said Bertie. "They have lots of blades, Mummy, and some of them have those things for taking stones out of horses' hooves."

"Don't be so ridiculous, Bertie," said Irene. "You've never even been near a horse, and you don't need to cut anything. If you do, then just ask Mummy to cut it for you with her nice scissors."

Bertie had said nothing more, knowing that there was no possibility of getting Irene to change her mind once she had made a ruling. She just did not understand, he concluded, and he thought she never would. Boys need to do certain things – to have penknives, and secret clubs, and bikes – but Irene would never accept this. That was because she had no idea of what it was like to be a boy. Irene thought that boys and girls were the same, or could be made to be the same. But that was wrong. If you were a boy, you just felt differently. It was as simple as that. For his part, Bertie was prepared to accept that girls felt differently about many things. He understood, for example, what it was like to be Olive. He understood why Olive hated Tofu, and why Tofu hated Olive. He understood why Olive hated to have her pigtails pulled by boys and why she thought that Hiawatha's socks smelled. Bertie could empathise with all this. Why, then, could his mother not see things from his point of view?

For a few moments after getting into the car after the party, Bertie had held his breath. But his mother, for come reason, did not seem to notice the jeans he was wearing and made no mention of them. When they arrived home, though, as they were walking up the stair at 44 Scotland Street, Irene suddenly let out a cry.

"Bertie!" she exclaimed. "What on earth are you wearing?"

Bertie's heart gave a lurch. "Jeans, Mummy," he said. "Do you like them?"

"Jeans!" shouted Irene. "Where are your dungarees? What have you done with your dungarees?"

Bertie swallowed hard. He had wondered whether he could tell her that they had been stolen and that he had been given the jeans by a kind passer-by, but he was a truthful boy and did not like the idea of lying, even to his mother. So he had decided that he would tell her exactly what happened and throw himself on her mercy. After all, she could hardly get the dungarees back now that property in them had legally passed to Tofu.

"I exchanged them with Tofu," he said. "He liked my dungarees and so I gave them to him in exchange for his jeans. I'm sure that the jeans cost more than the dungarees did. So it was a pretty good bargain."

Irene shook her finger at him. "You naughty, naughty boy, Bertie! Mummy is very, very displeased. Those were your best dungarees and you have no business letting some horrible rough boy, this Toffee person . . ."

"Tofu," corrected Bertie.

"This Tofu person take them off you," concluded Irene.

"I'm sorry, Mummy," said Bertie, looking down at the stairs below his feet. "I won't do it again. I promise."

"You certainly will not!" said Irene, as they resumed their climb up the stairs. "And the first thing we'll do is telephone them when we get in and arrange to go round and collect your dungarees."

"But we can't do that," wailed Bertie. "Everybody knows you can't take things back. That's the law, Mummy. You can't take things back once you've given them away."

"Nonsense," snapped Irene. "Those dungarees cost a great deal of money and they still belong to you. Toffee had no business getting round you like that."

Bertie hardly dared imagine the scene that was being prepared. It would be the ultimate humiliation to be dragged round to Tofu's house, to have to surrender his newly-acquired jeans, and to have to don, once more, his crushed-strawberry dungarees.

"Do I have to go?" he asked, his voice small and discouraged. "Can't we ask them just to drop them round?"

"No," said Irene, firmly. "We have to face up to the consequences of our acts, Bertie. You have created this situation and now you are going to have to get out of it again – like a man."

Bertie looked up at his mother. He wanted to act like a man – oh, how he wanted to act like a man. But men did not have to wear crushed-strawberry dungarees. Men did not have to go to yoga and psychotherapy. Men did not have mothers like Irene. And in the result, it was every bit as humiliating as he had feared. His mother referred to Tofu as Toffee throughout the encounter, and she even shook a finger at him. Bertie wanted to die. He wanted to close his eyes and go to sleep and never have to open them and see crushed-strawberry dungarees again.

72. Ink and the Imagination

Dr Fairbairn sat at his desk, a small bottle of ink in his hands. "Now, Bertie," he said. "I thought that today we would do something different. This is a bottle of ink."

He held up the small black bottle and shook it in front of Bertie. Bertie, wide-eyed, stared at Dr Fairbairn. It must only be a matter of days, thought Bertie, before Dr Fairbairn was taken to Carstairs, and he wondered how they would do it. Perhaps they could have men with a net drive into Edinburgh and they could throw the net over Dr Fairbairn while he was walking down Dundas Street in that blue jacket of his. Then they could bundle him into a van and take him off. Bertie had located Carstairs on a map and had seen that it was not far away. It would not take them long to get him there, and they would probably arrive in time for tea, which would be nice.

Bertie swallowed. "Ink," he said quietly. It was best not to say anything that would cause Dr Fairbairn to become more excited. Short words, uttered very softly, were probably safest.

"Yes," said Dr Fairbairn. "Good boy. Black ink."

Bertie nodded. "Ink," he said again. And then added: "Ink."

Dr Fairbairn smiled. "You may be wondering, Bertie, why I'm holding a bottle of ink."

Bertie shook his head. "No," he said, even more quietly.

"Well," said Dr Fairbairn. "There's a very interesting little game we therapists have invented. It's called the Rorschach Inkblot Test. Would you like to play it, Bertie?"

Bertie felt he had no alternative but to agree, and he did. This must have been the right answer, as Dr Fairbairn appeared pleased with it.

"Very well," said the psychotherapist. "I shall open this little bottle of ink . . . so. There we are. And now I shall pour just a little bit of it on to the middle of this piece of paper. So! Look. Now I shall fold the paper over, in half, like that. There!"

Bertie stared at the piece of folded paper. "Is it my turn?" he asked.

Dr Fairbairn smiled. "Hah! No, there are no turns in this game. You, Bertie, have to look at the ink blot that comes out and tell me what you see! That's what you do."

Bertie took the piece of paper and unfolded it with trembling hands. Then he examined the still wet ink blot.

"I see Scotland," he said quietly. "Look, there it is."

Dr Fairbairn took the piece of paper and stared at it. Then he turned it round.

"Funny," he said. "I'll do it again."

Once more he poured a small amount of ink on to the paper and folded it over. Again, he handed it to Bertie. "Now, we shall see," he said. "You tell me what you see. And don't hesitate to tell me, even if it's something very strange. Don't hesitate to speak your mind."

"I won't," said Bertie obligingly.

He took the piece of paper and unfolded it.

"I see the Queen," said Bertie. "Look, there she is, Dr Fairbairn. I see the Queen's head."

Dr Fairbairn took the paper from him and peered at it. He seemed put-out.

"I shall do it again," he said.

More ink was spilled, and the paper was folded. Bertie, now quite confident, although he found this game somewhat tedious, exposed the blot to view.

This time he stared at the blot for some time before he spoke. Then, handing the paper back to Dr Fairbairn, he said: "That's Dr Freud, isn't it? Look, Dr Fairbairn, you've made two Dr Freuds!"

Rather to Bertie's surprise, Dr Fairbairn now put away his bottle of ink and threw the pieces of paper in the wastepaper bin. "Perhaps we shall do that again, Bertie," he said, "when you are feeling a bit more imaginative. For the moment I think we can leave it at that. I need to have a quick chat with your Mummy before you go. You go off and read *Scottish Field* in the waiting room. Good boy."

Bertie sat in the waiting room while his mother went in to speak to Dr Fairbairn. Although he knew that he was meant to have an hour of therapy, he never really had more than ten minutes, as his mother would go in and talk to Dr Fairbairn for at least fifty minutes before she came out. What could they be talking about? he wondered. Surely one could not go on about Melanie Klein for fifty minutes twice a week? But that's what they seemed to be doing.

Inside the consulting room, Irene sat in the chair recently vacated by Bertie and listened to Dr Fairbairn.

"I did a bit of Rorschach work with him this morning," Dr Fairbairn said. "We didn't get very good results. He came up with very literal interpretations. I saw nothing of the subconscious processes. No light on the object relations issue."

"Oh well," said Irene. "We must persist. There's still a lot of aggression there, I'm afraid. He wanted to go bowling the other day. That's very aggressive."

"Maybe," said Dr Fairbairn, noting something down on a pad. "Maybe not."

"And then there's some sign of knife fantasies," went on Irene. "He keeps asking for a penknife."

"Worrying, that," said Dr Fairbairn. "Of course, boys do like that sort of thing, you know."

Irene looked at him. "Some boys may," she said. "Some males need knives. Some don't."

Dr Fairbairn thought for a while. "You know," he said, "I've been thinking a bit about Bertie, and I'm beginning to have a sense of what's going on. The dynamics. The splitting process. The good mother/bad mother schizoid bifurcation."

Irene leant forward eagerly. "Oh yes?" she said. "And what do you think is the problem?"

Dr Fairbairn rose to his feet. He looked down at the crumpled pieces of paper in his wastepaper basket and, on a sudden impulse, picked one out, uncrumpled it and showed it to Irene.

"What do you see there?" he asked.

Irene took the ink blot of Scotland and frowned. "A cloud of guilt?" she suggested. "Yes, a cloud of guilt."

"Hah!" exclaimed Dr Fairbairn. "That is Scotland!"

"Nonsense!" cried Irene. "That's a cloud of guilt."

Dr Fairbairn bent down and retrieved the ink blot of the Queen. "And this?" he asked, thrusting it into Irene's hands. "What's this?"

"Mother," said Irene, without hesitation.

Dr Fairbairn snatched the paper back from her. Then he turned to face her and spoke very quietly but firmly.

"You know something?" he said. "You know something? I've decided what the problem is. It's *you*!"

73. *Wee Fraser Again*

Bertie knew that something was wrong the moment that he heard shouting issuing from Dr Fairbairn's consulting room. He had been engrossed in a copy of *Scottish Field* and the time had passed rather quickly. But now the normal sedate silence of the waiting room was disturbed by voices raised in discord. Dr Fairbairn and his mother were having a row! Indeed, it might be even worse. Perhaps Dr Fairbairn had finally got out of control and might even now be assaulting his mother, possibly even throwing ink at her! Bertie dropped the magazine and sprang to his feet. He was not sure what to do; if he burst into the consulting room, then that might just make matters worse; if he stayed where he was then his mother could meet some terrible fate at the hands of the psychotherapist, all the while unaided by her son.

Bertie moved over and put an ear to the door of the consulting room. The sound of shouting had dropped, and now there seemed to be silence within the room. That was a very bad sign, he thought. Perhaps Dr Fairbairn was even now lowering his mother's body from the window, on a rope, with a view to hiding it in the Queen Street Gardens. But then, there was a voice, and another – voices which were no longer raised and seemed to be making casual conversation. Bertie heaved a sigh of relief. The row was over. They had got back to talking about Melanie Klein.

Inside the consulting room, Dr Fairbairn sat at his desk, his head in his hands.

"I don't know what came over me," he said remorsefully. "It was all so sudden. I don't know why I said it."

Irene looked at him. She understood how stress could affect people. Dr Fairbairn's job was undoubtedly stressful, dealing

with all sorts of harrowing personal problems. It would be easy
in such circumstances to say something rash and, as in this case,
completely unjustified.

"I understand," she said gently. "I really do. You mustn't
reproach yourself unduly."

She looked at him as he continued to stare down at the
surface of his desk. Of course this might be an opportunity
to probe a bit; there was a great deal she would like to know
about Dr Fairbairn and now might be the time to do that
probing.

"Of course, it might be better if you talked to me about it,"
she said.

Dr Fairbairn looked up. "About what?" he asked.

"About all the things that you're so obviously repressing,"
Irene said quietly. "About the guilt."

Dr Fairbairn was silent for a few moments. "Is my guilt that
obvious?" he asked.

"I'm afraid so," said Irene, trying to sound as sympathetic as
she could. "It's written very clearly. I've always sensed it."

"Oh," said Dr Fairbairn. It was like being told that one's
deodorant was less than effective. It was very deflating.

"Guilt has such a characteristic signature," went on Irene. "I
find that I can always tell."

She watched Dr Fairbairn from the corner of her eye. She
was not sure what his guilt was based on, but it was bound to
be something interesting.

"You can tell me, you know," she urged. "You'd feel much
relieved."

"Do you think so?" asked Dr Fairbairn.

Irene nodded. It was a time for non-verbal signs.

"I feel so awful," said Dr Fairbairn. "I've been carrying this
burden of guilt for so long. And I've tried to convince myself
that it's not there, but my denial has only made things worse."

"Denial always does," said Irene. "Denial is a sticking tape
with very little sticking power." She paused and reflected on the
adage that she had just coined. It was really rather apt, she
thought.

"And yet it's so difficult to confront one's sense of shame," said Dr Fairbairn. "That's not easy."

Irene was beginning to feel impatient. She glanced at her watch. What if the next patient arrived now? She might be prevented from hearing Dr Fairbairn's revelations, and by the time that they next met he might be more composed and less inclined to confess his guilt. "So?" she said. "What lies at the heart of your guilt?" She paused. "What did you actually do?"

Dr Fairbairn looked away from her, as if embarrassed by what he was about to say.

"I suppose at the heart of my guilt lies my professional failure," he said. "I've tried to tell myself that it was no failure, but it was. It really was."

Irene leaned forward. "How did you fail?" she asked. "Tell me. Let me be your catharsis."

"You've heard of my famous case?" asked Dr Fairbairn. "The study of Wee Fraser?"

"Of course I have," said Irene. "It's almost as famous as Freud's case of Little Hans or Melanie Klein's Richard."

Dr Fairbairn smiled, a smile that surrendered shortly to pain. "I'm flattered, of course," he said, "but in a curious way that makes what I did even worse."

Irene looked at him in astonishment. Had he falsified the case? Did Wee Fraser actually exist, or was he a fraudulent creation upon which Dr Fairbairn's entire scientific reputation had been built? If the latter were the case, then it would amount to a major scandal. It was easy to understand why the author of such an act of deception would feel a crushing burden of guilt.

"What exactly did you do?" Irene asked. "Did you invent Wee Fraser?"

Dr Fairbairn looked at her blankly. "Invent him? Why on earth would I have invented him?" He paused. "No. I didn't invent him. I hit him."

Irene gasped. "You hit Wee Fraser? Actually hit him?"

Dr Fairbairn closed his eyes. "I hit him," he said. "He bit me and I hit him. And do you know what? You know what? After I hit him, I actually felt a lot better." He looked out of the window, shaking his head. "And then the guilt came," he said. Then the guilt came, like a thief in the night.

And took from me my peace of mind."

74. *The Wolf Man, Neds, Motherwell*

Irene was rarely at a loss for words, but on this occasion, faced with the extraordinary confession by Dr Fairbairn that he had actually raised a hand to Wee Fraser, the famous three-year-old tyrant, she was unable to speak for at least two minutes. During this time, Dr Fairbairn sat quite still, privately appalled at what he had done. He had spoken about that thing which he had for almost eleven years completely repressed. He had articulated the moment of aggression when, his hand stinging from the painful bite which Wee Fraser had inflicted upon him, he had briefly, and gently, smacked the boy on the hand and told him that he was not to bite his therapist. Wee Fraser had looked at him in astonishment and had behaved extremely and uncharac-teristically well for the rest of the session. Indeed, had Dr Fairbairn not been as well versed in the dynamics of child behav-iour, he might have concluded that this was what Wee Fraser had needed all along, but such a conclusion, of course, would have been quite false.

Eventually, Irene spoke. "I can understand how you feel," she said. "That's a serious burden of guilt to carry around. But at least you've spoken to me about it." She looked at him quizzi-cally. "And, tell me, how do you feel now?"

Dr Fairbairn took a deep breath. "Actually, I feel quite a bit better. It's the cathartic effect of telling the truth. Like a purging."

Irene agreed. Dr Fairbairn actually looked lighter now; it was almost as if the metaphysical weight of guilt had been pressing down upon his shoulders; now these seemed to have been raised, lifted, filling his blue linen jacket with movement and strength.

"Of course you won't be able to leave it at that," she said, gently lifting a finger, not so much in admonition as in caution.

Dr Fairbairn looked momentarily crestfallen. "No?" he said.

"No," answered Irene. "The striking of Wee Fraser is un-finished business, isn't it? You need to make a reparative move."

Dr Fairbairn looked thoughtful. "Maybe . . ."

Irene interrupted him. "Tell me," she said, "what happened to Wee Fraser. Did you do any follow-up?"

Dr Fairbairn shook his head. "Wee Fraser had been referred to me by a general practitioner. She managed to get the Health Board to pay for his therapy after he had been involved in an unfortunate piece of exhibitionist behaviour in a ladies' hair-dressing salon out at Burdiehouse. He had been taken there by his mother when she went to have her hair done. Some of the other ladies were a bit put out and so she took Wee Fraser to the doctor to discuss his behaviour. Fortunately, the GP in ques-tion had the foresight to believe that psychotherapeutic inter-vention might be of some help, and that's how our paths came together."

"And the parents?" asked Irene. "Functional?"

"Oh, I think that they functioned quite well," said Dr Fairbairn. "Or they seemed to. They were a respectable couple. The father was a fireman and the mother was a receptionist at the Roxburghe Hotel. They were at their wits' end with Wee Fraser, I fear."

"And what happened to him?" asked Irene. "Did you not hear anything?"

"Nothing," said Dr Fairbairn. "But I should imagine that they're still there. Fraser will be fourteen now, I should imagine." He stopped. "You know, I saw him the other day?"

Irene's eyes widened. "Wee Fraser? You saw him?" She had read about how Freud's famous patient, the Wolf Man, had been found not all that long ago, living in Vienna, as a retired wolf man. The discovery had been written up by an American journalist who had gone in search of him. Perhaps it was time for Wee Fraser to be discovered in much the same way.

"I saw him at the East End of Princes Street," said Dr Fairbairn. "You see a lot of neds . . . I mean young men hanging about, I mean congregating, down there. I think they go shopping in that ghastly shopping centre at the top of Leith Street. You know the one that Nicky Fairbairn was so scathing about."

Irene sat up at the mention of the name. Nicholas Fairbairn. Why did Dr Fairbairn mention Nicholas Fairbairn? Was it because he was his brother, perhaps? Which meant that he must be the son of Ronald Fairbairn, no less – Ronald Fairbairn who had written *Psychoanalytic Studies of the Personality*, in which volume there appeared the seminal paper, 'Endoscopic Structure Considered in Terms of Object-Relationships'.

"Are you, by any chance . . . ?" she began.

Dr Fairbairn hesitated. More guilt was coming to the surface, inexorably, bubbling up like the magma of a volcano. "No," he said. "I'm not. I am nothing to do with Ronald Fairbairn, or his colourful son. I am an ordinary Fairbairn." He hesitated again. "We actually come from Motherwell originally."

"Motherwell!" exclaimed Irene, and then checked herself.

There was nothing wrong with Motherwell, nor with Airdrie for that matter. We all had to come from somewhere, even Motherwell. She herself came from Moray . . . Well, there was no need for anybody to go into that. (Moray Place, actually).

"Yes," said Dr Fairbairn. The confessions had given him confidence and now he looked directly at Irene. "Where do you come from, Mrs Pollock?"

"Moray," said Irene, prepared to continue to add Place (one should not lie, directly), but taking her time, and not having the opportunity to complete her sentence (no fault of her own).

"Moray!" said Dr Fairbairn. "What a pleasant part of the country. I love Moray, and Nairn too."

Irene said nothing. It was not *her* guilt that they were meant to be talking about; it was his.

"You have to seek out Wee Fraser," she said. "You know that, don't you? You have to find him and apologise for what you did to him."

Dr Fairbairn sat quite still. He had no doubt but that what Irene said was true. Reparation was of the essence; Melanie Klein herself had said that. He would have to go out to Burdiehouse, find Wee Fraser, and ask his forgiveness. It was a simple thing to do, but a very important one, not only for himself, but perhaps for Wee Fraser too.

75. *Cyril's Moment of Glory*

Irene had much to think about as she walked home with Bertie. The session with Dr Fairbairn had been a traumatic one and she needed to order her thoughts. She had been astonished when the psychotherapist had turned on her in that unexpected and vindictive way, suggesting that she, of all people, might be responsible for Bertie's troubles. Of course it was easy to blame mother; anybody with a smattering of knowledge of psychoanalysis thought that they could point the finger at mother; but to hear that coming from somebody like Dr Fairbairn, who had even held psychoanalytical office, was most surprising. And it was so dangerous too; she could cope with an allegation of that sort because she could stand up to him intellectually, and she was versed in Kleinian theory; but what if he had said something to an ordinary person? Such a mother could be extremely upset.

Of course the comment was an aberration, and Dr Fairbairn had been brought to his senses sharply enough by Irene's reaction, but their relationship had very clearly changed as a result of the incident. Seeing him sitting so miserably at his desk, his distinguished head sunk in his hands, had brought out the maternal in Irene. And then the penny dropped. Indeed, it dropped so sharply that Irene stopped in her tracks, some way down Dundas Street, and gave a half-suppressed cry. Of course! Of course! Dr Fairbairn had no mother. By coming up with the absurd suggestion that she was smothering Bertie, he was trying to divert her natural mothering instincts away from her son to himself. Do not be a mother to Bertie, he was saying, so that you can become a mother to me. It was quite clear. In fact, it was glaringly obvious.

Hearing his mother gasp, Bertie stopped and looked up at her.

"Are you all right, Mummy?" he asked.

Irene looked down at her son. She had been so immersed in her thoughts that she had forgotten Bertie was with her. But there he was, in his dungarees, smiling with that appealing smile of his. What an odd little boy he was! So talented, what with his Italian and his saxophone, but still encountering such difficulties in the object relations context.

"Yes, thank you, Bertie," she replied. "I just had a very important thought. You know how some thoughts are so important they make you go 'oh!'? I had that sort of thought."

"A moment of insight, you mean?" Bertie said.

Irene looked at him. She was occasionally surprised by Bertie's vocabulary, but it made her proud, too. All of this he got from me, she said to herself. All of it. Bertie is my creation.

"Yes," she said. "You could call it a moment of insight. I just had an insight there into what happened a little while ago in Dr Fairbairn's room. You won't know, but Dr Fairbairn and I had a tiny argument. Nothing serious, of course."

Bertie pretended to be surprised. "A wee stooshie?" he asked.

Irene frowned. "I'm not sure if I'd call it a stooshie, and I'm not sure if I want you using words like that, Bertie."

"Is it a rude word, Mummy?" asked Bertie. "Is it like . . ."

"It's not rude," said Irene. "It's more, how shall I put it, it's more vernacular, shall we say? It's Scots."

"Is Scots rude?" persisted Bertie.

"No," said Irene. "Scots isn't exactly rude. It's just that we don't use a lot of it in Edinburgh."

Bertie said nothing. An idea had come to him. He would start talking Scots! That would annoy his mother. That would show her that although she could force him to wear pink dungarees she could not control his tongue! Ha! That would show her.

"Anyway," said Irene, "we must get home. You have a saxophone lesson in half an hour, I believe, and you must do your homework before then."

"Aye," said Bertie quietly. "Nae time for onything else."

"What was that Bertie?" asked Irene. "Did you say something?"

"I didnae," said Bertie.

"What?"

"No spikkin," muttered Bertie.

"Really, you are a very strange little boy sometimes," said Irene, a note of irritation creeping into her voice. "Muttering to yourself like that."

Continuing down the street, they were now directly outside Big Lou's coffee bar. They reached it just as Matthew and Angus Lordie came up the steps to the pavement, their coffee conversation having been brought to an end by the sudden prolonged howling of Cyril. The canine angst which had produced this outburst had presumably resolved itself as quickly as it had come into existence, as Cyril now seemed quite cheerful and wagged his tail enthusiastically at the sight of Bertie. Cyril liked boys; he liked the way they smelled – just a little bit off; and he liked the way they jumped around. Boys and dogs are natural allies, thought Cyril.

When he saw Bertie, Cyril rushed forward and sat down on the pavement in front of him, offering him a paw to shake.

"Bonnie dug," Bertie said, taking the paw, and crouching down to Cyril's level. "Guid dug."

Cyril moved forward to lick Bertie's face enthusiastically, making Bertie squeal with delight.

"Bertie!" shouted Irene. "Get away from that smelly creature! Don't let him lick you!" And then, turning to Cyril, she leant forward and shouted at him: "Bad, smelly dog! Shoo! Shoo!"

As a dog, Cyril did not have a large vocabulary. But there are some words all dogs understand. They know what "walk" means. They know what "good dog" means, and "fetch". And Cyril knew, too, what "smelly" meant, and he bitterly resented it. He had seen this tall woman before, walking in Drummond Place, and he did not like her. And now she was calling him both bad and smelly. It was just too much!

Irene's ankles came into focus. They were close, and exposed. He hadn't started this, she had. No dog, not even the most heroic, could resist. He lunged forward, opened his jaws, his gold tooth catching the light, glinting wickedly, and then he bit Irene's right ankle. It was glorious. It was satisfying. It was so richly deserved.

76. Bruce has Uncharitable Thoughts about Crieff

Bruce had been deeply disturbed by what George had said to him over the telephone. He had been buoyed by his purchase of the Petrus at such a favourable price, but had been completely deflated by George's suggestion that the wine might be something quite different – an ordinary wine put into bogus Petrus bottles by calculating forgers.

At first, he had denied the possibility that George might be right. He had not even seen the wine in question; how could he pontificate on it? The problem with George, of course, was that he was so unadventurous. The idea of making an unconventional purchase, of buying something other than through the regular channels, was obviously alien to his cautious, accountant's personality. Poor George! He had always been the timid one, even at Morrison's Academy, where he would never do anything that was remotely likely to get him into trouble. What a mouse he was! But then mice sometimes had their uses, thought Bruce – especially if they had money.

But then, but then . . . perhaps George was right, to an extent at least, in saying that one had to be suspicious of bargains. If the Petrus was worth what it appeared to be worth, then why should Harry sell it to him at such a marked-down price? If it was worth more, and if, as Harry claimed, people were clambering to get it, then why should he sell it to him at such a reduced price? It was not as if he had given him an extra few per cent discount – the sort of discount one feels that one has to give to a friend – he had cut savagely into the market price. He had effectively given away the three cases of wine.

The thought that George might be right made Bruce very uncomfortable. He had paid a lot of money for the wine and he had done so out of his own bank account. He had also paid the first month's rental on the shop, again from his own account, and the debit side of the business would be mounting up rather sharply. And yet he had not obtained a single penny from George, even although George had assured him that the money would be available once he had sold the bonds. But how long did it take to sell bonds? Surely a call to one's broker was all that was required?

He spent his second day in the shop taking delivery of stock he had ordered from a wholesaler in Leith. It was good, knockabout wine, in Bruce's view – the sort of wine that Stockbridge people would buy to drink with their dinner or take to their parties – large Australian reds, various Chardonnays and even a range of sweetish German wines which he planned to place in a special section called Wines for Her. That last idea he considered rather good, and he thought it not unlikely that other wine shops would follow suit when they saw how appealing it was to women.

The shelves in his shop were now filling up. The New World was in the front, in accordance with Bruce's personal tastes, and France and Italy were at the back. Spain was only represented in a very small way – again based on Bruce's belief that Rioja was virtually undrinkable ("I wouldn't even gargle with the stuff," he was fond of saying; a rather witty remark, he felt) and there was a similarly small South African section. This was based on Bruce's dislike of the tactics of South African rugby, he being of the view that South African supporters had poisoned the All Blacks on more than one occasion when they were due to play the Springboks. "Entire rugby teams don't all get diarrhoea on the eve of a match by accident," he observed. And had the Scottish team been similarly poisoned? Bruce laughed at the question. "Who would bother?" he asked, bitterly.

The Petrus was not displayed. It was in the back room, under a table, three unopened cases with the keys of St Peter stencilled on the side. Bruce looked at them and felt a pang of doubt and regret. If the wine was not what it purported to be, then he would not be able to try to sell it. The last thing he could afford to do at the beginning of his new career was to get mixed up in that sort of scandal; that would obviously be the kiss of death. But how could he confirm these uneasy suspicions? That was far from clear.

Towards mid-afternoon, when he had almost finished stacking the shelves, Bruce decided to telephone George. He would have to arrange a meeting to sort out the financial arrangements so that he could pay the invoice of the Leith wholesaler – slightly over eight thousand pounds – which had to be settled within fourteen days.

George initially did not answer his telephone, but eventually he did, and agreed to come to the shop after work and meet Bruce there.

"I'd like to bring somebody," he said. "Somebody I'd like you to meet."

"Who?" asked Bruce.

"A friend," George replied opaquely. "A girlfriend, actually."

Bruce chuckled. "George! Got yourself fixed up at last? A real stunner, no doubt!" Which is exactly what he thought she would not be. He could just imagine the sort of girl George would end up with. She would be the absolute bottom of the heap; bargain-basement material. Sensible shoes. Markedly overweight. Dull as ditchwater. And probably from Crieff into the bargain! That girl he used to see – what was her name? – Sharon somebody or other, who lived with her parents in one of those little bungalows off the Comrie Road; that sort of girl. Poor George! Bruce was uncharitable about his home town. There was nothing wrong with Crieff, of course, but that was not the way he saw it. He had escaped to Edinburgh and he entertained the idea that one day he might even escape from Edinburgh to a wider world beyond that. New York? Sydney? Perhaps even Paris? Any of these was possible, he thought, if one has talent which, he told himself, he had. But poor old George! It was back to Crieff for him.

77. *Bruce Gets What He Deserves*

George and Sharon arrived at Bruce's new shop in St Stephen Street shortly before six. They were slightly late, which irritated Bruce, and indeed caused him more than passing concern. But at last there they were, standing outside the door, peering in through the glass panel. And it was that girl with him, Bruce observed. He had been right. That girl from Crieff, Sharon McClung, had finally got her talons into George. He smiled to himself as he went to open the door to his friend. We all get what we deserve in this life, he thought.

Now that was tempting the intervention of Nemesis! For Bruce, of all people, to invoke the principle of desert was asking for any lurking Greek goddess, underemployed, perhaps, because of the caution of others, to strike in a demonstrable and convincing way. And indeed it was Bruce's bad luck that Nemesis had been stalking around that part of Edinburgh at precisely that time, hoping to detect members of the Scottish Parliament managing their expenses accounts in a way which might be expected to attract her attention. She had failed to find anything but good behaviour, though, and so she was receptive to any reckless talk by the unworthy. And there it came in the form of Bruce's thoughts from St Stephen Street. Swiftly she turned the corner and poked her comely head into the basement premises into which a slightly fleshy couple had been admitted by the occupant. Nemesis took one look at Bruce and knew in an instant that here was one who had been in the long tutelage of her fellow myth, Narcissus. She rubbed her incorporeal hands with glee.

"George!" enthused Bruce. "Welcome to the shop!" He turned to Sharon. "And you Sharon! It's amazing to see you after how long? Yonks and yonks! And you're looking great, too!"

And he thought: look at her hair! Poor girl. And that haggis-shaped figure. Imagine being married to her. Mind you, he thought, poor George looks like a mealie-pudding himself, so perhaps it's a good match.

He moved forward and gave Sharon a peck on the cheek. Poor girl. How she had longed for him to do that all those years ago when she had sat there in the chemistry class at Morrison's Academy and stared at him in utter longing (along with nine other girls – all the girls, in fact, except one, and Bruce knew the reason why she was cool towards him. Oh yes, he did. With her short hair and her lack of interest in him. It stuck out a mile).

He shook hands with George. "So you and Sharon are an item! You kept that pretty secret!"

George smiled proudly. "Actually, Bruce, you're going to be one of the first to know. Sharon and I are getting engaged." He looked fondly in Sharon's direction and gave her hand an

254 Bruce Gets What He Deserves

affectionate squeeze. "We decided yesterday, didn't we, Shaz?"

Shaz! thought Bruce. Shaz! And what would she call him? You couldn't do much with George's name.

"But that's really great!" Bruce said. "Engaged. And . . ."

"And we're going to get married in March," George went on. "In Crieff."

"In Crieff!" said Bruce. "That's great. You'll be able to have all the old crowd there."

"With a reception at the Hydro," said George.

"A good choice," said Bruce, and thought: I suppose I'll have to go. He is my business partner, after all, and I'll be expected to be there.

He turned to Sharon. "Where are you living these days, Sharon?"

Sharon who had been looking at George, now turned to Bruce. She looked him up and down in a way which he thought was a bit forward on her part. Who was she to look at him in that way, as if passing silent comment on his appearance?

"Crieff," she said. "I've been working in Perth, but I've been staying with my folks. They're getting on a bit these days."

There was something in her tone which discomforted Bruce. It was as if she was challenging him in some way – challenging him to say that there was something wrong with continuing to live in Crieff.

"And what do you do in Perth?" he asked. "I'm a bit out of touch. You went off to uni in Dundee, didn't you?"

Sharon nodded, fixing Bruce with a stare which suggested that again she was challenging him to say something disparaging about Dundee.

"I did law," she said. "Now I'm a lawyer. I'm working for one of the Perth firms. I do a lot of court work."

"Sharon goes to court virtually every day," George said proudly. "The sheriff said the other day that she had argued a case very well. He said that in court."

"He's a very nice man," said Sharon. "He always listens very carefully to what you have to say."

"Great," said Bruce. He looked at George. "Now, I must show you the ropes round here. I've spent the day putting in stock. See. It took me hours. And see that section over there, Sharon, Wine for Her. See it?"

Sharon glanced at the four shelves pointed out by Bruce. Then she turned round and glared at him. "Why have you put Wine for Her?" she asked. "What's that supposed to mean?"

"It means that these are wines that women are more likely to enjoy," said Bruce.

Sharon glanced quickly at George, who shifted slightly on his feet. Then she turned back to face Bruce. "And why do you think women would want different wines from men? Have they got different taste buds?"

Bruce met her stare. He was not going to have this haggis talking to him like that. And he knew what sort of wine she would like: Blue Nun! Perhaps he would give her a bottle of it as an engagement present.

"Yes," he said. "Women like sweeter wine. And they like wine bottles with more feminine labels. Everybody knows that." He paused. This was a waste of time talking to Sharon. He needed to talk to George about business. "Anyway, George, we have to talk about this place. I've spent a bit of money on the stock, so that if we could talk about that side of things for a mo . . ."

Sharon said: "George has changed his mind, Bruce. Sorry. Now that we're getting married. We're going to buy a house in Stirling. We'll need the money for that. Sorry, Bruce."

Bruce said nothing for a moment. At the door, the faintest stirring of air, a slight shift of light, was all there was to indicate a triumphant Nemesis returning in satisfaction to the street outside.

78. Old Business

"You gave me your word," said Bruce, chiselling out the sentence. "You gave me your word, George. You told me that you would come in on this business with me. It was in the Cumberland Bar."

The words the Cumberland Bar were uttered with all the solemnity with which one might invoke the name of a place in which commercial promises are scrupulously observed – the words *the floor at Lloyds*, for example, might be spoken in the same tone. But on this occasion, even the mention of the locus of the conversation failed to have the desired-for effect.

"Actually, Bruce," said George, "actually, I didn't promise. I said that I was interested, but we didn't make any firm arrangements, did we? We agreed that we would draw up a partnership agreement, but you never showed that to me and I never signed it. We were talking about the prospect of going into business, not the actual mechanics. We didn't do a proper deal, you know."

"There's no proper deal," chipped in Sharon. "No contract. No deal."

Bruce turned round and glared at her. "Do you mind keeping out of things that don't concern you? This is between me and my friend, George. So please don't interfere."

"Oh!" exclaimed Sharon. "So what my fiancé does is no business of mine? Is that what you're saying? Well, I've got news for you: it's very much my business!"

Bruce bit his lip. He looked at George, but George was looking down at the floor, staring at his shoes. It was typical. A woman came in and tried to take over. And now this ghastly girl had taken control of this useless man and was twisting him around her pudgy little finger.

Bruce looked at her. "So you're calling the shots now," he said. "Little Sharon McClung has at last got hold of a man and is calling the shots big time! Pleased with yourself, Sharon? Pity you couldn't do any better."

George looked up from his shoes. "What do you mean by that, Bruce?" he asked. His voice was strained and his eyes were misty, as if he was about to cry.

Bruce sighed. "No criticism of you, George," he said. "It's just that you're letting Sharon push you around a bit, aren't you?"

"But you said: 'It's a pity you couldn't do any better,'" George insisted. "What did you mean by that, Bruce? What did you mean?"

"Yes," said Sharon. "What exactly did you mean by that, Bruce? Did you mean that George isn't much of a catch? Well, if you did, I can tell you what I think of that. I think that he's ten times, twenty times nicer than you. Nobody – nobody in her right mind – would look at you, you know. You do know that, don't you?"

Bruce sneered. "Don't make me laugh," he said. "Just don't make me laugh. You were happy enough to look at me back then in Crieff. Oh yes, don't think that I didn't notice you sitting there staring at me, along with all the other girls, mentally undressing me. I noticed those things, you know."

Sharon shrieked with indignation. "What? What did you say? Mentally undressing you? Are you mad?"

"Listen," said George mildly. "I don't think there's much point in talking like this . . ."

"Yes, there is," snapped Sharon. "I'm not going to stand here and listen to this self-satisfied creep saying things like that. I've got some more news for you, Bruce. The girls back in Crieff hated you, you know. They hated you. They really did. You should have heard the sort of things they said about you! You would have died of embarrassment if you had heard half of them. Did you know that there was something about you written on the wall of the girls' toilets for two years? Two years. And every time the cleaners rubbed it out, somebody wrote it back, and in the end they just left it there. And do you know what it was? You would hate what it said, I promise you. You'd just hate it. But I can't tell you – I'm too embarrassed."

"Was it written with one of those marker pens?" asked George. "Those can be quite difficult to rub off."

Both Bruce and Sharon looked at him. Sharon did not answer.

"You're a liar," said Bruce. "I would have heard about it. I never heard anything."

Sharon arched an eyebrow in amazement. "Do you think that anybody would actually tell you something like that?"

"It depends what it was," cut in George. "And anyway, I don't think that it's very fair not to tell him, Shaz. You've got him all upset now. You should tell him."

"No, Georgie," said Sharon. "I'm not going to tell him."

"Would you tell me then?" asked George.

Sharon thought for a moment. Then she leant over and cupped a hand around George's left ear and whispered to him. George's eyes widened. Then he let out a laugh. "Really?" he asked. "Did it really?"

Sharon nodded with satisfaction. "Yes, it did. Funny, isn't it?"

"Do you think it's true?" asked George.

Sharon shrugged. "Who knows?" She paused. "So that's it, Bruce. That's what we thought of you."

Bruce looked at George. "You're marrying this person?" he asked quietly. "You're actually going to go ahead and marry this person? This . . . this *haggis*?"

It was as if George had been given an electric shock. Pulling himself up to his full height – and he was considerably shorter than Bruce, and Sharon – he poked a finger in the direction of his erstwhile friend. "You are not to call my fiancée a haggis," he said. "Don't ever let me hear you call her a haggis."

And with that, he turned to Sharon, took her arm, and nodded in the direction of the door.

"Goodbye, Bruce," he said. "I'm sorry that this has happened. But you've only got yourself to blame. Come, Shaz. We must go."

Sharon gave Bruce a look of triumph. "Would you really like to know what was written on the wall? Would you?" She paused. She had spotted a piece of paper and a pencil on the counter and she went over to this and scribbled a few words. Then she folded the paper, passed it to him, and quickly rejoined George at the door.

After they had gone, Bruce sat down. He held the piece of paper in his hands, fingering it for a moment before he opened it and read what she had written. He crumpled up the paper and threw it across the room.

79. *At the Gallery*

Matthew came back from Big Lou's eager to tell Pat about what had happened. "Cyril bit somebody," he said, grinning. "There's a woman who lives in Scotland Street. One of your neighbours, I believe. She's got a little boy who looks as if he's seen a ghost most of the time. He was patting Cyril and Cyril was lapping it up and then this hatchet-faced woman said something to Cyril that he didn't like, and he bit her in the ankle! Not a serious bite. A nip really. I don't think he even broke the skin. But she howled and tried to kick him but Cyril backed off. It was the funniest sight. And we had to keep a straight face through all this. And Angus Lordie had to say how sorry he was and gave Cyril a wallop with a rolled-up copy of the *Scotsman*. Poor Cyril."

"I know her," said Pat. "Domenica can't stand her. She says that she pushes that little boy an awful lot. She makes him learn the saxophone and Italian. Domenica says that he's going to rebel the first chance he gets."

"Mothers can be like that," said Matthew. "They create a lot of problems for their sons. Anyway, it was a very amusing incident."

They returned to the business of the gallery. An auction catalogue had arrived with the morning's post and Pat had already perused it, noting down the lots in which she thought Matthew might have an interest. There were early 20th-century studies of Kirkcudbright Harbour which she thought he might go for, and Matthew was busy looking at photographs of these, wondering about the price at which he would be able to sell them on if he were to bid for them, when the door opened and a woman came into the gallery. For a moment he did not recognise her, but then he realised who she was. This was Janis, his father's new girlfriend, the florist with whom he and his father had enjoyed a somewhat less than satisfactory evening in the New Club. He rose to his feet and greeted her. He tried to sound warm, but it was difficult.

"So this is your gallery," said Janis, looking around her.

Matthew nodded. He wondered about her tone. Had she sounded a little bit dismissive? He was determined that he would not be condescended to by this woman, whatever her relationship with his misguided father was.

"Yes," he said, his tone becoming noticeably colder. "This is where I work."

"I hope you don't mind my dropping in like this," said Janis.

Matthew shrugged. "You're very welcome," he said, adding: "I might drop into your flower shop some time."

"Oh, please do," said Janis. "Any time at all." She cast an eye around her. "Not that we have much to interest you up there. Unless you're particularly keen on flowers."

"I don't mind flowers," he said. "In their place." It was an enigmatic remark, capable of interpretation at many different levels. In one reading, it suggested that one should not concern oneself too much with flowers; that there were better things to think and talk about. In another sense, it could be taken to mean that flowers should remain where they grew, and should not be picked. And in another sense altogether, it could be taken as implying that people who dealt in flowers should not take up with the fathers of those who dealt in pictures, especially when the father was considerably older than the florist.

"Well, I'm not sure," said Janis evenly. "Flowers bring a lot of pleasure to people – ordinary people."

This was itself an enigmatic observation. At one level, it might have been self-deprecatory: working with flowers made no claims to being anything special, unlike dealing in art, which gave pleasure to a slightly grander set of people. That was one interpretation. Another was this: at least people who sell flowers to people who buy flowers have no pretensions; they get pleasure from flowers and that is justification enough.

Whichever meaning Janis had in mind, she did not pursue it. Smiling politely at Pat, whom Matthew had not bothered to introduce to her, she made her way over to the far side of the room and began to peer closely at a painting of a girl picking flowers in a field.

"My father's girlfriend," whispered Matthew to Pat. "The florist. Note how she goes straight for the picture of flowers. Typical."

"I don't know," said Pat. "She seems nice enough to me. And that's a nice enough painting."

"You don't understand," hissed Matthew. "Can't you see the pound signs in her eyes? Can't you see them?"

"No," said Pat.

Matthew cast his eyes upwards in an expression of frustration, but said nothing, and returned to his catalogue. After a few minutes, Janis came over to his desk.

"You've got some nice paintings," she said. "That Crosbie over there is very pretty."

Matthew glanced at the painting in question. "Somebody may like it," he said grudgingly. "You never know."

"I thought that I might buy it," said Janis. "That is, if you'll sell it to me."

"You're welcome to it," said Matthew. "It's for sale."

"Then I'll take it," said Janis, adding: "It's a present for your father. I'm sure that he'll appreciate it."

Matthew hesitated. The purchase of the painting as a gift for his father was a sign of intimacy between the two of them. One did not purchase paintings for those with whom one had a casual relationship.

"He's not a great one for paintings," muttered Matthew. "Are you sure?"

Janis nodded. "I'm very sure, Matthew. I've got to know him quite well, you know."

Matthew said nothing. He rose from his desk and walked over to the place where the painting was hanging. Lifting it off its hook, he brought it back to Janis. He looked at the scene which Crosbie had captured so swiftly – a harbour-side scene with several fisherman sitting on upturned fish-boxes. It was a deft painting, a confident painting, of a subject that could so easily have appeared posed and trite. But that had been avoided.

Janis looked at the painting and smiled. "He'll like that, you know."

"I hope so," said Matthew.

Janis hesitated. "Would you mind if I did something?" she asked. "Would you mind if I told him that you chose it for him?"

It was Pat who answered the question. "You'd be very pleased with that, Matthew? Wouldn't you? Yes, he would."

80. Dogs and Cuban History

Two days later, Pat knocked on Domenica's door. Domenica had never appeared to be anything but pleased to see her younger neighbour, and today was no exception. Of course it was convenient; of course Pat must come in and have coffee.

Pat realised, of course, that Domenica liked conversation, but she had always felt that their encounters had been somewhat one-sided, with Domenica doing most of the talking. And that was because Domenica had just done so much more than she had;

more happened in sixty years than in twenty, as a general rule, although naturally there were exceptions. Some people did very little in their lives, and such habits of inaction could last for generations. She had read in a newspaper somewhere of the work of Professor Sykes, who had used the techniques of modern genetics to look at the roots of people who bore the surname Sykes. People called Sykes, he discovered, tended to come from a small village in England, and there were still people of that name there – families that in eight hundred years had moved no more than a few hundred yards. That was stability on a thoroughly heroic scale.

On this visit, Pat had rather more to say than usual, as the previous two days had been full of incident. There had been the reported incident of Cyril's biting of Irene; there had been the visit of Janis to the gallery and the resulting row with Matthew. And finally there had been the outing with Peter to the nudist picnic in the Moray Place Gardens, an occasion which she needed to talk about.

They sat in Domenica's study, Domenica in the chair that she liked to occupy at the side of her desk, flanked by a pile of books, Pat in the chair normally reserved for visitors underneath Domenica's framed photograph of her father.

Domenica had not heard from Angus Lordie of Cyril's disgrace, and was delighted with the tale.

"I wouldn't normally wish a dog-bite on anybody," she said. "However, in this case there is an element of poetic justice. I myself have wished to bite that woman for some time, and I can thoroughly sympathise with Cyril. I wonder whether she's learned anything from the experience. I doubt it."

"Matthew says that she provoked him," said Pat. "She insulted him in some way."

"Dogs are sensitive to insult," said Domenica. "And, you know, it's an interesting thing – dogs from highly sensitive cultures are more prickly about how they're treated. There's been a very interesting piece of research on that. Somebody from Stanford got it into his head that the behaviour of dogs reflected the national characteristics of the human culture in which the dogs lived. I think that the idea came to him when he visited New York and found that the dogs he saw were all highly-strung and neurotic – just like their owners. So that set him off thinking that these differences might be manifested at a national level too. A very interesting bit of research, but highly contentious, of course; almost eccentric."

Pat was intrigued. "And what did he find out?"

Domenica smiled. "He found out what he had set out to find out," she said. "Which always makes research a bit suspect. You have to keep an open mind, although you can have a hypothesis, of course. He looked at dogs in Spanish-speaking cultures – Colombian dogs, I think – and then he looked at Swedish, Australian and Japanese dogs."

"And?"

"Well," continued Domenica, "Swedish dogs showed themselves to be quieter and more cautious. Their behaviour, in fact, showed signs of depression. They sat around rather mournfully and did not bark to the same extent as other dogs. The Colombian dogs were very excitable. If you subjected them to stress, they made a terrible fuss. They were always dancing about and chasing things."

"And the Australian dogs?"

"They behaved in a fairly boisterous way, too," said Domenica, "although not as markedly as the Colombian dogs. They seemed less concerned about their appearance – they were much scruffier – and they were very outgoing. They were also very good at chasing balls."

"The Japanese dogs" she continued, "were very interesting – from the animal behaviour point of view. They were very sensitive. Very concerned with face."

Pat laughed. "All rather like their owners?"

"You could say so. And I suppose it shouldn't surprise us. Animals with whom we live in close proximity are bound to throw our behaviour back at us, aren't they? I'm not sure if we should be surprised by such findings."

"No," said Pat. "But it seems a little bit far-fetched."

Domenica looked thoughtful. "I had occasion to reflect on this myself," she said. "Last year, when I was in Havana. I recalled that bit of Stanford research while I was there. And I must say I thought that he had a point. But I'm not sure if you want to sit there and hear all this from me. You have that picnic to tell me about."

Pat wanted to hear about Havana. There would be time enough for Moray Place later on.

Encouraged to continue, Domenica picked up one of the books from the pile, glanced at it thoughtfully, and replaced it. "I wanted to go to Havana," she said, "before two things happened. The first of these is before the place fell down altogether. Do you know that over one hundred of their lovely old buildings collapse every year? And the second is before the Americans got their hands on it. I am not one of those people who are uncharitable about the Americans, but the truth of the matter is that the United States has been breathing down Cuba's neck since the early nineteenth century and continues to do so. I cannot believe – I just cannot believe – that if the average person in the United States knew how that lovely island has been treated over the years they would feel anything but shame. Pure shame. Indeed, everybody has bullied Cuba. The Spanish were simply murderous. Then they looted the place. We had a go at it. Then the Americans tried to buy it. They occupied it. They treated it as a private playground. Organised crime ran the place. They built big hotels. They had their meetings there. And then Castro and his crew appeared and we all know what happened then. Thousands and thousands imprisoned and held under the thumb. Poor Cubans. It's ever thus."

Pat wondered what this had to do with dogs, and Domenica sensed her puzzlement.

"You're obviously wondering where dogs come into this," she said.

"A bit," said Pat.

"Dogs have everything to do with this," said Domenica. "Cuban dogs are rather special, you see."

81. Havana

"I arrived in Havana at night," said Domenica. "That's a good time to arrive anywhere, because you don't see very much and then you wake up in the morning and open your shutters to an entirely new world. That's how I felt. There was a balcony to my room and this looked out over the rooftops to the most gorgeous tower I have ever seen. A tower on top of an ornate palace of some sort, with small arches and windows painted in that light blue they go in for in Cuba – almost a turquoise. And when I looked down and along the street to the front of my building, I saw nothing but three-or four-storey buildings with decorated stucco facades, all in faded white or yellow or pink. Ironwork balconies. I have never seen such beauty in a city. Never. Not even in Italy. Not even in places like Siena or Vienna. It's a wonderful, very feminine architecture.

"But the problem with the beauty of Havana is that it's so decrepit. So many of those wonderful buildings are on their last legs. The people can't afford to fix them. They have no money. When you don't even have enough money for food or soap or any of those things, then you won't have enough money for your buildings, will you?

"And so you walk past these buildings in which whole floors, or rooms within floors, have collapsed. And yet people who lead their lives in the rooms next to those that have simply fallen to the ground continue to live where they are. So you will see gaps in buildings, like missing teeth, and right beyond the gap will be a lighted window which shows that others are hanging on in the midst of the falling masonry.

"I had a friend who lived in one of those buildings. I had met her at an anthropological meeting in Jamaica a few years earlier, and we had kept in touch. They are desperate for friends, the Cubans. They are loveable, charming people and they want to belong to the world like the rest of us. And so they write when they can afford the stamp.

"She asked me to her flat, which was on the edge of the old city. The staircase which took you up to the top floor, where she lived, was distinctly suspect and there were large holes in it. You had to watch where you put your feet. And her flat had three rooms. A kitchen, and two other rooms. She lived in one with her young son, and her husband, from whom she was divorced, lived in the other. Yes, she was divorced from him on the grounds of his adultery and cruelty, and yet they were trapped together because you just can't move in that society unless you go through a very complicated and expensive system of exchanging flats. They couldn't afford this. So they still had to live under the same roof and share the kitchen and the bathroom, such as it was. And in order to get to his room, he had to go through hers, at any time of the night and day. Can you imagine it?

"And yet, like so many other Cubans, she had a dog, a little dog called Basilio. She wanted her little boy to have a dog, and so they had one. Every Cuban gets a ration of food, and you can't get anything else unless you have a lot of money to spend, which she didn't. So Basilio had to be fed out of the wretched, barely adequate food ration that she had. In other words, she gave him her own food.

"And when you went out in the streets or the plaza, you saw these bands of little dogs walking around with such good spirit. They were not really strays – they all had owners – and all of them were loved by somebody. In other cities, you would expect to see collarless dogs persecuted. Rounded up. Taken to pounds. And then executed by lethal injection. These dogs just wandered about perfectly happily.

"And in a way I thought of it as a metaphor for the society. These cheerful small dogs, these *perritos*, all getting by in the face of terrible material privation. And putting up with it in such good spirit, just as the people about them seem to do. All of them, dogs and people, smiling in the face of constant, grinding poverty.

"Which may be part of the problem, of course. Communism has failed miserably in Cuba, just as it seems to have failed elsewhere. It just does not seem to have been able to provide for the material needs of people. It has only survived through the denial of freedom – there are many charges one can levy against it. And if the people weren't so nice about it, then they would have risen in anger and demanded their freedom, demanded some more effective response to material needs, just as they did in Eastern Europe. But they haven't. They've continued to dance and play music and keep their sense of humour. It's quite remarkable, and really rather sad – sad to think that there must have been many people who genuinely wanted to create a decent society, people who believed they were doing the right thing, and then they found that everything went so wrong, the whole thing involved lies and distortion and repression, and had become so utterly shabby. And that happened. Even the signs that claim victory are falling down. And if people are given half a chance, they flee, out of sheer desperation, braving no matter what dangers.

"And waiting in the wings are those who are rubbing their hands and saying that it's only a question of time before the whole place is covered in fast-food restaurants, the ports crowded with the cruise ships full of spoiled tourists, the prostitutes and the pimps triumphant, and that charming, beautiful culture crushed in the deluge.

"Globalisation, my dear. And in this way, is our wide and entrancing world, our vivid world of songs and music and cultural difference, brought to an end by the crude, the false, the mindless, the imposed."

Domenica became silent. She was looking down at the floor now. Pat had not even begun to tell her what she wanted to tell her, but could not now, after a story of such sadness. So she finished her coffee in silence and asked Domenica to excuse her until another moment, another day. Domenica understood.

82. *A Great Sense of Purity*

Pat reflected, in private, over what had happened. Peter had left a note that afternoon, pushed through the letter-box at the flat, with her name written on the outside of the folded paper. That picnic – remember? – it's on! I'll come and collect you at five. If you can't make it, give me a call at this number.

She had retired to her room – there was no sign of Bruce – and re-read the note. When he had issued the invitation she had certainly not accepted it there and then. After she had overcome her initial surprise – it was not every day that one was invited to a nudist picnic, and in Moray Place Gardens too – she had said that she would think about it. That was all. And she had thought about it, and although she might have decided to go, she had not yet told him that.

She looked out of the window. It was a warm enough day – much warmer than one would expect for early September – and this must have encouraged the nudists to go ahead with their picnic. But the weather in Edinburgh was notoriously change-able and sunlight could within minutes become deep gloom, empty skies become heavy with rain, snow give way to warm breezes. There was simply no telling.

By five that afternoon, when the bell rang, she was in a state of renewed indecision, although, if anything, she was now marginally more inclined to decline the invitation. She would tell Peter that she did not feel ready to go to a nudist picnic just yet. Though when would one be ready for such an event? How did one prepare oneself? Perhaps nudists had a coming-out process in which they gradually came to terms with the fact that they felt more comfortable without any clothes. Or it could be a road to Damascus conversion, when the restric-tiveness of clothes suddenly came home to one with blinding clarity.

She went to the door and was just about to open it when the thought occurred to her: would Peter be clad or unclad on the doorstep? It was an absurd thought, and she dismissed it imme-diately. And when she opened the door, there he was, dressed quite normally in a tee-shirt and jeans. But he was carrying a small bag with him, and that, she assumed, would be for the abandoned clothes.

He greeted her quite normally, as if he had come to collect her for the cinema or a restaurant rather than a nudist picnic.

"We should be getting along there soon," he said, looking at his watch. "Things begin quite promptly."

And what, she wondered, were these things?

"I'm not quite . . ." she began. But he did not seem to have heard her. He asked her instead whether she had a bag which she could bring. "Or you can share mine," he said, pointing to his bag. "There's enough room in there for both of us."

"But . . ."

"No that's fine. This bag is big enough. You don't have to bring anything else. That's fine."

"But I was . . ."

He tapped his watch. "Really, we must hurry. It'll take us fifteen minutes to get there and I really don't want to be late."

She took the path of least resistance and left with him. After all, it was only a nudist picnic and everybody knew that nudists were harmless enough. So they walked back along Cumberland Street, Peter swinging the bag as he went, and Pat largely silent beside him.

"You're quiet," he said as they crossed Dundas Street. "You aren't nervous, are you?"

She hesitated. "A bit, I suppose. I've never . . ."

He smiled and playfully put his arm about her shoulder. It was only there for a moment, and then he withdrew it. "There's nothing to it. It's very easy, you know. You won't even notice it after a couple of minutes."

"Did it take you long to get used to it?" she asked.

"I was born to it," he said. "My parents were prominent nudists. Over in Helensburgh. We used to go on naturist holidays in Denmark each year. We had lots of Danish friends. I was brought up to accept it. I don't even think about it now."

"And how did you get involved with these people in Moray Place?" Pat asked.

"Through my parents," Peter explained. "When I came to university in Edinburgh, friends of my parents got in touch and asked whether I would like to come to a dinner party. The dinner party was in Moray Place and I discovered that it was a nudist affair. These people had a very nice drawing-room flat with views over the Dean Valley. It was a pretty stylish affair – a typical Edinburgh dinner party, except for the fact that nobody had any clothes on."

Pat tried to imagine it, but found it difficult. "But what did you talk about?" she asked.

"The same things that they talk about at any Edinburgh dinner party," said Peter. "House prices. Schools. So it was pretty boring for me, apart from one or two people of my own age who had been invited as well. They put us all together at one end of the table. The other end was full of lawyers and people like that."

Pat was silent. "And then?"

Peter shrugged. "After dinner we went through to the drawing room for coffee," he said. "We played charades for a while, and then we put on our clothes and went home. Pretty dull stuff."

Pat thought for a moment. Charades: did they act out the story of Adam and Eve, or was that done so often at nudist dinner parties that nobody did it any more? *Three words. From a book. First word . . .* The whole idea seemed so completely absurd, and yet there must be a reason why people did it. She looked at Peter. What went on in his head when he went to these things? Did he feel any different without his clothes on?

"Why do you do it?" she asked. "Does it do something for you?"

Peter laughed. "It means nothing in that sense, if that's what you're asking. No, it gives you a feeling of complete natural-ness. All falseness, all pretence stripped away. You feel as if a great burden of restriction and secrecy are taken off your shoul-ders. It's . . . Well, it's completely liberating. And pure. You feel utterly pure." He paused. "You do believe me, don't you, Pat? I really mean it. You'll find out for yourself when you try it. I promise you."

83. In Moray Place Gardens

When they arrived in Moray Place there was no sign, absolutely no sign, that a nudist picnic was about to take place. The great sweep of architecture, with its handsome facade and its high windows, was as dignified and discreet as ever. Those who were going about their business, walking on the pavement, parking their cars, or going in and out of their houses, were entirely clad.

"It's not those gardens," said Peter, pointing at the rather dull gardens in the middle of the circle. "We go round the back. The gate is at the very top of Doune Terrace."

They walked round until they came to the point where Doune Terrace sloped off to the north. At the top of this road, a small gate, discreetly set in the iron railings, gave access to the gardens that stretched down the steep side of the hill to the Water of Leith below. It was a magnificent set of private gardens, reserved for those who held a key. But now no key was necessary, as the gate had been propped open and there was a bearded man standing just behind it.

Peter led the way, shaking hands with the man at the gate. The man laughed and pointed up at the sky. There, rolling in from the north, were the rain clouds which had been nowhere in sight when they had left Scotland Street.

"The weather looks bad," said Peter as he and Pat went into the gardens.

"Will they cancel it if there's rain?" asked Pat. There was a note of hope in her voice, but this was soon dashed by Peter's response.

"It'll go ahead," he said. "It's just that it will be a bit different, that's all."

At that moment the rain started, not pelting down, but falling with insistence, blotting out the view of the town to the north, running in rivulets down the sharply dipping paths of the gardens. Peter looked at Pat and smiled. "Here's your mac," he said, taking two black plastic raincoats out of his bag and handing one to her.

Pat thanked him and began to put it on.

"Not yet," he said, wagging an admonitory finger. "You have to take your clothes off first. There'll be a couple of changing tents down there on the grass. Wait till then."

Two small white tents now came into view behind a hedge. And there, on the other side of the hedge, shielded from view until the barrier of the hedge was actually negotiated, was a group of about twenty people, all clad in voluminous mackintoshes. The mackintoshes were opaque, with the result that the only evidence that they were unclad underneath were the bare ankles sticking out below the lower skirts of the raincoats. The heads of the nudists were bare, though, and their hair was plastered to their skulls. They looked very wet and very uncomfortable.

"Welcome to the picnic," said a tall man. "The ladies' changing tent is over there. The men are in that one."

Pat made her way to the tent and drew aside the flap. Inside, a middle-aged woman was in the process of buttoning up the front of her mackintosh.

"This rain is such a pest," said the woman. "But we shall have our picnic come hell or high water."

Pat nodded. She slipped out of her clothes and donned her mackintosh. She did not feel at all exposed in this new garb; and indeed she was not.

"You'll need a bag for those clothes of yours," said the woman helpfully. "Here's a Jenners bag for you."

The sight of the plastic bag, stamped with the familiar Jenners sign, was a reassurance to Pat in these unfamiliar and challenging circumstances. There was something about the name Jenners that provided the comfort one needed in dubious situations. An occasion on which you were asked to take off your clothes and put them in a Jenners bag was inherently less threatening than an occasion in which one was asked to put them in any other bag.

Pat thanked the woman and stuffed her clothing into the bag. Then, leaving the bag in the tent, alongside a number of other bags (mostly from Jenners), she went out into the rain. On the grass ahead of her, in a cluster around a small portable table, a group of respectably-covered, mackintosh-clad picnickers were sipping on glasses of fruit punch. Pat was offered a glass and joined the group.

"Your first time at one of our little gatherings?" asked a man on Pat's left.

She looked at him. He was wearing a large brown raincoat,

the collar of which was turned up around his neck. He had a small moustache which was now wet through. Little streams of water ran off the edges of the moustache and on to his cheeks.

"Yes," she replied. "I came here with a friend. I'm not really . . ."

The man cut her short. "We have such tremendous fun," he said. "Last month we went to Tantallon and had a picnic in the dunes. Unfortunately, there was a terrible biting wind and we all ended up wearing sou'westers, but we did our best. On most occasions we at least manage to go about bare-footed, even if that's about it. That's the way nudism is in Scotland, I suppose. We can't actually remove our clothes. But everybody is very understanding about that."

Pat was about to ask what the point was, but the man continued. "Are you interested in stamps?" he asked.

Pat shook her head. "Not really," she said.

"Pity," he said. "I find stamps absolutely fascinating. I have a very fine collection. Do you not collect anything?"

"Not really," said Pat.

"I used to collect birds' eggs when I was a boy," he went on. "But then that became rather a bad thing to do and I gave up. So many people were raiding nests that some species were becoming a bit threatened. So I moved on to playing-cards and then to share certificates. That's my current enthusiasm. Scriptology. I go for South American railway bonds – that sort of thing. They have beautiful designs. Quite beautiful."

Pat looked into her fruit punch. Drops of rain were falling into it, creating tiny circles. Underfoot, the grass was becoming sodden; and now, from the east, a wind had started to blow. She looked about her. Peter was nowhere to be seen. But that did not matter, because she did not want to see him any more. She felt nothing for him, no interest, no antipathy, nothing.

She turned to the man beside her. "I have to go home," she said impulsively. "Good-bye."

84. The Memory of Pigs

Dr Fairbairn was grateful to Irene for making him face up to the guilt that had been plaguing him for so many years. He had suppressed the memory of his professional breach, and had done so effectively. Or so he told himself. The problem was that he knew full well that repression of that sort merely allowed the uncomfortable memory to do its work at another level. And it was inevitable that this would become apparent at a later stage, creating tension between the external Dr Fairbairn, the one the world saw, and the internal Dr Fairbairn, the one hidden from the world by that blue linen jacket with its special crumple-resistant qualities.

On the day that Irene had forced him to admit to himself, and to her, that he had actually struck his celebrated patient, Wee Fraser, Dr Fairbairn returned to his flat in Sciennes in the late afternoon and prepared himself a round of tomato sandwiches and a pot of tea. The flat was empty when he went in as his wife worked long hours and tended not to come home until well after seven. For this reason, they usually dined late – sometimes not until after nine – and Dr Fairbairn found it necessary to have a snack to keep hunger at bay.

Dr Fairbairn did the cooking. He had done this throughout their marriage, not only to show that he was a "new man", but also because he found cooking a relaxing and creative activity. Indeed, as he stood above his saucepan, adding cream to scallops or delicately re-inflating porcini mushrooms with a judicious measure of boiling water, all sorts of thoughts would go through his mind. This, he felt, was the time in which his unconscious could order the experiences of the day, before dreams took over that function slightly later on. This theory, that one should think through things before the dreaming mind began to function, was one which he hoped to develop in a book. It would be called, he had decided, *Pre-Dream Dreaming*, and he anticipated that it would be every bit as successful as his well-known book on Wee Fraser. Of course there were other books to write, and these were jockeying for position in his already busy schedule. One of these was *Eat your Way to Mental Health*, a title which had come to him during one of his sessions at the stove. He remembered exactly how it had happened. He had been lightly sautéing garlic in olive oil when it occurred to him that our attitudes towards food were often affected by our view of what other people would think about our eating the food in question. He stopped, and stared at the garlic. He liked the taste of garlic, as did his wife. And yet people, even garlic enthusiasts, were so cautious, almost apologetic about its use. Who – other than the French, of course – would even contemplate putting a clove of garlic in the oven, its head neatly chopped off and a drop of oil dribbled very gently on to the top, and then a few minutes later taking it out and eating it? With nothing to accompany it?

And yet why should one not do that? The answer, of course, lay not in any culinary realm, but in a social one. Garlic smelled. People who ate garlic smelled. And nobody wants to smell.

Now, most people would leave it at that. Dr Fairbairn, however, felt that social inhibitions of that sort – the desire not to smell – were probably much more harmful and limiting than people generally thought they were. A person who did not worry about how he appeared to others, or what others thought of him, would enjoy far more resolution, more inner tranquillity, than one who did. And one way of encouraging this resolution would be to get people to eat what they wanted to eat. If self-expression could be encouraged at the table, then self-expression would follow in other parts of a person's life.

On this particular insight, Dr Fairbairn had sketched out an entire theory of how inhibitions and anxieties could be addressed both in the kitchen and at the table. It would be called *food therapy* and it would become immensely popular. Other books would be written on the subject. There would be courses. There would be lecture tours. And he and Estelle, his wife, could leave Sciennes – charming though it undoubtedly was – and go and live somewhere like Palm Beach. That was a very pleasant prospect, and indeed gave rise to a new idea, an autobiography, which perhaps could be called *From Motherwell to Palm Beach*.

But now, sitting in an armchair in his flat in Sciennes, his tomato sandwiches on a plate before him, Dr Fairbairn thought of what lay ahead. Irene was right; he would have to seek out Wee Fraser and apologise to him for what he had done all those years ago. But first he would have to relive, in as vivid a way as possible, the precise sequence of events that had led him to raise his arm.

He had been in his room with Wee Fraser. He had given the boy a small wooden farm set, consisting of a couple of pigs, a tiny tractor, a stylised farmer and his wife, and some blocks out of which to make walls and pens. There was enough there to allow the child to portray a wide range of internal dynamics. But Wee Fraser had insisted on laying the pigs on the ground upside down, with their tiny porcine legs pointing upwards.

"No, Fraser," Dr Fairbairn had said. "Piggies go like this." And he had placed the pigs the right way up.

"Dinnae," said Wee Fraser, turning the pigs upside down again.

Dr Fairbairn righted the pigs, and at that Wee Fraser turned his head and bit him hard. Dr Fairbairn then smacked Wee Fraser.

That is what had to be redressed. He stood up. He would do it now. Right now. He would go to Burdiehouse and find Wee Fraser. He reached for his blue linen jacket.

85. Encounter, Catharsis, Flight

Dr Fairbairn left the flat in Sciennes and made his way to the nearby bus-stop on Causewayside. His mood was buoyant; now that he had made the decision to go, he was keen to be there as soon as possible. He was sure that he would find Wee Fraser. He had extracted the address from his original records and a quick search of the telephone directory had revealed that there was still a family living there by the name of Maclean – Wee Fraser's surname. If the bus did not take its time in coming, then he thought that he could be knocking on the front door of Wee Fraser's house just before six, which would be a good time to catch them in, as that was when ordinary people (as both he and Irene called them) ate their tea.

A bus arrived and Dr Fairbairn boarded it. Because of the time of day it was fairly full, and Dr Fairbairn had to move down to the back in order to find a seat. And even then it was a small seat, as he was obliged to perch beside a large woman in a floral dress. The woman looked at him with distaste, as if he had no right to sit down on space which she could so easily have flowed into. Dr Fairbairn caught her hostile glance and returned it. Schizoid, he thought.

He looked at the other passengers. He did not travel by bus very often – in fact he never went anywhere by bus – and it was interesting for him to look at the faces of the people and speculate on their psychological problems. On the bench on the other side of the narrow aisle were a young man and young woman, dressed in nondescript clothes. The man wore jeans, the knees of which had become distressed and ripped. Then he had a tee-shirt on which was written the word NO. The young woman had very similar garb, although her tee-shirt had a more complicated message. It said: I'M NOT DRUNK, IT'S JUST THE WAY I'M STANDING.

Dr Fairbairn stared at the tee-shirts and then at the faces of the couple. They were, he imagined, about nineteen or twenty, and reasonably composed in their appearance and manner. Why then did they wear tee-shirts with messages? Was it a question of fashion – others broadcast messages on their clothing and therefore they felt they had to do it too? That was a simple, but powerful explanation. The desire to conform in clothing was almost universal. Jeans were a statement that one was just like everybody else. They were the modern uniform, achieving a flat monotony of look that would have warmed the heart of Mao at his height of enthusiasm for the destruction of sartorial salience.

But messages, he thought, were different. In having something written on one's clothing – written on the outside, be it noted – one was effectively making oneself into a walking billboard. This meant that one's clothing could make both a passive and an active ideological statement. The red shirt with the head of Che Guevera said: *I sympathise with the struggle*. And if this message was not clear enough, one could add the words *la Lucha* underneath. If one was really radical, then an exclamation mark could be added to that. Thus people whose shirt said *la Lucha* were likely to be seen as far more credible activists than those timid souls whose shirts merely said *la Lucha*. And of course Spanish was mandatory for such messages. It didn't sound quite the same to have on one's shirt the word *küzdelem*, which is Hungarian for "struggle".

The whole point, though, of having writing on one's shirt was an exhibitionist one. To draw attention to oneself through clothing is exhibitionist, and of course, as Dr Fairbairn knew very well, exhibitionism was a substitute for real giving, real intimacy. The exhibitionist appears to be giving, but is actually not giving at all. He trumpets out the message *Look at me*, but he does that only to avoid having to engage in a real encounter, a real human exchange, with the other. The external is all that is on offer with the exhibitionist; the internal is hoarded, protected, Freudianter: retained. The last person you see when you are confronted with an exhibitionist is the real person inside. That person is not on display.

Dr Fairbairn glanced at the young man's shirt with its negative message. NO was perhaps not too bad a message to be proclaiming. At least it was modest. At least it was not like the obscene messages that some people wore on their clothing. Such people were shameless exhibitionists, but they were also polluters of our common space.

He shifted in his seat, which gave him a better view of the seats at the back of the bus. It was an average group of people: a young man in a suit (a bank-teller, perhaps, thought Dr Fairbairn), a person with a full shopping bag and a look of resignation about her (a woman, perhaps, he thought), an elderly man who had fallen asleep. And then, very near the back, sitting alongside his mother, whom Dr Fairbairn recognised after all these years . . . Wee Fraser himself.

Dr Fairbairn caught his breath. He had prepared himself for a meeting with Wee Fraser, but had not prepared himself for a meeting on the bus. And now, faced with the reality of this 14-year-old boy, with his short hair and his aggressive lower lip, Dr Fairbairn was not at all sure what to do. Should he wait until they got off the bus, at which point he could himself alight, or should he go and speak to them now? Would it be awkward to say what he had to in the bus, or would he need privacy?

He thought about this, indifferent to his surroundings, but when he looked out of the bus window he realised that they were almost at Burdiehouse. In fact, now they were there, and Wee Fraser and his mother were rising to their feet.

Dr Fairbairn waited for them to pass, before he got up. As they made their way past, Wee Fraser looked at Dr Fairbairn, and his eyes narrowed. Somewhere, in the very recesses of his mind, a memory was at work.

Dr Fairbairn stood up, and in so doing he inadvertently jostled Wee Fraser, who spun round, muttered aggressively and then, with extraordinary speed, launched his head forward and head-butted the psychotherapist.

Almost instinctively, but moved, too, by sheer rage, Dr Fairbairn raised his fist and hit Wee Fraser soundly across the side of his chin. There was a crack as the jaw broke.

"Maw! Maw!" wailed Wee Fraser, the words strangely slurred by the loosened jaw.

Dr Fairbairn pushed his way up to the front of the bus and burst out of the door. We repeat our mistakes, he reflected, as he made his way hurriedly down the road. Endlessly. In ways that speak so eloquently of our deepest inner urges.

86. In the Café St Honoré

Janis and Gordon met that night at eight o'clock at the Café St Honoré. Gordon had suggested dinner, and Janis had readily accepted, as she had been hoping for an opportunity to give him the Crosbie which she had bought from Matthew. The painting had appealed to her when she first saw it, and when she took it home, to her house in the Stockbridge colonies, she had become even more taken with it. She had wrapped it carefully in the red gift paper which she used in her florist shop, and had written a short message on an accompanying card. *For Gordon, who has made these last few months so happy for me – Janis.*

Gordon had suggested that he call for her in a taxi, but she had decided to walk up the hill to the dinner engagement, as it was a fine evening. The first signs of autumn could be detected by those on the look-out for them, a slight sharpening of the air, an attenuation of the light. But for now, on that still evening, there was still every reason to be out under the pale sky, every reason to be walking through the streets of Edinburgh with the prospect of conversation and companionship at one's destination. Which is what we are all looking for, thought Janis – in our various ways.

She thought about her day as she walked up Howe Street.

They had been busy at the shop, and she and her two assistants had been exhausted when they closed the door at six. There had been a large delivery for two weddings they were doing the following day and there had also been a steady stream of customers. In the mid-afternoon, a man had come in and chosen a large spray of roses. She had prepared the flowers and had handed them to him.

"They are for my wife," he had said. "They are for her."

Janis had smiled. "I'm sure she will like them," she had said.

The man had looked down at the flowers, staring at them for several moments, and then she had realised . . . and he had raised his head again and she had seen the tears. She reached out and placed a hand on his forearm, to comfort him, and thought: *We buy flowers for the dead. That is the one thing we buy for them.*

Such moments as those were part of the florist's day, and were handled as professionally as she could manage. But it was impossible not to be reminded in her work of the transience of human life and of how we can transform it by moments of kindness and consideration.

Gordon was already there when she arrived, seated in a table by the window. He rose to his feet, knocking over a glass as he did so. The glass rolled briefly on the table and then fell to the ground, splintering into fragments.

"I'm so clumsy," he said to the waiter who appeared to deal with the situation.

"It's nothing, sir," said the waiter. "People do far worse than this. Whole tables of things end up on the floor."

She smiled in appreciation at the waiter's kindness and then turned her attention to the menu which had been put in front of her. For a few minutes they discussed what they would have and then, in the brief silence that followed, she reached for the small parcel which she had placed at her feet.

"I've brought you a present. It's not a very big present, but I hope you like it."

His eyes widened. "But it's not my birthday."

"That doesn't matter."

She passed the red parcel over to him and he took it from her gingerly.

"Open it."

He slid a finger under a flap of the paper and peeled it back. The card was exposed and he took this out and read it.

"That's very kind of you to say that."

"I mean it."

"Well, thank you. I'm the one who should be giving you a present. These months have been happy ones for me, too."

He took off the rest of the paper and held the painting out at arm's length. He said nothing at first, and then he smiled at her. "I like harbours," he said. "And I particularly like this one."

"Matthew thought you would," she said.

He raised an eyebrow at the mention of his son's name. "My Matthew? He said that?"

"It was his idea," Janis said. "I wanted to get you something. He thought you would like this."

I'm not telling a complete lie, she told herself. Matthew had implied that he would like it and had not actively discouraged her from buying the painting. That, by a short leap, could be interpreted as being behind the idea. Gordon looked at the painting again. "That was thoughtful of him," he said. He paused. "How was he? I mean, how did you find him? The other night at the Club . . ."

Janis shook her head. "I understand," she said. "It can't be easy for him. People are jealous of their parents. They don't like to see them with other people. It doesn't matter if you're eight or twenty-eight. These feelings can be very strong."

He looked down at the tablecloth. "I don't know what to do. If we ask him to join us for anything, we'll just have a repeat of last time. Surly, immature behaviour."

"That's because he loves you. If he didn't, then he wouldn't care at all."

"But it makes it very hard for you, doesn't it?" he said. "And it'll be even harder when we tell him that we're getting married . . ."

He stopped himself. He coloured deeply. He reached for his

table napkin and the sudden action sent another glass to the floor.

"I'm so sorry," he stuttered. "That was a slip of the tongue. I wasn't . . ."

"But I accept," said Janis. "Don't worry. I accept."

The waiter reappeared, brush and pan in hand.

"I've done it again," said Gordon. "I'll pay for all these glasses. Please add them to the bill."

The waiter shook his head. "Doesn't matter," he said.

"Do you have any champagne glasses?" asked Gordon. "Not that I intend to break those. But I think we're going to need a bottle of champagne."

The waiter went off to fetch the champagne and the glasses. By the time that he returned, Gordon had discreetly opened his wallet and extracted a crisp Bank of Scotland fifty-pound note, which he slipped into the waiter's hand.

"You're very kind," said the waiter.

Janis thought: But there's 10,999,950 more where that came from.

87. Domenica Takes Food to Angus

Angus Lordie did not often receive a visit from Domenica, but every now and then she would call in on him, usually un-announced, and usually bringing him a small present of food, normally cheese scones, which she baked herself.

"I'm convinced that you don't feed yourself properly, Angus," said Domenica, placing a small bag of provisions on his kitchen table. "I've made you an apple pie and there's a pound of sausages from that marvellous butcher down at the end of Broughton Street – the one who makes the real sausages. You do remember that wonderful line from Barbara Pym, do you not, where one of the characters says that men need meat? Not men in the sense of people in general, but men in the sense of *males*. Priceless!"

"And yet you've brought me a pound of sausages," said Angus. "For which, thank you very much indeed. But doesn't that suggest that you, too, feel that men need meat?"

"Not at all," said Domenica. "Men can get their protein from anywhere in the protein chain, if there's such a thing. You'd be better off not eating meat at all, you know. Look at the statistics for the survival of vegetarians. They do much better. Perhaps I should take those sausages back."

"As long as they drink," said Angus. "Vegetarians who drink a couple of glasses of wine a day do terribly well."

"A thirty-five per cent improvement in mortality," said Domenica.

Angus Lordie peered at the sausages. "And yet the government can't exactly encourage us to drink, can it?"

"Certainly not," said Domenica. "We know that the government itself drinks, but on this issue it has to be hypocritical."

Angus Lordie, who had stopped painting when Domenica arrived, moved to the window. Picking up a rag, he wiped a small spot of oil paint off his hands. "I've never understood the objection to hypocrisy," he said. "There must be some circumstances in which it's permissible to be hypocritical."

"Such as?"

"Let me think," said Angus. "Yes. On the receipt of a present that one doesn't like. Do you really think that one should say how much one likes it?"

Domenica thought about this. "I suppose so. But is that being hypocritical, or is it something different?"

"Hypocrisy is saying one thing and doing another," said Angus. "If you say that you like the gift and say how much you're looking forward to using it or looking at it, or whatever, then surely you're being a hypocrite." He paused for a moment. "So, should a politician tell other people not to drink or not to eat sausages, and all the while he drinks and eats sausages himself, then he's being hypocritical. But it may be the right thing for him to do."

"But would you yourself choose to be hypocritical?"

Angus replaced the oily rag on a table. He smiled. "I'm as

weak as anybody else," he said. "I suppose I've told my share of lies. I've been hypocritical on occasions."

Domenica laughed. "Tell me, then. You don't like sausages."

"No, I don't," said Angus.

Domenica saw that he meant it. "You should have told me," she said.

"But I didn't want to offend you. And I can't stand apple pie either."

Domenica frowned. "But why not tell me? You would just have wasted them. I would have gone away thinking that you would be enjoying my little offerings and all the time you'd be putting them out in the bin."

Angus shook his head. "I would not," he said defensively. "I would have given the sausages to Cyril, and I would have put the apple pie out in the gardens for the squirrels."

"I will not have you giving my Crombie sausages to that dog of yours," said Domenica. "You presume on my friendship, Angus!"

"I didn't ask you to bring me sausages," said Angus peevishly.

"And I certainly shall not bring you any sausages in the future," said Domenica stoutly.

"Good," said Angus. "So, no sausages then."

They looked at one another reproachfully. Then Angus shrugged. "What are we to do about these sausages?" he said, gesturing to the package on the table. "I suppose you'd better take them back and eat them in Scotland Street."

"But I don't like sausages myself," said Domenica. "I can't stand them, in fact."

For a few moments they stared mutely at the package of sausages.

"Do you know anybody who would like them?" asked Domenica. "Any of your neighbours?"

"My neighbours would find it very strange if I started offering them sausages," said Angus. "We don't have that sort of relationship."

"I wasn't aware that there was a category of relationship which permitted the giving and taking of sausages," said Domenica.

"Well, there is," said Angus. "You have to know people quite well before you start giving them sausages."

Domenica said nothing. She knew that Angus occasionally became argumentative, and there was no point in engaging with him when he was in such a mood. "Well, let's . . ."

Angus cut her short. "Before we abandon the subject of sausages," he said, "I must tell you about an occasion on which I was obliged to eat sausages – and with every visible sign of enjoyment. It was at a terribly grand house in Sutherland. I went there for lunch one day and there were ten people round the table. We were looking forward to a good meal, but we certainly didn't get that. We had sausages with boiled potatoes. And that was it. But what I remember about that meal was that the subject of flying boats came up. I don't know how it did, but somebody must have raised it.

"And I said to our hostess: 'You know, Your Grace, you should get yourself a flying boat. You've got that great stretch of loch out there – it's ideal for a flying boat.' And you know what she said? She said: 'But we do have a flying boat somewhere or other.' Then she turned to the factor, who was sitting down at the end of the table, and she said: 'Mr Grant, have you seen the flying boat? Do you know where it is?'"

That was all there was to the story. Angus Lordie looked at Domenica. Then he burst into laughter, into wild peals of laughter. And Domenica laughed too. It was extremely funny for some reason. It may have been hard to put one's finger on the reason, but neither of them was in any doubt but that it was terribly funny.

But it was also rather sad. And again, to work out why it should be sad, required a measure of reflection.

88. Bruce Reflects

After his unfortunate experience with George and his new fiancée, Bruce returned to Scotland Street in what almost amounted to a state of shock. He had set off for his shop in a mood of confidence and optimism, but this had been conclusively shattered by the confrontation with his erstwhile business backer, now his former friend. There was to be no money from George, and with the disappearance of that support his liabilities now exceeded his assets. The payment to the wine dealer in Leith could not be put off for more than a short time, and now he simply did not have sufficient funds to pay. He would have to return all the stock, virtually every bottle of it, and that would leave him with empty shelves, including in that new section of which he was so proud – the innovative Wines for Her.

Pat was in her room when Bruce returned. For a moment he hesitated, unsure whether to knock on her door and offer to make her a cup of coffee. He did not want her to think that he needed her company in any way – she should be in no doubt that he could take or leave that as he wished – but eventually his need for comfort and reassurance got the better of him.

Pat greeted him politely. Yes, that was kind of him; she would join him for a cup of coffee in the kitchen in a few moments.

"So," she said. "The business. How's it going?"

"Great," Bruce started to say. "Just great . . ."

He broke off. He looked at the floor. "Actually," he went on, "it's going badly. Really badly."

Pat raised an eyebrow. "Is there a problem with that shop you're renting?"

Bruce shook his head. "No, it's more than that. In fact, Pat, it's awful." He sat down at the kitchen table, his head sunk in his hands.

Pat looked down at him. Poor Bruce – to be so vain and so pleased with yourself and then to become so obviously wretched. It was difficult not to sympathise with him.

"Money?" she said.

Bruce nodded miserably. "I've been let down."

"By?"

"By somebody I was at school with back in Crieff," said Bruce. "He should have stayed there."

Pat frowned. "Why are you rude about Crieff, Bruce? Aren't you proud of the place you came from?"

"No," said Bruce. "I'm not."

Pat thought about this. "May I ask why?" she said. "I don't see anything wrong with Crieff. In fact, I think it's really a very nice place."

"You would," said Bruce bitterly.

Pat almost let this remark pass, but decided that Bruce had gone too far. "Oh," she said. "Oh, you do think that you're superior, don't you? You think that by being rude about Crieff you can build yourself up. Well, you're wrong, you know. You're wrong about Crieff, completely wrong. Crieff is a great place. I know people who live there who like it very much indeed. And these are people with rather better judgment than yours, Bruce. By running Crieff down you tell me more about yourself than about Crieff. That's true, you know."

Bruce said nothing, while Pat fixed him with her stare. "The trouble with you, Bruce, is that you think nowhere and nobody is good enough for you. You think that you're too good for Crieff. You think that you're too good for your old friends. You think that this old friend of yours has let you down, but I suspect that it's exactly the opposite. I suspect that you've been trying to use him."

Bruce looked up abruptly. "And why do you think that, may I ask?"

Pat shrugged. "Because that's the way you do things." She paused. "But there's no point in my talking to you like this, is there? I doubt if you're going to change."

Bruce stood up. "No," he said. "There's no point. Because I have no intention of listening to you, Patsy girl, thank you very much."

And with that he left, crossed the hall into his room, and slammed the door behind him. Inside his room, though, the confidence which he had tried to show crumpled. He owed money, and he owed a great deal of it. The thought occurred to him that he could go back to his parents and ask them to lend him the money to pay the most immediate bills, including the one from Leith, but he simply could not face that. He could imagine what his father would say to him. He would be lectured about caution and misjudgment. He would be told that he should never have attempted go into business without getting the necessary experience first. And if he tried to explain about George, and how he had brought all this about, his father would probably just take George's side. He had always liked him, Bruce recalled, and had said that he thought he was the best of his son's friends. That shows how much judgment he has, thought Bruce.

He sat on his bed and considered his situation. Assets and liabilities – the fundamentals of business. He knew the assets and he knew the liabilities. The assets were the flat in Scotland Street, which was heavily mortgaged, a small amount of money in a deposit account at the bank, and . . . He had almost forgotten. There were three cases of Petrus. It was only George's view that these were not the real thing – but there was a chance, even if only a slim chance, that the Petrus was genuine and he remembered that he had read somewhere that there was a wine auction coming up in Edinburgh. They might be able to take late entries, and if the wine were genuine, then . . .

But who could advise him on that? If he asked the auctioneers, then that might plant a doubt in their mind. So he should seek a private opinion, and who better than Will Lyons! If anybody could distinguish between genuine and false wine then it would be him, and he had very generously given Bruce advice in the past. He would ask Will round for a glass of Petrus, not say anything to him about the price he had paid, and then see what the verdict was. It was a brilliant idea, and he would see if Will was free that very evening! How handy it was to live in Edinburgh, he reflected, and to have expertise so ready to hand.

89. *The Restoration of Fortunes*

Will Lyons had better things to do than to visit Bruce, but agreed, out of sheer kindness, to call in at 44 Scotland Street that evening shortly before eight. He would not be able to stay long, he explained, as he had work to do. He had recently agreed to write a history of the Edinburgh wine trade, and the manuscript was growing slowly beneath his hands. It was a pleasant sensation seeing the pile of pages grow higher, but, like every author, he knew that he had to guard jealously the spare hours in which he could write. There were histories to be written about those whose histories had never progressed beyond chapter one, or indeed the introduction.

Will sighed as he made his way up the stairs to Bruce's flat. He did not particularly like Bruce, whom he found both opinionated and ignorant in equal measure. He had tried to warn him about the drawbacks of going into the wine trade, but his warnings had not been heeded. It was clear to him that Bruce did not have even the basic knowledge that would enable him to run a wine shop. Nor did he possess the specialised knowledge and taste that would be required to run a wine shop in somewhere like Edinburgh's New Town, where the number of opinionated and demanding people was very high, and where many of these prided themselves on their knowledge of wine. Any enterprise of Bruce's was bound to fail, the only question being how long the failure would take, and how spectacular it would be.

Bruce opened the door to his guest and ushered him into the flat. He had been preparing coffee and it was into the kitchen that they now went and took a seat at the large, scrubbed pine table.

"I see that you have the original flagstones," said Will, pointing at the fine stone floor.

"For the time being," said Bruce. "I haven't got round to fixing that up yet."

"Fixing it up?" asked Will. "It looks in quite good condition to me."

"Modernising it," said Bruce. "I want an oak-look effect. There's a new sort of flooring that looks just like oak. I'd challenge anybody to tell the difference. It's a bit pricey, though."

Will kept his counsel. His eye had been caught by a bottle standing on a nearby shelf. Could it be? Was it possible?

"Yes," said Bruce jauntily, noticing the direction of his host's gaze. "Petrus. Would you like to take a look?"

"It's a very fine wine," said Will. "Many people would say that it's the finest wine there is, you know."

"Oh, I know that," said Bruce. "That's why I got in a supply."

"A supply?"

Bruce affected nonchalance. "Actually, I bought three cases for that new business of mine. I thought that Edinburgh being the sort of place that it is, there might be demand for it. There are a lot of wealthy people who live here, you know – people who will be prepared to fork out for this sort of stuff."

"Oh, I know that," said Will. He peered at the bottle on its shelf. "Would you mind if I took a look?"

"Of course not," said Bruce. "In fact, how about a glass?"

Will raised an eyebrow. "That's very generous of you," he said. "I wasn't . . ."

"Of course not," said Bruce, rising to his feet. "I've been looking forward to trying it myself and who better to share it with?"

He crossed the room to take the bottle from the shelf. Then he handed it to Will, who examined it closely.

"Lovely year," said Will. "I take it that you know that this is pretty valuable?" He hesitated. "I suppose that you must know that, if you bought three cases of it."

Bruce was not giving anything away. "Yes," he said, smiling. "This wine isn't cheap, by any means. But what's the use of having the stuff if you aren't prepared to have the occasional glass?"

He reached for a corkscrew and passed it to Will. "Care to do the honours?"

Will carefully exposed the cork and looked at the top of it. Then, as Bruce fetched the glasses from the cupboard, Will gently twisted the screw into the cork and drew it up the neck of the bottle. It emerged with a satisfactory plop and he immediately sniffed at it and smiled.

"So far, so good," he said. "Now if you pass me the glasses, we'll see what we have here."

Bruce's expression was anxious as he passed over the glasses. This, he thought bitterly, is the moment of humiliation – the crowning humiliation, in fact, coming on top of everything that had gone wrong for him in recent months – that business over that stuck-up American girl, the loss of his job at that pathetic firm of Macauley Holmes Richardson Black, and finally that terrible betrayal by George and his haggis-like fiancée. He closed his eyes briefly, hardly daring to look at the dark red liquid which Will was now sniffing at and swirling round his glass.

He watched in fascination as Will took a sip of the wine and moved it about his mouth, drawing in air through the lips. Nervously, he raised his own glass and sipped at the wine. It tasted all right to him – rather good, in fact – but then, in a rare moment of honesty, he said to himself: what do I know about this?

Will looked at Bruce. "What a stunner!" he said.

Bruce looked startled. "Stunner?"

"A beautiful wine," went on Will. "So supple and ripe – yet it has elegance and length. One can understand why this is seen as such a great wine. One really can."

Afterwards, when Will had left the flat, Bruce went into the bathroom and looked at himself in the mirror. His face was lit with triumph, and in his ears rang Will's parting words. His visitor had explained that he thought there would be no trouble in entering the remaining wine, now reduced to thirty-five bottles, but still a very impressive quantity, in the wine auction that was due to take place in a few days' time. And then he had said: "And I suspect that you'll clear at least thirty thousand for the lot, once commissions are taken."

Bruce looked back into the mirror and smiled at himself. "You're a stunner yourself," he said in self-compliment. "A human Chateau Petrus!"

90. Self-assertiveness Training for Civil Servants

It was about this time that the Scottish Executive decided that all civil servants above a certain level of seniority should receive self-assertiveness training. The reason why this training was offered only to those in more senior positions was simple: there appeared to be no need to increase the self-assertiveness of the more junior civil servants, whose confidence generally exceeded that of their superiors. Indeed, greater self-assertiveness in the higher echelons of the Executive was thought to be the only way in which policies could be implemented in the face of opposition from below. And in due course, it had been announced, ministers themselves would receive self-assertiveness training to assist them to assert unpopular policies in the face of widespread public opposition and thereby to force their acceptance. (This is not to say that these policies were bad. Indeed, many of them were good; it's just that the public cannot always be trusted to recognise a good policy when they see it.)

Stuart had signed up for a personal assertiveness workshop that would require him to spend two hours alone in the company of an assertiveness counsellor. He was looking forward to this, as he had gradually been reaching the conclusion that whatever level of assertiveness he managed to achieve in his working environment, this was far from adequate at home. In particular, he had concluded that if he was to do anything about his relationship with his son, Bertie, then he would need to stand up to Irene. And that was an alarming thought. It was all very well to have scored a minor victory with Bertie's attendance at Tofu's bowling party, but it would be quite another thing to achieve the goal of getting Bertie out of psychotherapy, of relieving him of the need to attend yoga lessons in Stockbridge, and to dismantle, as far as possible, the remaining planks of what Irene called the "Bertie project". And yet he owed it to his son. He had vowed that he would not let the little boy down: he would restore to him the tiny pleasures and idle moments of a happy boyhood. He would make his life whole again.

Stuart sat in Meeting Room 64A/3B/4/16 (west) in the offices of the Scottish Executive, awaiting the arrival of the assertiveness counsellor, who was already ten minutes late. Stuart passed the time reading a newspaper, and was immersed in an editorial when the door was opened by a slight man in his early thirties, wearing jeans and an open-neck shirt.

"You're Stuart Pollock?" asked the counsellor, glancing at a clipboard in his hand.

Stuart replied that he was, and extended his right hand to shake hands. The counsellor seized his hand and squeezed it tightly.

"Good to meet you, Stuart!" he said. "My name's Terry. You got a problem with that?"

Stuart blinked. "No," he said hesitantly. "Of course not."

"You see," said Terry, "some people think that the name Terry is a bit effeminate. Know what I mean by that?" Terry fixed him with a stare. "You don't find me short, do you, Stuart?"

"Not at all," said Stuart.

"And would it matter if you did?" asked Terry aggressively. "What exactly is wrong with being on the short side?"

"I didn't say anything was wrong with it," said Stuart. "You raised it, not me. And, anyway, I don't think your name is effeminate, Shorty . . . I mean, Terry. And your height is neither here nor there as far as I am concerned."

Terry continued to glare at him. "All right, let's sit down. I'm going to take this chair, right? This one here. That's my chair."

"That's fine," said Stuart.

"But what if you really wanted to sit in that chair?" asked Terry. "What if you wanted my chair?"

"I don't think that I would make a fuss about it," said Stuart. "It's exactly the same as this chair over here. All the Scottish Executive chairs are the same, actually."

"And that worries you?" asked Terry. "Have you got a problem with the Scottish Executive, Stuart?"

Stuart took a deep breath. Terry was extremely irritating, and they had had only five minutes of the two-hour session. He wondered whether he would be able to survive the full time; would it be entered on his file if he failed to complete the course? Would the conclusion be drawn that he lacked the requisite degree of assertiveness needed by a competent modern civil servant?

"No," he said in reply to Terry's question. "I have no problems with the Scottish Executive. The only problem I have at present is a slight irritation with you."

Terry clapped his hands together. "That's the spirit, Stuart! Well done! That's exactly what I wanted you to say. I wanted you to assert yourself."

"Well, there you are," said Stuart, relaxing visibly. "And I suppose, if I were to be completely frank . . ."

"Always be frank," said Terry. "Tell it how it is, Stuart. Don't conceal. Get it out."

"Well," Stuart continued, "I suppose that I do have a bit of a problem with my wife. She herself is rather on the assertive side."

"Assertive!" exclaimed Terry. "I bet she's assertive! She's emasculating you, Stuart. I've never met her but I can tell what's happening. I see it all the time. Virtually every man I meet in this job has been emasculated by some woman. It's endemic these days, absolutely endemic."

Stuart was surprised by the force with which the counsellor issued this judgment. By his own admission he did not know anything about Irene, and so how could he possibly judge her in such extreme terms? On the other hand . . .

"Is it that bad?" he asked mildly.

"You bet it's that bad," said Terry. "And it's time for men to fight back. Men are going to have to fight back, to reclaim their space before it's too late and they become the new victims, just as women used to be the victims of men. We have to fight back."

"So what should I do?" asked Stuart.

"Tell her what you plan to do," said Terry. "And if she objects, just ignore her. Leave the house. Women don't like that. They don't like it if you leave the house."

"Is that what you do?" asked Stuart.

Terry thought for a moment. "It's what I would do," he said. "If I had to, that is. You see, I'm not heavily into relationships. I live by myself. I'm a relationship-free man. It's the new thing."

"I see," said Stuart.

They talked for some time after that. There were exercises in self-assertiveness which Stuart was required to do – including assertive telephone techniques – and there was a lengthy discussion about assertive report-writing. And then, at the end, Terry placed an arm over Stuart's shoulder and wished him good luck.

"Do you feel better?" he asked.

Stuart thought for a moment. No, he did not feel better. He felt, if anything, more afraid. It seemed to him that the odds had suddenly been seriously raised. It was not just Bertie's future that was at stake – it was his own.

91. *Stuart Paints Bertie's Room*

Stuart finished his self-assertiveness workshop at four in the afternoon. He decided to leave the office immediately, rather than wait until five. This was assertive, but not unduly so. He had arrived at work early that day and in terms of hours he was well in credit. So he left the office and made his way to a hardware store that he had walked past on numerous occasions but of which he had never taken much notice. It sold paints and paint brushes, he knew, and it was bound to have what he wanted – a large paint-roller and two tins of matt-finish white paint.

He bought the supplies, thanked the shopkeeper, and began the journey home. He felt excited and anxious – in the same way as a schoolboy would be filled with a mixture of thrill and dread when planning some transgression. This, he thought, is how criminals must feel as they travel to the scene of the crime: hearts racing, mouths dry, every sense at a high pitch. And what he was proposing to do was, for him, almost criminal. He was planning to paint Bertie's room, unilaterally, without consultation, in complete defiance of Irene's wishes. It was she who had chosen the existing colour-scheme, opting for pink because of its alleged calming properties and its refutation of the culturally-conditioned assumptions about the preferences of boys. Boys don't like pink, was the conventional wisdom. Well, we would soon see about that! There was no reason why a sensitive boy, a boy brought up to eschew the straitjacket of narrow gender roles, should not approve of pink.

Stuart knew that Bertie did not like his room – or "space" as Irene called it – to be pink. He had told him as much and had also said that as long as his room remained pink he could not possibly invite any friends to the flat, not that he had any friends, of course.

Stuart had listened sympathetically to his son. "But you must have some friends, Bertie," he said. "What about that boy, Tofu? Isn't he your friend?"

Bertie looked doubtful. "I'm not sure about him," he said. "He may be my friend, but I'm not too sure. He keeps asking me for money and food – he's a vegan, you know. I think that he may like me just because I can give him the things he wants."

"Some friends are a bit like that to begin with," said Stuart. "But then they change after a while and become real friends – friends who like you quite apart from anything you can do for them." He paused. "And what about that girl, Olive?"

Bertie shook his head. "She thinks I want her to get lockjaw," he said. "And I don't. I don't want anyone to get lockjaw, Daddy. I really don't."

Stuart smiled. "Of course you don't, Bertie!" And then he had thought: but do I want anybody to get lockjaw? – and he had decided that the answer was that he did. There were public figures, and one or two so-called singers, he thought he would like to get lockjaw, which he imagined was the only way, even if somewhat drastic, of getting them to keep quiet. But such thoughts were uncharitable.

Now, climbing up the stairs to the flat in 44 Scotland Street, Stuart looked at his watch. Irene would be out, he thought, as she was taking Bertie to his saxophone lesson and they were both going to an extra yoga session after that. They would not be back until well after seven, which would give him a good two hours in which to paint Bertie's room. It was not a big room, and paint-rollers covered a lot of wall in a very short time. By the time Irene and Bertie returned, then, they would be faced with a fait accompli.

He let himself into the flat. To verify that the coast was clear, he called out to Irene. There was silence; just the ticking of a clock and the humming, somewhere in the background, of a fridge. Stuart deposited the tins of paint and the paint-roller in Bertie's room and then went to change out of his office clothes. He knew that Irene did not like him to leave his clothes lying on the floor, and so he tossed his shirt down on to the bedside rug and threw his dirty socks into a corner. As he did so, he thought of Terry, and of how proud he would have been of him to see this. He was sure that Terry left his clothes on the floor of his flat; mind you, being a relationship-free man, Terry would not have had anybody to object to the practice.

Once changed, Stuart went back to Bertie's room. He moved around the pink walls, taking down the pictures which Irene had pinned up. A poster proclaiming the merits of Florence, the periodic table, a picture of Mahler. He sighed as he took them down and, on sudden impulse, rather than fold the periodic table away for putting back up once the new paint had dried, he tore it up and tossed it into the wastepaper bin. Then, with the walls bare, he opened the first can of paint, poured it into a tray, and dipped in the paint-roller. Then he set to work.

It did not take long to cover the walls with the easily-applied white paint. Stuart worked feverishly, oblivious to the spots of paint which were appearing on Bertie's carpet. From time to time he looked at his watch, and listened for any sound from the hall. But no sound came, and he continued with his work until the entire room had been transformed. No pink was to be seen. It was gone. Now Bertie could bring any friend home and would never suspect that anything was amiss.

When he had finished, Stuart tucked the empty tins and the painting equipment into a cupboard. Then, having made a not altogether successful attempt to clean the paint off the carpet, he returned to the main bedroom and changed. The paint-spattered clothes he tossed to the floor in a heap. Then he went to the kitchen and poured himself a large whisky.

There was the sound of a key in the front door and voices.

"And remember, Bertie," said Irene, her voice drifting in from the hall to the kitchen where Stuart sat. "Remember that you've got extra Italian this week. That nice story about a little Italian boy who . . ."

There was a sudden silence. Stuart looked into his empty whisky glass. It would have been reassuring to have Terry with him at the moment, he thought.

92. Discussions Take Place Between Irene and Stuart

The silence was broken by Bertie. "My room!" he shouted. "Look, Mummy! My room's turned white!"

The joy in Bertie's voice was unmistakable and indeed became even more apparent with his next exclamation. He did not use Italian spontaneously now, but this was an occasion, he thought, when Italian seemed more eloquent than English. "Miracolo!" he shouted. "Miracolo!"

Irene, standing at the door to Bertie's room, surveying the transformation, was momentarily lost for words. But then she found her voice.

"What on earth has happened here?" she said. "Somebody has painted . . ."

She stepped into the room and noticed the periodic table, torn up and tossed into the bin. She picked it up gingerly, as a detective might pick up a piece of evidence at the scene of the crime.

"Isn't it nice?" asked Bertie, nervously. He realised that his mother was far from pleased and he dreaded the possibility that she would immediately repaint it in pink. "I think white is such a good colour for . . ." He was going to say "for boys" but he knew that would merely provoke his mother. So he finished by saying "for rooms".

"We can talk about that later on," said Irene grimly. "In the meantime, don't touch anything. We don't want you getting paint on your dungarees."

She turned on her heel and went through to the kitchen.

"Well!" she said, glaring at Stuart. "Somebody's been busy!"

Stuart looked at her coolly. "I thought it was about time that we redecorated Bertie's room," he said. "I did it quite quickly, actually. You got a problem with that?"

"What?" hissed Irene. "What do you mean have I got a problem?"

Stuart shrugged. "You seem a bit taken aback. I thought you would be pleased to discover that your husband's a skilled painter."

Irene turned and slammed the kitchen door behind her. She did not want Bertie to hear what was to come.

"Have you gone mad?" she asked. "Have you gone out of your mind?"

"No," said Stuart, adding: "Have you?"

Irene took several steps forward. "Listen to me, Stuart, I don't know what's come over you, but you've got a bit of explaining to do. What are you thinking of, for heaven's sake?"

Stuart held her gaze. "I decided that it was about time we let Bertie have one or two things his way. It's been perfectly apparent for some time that he did not like his pink room. Nor, for that matter, does he like those pink dungarees of his."

"Crushed strawberry," corrected Irene. She shook her head, as if to adjust a confused picture of reality. "I just don't know what you think you're doing. There's a reason why Bertie is being brought up to like pink. It's all to do with gender stereo-types. Can't you even grasp that?"

Stuart smiled. "There's something which I grasp very well," he said. "And that is this: it's about time we let that little boy just be a little boy."

"Oh!" said Irene. "So that's it, is it? You think that you know what it is to be a little boy? You, the inheritor of the patriar-chal mantle, passing it on to your son! Get him interested in things like cars . . ."

Stuart frowned. "By the way," he interrupted. "Where's our car?"

Irene, derailed by the question, stared at her husband. "Outside in the street," she said. "Where you parked it the other day."

"No it isn't," said Stuart. "You parked it."

"Nonsense!" said Irene. "You had it last. And you parked it in the street."

"I did," he said. "I parked it there the other day and then you used it to go somewhere or other. You're the one who parked it last."

Irene opened her mouth to say something and then thought better of it. He was right, she feared. She had driven the car recently and had parked it somewhere, but she had no recollection of where that was. But then, something else occurred to her; something which was more serious than the temporary mislaying of the car.

"Be that as it may," she said. "There's something that I've been meaning to raise with you for some time now. That car of ours. How many gears does it have?"

Stuart swallowed. He could see where this was leading, and suddenly the whole business of painting Bertie's room seemed to fade into insignificance.

Irene stared at him. "How many?" she repeated.

"Five," said Stuart, his voice now deprived of all the assertiveness which he had injected into it earlier. So much for courage, he thought.

"Oh yes?" said Irene. "Then why does it now have only four?" She waited a moment before continuing. Then: "So could it be that the car you brought back from Glasgow is not actually our car? Could that be so? And if it isn't, then whose car, may I ask, is it?"

Stuart was defeated. It had become perfectly obvious to him that Lard O'Connor had ordered the stealing of a car for him and its fitting up with false number-plates. And once he had discovered that, he should have gone straight to the police and told them what had happened. But he had not done that because he had been frightened. He had been frightened of what Lard O'Connor would do to him when he discovered that Stuart had reported him. So he had taken the easy way out and done nothing, denying the problem, hoping that it would go away.

Irene sat down. "Now look," she said. "We must settle this like sensible adults. We have several problems here, haven't we? We've got this problem of our car. And then we've got a problem of your interfering with Bertie's upbringing. Those are our two problems, aren't they?"

Stuart nodded. He felt miserable. He would have to abandon this wretched attempt to do things for himself.

"So," said Irene, her voice low and forgiving. "So, what you need to do, Stuart, is to let me sort everything out. You don't have to worry. I'll handle everything. But, as a quid pro quo, you just behave yourself. All right?"

Stuart nodded. He was about to say: yes, it was all right, but then he remembered the trip on the train with Bertie and what he had said to him. So now he looked Irene in the eye. "No," he said. "It's not all right."

93. The Gettysburg Address

"Six years ago," said Stuart, "we conceived a child, a son . . ." Irene interrupted him. "Actually, I conceived a son," she said. "Your role, if you recall the event, was relatively minor."

Stuart stared at her. "Fathers count for nothing then?"

When she replied, Irene's tone was gentle, as if humouring one who narrowly fails to understand. "Of course I wouldn't say that. You're putting words into my mouth. However, the maternal role is undoubtedly much more significant. And when it comes down to it, women do most of the work of child-rearing. They just do. Who takes Bertie to Italian? Who takes him to yoga, to school? Everywhere in fact? I do." She paused. "And whom do I see there, at these various places? Not other fathers. Mothers, like me."

Stuart took a deep breath. "That's part of the problem. Bertie doesn't want to go to Italian lessons. He hates yoga. He told me that himself. He said that it makes him feel . . ."

She did not let him finish. "Oh yes? Oh yes? And where would you take him then? Fishing?"

Stuart smiled. "Yes, I would. I would take him fishing."

"Teach him to kill, in other words," said Irene.

"Fishing is not killing."

"Oh yes? So the fish survives?"

Stuart hesitated. "All right, it's killing. But . . ."

"And that's what you want to teach him to do! To kill fish!"

Stuart looked out of the window. The evening sky was clear, bisected on high by the thin white line of a vapour trail. And at the end of the trail, a tiny speck of silver, was a plane heading west; a metaphor for freedom, he thought, even if the freedom at the end of a vapour trail was a brief and illusory one.

"I want him to have some freedom to be a little boy," he said. "I want him to be able to play with other boys of his age, doing the sort of thing they like to do. They like to ride their bikes. They like to hang about. They like to play games, throw balls about, climb trees. They don't like yoga."

The roll-call of boyish pursuits was a provocation to Irene. "What a perfect summary of the sexist concept of a boy," she exclaimed. "And what about ungendered boys, may I ask? What about them? Do they like to climb trees and ride bikes, do you think?"

"I have no idea what ungendered boys wish to do," answered Stuart. "In fact, I'm not sure what an ungendered boy is. But the whole point is that Bertie is not one of them. He wants to get on with being what he is, which is a fairly typical little boy. He's clever, yes, and he knows a lot. But the thing that you don't seem able to understand is that he is also a little boy. And he needs to go through that stage. He needs to have a boyhood."

Irene was about to answer, but Stuart, in his stride now, cut her off. "For the last few years I think I've been very patient. I was never fully happy with the whole Bertie project, as you called it. I expressed doubts, but you never let me say much about them. You see, Irene, you're not the most tolerant woman I've known. Yes, I'm sorry to have to say that, but I mean it. You're intolerant."

He paused for a moment, gauging the effect of his words on his wife. She had become silent, her face slightly crumpled. Her confidence seemed diminished, and for a moment Stuart thought that he saw a flicker of doubt. He decided to press on with his address.

"Then you were surprised," he went on, "when Bertie rebelled. Do you remember how shocked you were when he set fire to my copy of the *Guardian* while I was reading it? You do? And here's another thing, by the way: has it ever occurred to you that I was secretly pleased that he had done that? No? Well, let me tell you, I was. And the reason for that is that I was never consulted about what newspaper we should take in this house. You never asked me. Not once. You never asked me if I would like to read the *Herald* or the *Scotsman*, or anything else. You just ordered the *Guardian*. And that's because you can't tolerate another viewpoint. Or . . . or is it because you're trying so hard to be right-on, to have all the correct views about everything? And in reality, deep underneath . . ."

Irene, who had been looking at the floor, now looked up, and Stuart, to his horror, saw that there were tears in her eyes.

"Now look," he said, reaching out to touch her, "I'm sorry . . ."

"No," she said. "You don't have to be sorry. I'm the one who should be sorry."

"I don't know," said Stuart. "I'm sure you were doing your best."

Irene disregarded this. "I had so many ambitions for Bertie. I wanted him to be everything that I'm not. What have I done with my life? What have I ever achieved? You have a job – you have a career. I haven't got that. I'm just a woman who stays at home. Nothing I do ever changes the world. So I thought that with Bertie I could achieve something, at least have something that I could point to and call my creation. And now all that I've achieved is to get Bertie to hate me, and you too, it seems."

"I don't hate you," said Stuart. "I admire you. I'm proud of you. I love you very much . . ."

"Do you? Do you really?"

"I do." But he added: "I want you to loosen up. I want you to be yourself. I want you to let Bertie be himself. I want you to stop trying."

"And what if the self I should be is something quite different?" asked Irene, dabbing at her cheek with a corner of tissue. "What then?"

"That doesn't matter." But he was intrigued by the possibilities. Was there a side to Irene that he had never guessed at? "Are you different?"

Irene nodded. "I'm quite conservative," she said. "In my heart of hearts, I'm conservative. You see, Stuart, there's something I've never told you before. You don't know where I come from, do you?"

"Moray," he said. "You come from Moray."

"No," said Irene. "Moray Place." She paused, studying Stuart's reaction. He seemed to be taking it fairly well, she thought; well there was more news for him.

"And there's something else," she said. "I'm pregnant."

94. *Bertie's Dream*

That night, Bertie was reluctant to switch off his bedside lamp, so happy was he just to gaze at his newly-painted walls. He was still convinced that the transformation of his room had been achieved through some form of supernatural intervention, although he was not sure what precise form this had taken. One possibility was that the room had been painted by angels, as Bertie had recently read an account of the activity of angels which stressed that the heavenly beings frequently undertook good deeds by stealth. But ultimately it did not matter in the least who, or what agency, had effected the change in his colour scheme; the important thing was that he no longer lived in a pink room, but in a white one.

After he had been lying on his bed for half an hour or so, gazing dreamily at the walls, his parents came through to say goodnight to him, as they always did. His father was first to appear, looking shocked and dazed, and then, after he had gone, his mother, whose eyes and cheeks struck Bertie as being puffy and red.

"Are you all right, Mummy?" asked Bertie. "You haven't been crying, have you?"

Irene bent down and kissed Bertie on his brow. "No, Bertie carissimo. Not crying. Just re-evaluating."

"Good-night, then," said Bertie, snuggling down into his bed.

"Buona notte, Bertie," said Irene. She reached out to turn off his light and stood at his bedside for a few moments, wistfully, looking down at her young son. Then she turned away and left the room, leaving the door very slightly ajar to allow in the small chink of light that Bertie liked to have at night, against the greater darkness.

Bertie closed his eyes and thought of what he might do now that he had a white room. He might invite Tofu round some afternoon and give him bacon sandwiches to eat in the room. There was always plenty of bacon in their fridge and Tofu wouldn't mind too much if it were to be uncooked. And then he might even invite Olive. He wondered about her. He had felt very wounded when she had accused him of wishing lockjaw upon her, but he thought that it was now time for both of them to move on. He would forgive her for spreading rumours that she was his girlfriend (he had even heard that she had told people that they were actually engaged and that there would be a notice to that effect in the school magazine quite soon). And if he forgave her for that, then she should surely forgive him for the misunderstanding over lockjaw.

Lockjaw, of course, was not the only threat. Bertie had also heard about the dangers of cutting the skin between one's thumb and forefinger. That, he was told, induced immediate blood-poisoning, unless, of course, one had ready access to a frog, in which case the rubbing of the frog on the wound was a quick and effective treatment. Merlin, the boy in his class who was consulted on all physical matters, had reliably informed them that there was a special tank at the New Royal Infirmary where frogs were bred for this precise purpose, along with leeches, which, he explained, doctors used to treat patients whom they particularly disliked. Olive, Tofu said, would definitely have a leech attached to her if she were for any reason to be admitted to the Royal Infirmary.

Bertie eventually drifted off to sleep and during the course of the night had a dream. In this dream, which he remembered vividly upon waking, he found himself walking in a field of grass, alone to begin with, but first joined by a spotted dog, which trotted contentedly at his heels, and then by a friend. And this friend was Tofu, who walked beside him, his hand resting on Bertie's shoulder in comfortable companionship. Bertie felt proud to have a friend, even if it was only Tofu, and to have a dog, too, added to his pleasure. Above them was a high sky of freedom, unsullied by clouds.

Then suddenly the spotted dog ran away. It scampered off into the undergrowth and Bertie called out to it, but it did not come back. He felt bereft now that the dog had gone and he turned to Tofu for reassurance, but Tofu himself had skipped off, disappearing into a thicket at the edge of the field. Bertie called after him, just as he had called after the dog, but a wind had arisen, and it swallowed his words.

Now he was alone, but only for a short time, for his mother suddenly appeared round the corner of a path and she rushed towards him and lifted him up, smothering him with caresses. Bertie squirmed, trying to escape, but could not; his mother was too powerful; she was like the wind, a gale, an irresistible tide; she could not be vanquished. She held him in her grip, which was a strong one, and prevented him from moving.

But at last she put him down, and Bertie looked up at her and saw something which made his heart turn cold. Irene had a baby in her arms, and she held this baby out to Bertie, saying: "Look, Bertie! Look at this baby!"

Bertie stared at the baby and thought: Now I have a brother. "Yes," said Irene. "You have a brother, Bertie!"

Bertie did not know what to say. He stood quite still while Irene held the baby up to allow it to gaze down on Bertie, which it did with a smile, like one of those babies one sees in pre-Raphaelite paintings, slightly sinister babies. Then Irene turned. To her side there was a piano and a piano stool, and she put the baby down on the stool. The baby reached out and began to play the piano, its tiny, chubby fingers dancing across the keyboard with great skill.

Bertie watched. He was fascinated by the baby's ability to play the piano. My mother has forced him to learn the piano, he thought. And he is only six months old!

He looked more closely at the baby, who had reached a difficult passage in the music and was frowning with concentration. Then the baby stopped, and turned towards Bertie and smiled. And Bertie saw that the baby was wearing a baby-suit made of the same blue linen as that worn by Dr Fairbairn.

That was Bertie's dream.

95. *The Wind Makes the Trains Sound Faint*

When he awoke the next morning, Bertie was initially unwilling to open his eyes. He had gone to sleep in a room which had miraculously turned white; now he feared that it would have changed colour again overnight, back to the pink that he so disliked. But it had not, of course, and he was able to gaze, wide-eyed, at his new colour-scheme and confirm that it was true.

After he had dressed, Bertie went through to the kitchen, from which he heard the strains of an aria from *The Magic Flute* issuing forth.

"Good morning, Bertie," said Irene. "Do you know what they're singing about on the radio?"

"Catching birds," said Bertie. "Isn't that the man who catches birds?"

"Yes," said Irene. "Papageno. Do you know, I briefly considered calling you that when you were born? But then I decided that Bertie sounded better."

Bertie felt weak. It would have been impossible to live down a name like that, and he felt immensely relieved at his narrow escape. But if she had been thinking of calling him Papageno, then what would she have called that baby in the dream?

Irene looked at him. "Your father and I had a discussion last night," she said. "We talked a little bit about you."

Bertie looked at his mother impassively. She was always talking about him, although it was perhaps a bit unusual for his father to do so too. He reached for his porridge bowl and poured in the milk.

"Yes," continued Irene. "We talked about you and we thought that you might like to change things a bit."

Bertie looked up from his porridge. "Really, Mummy?" He thought quickly. Perhaps this was his chance.

"Could I go and live in a hotel, Mummy?" he asked. "There's one round the corner in Northumberland Street. I've seen it. I could go and live there. You could come and see me now and then."

Irene smiled. "What nonsense, Bertie!" she said.

Bertie looked back at his porridge. The milk was the sea and the lumps of porridge were tiny islands. And his spoon, placed carefully down on the surface of the milk, was a little boat. Perhaps he could go to sea. Perhaps he could sign on as a cabin boy in the navy and make the captain's tea. Bertie had read one of the Patrick O'Brian books and he made it sound so much fun, although the parts where the ships did battle were rather frightening. However, it wouldn't be like that these days, he thought, now that the European Union had stopped British ships firing upon Spanish or French ships. Perhaps they just met at sea these days and exchanged new European regulations.

"Yes," went on Irene. "We've been thinking, your father and I, that maybe you should do more of the things you really want to do. Would you like that, Bertie?"

Bertie smiled at his mother. "Very much," he said. He was pleased, but still rather doubtful. He was not sure whether his mother really understood what he wanted to do. Would he be let off yoga today?

"So, Bertie," said Irene, "I thought that although today is Saturday, and we normally have double yoga on a Saturday, we might skip it."

"Oh thank you!" shouted Bertie. "Thank you, Mummy!"

"And instead," continued Irene, "we shall . . ."

Bertie's face fell as he wondered what the alternative would be. Double Italian? Or perhaps the Floatarium?

"We shall get Daddy," said Irene, "we shall get Daddy to take you up to the Princes Street Gardens. You can climb that bit underneath the castle there and look down on the trains. Would you like that, Bertie?"

Bertie let out a whoop of delight. "I'd love that, Mummy. We could see the trains leaving for Glasgow!"

Irene smiled. "An unusual pleasure, in my view," she mused. "But there we are. Chacun à son goût."

Bertie finished his porridge quickly and then returned to his room to put on a sweater. It was a warm day for the time of the year, but by wearing a sweater he could cover the top part of his dungarees and people would not necessarily think that he was wearing them. From a distance, and if they did not look too closely, they might even think that he was wearing nothing more unusual than red jeans. That is what he hoped for, anyway.

Stuart emerged shortly after Bertie had got himself ready. After a quick breakfast, with Bertie champing at the bit to be out, they left the flat and Scotland Street and began to walk up the hill towards Princes Street. It was a fine morning and when they reached Princes Street the flags on the flagpoles were fluttering proudly in a strong breeze from the west.

"It makes you proud, doesn't it, Bertie?" said Stuart. "Look at the wonderful scene. The flags. The Castle. The statues. Doesn't it make you proud to be Scottish, to be part of all this?"

"Aye, it does that, Faither," said Bertie.

They crossed the road and made their way into the Gardens. Then, crossing the railway line on the narrow pedestrian bridge, they headed for the steep path that led up the lower slopes of the Castle Rock. After a short climb, they found a place to sit, half on rock, half on grass, and from there they watched the trains run through the cutting down below. As they passed, some of the trains sounded their whistles, and the sound drifted up to them, and the sound, to Bertie at least, meant the freedom of the wider world, the freedom of which he was now, at last, being offered a glimpse. And he was happy, even when the wind swallowed up the sound of the whistles and made the train sounds seem faint and far away.

"I had a very strange dream last night, Daddy," said Bertie suddenly.

"Oh yes, Bertie. And what was that?"

"I dreamed that Mummy had a new baby," said Bertie. "And the baby was dressed in blue linen, which is what Dr Fairbairn wears. It was very funny. A little blue linen baby suit."

Stuart looked at his son. Down below a train went past and sounded a warning whistle, audible for a moment, but then caught by the wind and carried away.

96. *The Ramsey Dunbarton Story: Part VII – Bridge at Blair Atholl*

Ramsey Dunbarton looked at Betty with all the fondness that comes of over forty years of marriage. "I don't think that you're finding my memoirs interesting, Betty," he said. "But don't worry, I'm not going to read much more."

"But they *are* interesting," protested Betty. "They're very interesting, Ramsey. It's just that it gets so warm here in the conservatory and I find myself drifting off from the heat. It's not you, Ramsey, my dear. You read on."

"I'm only going to read two more excerpts," said Ramsey, shuffling the papers of his manuscript. "And then I'm going to stop."

"Read on, Macduff," said Betty.

"Why do you call me Macduff?" asked Ramsey, sounding puzzled. "We have no Macduffs in the family as far as I know. No, hold on! I think we might, I think we just might! My mother's cousin, the one who came from Forres, married a man whom we used to call Uncle Lou, and I think that he had a brother-in-law who was a Macduff. Yes, I think he was! Well, there you are Betty! Isn't Scotland a village!"

"Do carry on," said Betty, closing her eyes. "I love the sound of your voice, Ramsey."

"Now then," said Ramsey, referring to his manuscript. "This happened about twenty years ago. I had a client, not Johnny Auchtermuchty, but somebody quite different, who had a large hotel in Perthshire. We acted for them in some Court of Session business that they had and I went up there one Saturday to have lunch with my client and to discuss the progress of the legal action down in Edinburgh. It was a very complicated case and I was not at all sure that the counsel we had instructed understood some of the finer points involved. I had suggested this to him – very politely, of course – and he had become quite shirty, implying that advocates generally knew more about the law than solicitors did, which is why they were advocates in the first place. I replied that I very much doubted this and to prove the point I asked him whether he could name, from the top of his head, a certain section of a statute to do with the sale of goods. He looked at me in a very rude way, I thought, and then he had the gall to tell me that the legislation to which I was referring had been repealed the previous year, and did I know that? It was not an amicable exchange.

"The client, though, was a very agreeable man, and it was a mark of his status in that part of Perthshire that just as we were finishing lunch at his house the telephone went and it was none other than the Duke of Atholl! Now deceased, sadly.

"The Duke was a very strong bridge player – international

standard, in fact – and they were just about to have a game of bridge up at Blair Atholl and they needed a fourth player. The Duke wondered whether my host would care to play. Unfortunately he could not, as he had a further engagement that afternoon, but then he turned to me and asked me whether I would like to go up in his stead. Now, my bridge is not very strong, but I had played a bit with the Braids Bridge Club and of course it was a great honour to be invited to play with the Duke, and so I readily agreed.

"I went up to Blair Atholl more or less straightaway. A servant let me into the house and showed me up to the drawing room, where I met the Duke and two others, a man and a woman who were staying with him as his guests – people from London whose name I did not catch, but who seemed quite civil, for Londoners. Then we all sat down at the bridge table, with me partnering the Duke. He opened the bidding on that first hand with one heart, and I rapidly took him up to four hearts on the strength of my single ace. Unfortunately, we did not make it, the Duke very quietly saying that he thought it was perhaps a slightly bad split.

"The game continued, and I must say that I enjoyed it immensely, even if the Duke and I were three rubbers down at the end. He did not seem to mind this very much, and was a very considerate host. We had a cup of tea after the bridge and we talked for about half an hour before the Duke had to attend to some other matter and I took my leave.

"Do have a wander round, Dunbarton," the Duke said very kindly. "Take a walk up the brae if you wish."

"I decided to take him up on this invitation since it was such a pleasant late afternoon. There was a path which led up a small hill and I followed this, admiring the views of the Perthshire countryside. Then the most remarkable thing happened. I turned a corner and there before me, charging through the heather, was a group of armed men, all wearing kilts and carrying infantry rifles. I stopped in my tracks – the men had clearly not seen me – and then I rapidly turned round and ran back to the castle. Beating on the door, I demanded of the servant who came to answer that I had to see His Grace immediately, on a matter of the utmost urgency.

"I was taken to the drawing room again, where I found the Duke sitting with his two other guests, engaged in conversation.

"'Your Grace!' I shouted. 'Call the police immediately! There's a group of armed men making their way down the hillside!'

"The Duke did not seem at all surprised. In fact, he smiled.

"'Oh them,' he said. 'Don't you worry about them. That's my private army.'

"And then I remembered. Of course! The Duke of Atholl has the only private army allowed in the country. I should have thought about that before I panicked and raised the alarm, and so I left feeling somewhat sheepish. But the bridge had been enjoyable, and I reflected on the fact that it would probably be a long time before I would be invited to play bridge again with a duke. In fact, I never received a subsequent invitation, but I have in no sense resented that. Not in the slightest."

97. *The Ramsey Dunbarton Story: Part VIII – I Play the Duke of Plaza-Toro*

"From real dukes," read Ramsey Dunbarton, "to stage dukes. And to that most colourful character, the Duke of Plaza-Toro, whom I had the particular honour to play at the Church Hill Theatre. Looking back on my life, which has been an eventful one by any standards, I might be tempted to say that that episode is probably one of the great saliences of my personal history.

"At the risk of sounding boastful, I have always had a rather fine voice. As a boy I sang in the local church choir, and had I auditioned for one of the great Edinburgh choirs, the choir of St Mary's Episcopal Cathedral, for example, I would probably have got in. But I did not, and so never sang in Palmerston Place. I did, however, join the Savoy when I was at university and was in the chorus of several productions. I am quite certain that I would have had principal roles were it not for the fact that the various producers who did those productions did not like me for some reason. It is very wrong when producers allow personal preferences to dictate casting. It happens all the time. People pick their girlfriends and boyfriends to sing the choice parts; it's never a question of merit. And I gather that you find exactly the same thing in the West End and on Broadway.

"After the Savoy, I joined the Bohemians, and appeared in a number of their productions, often at the King's Theatre, again in the chorus. There was *The Merry Widow*, which I always enjoyed very much, *Seven Brides for Seven Brothers*, and *Porgy and Bess*, to name just a few. In *Porgy*, I was an understudy for one of the principals, but was not called upon to sing. I must admit that it is very difficult not to wish ill on a principal in those circumstances, but I shall never forget the story told me by one of the Bohemians about how, some time ago, he had been an understudy for somebody in *Cav and Pag*, and had wished that the other singer would fall under a bus. Which he did. I'm not sure which number the bus was, but I think that it might even have been the 23, the bus which goes up Morningside Road. Fortunately, he survived, although one of his legs was broken, and of course the understudy felt so bad about it that he could barely bring himself to sing the part.

"After a break from the Bohemians, I joined the Morningside Grand Opera, an amateur group which put on a range of performances at the Church Hill Theatre each year. They were ambitious and even did Wagner's *Ring Cycle* one year, to mixed reviews, but they also did a lot of the old favourites, such as *The Gondoliers*. And it was in *The Gondoliers* that I sang my first principal role, that of the Duke of Plaza-Toro.

"It was a wonderful role, and I would have enjoyed it far more than I actually did if the other singers had been slightly stronger than they actually were. Only a day or two before the first night, I could not help but notice that a number of them had not bothered to learn the words correctly, and there was one young man, who sang the part of Luiz, who just sang *la, la, la* when he came to a bit that he had not learned. And as for the woman who sang the part of the old nurse, she only had two lines to sing (where she reveals that Luiz was really the baby), but she could not even remember those!

"The young man who played Luiz was particularly irritating. My feelings over his behaviour became quite strong at an early stage in the rehearsals, when I overheard him saying to one of the gondolieri that he, rather than I, should have been cast as the Duke of Plaza-Toro.

"If the whole idea had not been so laughable I would have remonstrated with him. One needs a certain gravitas to play the Duke of Plaza-Toro, and I had that and he simply did not. I was a WS, after all, and he was not. He was also far younger than I was and it would have been absurd to see him pretending to be the leader of the Ducal party.

"But it gets worse than that. He had a most annoying manner, that young man. I expected him to call me Mr Dunbarton (or perhaps 'Your Grace' in the circumstances!) but he actually used my first name immediately after we had been introduced. And then he presumed to shorten it, and began to refer to me as 'Ramps'. That was almost unbearable, particularly when he turned to me at one point in a rehearsal and said 'That's a B-flat by the way, Ramps!'

"I must also admit my doubts as to the casting of the Duchess. The woman who had the part was very friendly with the producer. I shall say no more about that. However, I did feel that a more appropriate person might have been cast in that role. In particular, there was somebody in the chorus who had been Head Girl many years before of the Mary Erskine School for Girls, when it used to be in Queen Street, where it had that wonderful roof garden for the girls to play on. That sort of background would have equipped her very well to play the role of the Duchess of Plaza-Toro, but do you think that the producer took that into account for one single moment? He did not.

"But these were minor matters, when all is said and done. The final production was not at all bad, and a number of people said that my own performance as the Duke of Plaza-Toro was the best portrayal they had ever seen of that role. That was very kind of them. It's so easy to be disparaging of other people's efforts, and I must confess that there is a slight tendency in that direction in Edinburgh. But I am not one to criticise Edinburgh, in spite of its occasional little failing. We are very lucky to live here and I for one will never forget that, bearing in mind what so many people have to put up with when they live in other places."

He put down his memoirs and looked at Betty. Her head was nodding in agreement, or, if one took the uncharitable view, sleep.

98. *Younger Women, Older Men*

Down the steps into Big Lou's coffee bar, the very steps down which Christopher Grieve had descended when books were sold there (in the days when coffee was instant, and undrinkable); down those steps went father and son, Matthew and Gordon. Gordon had arrived at his son's gallery without notice, had sauntered in, and indicated that he wanted to talk to his son. And Matthew, embarrassed by the memory of his churlish behaviour over dinner – behaviour which he somehow had seemed just unable to control – had said: "We must have coffee, Dad. I usually go about this time to a place over the road."

"Anywhere, son," Gordon replied. "You know my feelings about coffee."

Matthew frowned. "I don't, actually," he said. "I didn't know you had views on coffee."

"It's a racket," said Gordon. "All these fancy alternatives. Skinny latte with vanilla. Double espresso. Americano. So on. It's all just coffee, isn't it?"

Matthew thought about this. "But what about your malt whiskies?" he said. "You go on about fifteen-year-old this and twenty-year-old that. It's all just whisky, isn't it?" Gordon looked at his son with pity. "That's different, Matt," he said, adding: "As you well know."

Matthew had said nothing in response to this. He had never been able to argue with his father, whose tactic of defending a position was to imply that the other side knew full well that what he, Gordon, said was right. And there was no time for argument anyway, as they were now entering the coffee bar and Matthew had to introduce his father to Big Lou. A thought occurred to him, and made him smile: Big Lou would now be able to say of him *I ken his faither.* This was a useful thing to be able to say in Scotland, as it could be used with devastating effect to cut somebody down to size. And cutting others down to size, Matthew knew, was at the heart of Scottish culture. What better way of suggesting that the other person was just a jumped-up wee boy than to say that one kent his faither?

Matthew did not choose his usual table, as he was concerned that they might be joined by Angus Lordie, if he came in, or that vague woman from the flat above the coffee bar, that woman whose name he could never remember and who tried, unsuccessfully, to appear mysterious. Matthew knew that he had to talk to his father. He had to express the fears which had been preying on him since he had first met Janis and which would not go away. He was convinced that the florist was primarily interested in his father's money, and Matthew wanted to protect him from this, but until then he had been unwilling to broach the subject with him directly. Yet it could not be put off forever. Used they not to say in marriage ceremonies: *Speak now or forever hold your peace*? He would have to speak now.

They sat down together while Big Lou prepared the coffee.

She had smiled at Matthew's father and shaken his hand, and Gordon had responded warmly. "Nice woman, that," he had whispered to Matthew. "Lots of hard work in her."

"Yes," said Matthew. "Lou has certainly worked hard."

"There's nothing like hard work," said Gordon thoughtfully. "That's what makes money, you know, Matthew. Hard work."

Matthew pursed his lips. There was censure in his father's words, but he resisted the temptation to respond in kind. If they had an argument, then he would be unable to raise the issue of Janis. Of course, now that Gordon had mentioned money it gave him his opportunity.

"Yes," said Matthew. "You've worked hard for your money. Everybody knows that. I do." He paused, watching his father. Gordon sat impassively. Of course he had worked hard for his money, and he did not need his son to point that out to him.

"And that's why I wouldn't like to see anybody take it away from you," Matthew went on. He spoke hurriedly, rushing to get the words out.

Gordon frowned. "Naturally," he said. "But why do you think anybody would try to get my money away from me?"

Matthew's heart was thumping wildly within him. It was too late to stop now; he would have to complete what he had to say.

"Well," he said. "There are some people who try to marry others for their money. Gold-diggers, you know."

Gordon's eyes narrowed as Matthew finished. "I take it that you are referring to Janis," he said icily. "Am I correct? Are you?"

Matthew lowered his eyes. He had always found it difficult to hold his father's gaze, and now it was impossible. And of course he knew that this made his father consider him shifty and elusive, which was not the case. But he could not look into those eyes and see the reproach which had just always seemed to be there.

"Look, Dad," he began. "All I'm saying is that when a younger woman gets in tow with a . . . with a slightly older man, then one has to be a bit careful if the older man happens to have a lot of smackers. Which, I'm afraid, rather applies to you, doesn't it? You're not exactly on the bread line, are you? And the problem is that there have been one or two things in the press about how much you're worth. Eleven million, isn't it? Something like that? Janis can read."

Gordon was about to reply, but was interrupted by Big Lou bringing their coffee to the table.

"Here you are, boys," she said breezily. "One double espresso. One South American roast with double low-fat milk."

Gordon reached for his coffee, thanking Big Lou politely.

"Does my son here patronise your business regularly?" he asked.

"Every day," she said. "He comes in every morning. Sometimes stays for hours."

Matthew tried to catch Big Lou's eye, but the damage was done.

"Oh yes?" exclaimed Gordon, glancing at Matthew. "Sits here for hours, does he?"

Big Lou realised her tactlessness and looked apologetically at Matthew. "Not really," she laughed. "That's wishful thinking on my part. I'd like him to sit here for hours, but he doesn't really. Just a little joke."

Big Lou now went back to her counter, leaving the two men seated opposite one another, one glaring at the other.

"Let me get this straight," hissed Gordon. "Are you calling Janis a gold-digger? Is that what you're saying?"

"Yes," said Matthew. "I am."

99. *Janis Exposed*

Now I've done it, thought Matthew. I've very specifically accused my father's girlfriend of being after his money, and the accusation has gone down more or less as I thought it would.

And in that, Matthew was right. Gordon's face had coloured with anger.

"Tell me exactly why you have this low opinion of my friend,"

Gordon said. "If you're going to make allegations like that, then presumably you have some basis for them. Tell me, what is it? What evidence do you have? Or do you just throw things like that – insulting things – throw them about on the basis of suspicion or, and I'm sorry to say this, jealousy?"

Matthew thought. What evidence did he have? Now that he thought of it, none at all. So what was it? And at that point he realised that the reason why he took this view was simple. It was simple, but true. Janis did not love his father. You can tell when somebody loves another. It shows in the eyes; the attitude. There was none of that feeling in this case, thought Matthew. Any overt signs of affection on her part just did not seem to ring true. She was a gold-digger; it was obvious, and yet his poor father, infatuated because an attractive younger woman had shown an interest in him, simply could not see what her real motive was.

Matthew wondered whether he should tell his father this. It was a hard thing for anybody to hear – that love was unreciprocated. Many people would simply not believe that if they heard it. And yet, his father was an adult (offspring often have to remind themselves of that hard fact) and could not be protected from uncomfortable knowledge. So he looked at his father, met his gaze, and said: "Dad, she doesn't love you. I can tell."

At first, Gordon did nothing. He stared at his son, as if uncomprehending, and then reached for his coffee cup and took a sip of his espresso. He's struggling, thought Matthew. He's struggling with his dented pride (poor man) and with his *amour-propre*. This is very painful. This is very hard.

"So," said Gordon quietly. "So she doesn't love me, you say."

Matthew nodded. "She doesn't love you."

"And so when I asked her to marry me," went on Gordon, "and she accepted – that meant nothing, did it?"

Matthew sighed. "You've gone and proposed?" he asked. "Oh, Dad, Dad, Dad! You're making a big mistake. Mega-disaster all round. Oh, no, no, no!"

"Give me your evidence," said Gordon grimly. "Give me one

single shred of evidence you have that she doesn't love me. Show me. Just show me."

"But can't you see?" said Matthew, raising his voice. "Can't you see that there'll be no evidence as such? You sense these things. You know them. You can't necessarily find any evidence."

Gordon held up a hand to stop his son. "Right," he said. "You've said enough as far as I'm concerned. You've insulted the woman I love. I'm not going to stand for it, Matthew. I'm just not."

"I'm only trying to help you," protested Matthew. He reached out to touch his father, but Gordon sat back, out of reach. "Look," went on Matthew. "Try to think. Have you told her about your money? Did she ask you?"

"I've spoken to her," said Gordon. "She raised it with me."

Matthew's eyes widened. "She raised it?" he asked. "She did?"

"That's correct," said Gordon. "She asked me some fairly searching questions. And I gave her perfectly frank answers."

"Well, there you are!" cried Matthew. "It's just exactly as I said. She's interested in getting her hands on your cash. It's glaringly obvious."

Gordon shook his head. "You stupid boy," he said. "Sorry, but that's what you are, Matthew. She raised the issue because she wanted to talk to me about divesting myself of a large part of it."

"To her, I suppose," observed Matthew wryly. "Great tactic."

"No," said Gordon patiently. "You're one hundred per cent wrong there, Matthew. You see, Janis has persuaded me to set up a charitable fund. I thought I might set one up for golfers in distress. Then she has urged me to transfer a considerable amount of money to *you*, as it happens. She's suggested that I should, in fact, give away about seven million. Three to the fund and four to you."

Matthew was silent. He stared at his father. And then he bit his lip.

"Yes," said Gordon. "Do you know, when you were a wee boy you used to bite your lip like that whenever you were in the wrong over something. You just bit your lip.

And I see you doing it right now. It's funny, isn't it? – how we keep these little mannerisms over the years."

"Dad," Matthew began. "I didn't . . ."

"No," said Gordon, "you didn't know. Well, as they say, ye ken noo."

"Yes," said Matthew. "I ken noo."

"And can you think of any reason," Gordon asked, "why I should not reverse my decision to transfer that money to you? After all, you have such a low opinion of my fiancée. I wouldn't want to force a decision of hers upon you, would I?"

"I'm sorry," said Matthew. "I really am. I'm sorry."

Gordon stared at his son. My son has never been a liar, he said to himself. He has been lazy, maybe, and a bit weak, but he has never been a liar. And so if he says that he is sorry for what he said, then he is. And the least I can do is to accept that apology.

Gordon stood up. "Stand up, Matthew," he said. Matthew, shamefacedly, stood up, and Gordon walked round the side of the table and faced his son.

"That's fine by me," he said. He leaned forward, so that nobody else might hear what he had to say. "And do you know something, Matthew? Well, here's something you should know: I'm proud of you. I never told you that, and I should have. I'm proud of what you are. I'm proud of the fact that, unlike me, you've never trodden on anybody else, or even considered doing that. And that makes you more of a man than I am, in my book."

Matthew could not say anything. So he stood there with his father, and Gordon put his arm about his son's shoulder and left it there, to reassure him, to show what he felt but could not find the words to say.

100. Big Lou

Big Lou watched as Matthew and his father went their separate ways, Matthew to his gallery over the road and Gordon up the hill in the direction of Queen Street. It had been obvious to her what was going on: a reconciliation of some sort between father and son. That pleased her; Big Lou did not like conflict and estrangement – what was the point, she thought, in being at odds with those whom we should love when our time on this earth was so very short?

She stared out of the window on to the steps that climbed up to Dundas Street. The coffee bar was now empty, but a customer would no doubt soon appear. Angus Lordie, perhaps, with that dog of his, or one of the antique dealers from down the road, from The Three Estaits, who would entertain Lou with news from the auction rooms.

But it was the postman who arrived, a thin-faced man who came from Dundee and always asked Big Lou about Arbroath, although she had nothing to tell him. This morning he extracted a couple of letters from his sack and placed them carefully on the counter.

"Arbroath," he said, looking at Big Lou's face with searching eyes. "Did you know some people called McNair? He was a joiner there, a long time ago. Then they moved to Dundee."

Big Lou shook her head. "Sorry, Willy. It's been a long time." She glanced at the letters. Was it? Yes, it was.

"They had a daughter who went to Glasgow," continued the postman. "I think she trained as a nurse at Yorkhill." Scotland was like that; long stories, endless links, things that half-happened.

Big Lou was staring at the letters. "Oh yes," she said. "I didn't know anybody called McNair. They might have been there while I was, but you know how it is when you're younger. You just think of yourself."

"That's it," he said. "You're right there, Lou."

Big Lou looked down at the letters and then glanced at her watch.

"Won't keep you," said the postman. "Cheerio, Lou."

As he turned to leave, she reached for one of the letters and slit the envelope open with a bread-knife. The postmark had told her who it was, and now she unfolded the letter within and saw his characteristic handwriting, the same writing that had been on the letter which she had cherished for all those years, the years of his absence.

"Dear Lou," she read, "you know, don't you, what a bad letter-writer I am. This is not because I find it difficult to write things down – I don't. It's just because I find it hard to write to you, because I have treated you so badly. Well, maybe I haven't treated you badly, exactly, but I have not been very good about telling you things. And then there were all those years in which I never wrote to you at all although I knew that you must have been wondering what I was doing and when I was going to come back to Scotland.

"Well, I let you down on that, didn't I? When I wrote to you and told you that I was going to be in Edinburgh you must have wondered whether I was going to remember my promise to invite you over to Texas. And I had not even had the decency to write to you and tell you that I was married and that I had moved to Mobile. I'm sorry about that, Lou. I should have told you. Men sometimes don't think about these things and then they are surprised when women are upset about it. I want you to know that I'm sorry about that.

"I told you, didn't I, about how I had moved to Mobile and opened a restaurant which I was running with my wife? Well, we ran that restaurant for six months and then I discovered something really hard for me. My wife was carrying on with one of the waiters. I had no idea that this was happening until I discovered them together at a fun-fair. She had said that she was going to see her aunt and I believed her. But then I tele-phoned the aunt and she said that she wasn't there. So I knew that she was lying.

"I went out for a drive. It was a way of calming my anger that she should have lied to me, and by chance I found a fun-fair on a bit of waste land near this big causeway that we have in Mobile. I don't know why I stopped, but I'm glad that I did, as I found the two of them going round and round on the great wheel. I got into one of the cars behind them and up and round we went. They had not seen me, but I could see them and I could see him put his arm around her and kiss her. That was hard, Lou – it was very hard.

"I did nothing for a while, and then I shouted out: *I can see you*!

"She turned round and spotted me up above them and I thought she was going to fall out of the car. But she did not, and when they went down again they signalled to the operator to let them out and they ran off to the car park and climbed into his van. That's the last I saw of her. I shouldn't have married her, Lou. She was too young for me. Sixteen's too young for a girl to marry.

"So I divorced her and now I'm coming back to Scotland and I want to know two things. The first is whether you will be prepared to see me again. And the second is whether you will agree to marry me. That is what I want to know. I hope you do, Lou, because you are the lady I have always loved, even when I told myself that I loved somebody else. I didn't. I loved you. That's all, Lou. That's all there is to it."

Lou put the letter down, and then, fumbling with the strings, she tore off her apron, picked up a sign that said CLOSED, and half walked, half ran, out of the coffee bar and up the steps to the road above. She had to tell somebody, and Matthew would do. He would not be particularly interested, she knew, but she would tell him anyway. She had to share her joy, as Lou knew that joy unshared was a halved emotion, just as sadness and loss, when borne alone, were often doubled.

101. *In the Bookshop*

Seated on a comfortable blue sofa in the coffee shop of Ottakar's Bookshop, Domenica Macdonald was in conversation with her old friend, Dilly Emslie. Beside her, in a plastic shopping bag, lay Domenica's haul from her trip to the bookshop: a racy biography of an 18th-century German princeling (or Domenica hoped it was racy – the cover certainly suggested that, but covers were notoriously meretricious), a history of aspirin, and a novel about a young woman who went to London, discovered it was a mistake, and returned to her small town in Northumbria, where nothing happened for the remainder of the book.

"I almost bought a book about pirates," Domenica remarked. "Pirates are such an interesting subject, don't you think? And yet there are very few anthropological studies of pirate life."

"It must be rather difficult to do," Dilly said thoughtfully. "Presumably pirates wouldn't exactly encourage anthropologists."

Domenica took a sip of her espresso. "I'm not sure about that," she said. "Most people are flattered by attention. And remember that anthropologists have studied all sorts of apparently dangerous people. Head-hunters in New Guinea, for example. Those people became very used to having an anthropologist about the place. Some of them became quite dependent on their anthropologists – rather like some people become rather dependent on their social workers."

"But of course it's a bit late now, don't you think?" said Dilly. "Today's pirates must be rather elusive."

"There are more than you imagine," said Domenica. "I gather that the South China Seas are riddled with them. And they're becoming bolder and bolder. They even try to board tankers and ships like that. They're very piratical."

The two friends were silent for a moment. There was a certain incongruity in discussing pirates in George Street. But Domenica had a further thought. "Do you know that pirates used to be quite active, even in British waters? They used to plague the south coast of England, coming ashore and carrying off the local women into captivity. Can you imagine going about your day-to-day business in your kitchen and suddenly having a large pirate bursting in and carrying one off? What a shock it must have been."

Dilly agreed. It must have been very disruptive, she thought.

Domenica warmed to her theme. "Of course, it might have suited some women to be carried off by pirates. You know, the plainer sort of girl may have found it livened up her life a bit, don't you think? In fact, one might just imagine groups of plainer girls having endless picnics on likely-looking cliffs, just on the off-chance that a pirate ship might go past. Waving, perhaps, to attract attention . . ."

They both laughed.

"That's enough about pirates," said Dilly. "What about you, Domenica? What have you been up to?"

Domenica thought for a moment. What had she been up to? The answer, it seemed, was very little. She had gone nowhere, she had stopped writing the paper she was working on, and she had hardly even spoken to her neighbours for months. It was a depressing thought.

"Very little," she answered. "In fact, Dilly, I feel quite stuck. I'm in a rut."

"Impossible," said Dilly. "I've never known you to be anything but involved. You do so much."

"Not any more," said Domenica. "I'm stalled."

Dilly smiled. "You need a new project. A new anthropological study. Something novel. Something that will make waves."

Domenica looked at the ceiling. A new project was a good idea, but what was there for her to do? She had no stomach for further theoretical speculation on method and objectivity, and she had no idea of what opportunities there were in the field. New Guinea was stale these days, and the head-hunters were more concerned with human rights than they used to be . . . Besides, it was politically incorrect even to use the term head-hunter. They were . . . what were they? Head re-locators? Or, by some lovely inversion, personnel recruiters?

"I have an idea for you," said Dilly. "What about pirates? What about a pioneering anthropological study of the life and customs of modern pirates in the South China Seas? You could live with them in their mangrove swamps and then sit in the back of their boats as they dash out to commit acts of piracy. Of course, you'd have to be completely detached. You could hardly join in. But you anthropologists know all about detachment and disinterested observation."

Domenica, who had been cradling her coffee cup in her hands as Dilly talked, now put it down on the table with a thud.

"Do you know?" she said. "That's a very intriguing idea.

There are plenty of studies of modern criminals – even the Mafia has been looked into by anthropologists and criminologists. But, as far as I know, nobody has actually gone and lived with pirates."

"And would you?" asked Dilly.

"I feel like a change," said Domenica. "I'm fed up. I need a new challenge."

"This will be challenging," said Dilly, expressing a note of caution. "In fact, I wonder if it would be altogether wise. These people sound as if they are rather desperate characters. They might not appreciate . . ."

But it was too late for caution. Domenica had gone to New Guinea on impulse; she had carried out her ground-breaking study of bride-price procedures amongst the Basotho on the passing suggestion of a colleague; and she had spent an entire year among the Inuit of the North-West Territories simply because she had seen a striking picture of the Aurora Borealis, pictured from Yellowknife. Pirates now beckoned in exactly the same way, and the call would be answered.

"It's a marvellous idea," Domenica said. "I shall get in touch with the Royal Anthropological Institute. I imagine that they'll be positive about it."

"We shall miss you," said Dilly, "when you're with the pirates."

"Oh, I expect they're on e-mail these days," said Domenica. "I shall keep in touch." They said goodbye to one another at the front door of the bookshop and Domenica began the walk back to Scotland Street. On the surface, it was an outrageous idea; but then so many important anthropological endeavours must have seemed outrageous when first conceived. This would certainly be difficult, but once one had established contact, and trust, it would be much the same as any field work. One would observe the households. One would study family relationships. One would look at the domestic economy and the ideological justification structure (if any). It would, in many senses, be mundane work. But *pirates*! One had to admit there was a certain ring to it.

After Big Lou had burst into the gallery, full of her good news, and had burst out again, Matthew and Pat sat quietly around a desk, sorting out the photographs for a catalogue that they were planning.

"I'm very pleased for Big Lou," Matthew said. "She had written him off, you know. She thought she'd seen the last of him."

"She deserves some good luck," said Pat. "I hope that he's good for her."

"Big Lou can look after herself," said Matthew. "She's strong."

Pat disagreed, at least in part. "And it's often the strong women who suffer the most," she said. "You'd be surprised, Matthew. Strong women put up with dreadful men."

"Anyway," said Matthew, "the important thing is that Big Lou is happy."

"Yes," said Pat. "That's good."

Matthew looked at Pat. It made her uncomfortable when he looked at her like that; it was almost as if he were reproaching her for something.

"And I'm feeling pretty happy too," he said. "Do you know that? I'm feeling very happy this morning."

"I'm glad," said Pat. "And why is that?"

"That talk I had with my old man," said Matthew. "It was . . . well, shall we say that it was productive."

Pat waited for him to continue.

"I was wrong about Janis," went on Matthew. "I thought that she wasn't right for him."

"In what way?" asked Pat. "Too young?"

"That . . . and in other ways," said Matthew. "But I was wrong. And now I know that one shouldn't jump to conclusions."

"And you told him this?" asked Pat.

"I did. And he was really nice to me – really nice. He said something very kind to me. And then . . ."

Pat waited. She was pleased by this reconciliation – she liked Gordon and she had thought that Matthew had been too hard on him.

Matthew seemed to be debating with himself whether to tell Pat something. He opened his mouth to speak, and then closed it. But at last he spoke.

"He was very generous to me," he said. "He gave me some money."

"That's good of him," said Pat. "He's done that before, hasn't he?"

"Oh yes, he's done that before. But never on this scale."

Pat sighed. "My father gave me fifty pounds last week," she said. "How much did you get? A hundred?"

Matthew looked down at the desk and picked up a photograph of a painting. It was of a sheep-dog chasing sheep; the sort of painting that nineteenth-century artists loved to paint, on a large scale, for upwardly mobile purchasers. Nobody painted sheep-dogs any more, it seemed.

"Four million," he said quietly.

There was complete silence. Matthew put down the photograph, but did not look at Pat. She was staring at him, her mouth slightly open. *Four million.*

At last she spoke. "Four million is a lot of money, Matthew. What are you going to do with it?"

Matthew shrugged. He had no idea what he would do with four million pounds, other than to put it safely away in the bank. Adam and Company would be the safest place for that.

"I don't know," he said. He looked about the gallery. "I could put some of it into this place, of course. I could go to the auctions and bid for the expensive paintings. A real Peploe, for example. A Hornel or two. A Vettriano."

"You had a Vettriano," said Pat. "And then . . ."

"That was some months ago," said Matthew. "There's also Elizabeth Blackadder. People like her work. All those flowers and Japanese what-nots. Or Stephen Mangan, with those Thirties-like people; very enigmatic. People like him. I could have all these people in here now if I wanted to."

Pat reflected on this. "It could become the best gallery in town."

Matthew beamed. "Yes," he said. "There's nothing to stop us

now. The London galleries will be very jealous. Stuck-up bunch."

He looked down at the photographs on the table before them. The paintings seemed somewhat forlorn after the roll-call of famous artists he had just pronounced. Yet there was a comfortable integrity about these paintings, with their earnest reporting of domestic scenes and picturesque scenes. But they were not great art, and now he would be able to handle great art. It would all be very different now that he had four million pounds.

"It's odd, isn't it," said Matthew, "what a difference four million pounds makes? You wouldn't think that it did, would you? – and yet it does."

"Yes," said Pat. "I wouldn't mind having four million pounds." Then she added: "Are you going to buy a new car, Matthew?"

Matthew looked surprised. "I hadn't thought of that," he said. "Do you think I need to?"

Pat's reply came quickly. "Yes," she said. "You could get yourself something sporty. One of those little BMWs. Do you know the ones?"

"I've seen them," said Matthew. "I don't know . . ."

"But you must," said Pat. "Can't you see yourself in one of them? Shooting down the Mound in one of those, with the top down?"

"Maybe," said Matthew. "Or maybe one of those new Bentleys – the ones with the leather steering wheel and the back that goes like this. I wouldn't mind one of those."

"Well, you can get one," encouraged Pat. "Now that you've got four million pounds." She thought for a moment, and then went on, "And just think of the trips you can make! French Polynesia! Mombassa! The Caribbean!"

"That would be interesting," admitted Matthew.

"Well, you can do all of that," Pat concluded. "All of that – and more."

They returned to their work, putting aside thoughts of expensive cars and exotic trips, at least on Matthew's part. After about ten minutes, Pat looked up from her task of arranging photographs to look at Matthew.

"What are you doing tomorrow night?" she asked him.

"Domenica's having a dinner party and asked me. She said that I could bring a friend, if I wished. Would you . . . ?"

Matthew accepted quickly. He was delighted to receive an invitation from Pat, and had long hoped for one. Now, at last, she . . . He stopped. He stood up and walked over to the window to look out on the street. He looked thoughtful, for there was something very specific to think about here, something which sapped the pleasure that he had felt. There was something worrying to consider.

103. *All Goes Well for Bruce*

"So he's going away," said Dr Macgregor. "To London, you say?" Lying on her bed, talking to her father on the telephone, Pat gazed up at the ceiling. "Yes," she said. "He came back this evening looking tremendously pleased with himself."

"But that's not unusual for that young man," said Dr Macgregor. "The narcissistic personality is like that. Narcissists are always pleased with themselves. They're very smug." He paused. "Have you ever come across anybody who always looks very smug? Somebody who just can't help smiling with self-satisfaction? You know the type."

"Yes," said Pat.

"Apart from Bruce, that is," said her father.

Pat thought for a moment. There had been a boy at school who had been very smug. He came from a smug family in Barnton. All of them were smug. And what made it worse was that he won everything: the boys' 100-metre dash; the under-sixteen 50-metre breaststroke; the school half-marathon . . .

"Yes," she said. "There was somebody like that."

"And did you feel envious?"

"Yes," said Pat. "We all felt envious. We hated him. We wanted to prick him with a pin. Somebody actually did that once."

"Not surprising," said her father. "But it really doesn't help, you know. These people are impervious to that sort of deflation.

They're psychologically tubeless, if I may extend the metaphor."

"Bruce is exactly like that," said Pat. "He's undeflatable."

Dr Macgregor laughed. "So he announced his departure? Why is he going?"

"It's a bit complicated," said Pat. "He lost his job, you see. Then he started a business, a wine dealership. He says that he was let down by somebody who had promised to invest. He bought some tremendously grand wine at a knock-down price. He sold most of it today at a wine auction in George Street."

She remembered Bruce's triumphant return to the flat earlier that evening, brandishing the note of sale from the auction house.

"He made over thirty thousand on the wine," she went on. "He was very pleased. He said that he wouldn't bother with the wine trade now and would go down to London instead. He would live there for a while on the proceeds of the auction and then get a job. He said that he was keen to try commodity trading."

"And what about the flat?" asked Dr Macgregor.

"I'm afraid he's selling it," said Pat. "He's going to put it on the market next week."

"Which means that you're going to have to move out."

"Yes," said Pat. "That's the end of Scotland Street for me."

There was silence at the other end of the line. The world was a lonely place, a place of transience, of change, of loss; only the bonds, the ties of friendship and family protected us from that loneliness. And what parent would not have wished his daughter to say: "Yes, I'm coming home", and what parent with Dr Macgregor's insight would not have known that this would have been quite the wrong answer for Pat to give him?

"You're always welcome to come back here," he said. "But you'll want somewhere with other students, which would be much better. Will it be hard to find somewhere?"

"I've got a friend in Marchmont," said Pat. "She says that there's a place in her flat. It's one of those big flats in Spottiswoode Street."

"You must take it," said Dr Macgregor.

After they had concluded their conversation, Pat got up and went through to the kitchen. Bruce was sitting at the table, a newspaper spread out on the table in front of him. He looked up and smiled at Pat.

"Do you realise how much this place is going to go for?" he asked her. "I'm looking at some of the prices of places nearby. I'm going to make a packet, you know." He sighed. "Pity you can't afford to buy it, Pat. Then you could stay here instead of moving out to some obscure street on the South Side. Acne-Timber Street, or whatever it's called.

"Acne-Timber Street?"

"That's what I call Spottiswoode Street," Bruce said. "Where's your sense of humour?"

"Of course, if you buy something in London," Pat said, "then you're going to have to pay through the nose for it, Bruce. You won't get anything in Fulham for what you get for Scotland Street, you know. You're going to be in some dump somewhere, Bruce. Or Essex. You might even end up in Essex."

Bruce laughed. "No danger of that for me! I'm moving in with somebody in Holland Park. You know it? Just round the corner from that nice restaurant, Clarke's. You know the place? You can get a Clarke's cookbook. Everybody goes there. All the creative people. You get noticed there. I saw Jamie Byng there once."

Pat stared at him. They might part company on bad terms or good. If it was to be bad terms, then she could tell him now, before it was too late, what she thought of him. But what would be the point of that? Nothing could dent Bruce – nothing; it was just as her father had said. Bruce was perfection incarnate in his own eyes. It would be good terms, then. She was big enough for that.

"You're going to love London, Bruce," she said. "And you'll do pretty well there."

"Thanks," said Bruce. "Yes, I think it's going to go rather well. And this flat I'm moving into, very bijou – I'll be sharing with the girl who owns it. Her old man's pretty well-off. He likes me, she says. And she's got her views on that, too, if you know what I mean. She's a stunner. English rose type. Long, blonde hair. Job in PR. Who knows what lies ahead? Who knows?"

Pat nodded. "That's very nice for you, Bruce." She paused.

"And thanks, Bruce, for everything you've done for me. Letting me live here and so on."

Bruce rose to his feet. Taking a step forward, he reached out and placed both his arms lazily on her shoulders.

"You're not a bad type, Pat," he said. "And you know what? I reckon I'm going to miss you a bit when I'm down there. And so . . ." He bent forward and then, to Pat's astonishment, planted a kiss on her lips, not a gentle kiss, but one that was remarkably passionate, for Edinburgh.

Drawing back, he looked down at her and smiled. "There," he said. "That's what you've been wanting for so long, isn't it?"

Pat could not speak. Cloves, she thought. Now I smell of cloves.

104. Preparing Dinner

"Porcini mushrooms," intoned Domenica. "Place dried porcini mushrooms in a bowl of hot water and allow the mushrooms to reconstitute. Keep the liquid."

"Why?" asked Pat. "What are we going to do with it?"

"We are going to cook the Arborio rice in it," explained Domenica. "In that way, the rice will absorb the taste of the mushrooms. It's the same principle as in the old days when people in Scotland ate tatties and a pass. The pass was the passing of a bit of meat over the tatties. The father ate the meat and the children just got a whiff of it over their tatties."

"Life was hard," said Pat, slitting open the packet of mushrooms.

"Yes," said Domenica. "And now here we are, descendants of those very people, opening packets of imported mushrooms." She looked out of the window, down on to Scotland Street, to the setts glistening after the light evening rain which had drifted over the town and was now drawing a white veil over Fife. "And to think," she went on, "that the woman who lived in this house when it was first built probably had only one or two dresses. That's all. People had very few clothes, you know. Even the wives of well-to-do farmers – they might have had only one dress. Life was very different."

"It's hard to imagine," said Pat.

"Yes," said Domenica. "But we need to remind ourselves. We need to renew that bond between ourselves and them, our great-great-grandparents, or whatever they were. It's what makes us a people. It's the knowledge of what they went through, what they were, that brings us together. If we lost that, then we'd be just an odd collection of people living on the same little bit of land. And that would be my nightmare, Pat – it really would. If our sense of ourselves as a group, a nation, as Scots, were to disappear."

Pat shrugged. "But nobody's going to make that disappear," she said. "Why would they?"

Domenica spun round. "Oh, there are plenty of people who would be quite happy to see all that disappear. What do you think globalisation is all about? Who gains if we're all reduced to compliant consumers, all with the same tastes, all prepared to accept decisions which are made at a distance, by people whom we can't censure or control?

"I, for one, refuse to lie down in the face of all that," went on Domenica. "I want to live in a community with an authentic culture. They may sound trite, but I can find no other words for it. I want to have a culture that is the product of where I am – that engages with the issues that concern me. It's the difference between electronic music and real music. Between the pre-digested pap of Hollywood and real film. It's that basic, Pat."

Domenica reached for her recipe book. She sighed.

"I sometimes feel very discouraged," she said. "You must forgive me. I look out at our world and I just get terribly discouraged. And if I ever turn on a television set, which I try to avoid if at all possible, it only gets worse. All that crudity, that dumbing-down. Inane, mindless game shows. People laughing at the humiliation and anger of others. The most basic, triumphalist materialism, too.

"And the crassness, the sheer crassness of the characters who are paraded across the national stage to be jeered at or applauded. The vain celebrities, the foul-mouthed bullies. What a wonderful picture of our national life all this presents!

"And what voices are there in all this . . . all this noise? What voices are there to say something serious and intelligent? When the justice minister went to her own constituency to try to do something about the selling of alcohol to young teenagers, she was barracked and sworn at by teenage boys, and nothing was done to stop it. Did you see that? Did you see that shocking picture? That poor woman! Trying to do an impossible job as best she could, and that's her reward.

"I don't know, Pat. I don't know. I have the feeling that we've seen the dismantling of civilisation, brick by brick, and now we're looking at the void. We thought that we were liberating people from oppressive cultural circumstances, but we were, in fact, taking something away from them. We were killing off civility and concern. We were undermining all those little ties of loyalty and consideration and affection that are necessary for human flourishing. We thought that tradition was bad, that it created hidebound societies, that it held people down. But, in fact, what tradition was doing all along was affirming community and the sense that we are members one of another. Do we really love and respect one another more in the absence of tradition and manners and all the rest? Or have we merely converted one another into moral strangers – making our countries nothing more than hotels for the convenience of guests who are required only to avoid stepping on the toes of other guests?"

Domenica put down her recipe book. "I'm so sorry, Pat," she said. "You shouldn't have to listen to all this from me. I know that one could argue the exact opposite of what I've just said. I know that one might point out that moral progress of all sorts has been made – and it has. In many respects we are more aware of others' feelings than we used to be. And, of course, there's the ready availability of porcini mushrooms . . ."

They both laughed, and Domenica looked at her watch. "The guests will be here in an hour," she said. "And we still have a great deal to do. Open the wine, will you, Pat? We must let it breathe. It's very kind of you to bring those bottles."

"I found them in the cupboard," said Pat. "They belong to Bruce, actually, and I didn't have the chance to ask him. But he's always helped himself to my wine and replaced it later with cheap Australian red. So I thought I'd do the same."

"Quite right," said Domenica.

Pat stood up and went over to the table where she had placed the three bottles of wine.

"Chateau Petrus," she said, reading the label. "I wonder if they'll be any good?"

"No idea," said Domenica. "Never heard of it."

105. Farewell

They stood around the fireplace in Domenica's drawing room, glasses of wine in their hands, the guests of Domenica. They were her friends, and here and there the friend of a friend. Angus Lordie was there, wearing a frayed cravat and a jacket patched with leather at the elbows and cuffs; without Cyril, now, who was tied to a railing below and who was happy, nonetheless, with the smells of Scotland Street in his nostrils and the occasional glimpse of a furtive cat on the other side of the street. And standing next to Angus, smiling at a remark which the painter had made, James Holloway, Domenica's friend of many years, and Judy Steel too, perched on the arm of a chair and talking to one who was sunk within the chair, Willy Dalrymple, who had been the only one to recognise the Chateau Petrus and had complimented Domenica on it. And then there was Olivia Dalrymple and Pat herself, and Matthew, who had come as her guest, and who stood on the other side of the fireplace, curiously remote in his attitude towards her, Pat thought – but Matthew had his moody periods, and this must be one.

The conversation had ranged widely. They had considered the question of the Reverend Robert Walker skating on Duddingston Loch and had been equally divided. Some believed that it was beyond doubt by Raeburn; others were convinced by the Danloux hypothesis. The summer: some believed that it had confirmed that global warming had arrived; others felt that the summer had been indistinguishable from any other summer of recent memory. And so the areas of potential agreement and disagreement had revealed themselves, to be dissected and discussed and passed over for the next topic.

At nine o'clock, Domenica led her guests through to the dining room, where they sat about her large mahogany table while she and Pat went through to the kitchen to collect the first course.

"That wine is quite delicious," said Domenica. "Willy seemed to imply that it was something special."

Pat felt a momentary pang of doubt. Bruce had told her that she could help herself; she clearly remembered his saying so, and he had himself taken two bottles of her Chilean Merlot on one occasion. So she had nothing to worry about, and she put the thought out of her mind.

The risotto was perfect, acclaimed by all, and after the plates had been cleared away, Angus Lordie tapped his glass with a spoon. The glass, which was empty, the Chateau Petrus having been consumed to the last drop, rang out clear across several conversations and brought them to silence.

"Dear friends," he said, "we are coming to the end of something here. When I was a little boy I hated things to end, as all children do, except their childhood – no child, of course, wants his childhood to go on forever. And when I became a young man, I found that I still hated things to end, though now, of course, I was learning how quickly and hard upon each others' heels do the endings come.

"Today, our dear friend, Domenica, told us that she was proposing to go away for some time. She is a scholar, and she obeys the tides of scholarship. These tides, she told us, now take her to the distant Malacca Straits, to a particularly demanding piece of fieldwork. I have my own views on that project, but I respect Domenica for her bravery in going to live amongst those whom she intends to study.

"We who are left behind in Edinburgh can only imagine the dangers which she will face. But tonight we can assure her that she goes with our love, which is what we would wish, I'm sure, to any friend about to undertake a journey. You go off clad in the clothes of our love. For that, surely, is what friendship is all about – about the giving of love and the assurance of love."

Angus stopped, and there was silence. He looked at Domenica, across the table, and she smiled at him.

"Dear Angus," she said. "A poem is called for."

"It is," said James Holloway.

Angus looked down at his plate, at the crumbs that lay upon it; all that was left.

"Very well," he said. "A poem about small things, I think."

He stood up, closed his eyes briefly, and then opened them as he began to speak.

Dear one, how many years is it – I forget –
Since that luminous evening when you joined us
In the celebration of whatever it was that we were celebrating – I
forget –
It is a mark of a successful celebration

That one should have little recollection of the cause;
As long as the happiness itself remains a memory.
Our tiny planet, viewed from afar, is a place of swirling clouds
And dimmish blue; Scotland, though lodged large in all our hearts
Is invisible at that distance, not much perhaps,
But to us it is our all, our place, the opposite of nowhere;
Nowhere can be seen by looking up
And realising, with shock, that we really are very small;
You would say, yes, we are, but never overcompensate,
Be content with small places, the local, the short story
Rather than the saga; take pleasure in private jokes,
In expressions that cannot be translated,
In references that can be understood by only two or three,
But which speak with such eloquence for small places
And the fellowship of those whom you know so well
And whose sayings and moods are as familiar
As the weather; these mean everything,
They mean the world, they mean the world.